the Carpenter's daughter

JENNIFER RODEWALD

WORDS THAT EDIFY
Rooted Publishing

ISBN: 978-0692654545

Printed in the United States of America

First Printing, 2016

Edited by Dori Harrell of Breakout Editing

Cover design by Jennifer Rodewald and Roseanna White Designs, www.RoseannaWhiteDesigns.com
Cover photo by Lorie Jerome
Cover model: Joanna Jerome

Author photo by Larisa O'Brien Photography

Published by Rooted Publishing
McCook, NE 69001

Song references from:

Chris Tomlin/Reuben Morgan/Ben Glover, "Jesus Loves Me," *Love Ran Red,* 2014. Used by permission.

Kari Jobe/Marty Sampson/Mia Fieldes/Ben Davis/Grant Pittman/Dustin Sauder/Austin Davis, "I Am Not Alone," *Majestic,* 2014. Used by permission.

Scripture quotations taken from the New American Standard Bible®, Copyright © 1960, 1962, 1963, 1968, 1971, 1972, 1973, 1975, 1977, 1995 by The Lockman Foundation. Used by permission.

For all of the sweet girls at MEFC I've been honored to watch
become beautiful young women.
Jesus loves you.
Don't ever forget it.

JENNIFER RODEWALD

Chapter One

SARAH

"I think it's a woman."

My world stalled as those words swirled behind me, sent into the air by a woman I'd never met.

I had stepped through the Subway door two minutes before, my only thought centered on satisfying my howling stomach. Cold air had kissed my sunburned cheeks, and I shivered as the sweat on my back cooled. A crowd had gathered in the restaurant for the Saturday dinner rush. Weekend warriors and little-league fans lined the length of the counter. I'd taken a place at the end of the line and was reading the options posted above the sandwich counter, right up to the moment that gashing remark registered in my brain.

Me. They were talking about me.

"It's a woman," the not-so-quiet woman hissed. "She's wearing a bra."

"She's certainly trying to disguise it," another female responded, her whisper not much lower than the first. "Why are so many young women going butch these days?"

"Well. She *isn't* very pretty."

"Nobody would look pretty in that getup. Men's clothes, clunky boots, and hacked-up hair barely hanging below that filthy hat? Come on. She's trying *not* to look pretty. Butch, I'm telling you. She's just butch."

Heat raced across my face, which had nothing to do with the fact that I hadn't worn my "filthy" hat on the roof most of the morning. Never in my life had I felt spat on by a conversation.

Minden, Nebraska, wasn't a big town, and I was known there. Dad was a respected general contractor, and I'd been his foreman for three years, since I turned eighteen. Nobody ever thought anything about my appearance. In fact, few seemed to notice me at all.

But we weren't in Minden that week. A job had us on the road, working in a town a hundred miles west.

I tugged on my hat bill, trying to hide. Staring at my reflection in the Plexiglas separating people from food, I took in my grimy face. Yuck. My examination dropped to my man-hands. Ugh. My gaze fell further, until it settled on my steel-toed work boots.

Butch. My throat constricted with strangling force.

"Can I help you?"

I swallowed. "Um—" I scanned my brain, feeling more stupid with every awkward moment. I couldn't remember what I'd decided to order. "Uh, three footlongs, please."

The teenager in uniform rolled his eyes. "What kind?"

"Oh yeah, sorry." This horrible scene kept getting worse. I licked my lips and swallowed again. "Cold cut, I guess."

"Bread?"

I blinked. Of course I wanted bread. What was the kid talking about?

He huffed. "What kind of bread?"

"Wheat." I cleared my throat and commanded my attention back to the errand.

Butch. My pulse throbbed.

A torturous amount of time passed before I had the bags of food in one hand and three Cokes precariously positioned in the crook of my other arm. I wanted to run out the door.

Don't look at them.

Pushing the exit open with my backside, I involuntarily rebelled against logic.

Two women stared back from the middle booth. One had dyed blond hair cut short and trendy, and the other's longer black hair had been styled and sprayed to perfection. Early to midfifties. Flawless skin on both faces, which contrasted dreadfully with their contemptuous eyes. The darker of the two actually shook her head.

My stomach hurt, like a rope had been looped around it and yanked tight. I spun out the door. A pair of large, rough hands caught me as I smashed into the solid barrier of a man's chest.

"Whoa there." His voice grabbed my attention and pulled it upward. Of all the horrible moments to bump into—literally— a good-looking guy.

"I'm sorry." He smiled.

I trembled inside.

"Let me help you." He reached for my bag of sandwiches.

I juggled the cups against my middle. The icy soda seeped through my T-shirt. *Add slob to butch.* Covering a groan, I looked into the man's vivid green eyes, which were framed by chocolate-brown brows. His easy grin seemed genuine. Something inside my chest fluttered—an odd and ridiculous sensation. Especially for a butch girl.

Fire crept up my neck. I hung my head, hoping the bill of my hat hid my flaming face. "That's all right. I've got it. Sorry I ran into you."

I lurched away and double-timed it to the truck, agonizing over both humiliations. Maybe Subway was the only fast-food joint in town, but there was no way I was going back. Dad and Uncle Dan would have to deal with Wonder Bread and peanut butter.

JESSE

She skittered away as if I'd burned her, her head down so far that I wondered if she could see where she was going.

I stood frozen, still holding the door. Were those eyes really that blue? Impossible. She must wear tinted contacts. Nobody had sapphire gems like that.

I should have helped her to her truck. She carried a bag stuffed full of footlongs, and had somehow managed to arrange three full cups in her arm. A gentleman would have helped. Usually I was—I tried to be. That was how my mama raised me. But a dumbfounded moment kept me glued to the sidewalk like a brainless mannequin.

One glance and her face etched into my head. Skin the color of creamed coffee, tanned from the early summer sun. Straight, narrow nose that ended with a small, upward curve. Short nearly black hair hidden under a well-worn baseball hat. And those eyes... *Sapphira.*

Nut ball. You shouldn't assign names to people whom you've never met.

I could've met her. I could have jogged over, caught her before she fired up that beat-up old truck, and said, "Hey, I'm sorry. I really should have helped you. I'm Jesse. You are..."

Sapphira.

That would be funny.

I shook my head as I moved into the restaurant, chuckling. Total nut. Except...well, it'd be nice to meet a woman like that. Sturdy build. Definitely *not* prissy. She looked like she knew how to work and didn't mind doing so. A woman like the kind Mom had been.

Opportunities lost. Life went on. I reached the counter and ordered a meatball sub, toasted.

"Jesse Chapman." A woman's voice beckoned from behind. "I'd know that ragtag hat anywhere."

Turning, I fixed a grin. I ran into people I'd met over the years and miles all the time. Came with the work, and suited me pretty well. I sought a familiar face and recognized the middle-aged woman with longish black hair.

Don't groan.

"Mrs. Kellogg." I made a silent note not to let my grin falter. "How are you?"

"Surprised to see you here." The woman wiggled herself straight and smiled. "I didn't know Homes For Hope was building in this little town."

I shoved my hands into my jeans pockets. "We're not. Not this year, anyway. I'm on my way through. Heading north."

"Not west?" She pushed out her bottom lip. "Such a shame. Shelia will be home from college this week. I know she'd love to see you."

Oh boy. Here we go again. For three years running, I'd come across Marta Kellogg when Homes For Hope worked in the area, and the woman always scheming. Poor Shelia. The girl seemed as appalled as I was uncomfortable with the constant and not-so-subtle setups her mother arranged.

It was a compliment, really. I ought to thank her for it and then set the record clear—for both Shelia and me. Shelia was a good seven years younger, just started college, and exceptionally shy. All that would be fine, except...well, I wasn't interested.

I was a construction guy. Shelia was the fragile type. She liked frills and manicured nails and expensive seafood. I wore the same pair of jeans until they could almost walk themselves to the Laundromat, scrubbed my blackened fingernails to no avail, and honestly preferred a double-bacon cheeseburger to just about anything else that could come out of a kitchen.

Add to all that, Shelia wasn't interested either. She tried to be, for her mother's sake, but the girl had ideas of her own, even though she kept them locked behind a compliant smile.

"I'm sure Shelia has plans for her first week of summer break." I forced a smooth tone, tucking irritation into a box labeled *Really Doesn't Matter.*

"Oh..." Mrs. Kellogg shook her head. "I know she'd set everything else aside. Why don't you come on through? We're an easy forty miles down the road. You could stay with us tonight. Save yourself one night's sleep in a cheap hotel. In fact, stay the weekend. You could come to church with us. Shelia would love that."

Heavens. I kept the sigh bundled in my chest. "Thanks, but I've got a job waiting."

Thank goodness.

As I turned back to the counter, my mind flitted to the woman I'd bumped into on my way in. Why couldn't I meet that kind of girl?

Chapter Two

SARAH

"You okay, Sarah?"

I leaned back against the plastic hotel chair, forcing a smile. "Fine, Dad."

Uncle Dan squinted my way from his side of the table. "You look a little done in, kid. Maybe a touch of sunstroke?"

Sunstroke—not hardly. I'd been working in the heat day in and day out for my whole adult life, and then some. Never once had I wilted.

"I'm fine."

"Why'd you get a cold cut? You don't like ham." Dad watched me while I searched for an answer. His brow furrowed a little more with every silent moment.

Dad and I were straight with each other. Neither of us had anything to hide. But this... I needed to sort through it on my own. For now.

"It...it was busy," I stuttered. "I didn't get a chance to make up my mind, so I thought it would be easiest to order three of the same."

Dad eyed me with a suspicious mask. "Are you sure you're okay?"

I sighed. Didn't want to talk about it. "Yeah, I'm okay. Think I'm done for the day." I folded up the paper our sandwiches had been wrapped in and stopped at the garbage on my way out of Dad's room. "See you both in the morning."

I left before they could pester me more, heading down the hall. Jamming the key card into the door, I let myself into room eight. It was uninspiring. Cream walls that needed fresh paint set the backdrop for out-of-date décor that had probably been bought at an auction. It smelled faintly of mold and smoke, despite the No Smoking sign on the door.

People rarely offered their best when a profit margin could be damaged. We'd stayed in enough lousy hotels to know that was a simple fact. One in particular stood out in my memory. The man at the front desk threatened me if I touched more than one bed. How dumb. Why would I sleep in two different beds? Anyway, it didn't matter. I never actually slept between hotel sheets. Yuck.

I reached to the chair across from the bed, snagging the sleeping bag I'd rolled up that morning. With a flick of one hand, I pulled the cover off the bed and, with an easy flip of the other, unrolled the bag in its place. There. The bed was ready. I dropped onto it and bent to remove my steel-toed boots.

How many women wore these things?

Butch.

I pushed the harsh voice away. Heading to the shower, I hoped the low-pressure water would wash away more than just the day's sweat and grime.

Fifteen minutes later, the steam slowly melted from the small square mirror as I brushed my teeth. I studied my reflection. Clean, but not really better. For the first time in my life, I wondered what people thought of me. I mean, really thought. Maybe they rated me about like I did this bathroom. Hard-water stains, rust, and poor upkeep made it completely unattractive. Ugly.

My nose stung. I'd worked hard every day of my life, doing a job most women couldn't. Ugly was all I could say for it?

A knock at the door interrupted my spiraling thoughts. I pushed away the unwelcome tears and sniffed. It'd been years since I'd cried, and never about something so superficial. I scowled at my reflection, leaning closer to the mirror. "You've never seen much value in appearances. After twenty-one years, why start now?"

That was only partially true. I didn't see much value in the appearance of *people*. Architecture was entirely different. A good design led to a solid build. And a well-built project was more than satisfying. It was a source of pride, of dignity.

The knock beckoned again. I left my musings at the sink and went to the door. A quick check through the peephole, and I found Dad pacing in the dim hall.

I resisted the urge to yank on the door, pulling it open as though nothing brewed inside. "Hi, Dad."

"Hey." He entered and stepped to the only chair in the room.

I followed, pushing the entry closed after he'd passed through. He waited until I sat on the bed directly across from him. Dressed in baggy gym shorts and an old T-shirt, and sitting with my legs crisscrossed, I felt like I had when he'd coached my high school basketball team.

A long time ago. But in reality, not much had changed. Was that good or bad? I'd been happy. Well, maybe happy was an overstatement. But up until about an hour ago, I hadn't been unhappy.

"What's going on, Sarah?"

I didn't want to look at him. What if he was disappointed in me? He always said what other people thought didn't matter. Work hard. Be honest. Treat people right. Those were his standards. *Pretty* was a word he'd probably marked out in his dictionary. If he had one.

I glanced to the shabby headboard. "Nothing."

"Let me see those blue eyes." He leaned both elbows against his knees. "We don't lie to each other."

Blue eyes. They were Mother's. The only part of her that remained in our lives. Sometimes I hated that I had her eyes.

When I was small, Dad could hardly look at me, especially when some well-meaning person would comment on how much my eyes looked like my mother's. He probably thought I couldn't remember those days. I wasn't gonna tell him I did. We'd made it, me and Dad. Through a whole lot of garbage, we were strong together. I wasn't going to dishonor that by dragging up old wounds.

"Sarah?" He expected an answer. An honest one.

Frankly, I didn't know how to lie to my dad.

I ran my rough man-hand through my wet black hair, which still clung to my neck. *She's trying not to look pretty.* Why did I care what some middle-aged woman who was clearly desperate to recapture her own youth had said?

Huffing, I finally looked Dad in the eye. "I'm not pretty."

Dad's jaw dropped. So, so stupid. This was just stupid. I was a steady and levelheaded woman. Because that was what Dad raised me to be. *Pretty* belonged to empty-headed, mean-spirited girls who couldn't see anyone but themselves—because they were too busy looking in the mirror. I wasn't one of those.

"Why are you worrying about that?"

See? I knew it. He was disappointed. "I didn't know before." My voice faltered. I hated it. We had real work to do in the morning. Sleep was necessary—not for beauty, which, as Dad said, went about as deep as a mud puddle. I shouldn't waste my energy on something so stupid. "I found out today. I never thought about it before."

"What?" His eyebrows drew together.

"I never gave it a thought before tonight." I shrugged, wishing the whole deal was easily brushed away. "I barely look in the mirror. We're off to work before my eyes can focus in the morning, and I come home covered with dirt and sweat. By the time I shower, I'm too tired to care about what I look like. So, I've never thought about it. But now I know. I'm not pretty." Crying? I was crying now? "I'm sorry, Dad. I don't know what's wrong with me."

He leaned back against his chair, looking like I'd kicked him in the gut. "Why do you think you're not pretty?"

I rubbed away the dumb tears and shook my head. *Just let the stupid thing go.* My lips quivered. "A woman at Subway said it. She called me butch—said I was trying to hide the fact that I'm a woman."

Dad covered one fist in the tight squeeze of the other. His knuckles paled. "Women." The word sizzled from his lips.

My eyelids slid closed, and something high pitched rang in my ears.

"Not you." Dad reached across the space and gripped my hand. "I didn't mean you." He searched my face, a fierceness in his eyes.

Dad adored me. I'd known that since the day he taught me how to pound a nail straight. But he didn't raise me to be like *them.* Like *her.* No sir, he raised me with a determination that I would know what things were important, which things had true value. Vanity was never part of his agenda.

Silence dangled awkwardly between us, and I wished I'd left it all unsaid.

Dad sighed and pushed to his feet. "Don't let some cat get to you."

Right. I knew that.

He paused, dropping a hand to my head. "You're better than them."

Was I?

Dad shoved his hand into his pocket and moved to the door. "Sleep it off, kid. They don't know you, so it doesn't matter."

The latch clicked behind him, and emptiness settled in my room. I left the bed to flick the light switch, but caught my reflection in the mirror near the door.

Butch.

They don't know you...

That was when I realized it. I didn't know me either.

I couldn't sleep it off. I couldn't sleep at all.

DALE

I paced the worn-out carpet in my room, my fist clenching the phone with a grip that might have killed.

"Who said that?" Darcy's indignation spewed hot over the line.

My sister and I shared the same temper, which meant it heated up in a hurry. Mine was already above boiling point.

"I don't know, just some woman."

"Why would anyone say something like that to a stranger?"

"I don't know." If I did, I wouldn't be standing in the hotel talking on the phone. I'd be in someone's face. "It doesn't matter, Dars. I need your help. I don't know what to do."

"Seems a few years late."

"What's that mean?"

"No. Not your asking for help. Sorry." Darcy sighed. "I meant this whole ordeal. She made it all the way through school without having to deal with this garbage. Seems like a rotten deal that it comes up now."

"She was quiet in high school."

"Sarah's quiet now. What's that got to do with it?"

"I think people were afraid of her. The strong, silent type."

"Dale." Her voice carried an eye roll. "You can't assign a male stereotype to your teenage daughter. Or your grown-up one, for that matter."

Lectures from my big sister. Some things never changed.

"What do I do?"

"I'm not sure." Darcy sighed again. "Do you want me to call her?"

"Would you? Maybe you could do a girls' weekend or something? Take her shopping or whatever it is women do on those things."

Her eye-roll voice carried over again. "Dale, new clothes and a tube of lipstick aren't going to fix this."

Who said anything about lipstick? "Like she'd wear that junk anyway. That's not what I was saying. Look, just take her out."

A long pause made me doubt Darcy's concern. Darcy was the closest thing Sarah had to a mother. She ought to be concerned. At least a little. I couldn't handle this. All this junk was nowhere in my playbook.

Finally, in a soft, tender voice, Darcy spoke. "Did she take it hard?"

The moment tears seeped from Sarah's eyes replayed. She was a steady girl, not a bundle of emotional explosions. I rubbed the bridge of my nose. "She cried."

Darcy's voice cracked. "I'll call."

I grunted a thanks, and that was that. Should take care of it. Except, the whole thing kept looping through my mind.

I'm not pretty.

I lowered onto the lumpy double bed in my room, still dumbfounded that *my* daughter said those words. Sarah wasn't that kind of woman. She wasn't shallow. Wasn't frail. And wasn't ugly.

She looked like the best combination possible of Cassie and me, and Cassie was a looker.

Cassandra von Holtzhausen, or locally known as Cassie Holtz, had made it. She'd achieved exactly what she'd abandoned us for—fame and envy among the vain and superficial.

Sarah didn't know her mother's adopted and very well-known last name, which was for the best. She didn't need to know that her mother had taken three other husbands, squandered her wealth built from face-lifts, updos, and scandalous photos. And she especially didn't need to know...

All Sarah knew was that she had Cassie's eyes. That was enough. She didn't need anything else from the woman.

I reached for the TV remote. I was too old for this. And too...blue collar. That was why Cassie left. She didn't want the ordinary life I could give her. That, and she'd cracked. All of the crap her faith-freak dad had dumped on her finally split her right in two, and she lost it. Crazy didn't just happen.

Old reels of events I'd rather forget started ticking, flashing my most hated memories with cruel accuracy.

We were eighteen and in love. I was in love, anyway, even if I couldn't figure why Cassie wanted me. Maybe because of basketball. She thought she'd latched on to a star who could lift her out of the nightmare she'd lived in.

Me. Imagine that. The son of a drunk and of a floozy who'd run off and killed herself. My future was sealed before I drew breath—I wasn't going anywhere special, and I sure couldn't fix her mess. Even if Kansas State thought I'd be a game changer on their basketball court.

The scholarship offer was revoked, proving the unspoken prophecy. I'd failed the drug test, which was stupid. I never tried cocaine again. Especially after I found out Cassie was pregnant.

That vivid and horrific moment still haunted me. I'd found her in her father's basement. In the nine months we had been together, I'd learned that when she went missing, she was probably down there, raw knees pressed to the concrete floor, facedown, hands covering her hair. Repenting. That was what her father called it.

I called it abuse.

Sure enough, that was where I'd found her. Except she hadn't been face-to-the-floor prostrate. In her white atonement dress, she was huddled in a corner of the dark, abandoned coal room, blood staining the sleeves of the snowy material.

I remembered my stomach twisting hard, the taste of puke in my mouth as I bolted to her side. Her hands dripped red, and in between trembling fingers, she'd gripped a paring knife.

With torture in her eyes, she looked up to me and moaned. "I don't want to go to hell."

"God, Cassie, what are you doing?" I ripped my jacket off and knelt to wrap her wounds. Engraved in both of her forearms, cuts climbed like ladder rungs to her elbows. Sweat broke out over my forehead and neck as she fought against my help.

"I don't want to go to hell," she cried.

"Then why are you trying to kill yourself?"

She pulled in a shuddered breath and set her agony-soaked expression on me. "Not." She leaned heavily back against the cold wall. "This is atonement."

Something cold and hard snapped inside of me. Atonement. Her father's word. The first time I'd ever heard it, Cassie had been missing for three days. We'd gone to a Friday night football game together, and I'd found the group with the goods. Cassie drank a little, but she didn't get drunk. Didn't matter— drinking was apparently a vile sin. Her father had her *repenting* for three days solid. I didn't drink with her again.

"Cass." I tried to measure the rage in my voice. "This is crazy. Why are you—"

"I'm pregnant." Tears seeped from the corners of her eyes. She tried brushing them away, leaving a crimson streak across her face.

What kind of a father did this to his daughter? What kind of a god would require it?

My mind set right there in that nightmare of a moment. Cassie wouldn't live like this, and neither would our child. And as for this god? Who needed that? Not me. Not Cassie. Not our kid.

We got married a week after graduation, and I took a job with a local contractor. Found out that I liked the work.

I thought maybe we'd have a future after all. Like I said, I loved her. I loved the way her eyes burned into my mind so that even when I drifted off to sleep, I could see their mesmerizing color. I loved the way she laughed at my jokes, the way she said I'd be something someday.

Those things ended though. We moved into a shack that looked more like a toolshed than a home, and Sarah was born. Cassie didn't even stick around for Sarah's first birthday.

I'll never forget that day, much as I'd trade anything to erase the memory. I came home from work to a howling baby and a note stuck on the refrigerator.

I can't do this.

Ignoring little Sarah, I hopped in my pickup and searched the town. I exhausted every possibility—her father's basement, the bar, the train station, every store in a reasonable radius—and finally went to the police. When I got home, Mrs. Lockwood, the old lady next door, was sitting in my living room, rocking my daughter.

"Young man, you're a father." She continued her rhythmic back and forth, back and forth. "Doesn't matter if that girl's packed up and gone. You're a father. You take care of this baby, or give her to someone who will."

Weeks went by. I tried to take care of Sarah, but I couldn't do it without looking at her. And she looked like Cassie. So I called Darcy.

Growing up, my older sister had more responsibility than any girl ought to have. I felt guilty pressing more on her right after she'd been married and was starting out a new and better life. But what else could I do? I wasn't a father—not a good one. I wasn't anything.

Darcy came. "I'm staying two weeks, Dale. Two weeks. And we're gonna work on this. But you start thinking right now, start remembering what it felt like to be abandoned by our father. What it felt like to know our mother didn't want us. You think about it while you work. Dream about it while you sleep. And see it from the life of your daughter."

I did, but not because I wanted to. I couldn't escape it. And by the end of those two weeks, I knew I couldn't pass that legacy on to my daughter, no matter what her mother did.

I made arrangements with Mrs. Lockwood for babysitting, and I set out to be the father my dad wasn't. I didn't know how to be one, but I was pretty sure how *not* to.

Then one day a little bit down the road, Sarah climbed into my lap. "I wuv you, Da-ie."

Took my heart right out of my chest and kept it in her miniature hands.

Somehow the years had trickled by. Thinking about Sarah as a grown woman, I felt a heavy failure. Grown up, yes. But not on the inside. I'd crippled her.

A deep warning surged through my chest. Life was about to change.

Chapter Three

JESSE

A train horn blared through the heavy summer air at the same moment my cell jingled. I passed through the glass doors of the small market, letting the blast of air-conditioning fully envelop me. The phone sounded again. Tugging it from my belt, I was pretty sure I knew the caller. A quick glance to the screen confirmed my guess.

"Hey, Shane." I moved toward the back of the store. "What's happening?"

"Not much. Where are you?"

"Just pulled into North Platte." Reaching the floral department, I turned right.

"Thought maybe you'd be about that far." Shane paused. I imagined him cocking his head just a bit. "How you doing?"

"Fine." My boots clunked against the floor until I came to the Memorial Day stock. "It's warm here. Nebraska's funny that way. You never know what you're gonna walk into."

"Yeah?" Shane paused again. He hadn't been asking about the weather. "Did you stop?"

I combed my fingers through my hair. "Not yet. I'm buying a new marker."

Silence hung in my ear. My mind traveled back five years, landing on a sunny spring morning, which I'd always thought ironic. Rain had been predicted that day. Would've been more appropriate. God was quirky like that.

"Just wanted to check on you," came Shane's voice over the phone again. "Call us tonight, after you stop."

"I will." I reached for a yellow wreath, followed by a red one. "Thanks, Shane. Tell Mia and the girls hey for me."

"Will do." Shane always remembered, always called. While awkward, it made me feel like God was still watching and that my parents hadn't been forgotten.

The wreaths were my only purchase, so I paid with cash. Sultry heat slapped my face again as I left the store, making me grateful for an air-conditioned truck.

Another tug from a diesel train ripped through the humidity, this time closer. Must be a challenge, living and sleeping in this rail town. Engines constantly chugging, rails always rumbling, horns forever splitting the sky. But people adjusted to lots of things. Some by choice, others by circumstances.

Pulling back onto the highway, I continued north over the viaduct spanning more rail tracks than I could count, and past the industrial part of town until I reached the North Platte River. The banks were high, water from the spring melt in Wyoming pushing through the artery of Nebraska. They would recede in a month, and sometime in July I'd pass over the comparative trickle splotched with sandbars and water reeds.

Two miles past the bridge, I pulled onto the highway shoulder and eased to a stop. Twenty feet off the road, two wreaths rustled in the breeze, faded and wind torn from a year of exposure. I cut the engine and pushed back against the bench seat. Glancing to the fake memorial flowers I'd purchased, I swallowed, wrapped a fist around both circles, and pushed out of the vehicle.

Stopping at the toolbox anchored in my truck bed, I grabbed my hammer. This was the only place on earth I hated the feel of its smooth, wooden handle.

21

A Blazer passed, heading south. I raised the hand with the hammer in it—waving was pretty standard around here. Grief didn't excuse rudeness. I walked over the new blades of springtime grass, avoiding the happy daisies that bounced with blissful ignorance. Mom wouldn't want me crushing their snowy petals.

I reached the faded markers and dropped to my knees. Cool moisture seeped through my jeans. It must have rained in the near past—the sandy dirt didn't hold water long. With the claw of the hammer, I tugged on the anchor holding the worn wreaths steady in the ground, releasing them from their yearlong vigil. It took only minutes to replace them, but I remained on the ground long after I'd pounded the new anchors deep into the grainy soil.

"Another year." I settled back against the heels of my boots. "Five now. Sometimes it feels like so much longer." I shook my head and tossed a glance toward the blue sky. It was probably crazy to talk to myself. I was twenty-six, after all. But I couldn't help it. They were not there, and this was the closest I felt to them. "Bet you thought I'd have a new life plan by now, a future all set to get started on."

Rubbing my hand against my leg, I watched as the grains of dirt released from my skin and dropped back to the ground. "Me too." A tiny chuckle vibrated my chest. Strange how one laughed like that when sad. "I sure didn't think I'd be an orphan already."

I pulled my legs forward and dropped to my backside. "Not that things are bad. Just fuzzy. Shane is doing well, but you probably already know that. He's keeping the business up—is always saying how grateful he is to you, Dad. And says I can jump in anytime. I'm just not feelin' it though."

Sighing, I rubbed the back of my neck. "I don't know if this is what you intended. Probably not, you weren't expecting to die—" My voice broke. I was glad I was alone. "But I want to honor your legacy. I hope I'm doing it well. And don't worry, Mom. I know God is still good."

I pushed to my feet, brushing at my damp jeans. "Miss you both."

Bending just enough to reach the tops, I brushed both wreaths with the tips of my fingers. It always felt like a fresh good-bye. Good thing I had a three-hour drive to work through it. I'd call Shane back when I got to Valentine. Should feel normal by then.

SARAH

The quilt spread over the basement guest bed felt heavy and warm. I snuggled under it, pushing deeper into the mattress. This plan Darcy had hatched up made me nervous. No, let's be honest. I was terrified, and a little mad at my dad for telling Darcy about the Subway incident. Like I didn't feel dumb enough.

But up to that point, all was okay. Jeff and Adam, my cousins, stayed in that Friday night, and we hung out. A round of pool and an outdoor barbecue set the background for a good night. Maybe a break from the norm was what I needed. I could pack up Sunday morning, go home, and move on with life.

The day gone, I lay clean and tired and soaking in the feeling of family. Right there my contentment turned sour. I had my dad and Uncle Dan, who was around more often than not. But somehow it wasn't the same. A deep hunger moaned inside me—the ache of something missing.

Great. First I was worried about my looks, and now I was thinking I might be lonely? I needed to get out of the fairy-tale mode. There was nothing wrong with my life.

No more nonsense. Go to sleep and dream of—

Of what?

I loved Aunt Darcy's house. She and Uncle Rick were happy. Content. Jeff and Adam, both a bit younger than me, were fun.

It wasn't their house I loved. It was their home. It felt like home. That was weird. Home felt like home, but a different kind. Maybe the kind I'd like to grow out of, and into something more. Something deeper, richer. Like Darcy and Rick's home.

I hoped that was what I would dream of.

Waiting for sleep to claim me, the phone call between Darcy and me replayed in my mind. She'd called me the day after the incident and tried to play it off as coincidence.

I wasn't dumb—too much.

"Dad told you, didn't he?" I said.

She hesitated, then sighed. "Yeah, he called me. Why don't you come here for the weekend? We can talk."

I didn't want to. But... maybe I did, because I started in on it right there on the phone.

She listened until my story was done.

"Some people are just mean. Or self-righteous. Or maybe scared," she'd said. "You live a different kind of life than most women. Some don't know what to do with that."

But they called me butch.

I wanted to say it out loud, but I thought she'd ask me why that bothered me so much. Girls used to be snippy to me back in high school. Called me *carpenter girl* and *gym rat.* The thing was, those things were true. I'd been a carpenter girl since Daddy taught me to swing a hammer, way back almost before I could walk. And back in those school days, when I wasn't working in the shop, I was throwing a ball up at a hoop in the gym, so that was true too.

Did that mean I was butch? Were those women, looking put-together and intelligent, right?

I couldn't answer. Not on the phone, not in that bed.

Sleep crept over me, and I dreamed of mirrors. All around me—they surrounded me, mocking me as I stood like a rabbit trapped in a circle of coyotes. My reflection bounced a million times—me in every direction for all eternity. A pink frilly dress hung over my awkward body, the skirt reminding me of the kind you'd see on a ballerina. The top was satiny and cut close to my small, not-very-womanly curves. Black dirt smudged the shiny material covering my body, and there were brown sweat stains under my arms. I wore my ball cap and steel-toed boots. The mirrors laughed as they closed in on me. Closer. Louder. Their chorus of ridicule crashed over me.

I woke up with sinister laughter sickening my stomach. It sounded like the Joker from the old Batman movies.

While I showered, I tried to think of something to hum. Anything to drown out the awful chuckles. The alphabet song was all I could summon. I hoped Jeff and Adam couldn't hear through the closed door.

What kind of simple-minded woman was creeped out by a stupid dream? The kind who couldn't figure out who she was in life.

We went shopping, Darcy and I. I never liked the activity. Always made me feel like a dirty pig at a tea party. I tried harder this time though. It didn't start off so well, because I asked to get my hair cut first.

"Who has butchered you, girl?" asked a woman with painted eyes and a pair of scissors in her hand.

Maybe the stylist meant to give me an opportunity to gain her sympathy. Certainly she expected me to say that some yahoo at a podunk beauty school had taken a dull knife to my locks of black hair.

I met her eyes for the tiniest breath. "I cut my own hair."

Seemed like that kind of moment a person ought to feel a bit sorry for smacking your face with her tongue. The girl stared at me in the mirror's reflection, then raised her eyebrow with all of the condescension of an unsympathetic teacher looking at a kid who'd wet his pants.

I squirmed in the purple-cushioned twirly chair.

"Don't *ever* do that again." She sighed and shook her fashionable but nonfunctional bangs out of her eyes.

Why did people wear their hair draped over their line of sight like that?

25

"Okay," I mumbled.

"Huh." The girl's frowned deepened. "Let's see what I can make out of this." She ran her fingers through my hacked-up hair, tugging it this way and that. Parting it to one side and then the other. She sectioned off some in the front and lifted her scissors.

I sat up straighter. "No bangs."

She lowered her scissors but kept them in her fingers. "You need some kind of style. Since I don't have much to work with, bangs make sense."

"No." I met her eyes again. "I'm in construction. I wear a hat almost all the time. Bangs won't work."

"Oh!" She grinned, taking on the persona of a friendly adviser. "Bangs look so cute with a hat! And we have such adorable options over by the front counter. You simply must take a look. Buy a couple. You'll be the fashionista of construction."

Fashionista. Yep, that was exactly what I was going for. I glanced over to the "hat" section of the feminine boutique. Plaid prints, twisted rosettes, and bows embellished the useless headgear.

"I wear real hats. The kind with a useful bill to keep the sun off my face."

Her eyebrows pulled together.

"Skip the bangs," Darcy intervened. "They're really not going to work. What about an asymmetrical bob?"

"The *Kate-do*?" The snippy snipper looked horrified. "That's so tired. Gone. Nobody does their hair like that anymore."

The Kate-do? What the heck were they talking about?

"Look." Darcy sighed and came to my side. "We need something that's functional. Don't make it as drastic as Kate Gosselin's was. Try something more like, umm...Kelly Ripa."

If only I knew who these people were.

The scissor snob propped her hands on her hips. "Kelly Ripa's hair is longer."

Darcy's mouth drew a tight line. Oh, I knew that look. She gave it to Jeff when he argued about doing something he didn't want to do. She gave it to Dad when he was being stubborn about eating raw vegetables or going to the doctor. Snippity-Sue was about to be put in her place.

"So do a shorter version. Every minute we've stood here in debate has cut your tip." Darcy gave her a stern eyebrow raise. "Do keep in mind that Charlotte is a friend of mine. I'm sure there's a waiting list for your chair, so let's not continue with this any further."

Charlotte? The boutique owner, I presumed. Huh. The moments when Darcy showed her Sharpe side always left me a bit in wonder. She was as pleasant as a monarch on a late summer day unless you set her crisscross. Then she left no doubt—she and my dad were definitely related.

My hair turned out...uh, wow. She cut it so it didn't lay like a clump of soggy weeds against the back of my head. The back puffed up a bit, and the front framed my face. I liked it. Seemed our outing was taking a turn for the better.

And then came the clothing.

I wore jeans. And old T-shirts from my basketball days. Or from my dad's closet. They were baggy enough to move in, and dirty and worn, so I didn't feel bad when they ended up ruined. Because they got ruined all the time.

"Let's start in Von Maur." Darcy slammed her Buick door shut and stepped toward the mall.

"Who?" I double-timed it to catch up.

She laughed. "Not who. Von Maur is a store."

I looked at her, feeling a scowl pinch my face.

"Okay, maybe not." She grinned again and looped her arm through mine.

We didn't go to Von whoever. I peeked through the giant glass doors as we passed. Any store that had a grand piano centered under an enormous crystal chandelier as its focal point was not a store I belonged in.

After several smaller shops, I left with three new pairs of jeans and a few shirts that were several steps above my gnarly gym tees. Darcy said they were all casual wear.

Casual was rather subjective.

"We need to find you some work clothes, and a dress."

I snickered. Work clothes and a dress. Two nouns that didn't belong in the same sentence. "I don't wear dresses."

"Haven't." Darcy tossed her long dark hair as she passed me an ornery grin. "You haven't worn a dress. Yet. That doesn't mean that you don't."

I eyed her, sending the silent but definite *no* look.

"Every woman needs at least one dress. And a pair of heels."

Heels? I clumped around in work boots or worn-out tennis shoes. My feet didn't belong in any heeled slipper. Ever.

Darcy ignored my obvious aversion. "So, we'll venture into a store with dresses and then—"

"Not Von Rich."

She laughed. "Okay. Not Von Maur. After we find you a dress"—she gave me that motherly *this is not a discussion* look—"we'll go over to the Goodwill. I'm sure we'll find feminine work clothes there, and you won't feel bad about putting them over your sweaty body for a good day up on a roof. Or whatever."

I didn't like the idea of a dress—but not because I didn't like the idea of wearing one. I didn't know *how* to wear one. What if the wind blew the skirt up? How was I supposed to sit?

What if I looked like a total fraud?

Look—there's that butch woman, trying to hide the fact that she's butch.

Why did that word repeat in my head like that crazy "It's a Small World After All" song? Never ending. What did it mean, anyway? Butch, I meant. Well, actually, that song too.

The dream flashed through my mind—faint laughter building in a distant corner of my subconscious and making my skin prickle. I set my determination. No matter what Darcy said, we were not putting anything pink on this body. I couldn't endure a bubblegum nightmare come to life in a dressing room.

What on earth was I doing? Shopping for dresses? I should have been swinging a hammer somewhere. Measuring, cutting, creating...not chasing down some ridiculous image of a self I didn't know.

"Here we are." Darcy steered me into another medium-sized shop. The kind with good-looking young adults plastered all over the advertising posters, looking confident and fresh and...sexy.

Whoa. We just stepped onto Jupiter. No, wait, I don't think you can do that, actually—isn't it a gaseous planet? See, I didn't belong in a mall. I couldn't think straight.

"We'll find something perfect. A summer dress, I think. You can wear it to church tomorrow."

Wait, what? Did I say I was staying long enough to go to church? I'd never been to church. My Omaha trips usually ended bright and early on Sunday morning. Why did Darcy assume I'd be going to church?

"Adam's getting baptized tomorrow." Darcy chattered on, assuming my head was still with her. "I know he wants you to come. You'll stay, right?"

I failed to see why that would matter to me. Except it seemed to matter to Darcy.

"Okay." Guess I was staying.

So, we got the dress. A light-bluish thing—Darcy called it teal. I stuck with primary colors, so it was blue. Ish. Maybe green? Whatever. It strapped around my shoulders and left my back bare. I felt naked. She said I looked gorgeous. Hmm, I did look different. That couldn't be a bad thing.

The heeled shoes were like walking on cobbled torture. Why did women wear them? Darcy snagged a pair of *ballet flats*. I had no idea what they were, but she kneeled on the carpet in the shoe store and slid them over my troll feet. Plain black, they didn't wobble when I stood to walk, so I agreed. Couldn't wear my work boots to church, could I? The flat deals were way better than the foot-torture-on-a-spike shoe.

Exhausted, we left the cursed mall—why were there so many of those?—and drove to a quiet diner thing. Bistro, that was what Darcy called it. It was a far cry from the truck stops and Grandma Jones's diner where Dad and I usually ended up eating. She ordered a chicken salad, and since I didn't know what I was doing, I did the same.

It was good. I'd have to Google a recipe. Because I cooked so much. Me in the kitchen? Well, it happened, because we couldn't eat at the diner every night. But my cooking went from the freezer to the microwave and onto the table in about ten minutes.

I remembered that home I was supposed to be dreaming of. The one like Rick and Darcy's. Who was I kidding? That kind of life didn't happen. Not to my kind of people.

Chapter Four

JESSE

First day back on the job. Mark it in the books.

I arched my spine backward, the stretch pulling the muscles all the way down to the back of my knees. The dull ache felt good after being bent forward on a roof all day.

Mack slapped my shoulder. "You're gonna age that body long before your time if you keep up this pace, Chapman."

I grinned. "Didn't harm you much, old man."

"Oh, I'm as rickety as the Tin Man." Mack started toward his truck, unfastening his leather tool belt as he moved. "Better not tell anyone."

I walked beside him, my roofing gun still hanging from my right hand. "They'd never believe me anyway."

"Good." Mack tossed his tools into the steel box in his truck bed. "And as long as you're the one scrambling up and down those ladders, I'll be able to avoid that knee surgery the doctor keeps pestering me about."

Chuckling, I put my attention to coiling the air hose.

"Seriously, Jess." Mack touched my shoulder again, and I paused. "It's good to have you back. Every spring, I think, *He's not coming this year. Can't keep hoping he'll keep his life on*

31

pause forever, and then you call, telling me you'll be up in a week or so. It means something to me."

"Means a lot to me." I made a brief connection with the leathery old man's eyes. The tough world of construction often made for crass men. But even with a gruff, hard exterior, Mack wasn't one of them. Which would explain why Homes For Hope board members retained him as their regional building coordinator. He had the uncommon combination of know-how and heart for the job.

"Your parents would be proud." Mack made a fist and gave me a small pound on the side of my arm.

I hoped they would be, and it propelled me daily. Emotion knocked on the front door of my heart. I let it go unanswered. We had things to do—a job to clean up and another day of work tomorrow.

"You going to Avery's tonight?" Mack moved on. Thank you very much.

"Yep." I nodded, though I walked toward my own truck as I spoke. "Wouldn't miss her chicken fried steak." My phone chirped as I set my gun and air hose in the bed.

Mack nodded and lifted a hand. "See you there."

I returned the wave as Mack climbed in his truck, and then answered my phone. "Hey, Shane. What's happening?"

"You always ask me that." Shane's voice seemed to smile. "And the answer's always the same. Nothing."

"Well, you call me all the time. I'm always hoping there's some kind of action going on so I don't feel like a teenage boy you're keeping tabs on."

Shane chuckled. "You need it. Plus, I promised your dad. How are you?"

"Dirty. Tired." I closed my toolbox. "Good."

"Standard answer. Have plans tonight?"

"Yep." I knew exactly what Shane was fishing for. Didn't know why. That pond didn't seem to have any life. "Going to Avery's for dinner."

"Yeah?" Shane's grin traveled clear over the phone. "Who's Avery?"

I hopped into the cab and pulled the door shut. "I told you about Avery." I slid the key into the ignition but didn't turn it. "She's about sixty years old and adopts the crew, whoever shows up, every season. She makes a good chicken fried steak."

"Oh." Shane's voice dropped flat. "That one. What's with you and all the old women?"

"They love me." I laughed. "Kind of a lost-dog syndrome, I think. But hey, it works. I get some good home-cooked meals."

Shane grunted. "What ever happened with you and what's her name? Mia's friend."

"Angela?"

"Yeah. She was nice. And closer to your age."

"She got married. Last fall." *Way to keep up, Cupid.*

"What? Who'd she marry?"

"I dunno." Didn't care all that much either. She was a nice girl, but not my type. Why would Mia set me up with a girl who had *manicure* on her weekly schedule? "Some doctor, I think."

"Ouch."

"Nah." Turning the key, I shook my head. The truck coughed itself to life. I pulled away from the job site and found my way back to Valentine's main drag. "It's fine."

"How do you keep striking out? Mia says you're a looker— which doesn't thrill me, by the way. Do you tell them you're living off a trust? Might help."

"Good idea. I'll just throw it out there that my parents left me a large amount of money and I'm set for life. That's exactly why I want a woman interested in me."

"Huh." Shane cleared his throat. "I don't understand it. You're everyone's favorite guy. What's the hang-up?"

"Maybe my life." I turned left at the highway and followed it until it bent south. The hotel came in sight, and I had a sudden urge for a hot shower. "Vagabonds aren't real high on a nice girl's wish list."

"Could be. You know, you could stay here—"

"I know." I turned into the lot. "Not yet. I'm not ready."

"Jess, it's been five years. At some point you need to go through the house. You need to reach some closure."

"I've got closure." I put a cap on a surge of irritation. "That's not why I don't stay. They had a plan, a purpose for the money. I'm bound to that plan, and I happen to like it."

"What about the house?"

Yes, the house. Dad's craftsmanship shouldn't have been neglected. And I hated to think about what had become of Mom's gardens. But...

My boots hit the parking lot as I sighed. "I'll do it this fall."

Shane held quiet for a moment—long enough for me to reach the door to my room. And to wonder if he'd push harder.

"I'm not trying to run over you."

"I know." I found the remote to the old-school television, which took up the entire space on the dresser. "You were Dad's right-hand guy. He'd appreciate you looking out for me."

"Look, we're here, Jesse. Whenever you're ready to come home and to go through their house, we'll help you."

"Thanks." I folded onto the bed, flipping the remote in my hand.

Shane was the closest to family that I had left. His girls even called me Uncle Jesse, which, I'm unashamed to admit, completely melted me. He worried about me like the older brother I didn't have. But I wasn't running from anything. He didn't seem to believe that.

"I'm really okay, Shane. You do know that, right?"

"I think it, sometimes. Doubt it others."

A squeal in the background stole my attention. He must have just walked in from work. The girls would be wrapping themselves around his ankles, their sweet, high-pitched voices saying "Daddy's home!"

How could I explain what I was doing with my life to him? He couldn't understand. I wasn't running from the past.

Just looking for a future.

***

Avery's house smelled like a good old southern kitchen. Like my grandma's. Maybe that was why I loved landing at her place.

Avery wore Jesus like a prized coat. The Spirit of God dwelled in her home. I knew it from the first time I'd walked through her front door five years before. I was a grieving boy back then, traveling my parents' circuit because I didn't know what else to do. Avery touched my pierced soul with her gentle love, her hospitality, and her good food. Some people said you couldn't share Jesus with cookies. I disagreed.

I kicked my boots off at the front door and followed my nose to the kitchen. Avery had an open-door policy. If she was expecting you for supper, you'd better just let yourself in. And if you dropped by for a chat, you didn't stand in the doorway to do it. She'd have you sitting down in the vaulted dining room and settled with coffee and cookies before you could find out how she'd been.

She was gifted. Hospitality. I wasn't sure if that was on the list of spiritual gifts, but either way, she had it.

"Jesse, my boy, I'm so glad you're back." Avery left her stove to wrap her thin arms around my waist. She felt small against me. Not frail, but small. "I've been praying something fierce for you these past few weeks. Spirit's been pulling you to mind with urgency. Is there a reason?"

Mack, already seated at the big, wide-planked farm table, cleared his throat. He did that often when churchy things came up. Whenever I went back south in the fall—they called me the snowbird roofer because of it—I'd shake his hand and say, "I'll be seeing you, Boss. Until then, I'm praying for you." And then he'd clear his throat. "Drive safe." And that would be that.

"No reason I can think of, Avery." I squeezed her again. "But we never know about the things we can't see, do we?"

She laughed. She sounded like Dolly Parton, which made me feel all the more at home.

She pushed away, patting my arm as she moved. "You know where the coffee is, and I know where your favorite spot is. So you grab a mug and find your place. We'll eat in a bit."

I filled a stone mug, my favorite at Avery's, and stepped through the adjoining dining room and out the back sliding door. Her deck needed to be refinished, but it was still solid, and it hosted the best seat in the house, overlooking the river.

The Niobrara cut through northern Nebraska and created an ecosystem unique from the rest of the state. I eased into an Adirondack chair and looked over the forested ravine. Didn't look a thing like the wide-open Sandhills that hid in the heart of Nebraska. The contrast amazed me. Miles and miles of treeless rolling hills dotted with spring-fed ponds and sand blowouts and covered with a mat of green grass. Then suddenly the landscape met the river, and the ecosystem changed. The waters cut deep into the land, and trees thrived in its life-sustaining ravine.

Avery's house was perched on a pasture overlooking it all. From her deck I could see where the ecosystems collided. One so very different from the other, and independently, each with a unique beauty. But together—wow. The collision created a scene of spectacular magnificence.

Leaning against the slanted backrest, I breathed in the quiet eloquence. Not many see this tucked-away scene. Not many saw a lot of what I saw. I lived a unique life.

Sometimes it isolated me.

A tug, slightly painful and definitely startling, pulled inside my chest. Not like a heart attack—because it wasn't really physical. Undefined emotion thickened in my throat.

Spirit's been pulling you to mind with urgency. Is there a reason? I looked over the river's wandering. Was there a reason?

Something had shifted in that moment. I couldn't identify what, but it was as certain as the cooling temperatures of the fading evening. A breeze set the trees in motion in the river valley below. Sitting up, I leaned my elbows against my knees, and casting my vision upward, I waited.

I'm listening.

Another small gust swirled through the gulch, building as it touched the river base, and then it climbed the steep cliffs.

Swirling air rose above the treetops, rustling their leaves as it passed, and swept over the pasture grasses. I could see it travel, its invisible force made known by the movement of grass bending to its will.

When the force of air reached me, it blew on my face and pushed against the bill of my hat. I snagged it before it tore off my head, leaning down against the wind.

Do you trust Me?

The gust passed, and the land returned to stillness.

SARAH

I stayed for church—for Adam's baptism, because Darcy talked me into it. Adam was nineteen years old—what was he doing getting baptized?

Dad was right. Religion was weird.

Yet there I sat in a cushy chair with cushy people who looked a whole lot like those women at Subway. Not a hair out of place. Perfectly applied makeup. Every fingernail scrubbed clean.

This had been a mistake.

"What possesses people to do the most unbelievable things?"

The question posed by the man up on the stage gripped my attention.

What was he talking about? Maybe he meant, why did people drag themselves out of bed on a Sunday morning to impress each other before some imaginary god? No, that couldn't be what he was sermonizing about. I forced myself to ignore the sea of well-dressed people who definitely didn't want to know a girl like me, and looked at the guy talking.

"For what cause did Paul endure shipwrecks, beatings, and imprisonment? Why did Peter forfeit his life? Why did any of the disciples of Christ suffer imprisonment and unnatural deaths?

"Nothing less than total enthrallment would send a boy to a bloody battlefield to face a giant. David was captivated by the glory of God, and that alone propelled his sling.

"Moses stood upon holy ground, and his eyes beheld the burning glory of God. The rest of his life was marked by this revelation, and God did through him more wonders than any other man recorded in the Word. His entire life was a compass pointing to the glory of God.

"Abraham left the known for a life uncharted. He believed the impossible promises of God and was credited righteous for that faith. The glory of God was more important, more substantial than the facts and realities of life."

I held my breath, which didn't make any sense. The question was not only new, but the stories completely unfamiliar. Who were all these people? I faded out as some kind of surreal wonder possessed me. They lost their lives? Stood up to armored men with rocks? Left home for something unknown?

People didn't do that. Not sane people.

The steady, deep voice of the pastor reached me again. "Are you captivated by the glory of God? Perhaps you've not considered it..."

Not once. Ever.

I couldn't move.

Nothing in life mattered that much to me. Hearing the utter conviction in the preacher's voice made me feel vacant. Once again the melancholy pressed in. It wasn't just loneliness. Suddenly, in light of such passionate lives, mine lost all purpose.

The emptiness felt like drowning. We couldn't leave the church fast enough.

Darcy rode with me in my truck after church. I didn't try to chat. My thoughts kept dancing around the amount of purpose that the preacher's words had drained from my existence.

"What's on your mind?" Darcy interrupted my clumsy, whirling thoughts.

I wasn't ready for a conversation about things that wouldn't level in my head.

"The...the drive back," I blurted. "Figuring out the best way to get home."

"Really?" She laughed softly. "So, is it I-80 or...I-80?"

Yeah, she bought that. My transparency made me feel like I was scaling some wobbly rafters. Naked. My stomach quivered.

That was dumb. I wasn't a little girl. I was a fully functional, productive twenty-one-year-old woman.

I glanced into the rearview mirror and then did a double take. Whoa. Me?

Darcy had found Charlotte after Snappy-Sally finished with my hair yesterday, and Charlotte showed me some makeup tricks. Simple ones, because I needed baby steps. A smudge of eyeliner, a wisp of black mascara, and light lip gloss. I tried them this morning, and the woman in the mirror shocked me.

I couldn't resist a grin. I hadn't worn the dress we'd bought—that was going too far—but the black silk tank, studded with sterling bling along the neckline, paired with dark jeans, looked pretty darn good, if I did say so myself. Pleasure pulled my smile wider. I actually felt pretty.

For today. A momentary exit from my carpenter-girl self. Tomorrow...back to torn jeans and worn T-shirts.

What if I didn't go back to that life?

Not possible. Building was what I knew.

I took the last turn down the quiet street to Darcy's house. We passed three driveways on the left, and then we pulled up to her house.

Darcy unsnapped her seat belt and then sat back. "You know you can talk to me, Sarah."

Naked again. But who else was I going to talk to? I drew a breath, hoping I wasn't going to regret my honesty.

"I need direction, Dars." I shifted my eyes from the windshield to her. "Not the religious stuff. I need something tangible. I go to work with Dad, come home, and make something that passes for supper, and then drop into my bed. That's my life. But I don't know who I am, or if I'm who I want to be. I want..."

What did I want?

Continuing to stare out the windshield, a single word popped out of my mouth. "Purpose."

Yeah. That was it. Purpose to fill the void.

After a tortuous silence, Darcy drew in air as if she were about to plunge into deep waters. "Maybe if you get outside of yourself."

I frowned. "What does that mean?"

Darcy met my eyes with hesitation written in her expression. "Everything you do is about you. Work. Home. There's nothing in your life that makes you see beyond yourself. Perhaps you need to be useful to someone who has no way to pay you with anything more than gratitude."

Usefulness. To matter to someone else without being paid for it. Could work.

"Sarah." Darcy reached for my arm, her voice a warning. "I know you don't understand, but I have to tell you even usefulness by itself will not satisfy your soul. It's a good place to start, but I don't think that you'll find the contentment you're searching for."

"I want purpose." Resolution solidified in my mind. "That's all."

I reached for the door before Darcy could go into the Jesus stuff. Didn't need Him.

I'd do this on my own.

DALE

Trouble.

I scowled at the computer screen, counting the calendar dates. The Kearney account was huge, and we couldn't let a scheduling conflict set us back. My reputation was built on met completion dates and accurate bids. This job could open several doors for Sharpe Contracting, and with the economic climate teetering, I had every intention of ensuring business through the imminent trough. Something needed to give.

I hovered the cursor over the weekend blocked out in blue— Dan's color. A bubble appeared over the blocks *Homes For Hope, Valentine.* He did that a few times a year, volunteered for Homes For Hope. I appreciated it too. Made the whole business look good and put our name out there. But this weekend wasn't going to work.

"Dan, I need you this week. The whole week."

"Come again?" Dan looked up from his laptop.

"I need you in Kearney. I know you told Mack you'd be in Valentine, but I need you on our site."

Dan stared at me, none too pleased. Sarah looked up from her CAD drawings, silent, as the office suddenly felt tight. Dan wasn't angry yet, but he was frustrated, which wasn't a long trip from mad. We Sharpes tended to have a way of standing our ground. Well, Dan and I did. Sarah usually held her peace. I'd always thought that was a good thing, until last week.

Never mind. One problem at a time.

"Mack needs a master, Dale." Dan leveled his gaze on me. This could get hot. "I can't let one guy down to save face for another."

Thing was, Dan was not my employee. He was my partner. I managed the jobs, ran the business, but he had as much invested in this as I did. I didn't have much of a right to bully him. But there was no way around this. I couldn't afford to *not* have him on site.

"I know." I worked at diplomacy. Not a strong point with me. "But I've got to keep this job on track, and the rain last week set us back. The foundation will be ready, and we've gotta get that shell up. I need you there."

Dan's thick eyebrows pulled in. He didn't flinch, which meant he wasn't moving on this. "I've got commitments too, Dale. Commitments that define my reputation, not just Sharpe Contracting. You knew this was coming."

I leaned forward, matching his challenge. "I didn't know the rain would set us back." So much for diplomacy. "This is the job. It is what it is. I need you next week, and that's that."

Dan rose from his chair. His temper was like the simmering of a pot. It came slow and subtle before it exploded into a full-on boil.

"What if I go?"

My attention snapped to Sarah. She'd witnessed plenty of these office standoffs. Seen Dan and me go nose to nose countless times over the years. Never once had she interfered.

Her blue eyes looked up from under the brim of her hat, timid and yet determined. "I can go to the Homes For Hope in Uncle Dan's place."

Something strange was happening here.

"I need you there too, Sarah." End of discussion. Heartburn sizzled in my chest. I wanted better for her. She deserved it. But I needed her.

"I have the drawings right in front of me."

She was arguing?

"I can build the interior walls in the shop this weekend, and you can take them on the flatbed when you leave Thursday. As long as you don't change anything last minute, it should be nothing for you to install them without me."

I stared. She never argued. Never complained. Never left me for some unknown job with a group of strangers. What had that cat-woman ignited in my daughter?

Dan cleared his throat. "I only promised Mack Friday and Saturday, Dale." I turned my attention to him and scowled. He persisted anyway. "Sarah could meet us in Kearney on Sunday and pick up from there. It'd only be the difference of two days— and the panel idea will work."

Sarah continued to look at me. This was way outside of her character. The whole thing was a massive puzzle. Wasn't the whole rebellion-independence thing supposed to have passed by now?

She wasn't being rebellious. She wasn't really asserting her independence either. She was searching. Her eyes held me, uncertain and yet pleading. What was she looking for?

"You've got three days to get those walls ready." I barked more than I meant to.

She dropped her gaze, hiding beneath the brim of her hat.

The ball of indigestion grew in my middle. I moved to her desk and dropped my hand on her shoulder, forcing a softer tone. "That should be an interesting challenge."

Sarah settled back and pushed out half a grin. The smile didn't settle in her eyes. She was terrified. I could hear her thoughts as clear as if she'd called them out. *What was she getting herself into?*

Chapter Five

SARAH

What was I thinking, telling Dad and Uncle Dan I'd go? I'd gone loopy over the past few weeks. Shopping for *dresses*? Buying makeup? And now volunteering to travel by myself to a place I'd never been, working with a bunch of guys I didn't know?

Get outside of myself, that was what Darcy said. This was what I got for asking. I was nearing Valentine, ending what had been an agonizingly long four-hour drive, and seriously considered making a U-turn to head back south. This whole scenario was not me.

My stomach twisted like it'd been caught in my power drill. Going home would have been the best option, but my truck kept traveling the onward path. When I hit Highway 20, I took a left, and in less than an hour I was pulling into a town of three thousand people. Following the directions, I took a right and saw the job site, buzzing with people, mostly guys already sweating from work.

Peachy. Uncle Dan told me if I showed up around ten, I should be fine, but the frame was already up. Why exactly had this Mack person needed a framer? Somewhere a message got miffed. Which was what I was as I pulled up to the house-in-progress.

I tugged the bill of my hat until the band sat close to my eyebrows as I stepped out of my vehicle. The late-May sun beat warmth onto my skin, bordering on hot. Normal. Except that day I resented it. I was already hot.

Appraising the situation, I stopped short of the activity. My directions were to check in with Mack. Big guy, probably sporting short gray whiskers, and walked with a mild limp. Huh. Most of the older guys in construction that I knew walked with a hitch. Bad knees or back—or both, the lot of them.

Dan also said that usually Homes For Hope workers were volunteers, often of the inexperienced variety. Easy to spot. They were the ones wearing clean shoes that belonged on a track or basketball court, and their jeans were all in one piece. No patches, no holes. Many of them held hammers by the necks, gripping them like they thought strangling the things would help drive nails faster.

I picked out those I was pretty sure would be Homes For Hope's masters. Supposedly there were usually four or five on site, counting Mack.

The middle-aged guy with a tool belt wrapped around his jeans could have been a master. He pointed here and there, up and down, as different volunteers approached him. I couldn't tell for sure though. He directed traffic more than anything.

The roofer, for sure that guy was a master. He squirreled around the nearly covered rafters, pulling sheeting like he'd been doing the job since he was two. He looked familiar, but even as I filed through the jobs Sharpe Contracting had done over the last year, and the crews I'd met in the process, I couldn't place him.

And the third—my target. Big guy dressed in a gray T-shirt and jeans with about five patches gathered in the general knee area. His hard face sported a rough, silver beard, and his eyes crinkled at the corners. He strode the site like a man on a mission. Had to be Mack.

I gulped in air, willing confidence into my posture. It wasn't like this should be a big deal, not like going to church. I belonged there. This was me. I thought.

Making my feet move, I rehearsed in my head what I would say when I reached him. *Mr. Mack, I'm Sarah Sharpe, Dan Sharpe's niece.* How pathetic. Who would have to practice a thing like that?

Big guy looked right at me, not smiling, as I walked nearer. "You here to help?"

"Yes, sir." I swallowed. "I'm—"

"Good. Grab a broom." He pointed toward the northwest corner of the framed house. "I need the floor cleared. My framer's due soon, and I need to make sure the rest of the interior walls can be set without delay."

I stood with a dry mouth and a tied-up tongue.

He scowled "You gonna work?"

"Yes, sir." I licked my lips. *I'm Sarah Sharpe, your framer...* My voice wouldn't cooperate. Oh well. I could sweep up the debris, then clear up this misunderstanding. Not my first dance with a broom.

I spied a push broom and got after it. Sweeping the plywood subfloor gave me a chance to examine the build. A few closets, some work in the kitchen, and then the bones would be complete. My purpose here didn't seem very purposeful at all.

Chalk one up for misdirection. *Note this: don't ask Darcy for any more life pointers.*

I pushed around the broom for sixty-three minutes, making sure my menial task was completed thoroughly, and then looked around for the guy I assumed was Mack. He'd disappeared. Gone.

Great. What was I supposed to do next?

Volunteers moved to the backyard area. I followed at a distance, searching faces for the one person I'd had verbal contact with. Still AWOL. I glanced to my truck. Leaving seemed like a real option. I wasn't needed. Wouldn't be missed.

I looked back to the gathering, the assembly making sense now that I saw food being set out on the slapped-together tables. Lunch. I'd been around for a little more than an hour, and it was already lunchtime. I wasn't hungry. Wasn't tired. And I wasn't sure what I'd do in a crowd of twenty strangers.

My steps veered to the north end of the structure, where a tiny scrap of shade would shelter me from the cloudless sky. An aluminum ladder leaned against the house, extending all the way up to the roof. I suddenly wondered about the other master, the roofer. Pretty young to be in this gig—volunteering his expertise in Nowhere, Nebraska, on a weekday. Probably a local. Even at that, a generous move. The guy's gotta make a living.

I'd seen him before. I knew it. I couldn't place it, but I knew we'd met.

Heat raced over my body. Weird.

I took my hat off and let the moving air cool my sweaty scalp as I peeked around the corner of the house to the backyard. Laughter punctuated the buzz of several conversations while people milled between the food table and each other.

How was it that everyone else on the planet could slide into a crowd like a fish into a pond? If that was the case, I must be a bird. An ugly one, like those turkey vultures that circle around the railyard back home.

Peachy. On that happy note, I set a foot on the bottom rung of the ladder. If I wasn't going to frame and wasn't going to eat, I might as well be useful somewhere else.

The roof was lonely and waiting for coverage. Finally, a place where I'd fit and a job that met my skills.

JESSE

The hiss-pop-pop of a roofing gun gradually gained my attention as it echoed from the roof. I was not on the roof, and that was *my* gun. None of the local volunteers had brought one.

I bumped Mack's shoulder with my fist, making him delay the bite of sandwich his mouth had been set on. "Did you send someone up?"

Mack looked up to the roof. No one was visible from our side of the gable. "No." Another pull echoed from above. Mack's brows scrunched. "Huh."

I set my sandwich on a paper plate and left the remains of my lunch on the table created from sawhorses and plywood. Mack wasn't far behind, but I didn't expect he'd follow me when I climbed the aluminum ladder.

I headed to the peak, mostly curious, but a little concerned for the overachiever's safety. Roofing guns weren't toys. Plus, to be honest, it was my gun, man. Rules of the job site: start when it's cool, always clean up your mess, and never, ever mess with another man's power tools.

Cresting the rise, I stopped short. *Whoa.* A woman rhythmically slapped down shingles and nailed them in place. Work code aside, I watched in fascination. She didn't miss a beat as she lined the roofing felt with straight, even rows of dog-eared shingles. Clearly she knew what she was doing.

"Who is she?"

I jumped a little. Hadn't heard him sneak behind me. "What are you doing up here?" I pried my eyes from this roofing wonder-woman. "You'll be in for that surgery if you're not careful."

"Shut up. We're not talking about that." Mack crossed his arms. "We're talking about her. Who is she?"

"You're the coordinator. You tell me."

"I've had hundreds of volunteers work for me. Don't know." He returned my challenge with a raised brow. "You're in charge up here, so you're supposed to know who's doing what. Especially with your gun."

Propping my hands on my hips, I grunted. "You'd better get off the roof before you hurt yourself, old man. I've got this."

"Set 'er straight." Mack smacked my shoulder and grinned.

As if I'd set anyone straight. Not the way Mack meant it. Dad always said I was too nice to be a foreman. I wasn't sure that was the truth—I hated conflict, was all. Not built for the stern, barking roll of supervisor. Course, Dad wasn't either. He'd agonized when he had to let a man go, and when it came to the few disagreements he'd encountered with a client, he'd rather eat a loss than damage a relationship.

Made him a dang good boss. Which was why Shane stuck with him for forever.

Made him a good dad too. But I wasn't going any further with that reverie. I had a gun-snatching girl to set straight. According to Mack.

I pulled in a long breath, as if filling my lungs would lend some kind of firmness to my lack. The woman looked up, and I caught sapphire eyes peeking beneath her faded cap. I couldn't stop my smile. I knew those eyes.

Sapphira.

I chuckled as I moved forward.

She snatched the protective earphones off her head and slowly laid down my gun.

I squatted. "Have I been replaced?"

"I don't know." Her eyes darted from me to the roof. The mild pink on her cheeks stood out clearly against the nearly black hair ruffling from the sides of her hat. "I'm not in charge around here."

I laughed. "Well, you obviously know what you're doing, although I have to tell you, I rarely let anyone touch my roofing gun."

"Oh, I'm so sorry." The pink darkened to red. "I like to stay busy, and I don't know anyone down there." Her head nodded in the direction of the crowd enjoying lunch on solid ground.

"Don't worry about it." I kept grinning. Like an idiot. Man, those eyes... "Looks like you've saved me a half-hour's worth of work tonight." I caught a hint of a smile tugging on her lips before she ducked her head.

"Here." She nodded to the nailer sitting between us, keeping her head low. "Sorry."

I wanted to reach out to lift her chin. That'd be awkward.

"Really, it's fine. I appreciate the help." I dropped to my backside, hoping she'd flash those gems my way again. "Are you from around here?"

"No." Not looking up, she tucked her hands close to her middle as if she didn't know what to do with them. "I'm from Minden."

I'd been through there a couple of times. Big collection of pioneer stuff in a museum, as I recalled. Didn't matter. I wasn't fishing for an address. A name would do. And maybe a smile aimed my way.

I tried a little harder. "Are you a master?"

Her head came up, but only enough for me to see a timid grin trying to peek from beneath the bill of her hat. "I am, but roofing isn't really my thing."

Not her thing? I examined her work. Straight lines, perfectly spaced nails, and the area she covered in such a short amount of time could only be the product of experience. Lots of experience. "What *is* your thing?"

"Framing."

I jolted straight. Mack had been whining before lunch that his master framer had been a no-show. Apparently he hadn't looked hard enough. "What's your name?"

"Sarah Sharpe."

Enough of the shy stuff. I needed to see those eyes.

"Sarah Sharpe." I extended my hand toward her. Certainly she wouldn't avoid a direct greeting. "I'm Jesse Chapman."

She looked up. Boom. Yep, they were really that blue. Wow.

Staring was pretty schoolboy, but I couldn't help it. Her eyes had resurfaced in my mind all week. Now here she sat, in the flesh, and looking...uncertain.

Interesting. A woman with enough confidence to scale a ladder and attack a roof all on her own shouldn't look terrified to say hello. Then again, that day at Subway, she'd trembled under my hand. I had thought because I'd scared the dickens out of her, running into her like that, but...

Maybe I needed to get to know this blue-eyed carpenter princess.

"I think you've been overlooked." I smiled, hoping it would be enough to keep her attention from falling back to her hands. "Was Mack expecting you?"

Her shoulders relaxed and—hallelujah!—she kept her eyes on mine. "I think so. My uncle's worked with him, but he's caught up in a project right now. I came in his place. I thought he called ahead to let Homes For Hope know."

I stood and held a hand to her. Sarah shielded her eyes with her hand and stared at my hand.

"Come on." I felt like I was coaxing a kitten from a tree. "We'll go clear this up."

She tucked her chin down, and I thought for a moment that she'd tell me to take a hike. Her head came back up, though, and her grip slid into mine.

After she stood, she snapped her hand to her side and cleared her throat. "I take it you're the master roofer."

"For the moment." I sent her a wink.

She looked away, crimson filling her cheeks.

Maybe that was too bold. Oh well, no going back now. "If my job's in danger, you and I may not be friends."

Her face darted upward again, and her eyebrows folded in.

I chuckled. Couldn't help it. "You're not after my lofty title, are you?"

"No."

Did she know I wasn't serious? "Good." I dropped a hand on her shoulder. "Then we can be friends."

A tiny sound drifted from her mouth to my ears. A mouse laugh—which, by some quirk, I found adorable.

Who would have thought I'd meet an adorable roofer? Correction, framer?

"Come on, then." I moved toward the peak, and she stepped beside me. Up and over, then down the ladder we went. I caught a glimpse of the gathering of trees in the river valley before I descended, and I thought about the other night on Avery's deck when I'd stewed over the Spirit's hint of changes in my life.

I grinned. If this was it, I had nothing to worry about.

SARAH

I couldn't place him. Wished to high heaven I could so I'd have something intelligent to say. Talking would give me a reason to stare into his face. And his face was worth looking at. Did all men smile like little boys? I'd never noticed. But this Jesse Chapman, he grinned like a ten-year-old on the Fourth of July, and he teased like he'd been the class clown.

Why would he tease me? No one ever teased me. Must have looked like a snot because I didn't know what to do with his impish humor.

We hit the ground, Jesse right behind me, and he slipped a hand to my elbow. As if I were a lady. Was that a joke? Irritation wrestled with the pleasure incited by his hand against my skin. I decided not to take it as a joke. I liked the race of tingles in my arm way too much to spoil it with suspicion.

We headed toward the picnic, which stirred hesitation in my gut. Didn't he hear me? I didn't know anyone there.

"Mack." Jesse spoke loud enough to gain the big guy's attention as we walked.

Mack turned from a conversation and took three steps to meet us. "So, did you solve the mystery?"

"Two of them, actually." Jesse grinned. Impishly. "Mack, this is Sarah Sharpe. She's not only a capable roofer, but she's your master framer."

Jesse winked. Again. Heat flared in my face. What was this guy after? Whatever it was, he could certainly do better than me.

"Sharpe?" Mack clarified.

"Yes, sir." I commanded my brain to an intelligent state and thrust my hand toward him. He shook it, but doubt punctuated his flimsy grip. I squeezed his muscled hand. Dad always said a firm handshake left a lasting impression. "Dan Sharpe is my uncle. He was supposed to come, but he's tied up with work this week. I came in his place."

Mack listened, but I had the distinct impression he wasn't thrilled. His eyes shifted to a spot behind me, and I knew the look he was communicating to Jesse. The *I don't have time to babysit* look.

"She could easily replace me." Jesse's voice took on a hard quality, and the air tensed.

I glanced back, finding the teasing light in his green eyes had darkened.

I knew when two guys were about to have a stout disagreement. Between my dad and uncle Dan, I'd seen it all my life.

Mack crossed his arms. Jesse scowled.

I wanted to sink into the dirt. "I don't mind doing whatever needs done."

"What *have* you been doing, Sarah?" Jesse crossed his arms.

I stepped back. "Sweeping the back rooms."

Jesse shook his head, frowning at Mack. "Talent and skill shouldn't be wasted, especially when Homes needs them both." He didn't wait for a response, but strode back to the house and mounted the ladder. Leaving me to deal with the big guy.

Thanks. Next time I'll do my own talking.

Well, probably not. I'd had my chance when I'd arrived, hadn't I?

"Dan's daughter, huh?" The big guy turned his glare from Jesse to me.

I swallowed. "No, niece."

"Why'd he send you?"

"Like I said, he's on a job and he couldn't get away—" I tucked my clammy hands behind me, hoping he didn't notice that they shook.

"I need a carpenter—a framer. Not a girl."

A girl? That was nice—a step up from butch. "I've worked with my dad my whole life, sir. Framing is my specialty, but I can do anything you need."

"Your dad?" Mack spit toward the dirt at our feet. "I thought you said Dan was your uncle."

"Right. He and my dad work together. Sharpe Contracting."

He grunted, which sounded more like a growl. "You familiar with the codes?"

"Yes, sir."

I could feel his doubt like a cold bucket of water dumped over my head. This had gone on long enough. I wasn't sure who exactly I was as a woman, but I knew I was pretty dang good with a set of building plans and a hammer. Gumption nearly loosed my tongue, but before it came unhinged, Mack stepped toward the house.

"Come with me."

I pushed my shoulders back. I'd run a crew before, for heaven's sake. Why had I been cowering as if I didn't know the differences between a common nail and a finishing tack? Setting my stride to match his, I determined to keep up.

"Ed." Mack spoke to the guy I'd seen earlier, the one I couldn't decide whether or not was a master. "Our framer's here. This is Sarah Sharpe. Show her where you're at, and run the changes by her."

Ed, who had turned and given me a once-over, raised his eyebrows. Mack didn't respond before he walked away, leaving me stuck with yet another skeptical hurdle. I pushed panic back down my throat. Whatever I was not—which was sure to be a long list—I was a capable carpenter. If only I could remember that fact when these boys glared at me like I'd spattered paint on their new truck.

Forcing my hand forward, I made myself speak. "Ed? It's nice to meet you."

One eyebrow tipped up as he took my hand. Another weak grip. "Sharpe, is it?"

I squeezed. "Yes, sir."

"And you're a carpenter?"

"Yes, sir."

He dropped his flimsy hold. "Huh. Desperate times..."

Really? I ground my teeth. "What are we starting on after lunch?"

He held me with a cool gaze. With an enormous amount of determination, I maintained one of my own.

"The kitchen." He pointed in the general direction of that room. "The owners want it a bit different. A little more open. Shouldn't be a problem."

That was speculative. Moving walls wasn't like rearranging furniture. "Let's have a look."

Ed's cool stare turned to an outright glare. "Fine."

Clenching my fists so that no one would see my hands tremble, I followed him. He pointed to the wall that divided the kitchen from the living area. "They'd like this open. More modern."

"Sure." I nodded. That would make sense. Why was Homes For Hope building a chopped-up box anyway? That trend died a while ago. "That's doable, but we'll need a better header."

"Right." Sarcasm lilted his voice as he pointed to the far outside wall. "I've got one put together."

He'd slapped a couple of two-by-fours together with common nails. Not good enough. "If they want this open, that'll create an eight-foot gap on a load-bearing wall. That'll require something more substantial."

Ed crossed his arms. "Look, girlie. I don't know why Mack is playing whatever game you're up to, but you're not impressing anyone. Let the men handle this, and you go back to picking out fabric and paint colors."

My chin fell slack. Did he just call me *girlie?* "Where are the building plans?"

He clamped his jaw.

I huffed. "You can't put that rigged header in that wall and call it good. It won't pass inspection."

"I've done lots of building, chica. I know what I'm doing."

Building what? Chicken coops?

"Do we have a problem?" Jesse strode across the plywood from the would-be front door to where Ed and I stood.

I didn't know how long he'd been listening, and my face flamed at the whole scene. "No."

Ed unfolded his arms and looked at Jesse as if they shared a joke. "Girlie here thinks we can't make this an open-concept space."

"I didn't say that." I scowled first at Ed and then Jesse. "I said it shouldn't be a problem, but we needed a better header."

Jesse glanced at the wall. "How big an opening?"

"Eight feet." I wanted to spit on his boots. *No, Jesse Chapman, we will not be friends.*

"I've got a header ready to go." Ed's tone added the nonverbal *so there* as he stuck a finger in the direction of the slapped-together header.

Crossing the room to where Ed had pointed, Jesse made a quick inspection of the header in question. "Sarah's right. That's not going to do it."

Ed snorted. "You're playing too, huh? What's the deal—she your girlfriend?"

Jesse scowled and laughed at the same time. Crossing back, he dropped an arm over Ed's shoulders. "Probably better drop this, buddy, before you embarrass yourself. You're working with people that know what they're doing."

I looked to my boots, to the two-by-fours, to the plywood surrounding the house. The one place in life I felt confident, and I discovered I was an oddity there too. Instead of feeling like a person with purpose, I'd discovered I didn't fit in anywhere.

Thanks for that, Aunt Darcy.

JESSE

Most of the crew had left—gone home where dinner and family were waiting. That left the traveling crew to wrap up the day and to do the jobs that required more precision and focus. Mack, Sarah, and me, to be exact. That bit was a piece of luck. Or providence.

I leaned against the framed-out doorway at the front of the house, watching Sarah work. Definitely proficient. And particular. *Measure twice, cut once.* That was generally the rule, but Sarah measured every step along the way, squared every corner as she set the frame for a kitchen island. Another alteration to the plans, at the owner's request.

I pushed off the studs and stepped forward. "Looks good."

Sarah glanced back before she finished pounding in a nail. One solid swing and the shaft sank into the two-by-four with the squeak that came from dead-on impact. Pretty sure she could make the nails sing like that with every drive.

"Thanks." Her hand slid from the end of the hammer to its neck before it dropped into its appointed loop on her tool belt. She moved like a gunslinger holstering a six-shooter. I didn't think I'd want to face her in a draw.

On second thought, that was an idea...

"Did your day iron out?" I stopped in front of the U-shape frame she'd created. When it came time for finish work, someone would set a couple of cabinets in the space and then drop a countertop over the whole structure.

She shrugged and looked up to the properly designed header, which had been set in place of the wall studs that had been removed. "It'll pass code."

"Where'd you find the two-by-eights?"

A tiny smile curled her lips. "Mack. Showed up with them about fifteen minutes after you left." She squared her eyes on me. "You didn't have anything to do with that, did you?"

"Could be." I tugged my hat off and ran my fingers through my sweat-drenched hair.

She stared.

I couldn't tell if her gaze was approving or appalled. This was where I was always going wrong with women. I couldn't read them. I needed thought bubbles hanging over their heads, and even at that, I probably wouldn't understand. Why were they so mysterious?

I gave my grimy mane—which was in need of a pair of sharp scissors, by the way—a shake. "Pretty nasty, huh?"

"What?"

Confusion looked cute on her. I felt not entirely alone in my ineptness, which made me grin. "I'm pretty disgusting after being up there all day." I pointed toward the trusses overhead.

"I wasn't thinking that." She turned her face down.

Actually, I was pretty sure that was exactly what she was thinking, which siphoned some of my confidence.

She pulled her hat off, exposing her dark wet hair, and then cleared her throat. "I was wondering if that's what I look like after I've been on a roof all day."

Relief tickled, and I laughed. "I doubt it." Because even in her end-of-the-day grunge, her eyes kept me mesmerized, and her smudged face maintained a raw attractiveness.

This was why every time Mia had assumed Cupid's job, she'd failed. She didn't understand my way of thinking. Bless her, Mia had an obsession with the magazine-kind of pretty. She was always made-up, her hair always styled, whether it was Sunday or laundry day. Her hands were always scrubbed, nails painted, and fingers jeweled. Those were the kind of girlfriends she kept and the kind of women she'd arrange for me to meet. Nothing wrong with them, but it didn't do it for me. I wasn't saying I went for ugly—and Sarah definitely wouldn't slide into that category—just not high maintenance.

A blush made a slow trail from her neck to her cheeks. I tried not to chuckle. She glanced anywhere and everywhere but at me before she began packing away her tools.

Door closed. Huh. Where'd I go wrong?

Mack clumped up the two stairs and through the front door opening. I slouched against the island frame. Opportunity deflated by the second, and he could be the final pin.

"Did you get done?" he asked Sarah.

"Yes, sir." She straightened from picking up a stray Wonder Bar. "Walls are ready for your electrician."

"Thanks." Mack's gravelly voice paused. "I'm sorry about the mix-up. You did a good job."

Those blue eyes grew, and her lips parted. "Thank you."

Her glance caught me for a tiny moment before returning to the floor. I thought she might have been smiling under the cover of her hat. Wished I'd seen it.

Mack kept a look fixed on her, a hint of appreciation tipping his lips. He caught me looking and smothered his approval. "I'll see you tomorrow, Jess."

"Yes, you will." I couldn't help an all-out smile. "Have a good night."

Mack scowled and walked away.

How about that? This day had presented all sorts of interesting quirks. Keeping my chuckle under my breath, I turned back to our newly discovered Hammer Shelia. An unnamed black-and-white flick rolled through my head, one where two gunslingers stepped off ten paces and drew. I rested my right hand on my hammer, still hanging in my tool belt, and bit the inside of my lip.

Yep. Could be a good idea. Worth a shot. "I don't suppose you brought a roofing gun of your own?"

"No." She dropped the remaining tools in her box, along with her belt, and looked back to me. "Sorry."

I cloaked my hopeful eagerness with a shrug. "Just thought I'd ask."

My silence served as bait.

"Are you behind?"

"Not really, but it's supposed to be a scorcher tomorrow. I'm going to keep working for a while, and I thought maybe..." Catching her eye, I held on to the last vowel as if it were a lure.

A smile bloomed full, along with a rose on her cheeks. "I'm pretty good with an old-fashioned hammer."

Snagged. "Are you sure?" Like I was going to let her wiggle off the hook. Sounded nice though, and it kept the smile on her face.

"Sure." She bent to take up her tool belt again. "I haven't anything else to do."

I waited, trying not to look like a little boy on the winning soccer team while she fastened her tools around her waist. We made our way outside and up the ladder, and I ripped open another package of shingles.

Setting half of the stack in front of her, I hiked an eyebrow toward my hat. "So, how good are you?"

Sarah mirrored my expression. "Do you honestly expect me to answer that?"

I laughed. "Let's see it."

"I'm not a circus monkey." She ironed her features, but amusement sparkled in her eyes.

"Certainly not." I set aside my nail gun and snagged the good ol'-fashioned hammer out of my tool belt. "How about a race?"

She snorted. "I think the nailer would be faster."

Raising my eyebrows, I challenged her in silence, and she smirked. "All right. Ready, go."

Her hammer popped from its loop, and she somehow managed to grab a shingle and a nail nearly simultaneously. She had one nail completely sunk and another started before I hit my knees. I snagged my hammer and set my rhythm to match hers. She stayed ahead of me though. Competitive drive aside, I was pretty sure losing this draw would be the most fun I'd have all summer.

Or maybe not. A guy could hope.

We covered the remainder of the east facing eave as the sun tapped the horizon. Perfect timing. We still had enough light to clean up.

"I think it was a tie." Sarah swiped her forehead.

Generous. She'd kicked my tail.

"Uh-uh." I shook my head. "I won."

"How do you figure?"

"I got you to do half my work."

"Nice." Trying to look irritated, laughter bubbled from her mouth instead. It sounded like a light spring rain against the covered porch at my parents' home. Or the rustling of trees in a summer breeze below Avery's back deck. Or the swishing grass on the Sandhills in late spring.

Favorite places. Favorite sounds.

I plopped down next to her, and she didn't hide under the bill of her hat. "So, I think I owe you dinner or something."

Her back jolted straight. "I don't think that's necessary."

Dang. Wrong turn again. *Thought bubbles, please. I need a little help.*

I leaned back on my elbows and watched her. Alarm melted into confusion. Maybe she was as bad at this as I was. If that was the case, persistence might be worth the risk. I got her on the roof, didn't I?

"What's your story, Sarah Sharpe?"

"My story?" Her eyebrows gathered, wrinkling the skin above her nose. She stared, and I stared back. Licking her lips, she relaxed a bit. "What do you want to know?"

"Let's start with who taught you to swing a hammer, and see how far you get before I finish my hamburger."

Her brow wrinkled again.

Maybe I was coming on too strong. Oh well—no going back now. I could play it easy, and maybe she'd relax. "There's a small-town grill by the Skyline Inn. Their burgers are great, and I'm starving."

Sarah bit her bottom lip. I pretended not to notice. I hopped to my feet and gathered my gear, lowered my gun down to the ground, and then headed down the ladder. She had nothing to do but follow. We wound cords and replaced tools, and when the work was done, I walked her to her truck.

"It's down on Highway 20." I made my voice matter of fact. "Right by the motel. You can't miss it."

Her eyes held protest. But her silence hinted indecision. What was this girl's story?

I opened her door, and she settled behind the steering wheel, still mute.

After shutting her in, I laid an arm across her open window. "You're not going to stand me up, are you?"

Her eyes widened. "I didn't agree to go."

Yeah, I hadn't missed that. But I'd determined to play it cool—all the way to the point where she said, *Thanks, but no thanks.*

"I guess I'll have to wait and find out." I bumped her door with a fist and walked back to my own pickup.

Sarah turned the engine over, and I wondered if I'd ever see her again.

Chapter Six

SARAH

My stomach grumbled as I started my truck. I'd noticed JJ's Grill as I pulled into town this morning—looked like a decent place to land for supper. And maybe the only place. Didn't mean I was going.

Had I just been asked on a date? Didn't sound like a date proposition, but this Jesse Chapman wasn't a common guy. At all. Sticking up for a strange girl on the job? Hanging around me when there was still work to be finished? Not normal.

He couldn't have been suggesting a date. Men didn't date a woman who'd schooled them on a roof. Did they?

My mind ran circles, like a dog chasing its tail. Meeting him at the grill wasn't going to alter destiny. It'd only be a burger with a guy from the crew. That wasn't completely out of the ordinary.

I'd go. I was going.

Maybe.

Maybe not.

Growling at my feeble brain, I shifted into drive and set the tires for the highway. One thing was for sure—I wasn't going into anywhere without a shower first. Whatever this Jesse character was thinking, he'd have to wait for me to clean up. If I was going at all.

I showered at the motel, hoping the steam would evaporate the wispy daydreams that managed to invade my logic. Fancy thoughts of green eyes glued to mine, filled with admiration and... And nothing. The hot water wasn't effective on my wild imagination, so I shut off the valve. My stomach complained of its empty condition as I dried my hair—a deviation from my wash-and-go routine. I'd seen a McDonald's on the other side of town. I could go for a couple of McDoubles and call it a meal.

You're not going to stand me up, are you?

That would be mean.

I walked into JJ's Grill, reconsidering the McDonald's option. *What on earth am I doing?* A rather round woman at the front greeted me before I could retreat. I was stuck.

"Are you going solo this evening?" She smiled.

Yes. The word hung on my tongue, but Jesse's voice came from around the corner.

"Dark hair and blue eyes?"

My mouth dropped open.

The hostess smiled, sending me a conspirator's wink. "I don't think this is who you're waiting for, Jesse. She looks perfectly sane. And young. Not your type at all."

Jesse made an appearance from the dining room. "Are you insulting me, Shelly?"

The woman smiled innocently. "And here I was all prepared for your usual crew of sweaty men with monstrous appetites."

He smiled like a boy showing off a new toy. "Come on, Sapphira. I'm starving." He gestured with his head toward the booth he'd already claimed.

Sapphira?

I followed him, hoping my face didn't look as dumb—and flattered—as I felt.

Maybe this was a game. Who acted this friendly to someone they'd just met? Players. Desperate men.

I watched Jesse slide into the booth. Strong build. Deep tan. Amazing green eyes. Winning smile. Desperate? That couldn't be right. What was he up to?

I didn't play these kinds of games. I didn't know the rules, and I'd be lousy at them even if I did.

"What can I get you to drink?" Shelly asked.

"Water's good, thank you." I slipped into the bench across from him, a mixture of unease and hunger turning my stomach.

"So..." Jesse folded his arms on the table and leaned in. "I wasn't sure you were going to come. I thought maybe I scared you or something. I come on pretty strong. I'm a people person."

Was that it? I looked at my hands, a smile threatening to spread across my lips in spite of my doubt.

"You're not though." His steady gaze held on me, like this situation was nothing out of the ordinary.

He made me jealous. And hungry.

"Not really." My voice sounded strange, like I didn't use it much. "I usually stick to what I know."

He chuckled. "I could have guessed. Hiding on a roof to avoid strangers screams introvert."

Did it scream *easy target* too?

"So, you're a builder." He leaned back, sprawling his arms across his side of the booth.

Conversation couldn't hurt. It'd be better than sharing a meal in awkward silence. "My dad's a contractor in Minden." I twisted my fingers together in my lap. "I grew up with a hammer in my hand and a tape measure in my pocket."

"And Homes For Hope managed to snag you?"

Did he have cue cards? How did he know what to say so quickly?

"Not really. My uncle worked with Mr. Mackenzie on several unrelated projects, and then on a few of the Homes For Hope houses after Mack became the regional supervisor. Dan was going to come—Mack asked him specifically—but a job came up that he and my dad didn't think they could pass up."

"But they could spare you?" Jesse shifted again, pressing an elbow on the table and dropping his chin in his palm like whatever I had to say was exactly what he wanted to hear.

Did he practice in front of a mirror?

I shrugged, words stalling somewhere between my brain and my mouth. I wasn't about to explain to this man the events that had been pushing me over the past few weeks. I chose to avoid the question entirely. "Honestly, Homes For Hope didn't need a framer on this job. The walls were already up. Most of the technical stuff was done. I'm not sure why I made the trip."

"Maybe so I could meet you."

My head snapped up, and my jaw hinged loose.

Jesse laughed. "Too bold." His eyes did some kind of merry twinkle.

I was desperate to know what he was all about. If I could just find the same audacity that he seemed to have stored up in buckets, I'd ask him flat out why he was so friendly, what he wanted with me.

He moved the conversation along. "Sometimes there's a local volunteer who can do what the masters are brought in to do. But to ensure everything passes code, Homes asks for a supply of professionals."

"You work with Homes For Hope often?" Aha. I could do this. He talked. I answered. Like a ball game. I tried to relax against the seat.

One of his shoulders lifted. "Most of the year."

Now I had the ball. "I didn't know they hired masters outside of the supervisors."

"They don't."

My turn again. Now what?

Shelly returned with my water, and a Coke for him. "What's it gonna be, Jess?"

She was certainly personable with him. Was that what being a "people person" accomplished? How did I get some of that?

"The usual, Shell, and go heavy with the bacon."

"Right." Shelly turned to me. "And you?"

I hadn't even opened the menu. Heavens, I was good at looking stupid. "The same, I guess."

Shelly nodded and spun away. I waited for Jesse to toss a new pitch. He sipped on his Coke with his green eyes nailed on me. Weird.

I guessed this inning I was supposed to toss the first ball. I could do this. I had to, or he might stare at me all night. What was he looking at anyway? I wiped the bottom half of my face with a napkin and forced my brain to rewind. We'd been talking about...about him working for Homes For Hope, apparently for free.

"How do you live if Homes For Hope doesn't pay you?"

He crossed his arms loosely and leaned on his elbows, his look indecisive. I'd thrown a curve ball, and he wasn't swinging. I smothered a sigh. "I'm sorry. That was nosy."

"Not at all." That easy smile spread over his mouth again. "I just don't want you to think it's a big deal or anything. My dad was a contractor too, and my mom was a landscape designer. They worked hard their whole lives and were careful about the way they lived. They had a plan, a dream for when they retired. They wanted to be able to travel around doing relief work, using their skills to help people, and they wanted to be able to do it without asking for financial support. So they saved and invested to that end."

That was the strangest thing I'd ever heard. "Did they do it?"

"They retired seven years ago, and yes, they did. They discovered that their ideas and expertise were best suited to Homes For Hope. For two years, they traveled and worked with Homes. One night they were on their way to North Platte for a build, and a truck hit them head on. Both were killed instantly."

Unbelievable. Watching Jesse's face, I found it both amazing and confusing that while he looked as though his parents' death saddened him, he wasn't angry. The pleasantness about him never left. I couldn't reconcile the paradox.

Jesse took another swallow from his straw. "I was the sole inheritor of their trust."

Dumbfounded, I had nothing to say. Who was this guy? Something was wonderfully odd about him. Hunger carved deeper.

Amazement overrode my hesitancy. Surely I'd misunderstood. "Now you do what they dreamed of?"

He nodded, and was saved from more explanation by the arrival of our food.

I continued to stare. "That's really generous of you."

"Don't pin me as a saint or anything." His eyes, serious and commanding, caught mine as if it was important I understood. The stiff air held for a moment before the intensity of that look melted back into the easygoing character I'd met. "It's actually a pretty good gig. I get to travel all over and meet all sorts of people, and they're almost always glad I'm there."

I nodded, but I couldn't understand. What about his plans? Didn't he have any of his own dreams to chase? I reached for a fry for something to do as I laid out the pieces of the Jesse puzzle.

"Do you mind if I pray?" Unashamed, he waited with perfect ease.

"No." What else did you say when someone asked that? Religion. So many rituals. So many rules.

His head dropped forward, and he plunged away. "Lord, thank You for the work You've given us today and the ability to do it. I ask that You would bless our food and conversation. In Jesus's name, amen."

Huh. Simple and to the point. Like he was talking to a friend. Not unlike Rick and Darcy. I squirmed. Jesse was not the clean, well-dressed, white-collared kind that couldn't relate to my world. He worked right alongside me. He swung a hammer, wore a ratty T-shirt, and wasn't offended by filth.

He was one of my kind.

But my kind didn't need imaginary friends. We lived with grit, worked with our hands, and lived by a code not handed down from heaven.

And my kind didn't work for free—not on a regular basis.

So, he was not my kind. That made more sense. He was, after all, living off a trust. Blue-collar people didn't have those, let alone survive on one.

No, that wasn't right either. He worked like a minimum-wage survivor—I saw him do it. Why would he do that? Easy street was a quick right turn on his life map. He didn't need to be among the working lower-middle class.

What was the deal with this guy?

JESSE

I'd confused her. I wasn't sure how I'd managed that, but she was sure-as-shootin' confused. Was it my nomad life or...praying?

Praying. She'd looked a little befuddled before that—which was a normal response when people drew out my story—befuddled or gushy, the latter of which I found annoying. But Sarah hadn't been all-out confused until I'd prayed.

Bummer. That meant more than likely she wasn't a believer. My chest caved. Hardly seemed fair. Do you know how many women were *not* like the lovely Sapphira? Most of them, that was how many. I'd met the one unique girl I'd been hinting to God about, and though apparently available, she wasn't for me.

I wanted to sigh. Rules.

No. Not rules. I fixed my posture as I ordered my thoughts properly. God wasn't about a bunch of rules. He gave boundaries to keep His flock safe.

I could still be her friend. She seemed like she needed a friend. And I was fascinated. That was safe and not tipping over the boundary.

"So, Sarah." I leaned back against the booth, settled in my mind about what this could and couldn't be. "You've managed to pull my story out, and we haven't even eaten yet." I grinned, wrapping my hand around my juicy burger. "Not bad for an introverted carpenter girl."

Her eyes rounded before she breathed a small laugh. "It was an accident. I don't know what I'm doing."

That made two of us. "Since you're making such great strides tonight, how about you tell me about you?"

Blushing, she glanced away and then fiddled with a fry.

I took a healthy bite of my unhealthy greasy burger. I'd probably die before I was sixty-five, with my high-cholesterol diet. Then again, Mom was the most health-conscious person I'd ever met, and she died young just the same. Had nothing to do with clogged arteries.

"Um—" Sarah folded her bottom lip under her teeth. "I already told you pretty much everything. My dad's a contractor. I learned how to build from him. I usually work with him. This"—she waved her hand toward the window, indicating the town in general—"was a...a new thing for me."

I swallowed my oh-so-good beef, cheddar, and bacon. "That's good. New experiences help us see past ourselves. And Homes For Hope is a good program. They really need skilled workers to come alongside the volunteers. It makes the work go faster, which gets people into their homes sooner."

Her expression froze somewhere in the middle of that. How had I startled her? Man, I was such a klutz at this—and *this* wasn't even *that* anymore.

"What's that look for?"

"What look?"

"The *I can't believe he just said that* look." I ran a napkin over my mouth. "What'd I say?"

"Oh." She ducked, apparently used to hiding beneath a hat she wasn't currently wearing. "It didn't mean that. It's—" Her head came back up, and she searched my face.

I imagined what she'd say if I asked her what she was looking for.

Sarah: Can I trust you?

Me: Yes, I promise. I was an honest guy, a good friend.

Sarah: Will you tease me?

Me: Not if it would hurt your feelings. I liked a good laugh, but not at

the expense of another person's dignity.

Sarah: Do you think I'm strange?

Me: Only in the best way.

I'm a nut. I know. But I swore that conversation happened in the silence of that look. Made me feel like we'd sealed a true friendship.

"It's what, Sapphira?"

Her eyebrows scrunched together. "Why do you call me that?"

I was so in left field on the female ballpark. "Your eyes?" Did that sound as dumb to her ears as it did to mine? Whoa there, did it matter? I was blazin' a friendship here, that was all.

Whew. Glad to get that straightened out. Again.

She stared at me, and then, after I held my breath for longer than normal, the skin around those eyes crinkled.

Safe. How far could I push and still stay on that plane? She may as well know how goofy I really was.

"That's what I named you when I bumped into you last week."

Again, the incredulous look. "We've met before?" She leaned forward. "I mean, I thought you looked familiar, but I don't remember..." Crimson crept over her cheeks.

"Nah, we didn't really meet." I hoped my smile would rescue her. "I nearly ran over you when you were coming out of Subway the other day, and wasn't gentleman enough to help you to your truck."

Her mouth opened, and her face flamed deeper. Why was that embarrassing? Maybe she'd been mad that I'd been so clumsy and then rude.

"Sorry about that," I said.

"What?" Her stare drifted over my shoulder and then fell to her plate. "No, you don't need to apologize."

Hmm. This was an interesting reaction. I thought she'd laugh. If not about the incident, then at least about my naming her. She continued to study her half-eaten food, not looking at me.

"You okay?"

"Huh?" Her face snapped back up to me. "Oh, yeah. It was—" She licked her lips, her eyes wandering back over to some vacant spot behind me. "That was a bad day."

Super. I'd made her slop soda all over herself at the end of what had been a bad day.

"Why did you say what you said earlier?" Her soft voice mimicked her lost stare.

"What did I say?"

She refocused on me. "About seeing past yourself. What made you say that?"

Full circle. Intriguing. "Let me think—you said this was a new experience, and I said new experiences are good, right?"

She nodded once, expectation painting a solemn expression. "You said they help us see past ourselves."

"Right." This was important? "I think we get wrapped up in our own world, with our goals and problems and everyday stuff, and then it's hard to see other people. When we serve others, it's like taking blinders off. We can see past our tiny little lives and become useful to others."

She held eye contact, but her mind had sailed to somewhere else. I wished she were the talkative type—the kind who needed a sounding board to process through her thoughts. I'd gladly volunteer for the job. But Sarah seemed to be not only introverted but introspective.

Exactly my opposite. In personality, in thought, and probably in action. But we needed an opposite every now and then. Someone to open our eyes to things we didn't understand on our own.

"Maybe you're right." She'd returned from the labyrinth of wherever she'd gone, a tiny smile poking at the corners of her mouth. But that was it. No explanation. No details about her thoughts.

I chuckled. My thoughts were forever coming out of my mouth before they were fully formed. I definitely could take some lessons from an opposite. And I was pretty sure God sent her to be my teacher.

"Does that mean you'll be showing up at the job site tomorrow morning?"

"I'd planned on it anyway, though I'm not sure what I'm supposed to do."

Roofing. That was what she'd be doing. With her pace, we'd be done before lunch, and then perhaps we'd hang siding. The job would slide along the current of her ability and work ethic, and we'd be way closer to completion than we'd expected.

"I'm sure you won't be bored."

Chapter Seven

SARAH

The squeal of screws penetrating fiberglass punctured the air where we worked. I hated siding. It wasn't hard work, but it took the least amount of creativity, and the noise was flat-out awful. But after we finished the roof, Jesse asked me to stay and help him with the siding. I was pretty sure he usually got what he wanted. Not because he was pushy, but because he was charming.

Actually, charming wasn't the right word. That implied manipulation. Jesse was definitely *not* manipulative. He was like a light on a hill on a dark night. Intriguing, and something that you couldn't help but stare at.

I decided our dinner wasn't a date. He paid, didn't even leave me the option of going Dutch, but he didn't act like it was a date beyond that—not that I would really know what to expect. Strangely, that conclusion didn't disappoint me. Working with him was comfortable.

"Hey, Sapphira." Jesse stopped the miter saw and caught me before my drill screeched another screw into the house. "Are you good at angles?"

I liked his nickname for me. It came off his tongue with a casual ease, making me feel feminine. Way better than butch.

"Not bad. Why?" Actually, I was pretty good, if I did say so myself. Math in general rolled from my mind like a ball down a hill.

"I hate angles." He tilted his neck in a *come here* gesture. "We've gotta do the peak next, and I never get the angles right."

"How do you work construction and not know angles?"

"I'm a roofer." He grinned as if that was a sufficient answer.

"Okeydokey, genius." Laughing, I held the drill out to him. "If I have to do the math, you have to endure the screeching witch."

"Man, this is not a good deal." He took the tool, pretending to pout. "I'd better go back to school."

A hint of jealousy zipped through me. I should have gone to college, finished the drafting classes I'd started in high school. If only it hadn't been so far away and required me to live with strangers. More and more classes were offered online. I wondered if that included architectural drafting.

I took a sheet of siding and laid it out on the makeshift plywood bench set up by the saw. Jesse had the plans duct-taped to the corner of the wood, so I had easy access to the roof pitch, which I needed to calculate the gable's plane. Making a quick sketch of the triangle directly onto the wood, I inserted the known numbers and scribbled out my calculations. The math was pretty easy, and the cuts came out to what I would have guessed eyeballing it, but eyeballing on a build was never a good idea.

My mind drifted back to school. How much education did Jesse have?

"Did you finish?" I asked.

He glanced at me over his shoulder, his eyebrows raised. "I just got started. What kind of crew are you used to?"

The temperature in my face spiked. "No, I'm sorry. I was still thinking about school. Did you finish college?"

"Oh." He chuckled. "Yep."

I slid the siding to the edge of the table and marked where I needed to cut. "Was it worth it?"

Jesse pushed another screw through the siding, so I waited for the ungodly zing to stop. Finished with that strip, he walked back over to the pile of siding near me. "Depends on what you're asking. Do I regret going to school? Nope. Am I using my degrees? Nope."

"*Degrees?* As in plural? What did you study?"

That little-boy smile stretched as he stopped his movement to look at me. "Business and English literature."

"English lit?"

"Now you know why I'm not good at angles."

"How does an English lit guy wind up as a professional roofer?"

"I don't get paid, so I'm not pro." He walked back to the house to resume siding. "I worked for my dad for as long as I could pound a nail. Usually on a roof. That's how I paid for college. Dad said that three legs made a sturdy stool, and he encouraged an additional business degree when I told him I wanted to teach English. In case I needed something to fall back on. I liked school, so even though some of my business classes were a struggle, I went with it."

Business. English. And construction. The most well-rounded person I'd ever met. "What'd you struggle with?"

He turned from the house to flash me a smile. "Math."

Funny.

By the end of the day, my ears rang, echoing the screeches from our job. It'd take hours for the loop of noise to dissolve from my hearing.

"So, I have a proposition." Jesse wound the extension cord for the saw while I gathered the scraps of siding to toss into the Dumpster out front. "I'll buy you dinner again if you promise to stay and help with the soffits tomorrow."

Yuck. Soffits were worse than siding. The same horrible sounds with the added pleasure of having to tilt your head at an awkward, almost upside-down angle. Talk about a headache.

"I'm going to have to pass."

"Oh, come on. Soffits are so much fun." He tipped his head to complete the best puppy-pleading expression ever.

Tempting. I couldn't help but grin. "Can't. Sorry. I promised my dad I'd be in Kearney tonight."

"Come on. One more day. He'll understand." Jesse propped his hands on his hips. "Surely your dad knows how delightful it is to hang soffits. He wouldn't deny you that kind of joy."

Laughter escaped, and I shook my head. "You are persistent. But I really can't. My dad wasn't very happy about me coming in the first place."

He sobered, his eyebrows dropping in a quizzical expression. "Why?"

"He's got a big job down there, and I'm his framer. I only convinced him by having the interior walls prefabbed and ready for installation. If I don't get there to make sure it all goes smoothly, he'll—"

Jesse's forehead wrinkled. "He'll...be really mad?"

"No." How had he managed to pull so much out of me? "He won't let me try that again."

"What?"

"Panels. I've been looking into the panelized systems—do you know anything about SIPs?"

Jesse nodded. "Structural Insulated Panels, right?"

"Right. I think they're a good idea, and I think we can build with them—maybe even distribute them."

"And your dad?"

I shrugged and looked to the ground. "He's old school. Likes to stick with what he knows."

"Aha." His voice carried a smile. "You're an entrepreneur."

"No." Not even close. The idea of doing something risky on my own made me want to vomit. "I'd never try anything like that by myself. But I think they're a good idea, and if I don't get to Kearney to make sure my two-by-four panels get installed correctly, he'll never give it a go again."

I hoped he wouldn't go into a big *you should try it anyway* speech. I wasn't made of that kind of stuff. Tough on the outside, but inside...well, I wasn't sure what I had on the inside.

"Okay, no soffit party tomorrow."

Good, he'd moved on. So intuitive.

"I'll still pay for that dinner though, with a different condition."

And yet so relentless. "What could you possibly want with me?" Oh goodness. Did I just say that? Talk about setting yourself up for trouble.

"You show up at the next job site." His green eyes invited with warm friendliness.

I'd never felt wanted like that. Obviously not a romantic kind of wanted, but like I had...value. How could I turn that down?

I bit my lip. "Where is it?"

"Down your way, actually. It'll be perfect." He finished with the cords and dumped them into the rubber tote marked *Chapman.* "We'll be in Holdrege."

Not even an hour away from home.

"When?"

He flashed his *I'm the winner* smile. "We'll finish the structural work up here on Wednesday. If everything stays on schedule, we'll head south on Thursday."

"Do you have an address?"

"Nope. I follow Mack." He picked up some of the stray pieces of siding I'd missed, and we walked to the Dumpster. "If you give me your number, I'll let you know."

I flung my armful of siding into the bin. Handing out my number? That was new.

It was for a job. Not anything to get my pulse up about.

"Is it a deal?" Hanging on to a smaller piece, he tossed his handful of scraps.

What could I lose? Maybe Darcy had been right. "Okay."

"Good." His eyes danced as he pushed a small scrap of siding toward me.

What was I supposed to do with that?

He reached to his back pocket and produced a nub of a pencil. Common carpenter equipment.

What kind of girl gave her number out on a piece of vinyl siding? My life was so not normal.

DALE

She made it. Thank God—or something. I half expected Sarah to come back with her head low, face to the ground. She didn't.

I grabbed another slice of pizza. Sarah had wandered into the hotel as our food had arrived. "How's Valentine?" I asked.

She shrugged, plopping onto the chair across from me, but her eyes gleamed a little bit. "Fine. Mack didn't know I was coming, but it worked out."

"Are you going to eat?" I gestured toward the box of pizza.

"No, I ate before I left."

"Worked pretty late. Sun's down already. I thought you'd be here sooner."

"Sorry."

That was it? How was I supposed to pull out details when she stuck to uninformative sentences? "Where'd you eat?"

Her eyes flickered, and she hesitated. "Just a local joint."

Vague again. This wasn't my girl. What was going on here? Holding my half-eaten slice, I scowled. "That's all you've got?"

"What are you fishing for, Dale?" Dan was always interfering. "She didn't do anything wrong. Never does. What's with the inquiry?"

"Can't I ask my daughter about her trip?"

"Sure, if you're only looking for a conversation." Dan leaned forward on the couch, reaching for more food. "You look like you're waiting for a confession. What do you think she's done?"

I didn't know. Truth was, I didn't like this quest for self-definition. It was drawing out too long, and Sarah...she was starting to change.

That terrified me.

"I don't think she's done anything," I snapped, "but I can't know, because she's not talking."

Sarah huffed. "I'm still sitting right here."

I shifted my glare and settled it on her. Raising my eyebrows, I waited.

Her shoulders slouched. "What do you want to know?"

"Anything." I immediately wished I could take back the bark in my voice. "Tell me what you did."

"Worked on a house." She shook her head and pushed herself out of the chair. "It's been a long drive, and I'm tired. I'll see you in the morning."

She walked out of the door without looking back. I was losing her.

Just like her mother.

Chapter Eight

JESSE

Anticipation was almost foreign to me. Not that I didn't look forward to a new day, but eagerness didn't usually smack against a wall of impatience the way it did that week. I liked to live each moment—take every day and savor whatever came at me. Those six days? Not so much.

I had a Polaroid of Sapphira's face, not only those amazing eyes, burned in my mind. The image made the hours tick by like a worm crossing a dry gravel road. Slow. Unbelievably slow.

Owning a distinct attraction to this odd little carpenter girl wasn't going to make pursuing a friendship simple. Black-and-white judgment would have probably said to lose her phone number and continue on down our divergent life courses. But wisdom wasn't always black and white, and I was convinced that our paths intersected by design.

Wednesday night finally rolled around. When it came to punching her number into my phone, I'd forced restraint since the night after she left. There was nothing wrong with calling to make sure she'd made it to Kearney okay on Saturday night, but the more cautious, and probably reasonable, side of me said to practice a little self-possession. Didn't need to give Sarah the wrong impression. But it was Wednesday, and reasonable to make contact to make sure she'd be coming sometime in the near future. Thank goodness.

I tugged a clean white T-shirt over my wet hair and walked barefooted across the Super 8 room I would call home for the week. Snagging my work jeans, my truck keys jangled from the right pocket. A pungent mix of sweat and roofing tar wafted to my nose. Penance for disrupting the stack of filth that needed a visit with the local Laundromat. Dang. Was this what I smelled like on a regular basis?

Skip it. I fished in the pool of stench and dropped the offensive apparel after I had my keys in my grasp.

The scrap of siding, trimmed into a smooth rectangle and with a hole punched through one side, hung on the loop with my keys—308-564-8258. Ten numbers.

I stared at my phone. Ten numbers and then Call, and I could talk to her. Uh, what was I going to say? *Me again, that super-forward guy who probably scared you away from Homes For Hope for life. Just checking to see if you were coming despite my freakishly forward demeanor.*

My high school speech coach would be proud.

What was I—eighteen? She was a colleague. Another master I needed to touch base with.

Right. Dial the number.

Oh no. I dialed the number. The ringtone buzzed its foreboding little tune, and I wondered if women knew what guys went through when they actually called them. Not that this was that.

"Sharpe Contracting."

Oh heavens. She answered. "Uh—"

"Hello?"

I swallowed. What the heck had possessed me? I wasn't shy. Scared. Whatever. "Sapphira?"

A small breath crossed the airwaves—her tiny laugh. I exhaled, which apparently I hadn't in the previous forty seconds.

"This must be Jesse." Her voice smoothed my anxiety. Hesitant but not edgy. More shy than anything.

I could picture her sitting across from me at JJ's. Showered, and her head no longer covered by a ball cap, her dark hair had gleamed with almost a blue hue under the florescent lights. She'd been reserved at first, like she was pushing me to a safe distance, which for her seemed to be on the other side of the room. But she'd warmed up. She really was extraordinarily shy.

And lost.

That was where I came in. I thought. Not that I knew everything. But I did know purpose, and I had the impression that was what she was looking for. I knew the God who forged our beginnings and wrote our ends, the God who could breathe purpose into her life.

"Yeah, it's me." I sank onto my king bed, stacking the pillows against the headboard for a backrest. "I told you I'd call."

A beat of silence allowed doubt to poke around where confidence had risen moments before.

"I didn't think you would," she finally said.

Confidence restored, and fed. "Here's what you should know about me, Sapphira. I don't get drunk, I don't gamble, and I never lie. I'm a God-fearing kind of guy, and I try to live by His standards."

Again, quiet on the airwaves. I thought I heard her swallow. "Okay…"

"So, you said you'd help us this weekend." I moved forward quickly. On the chance that I'd totally freaked her out, I didn't want to risk talking to a dial tone.

"Yeah, I was planning on it." She paused. "If you called."

I grinned wide. "Well, this is your confirmation call. Do you need directions?"

Her breathy chuckle surfed into my ear. "No. Just an address. I know Holdrege pretty well."

I relaxed against the pillows. She was coming.

She'd be there. Day after tomorrow.

SARAH

Why did my stomach have to bind itself into cords of pain? I wasn't going to the moon—just Holdrege. It was only a job. Everything was fine.

Dad wasn't so fine. He'd been, uh, not right. Used to be I could do nothing wrong in his eyes. Now he was looking for me to mess up at every turn. He'd drilled me about this trip—clearly didn't want me to go. I was all grown up. Why was he freaking out?

"Did you meet someone?" he'd asked the night before. Actually, it wasn't really a question. More like a demand for a confession.

I didn't know how to answer. Yes, I did, but not the way he meant. And even if I had, why would that be a bad thing? He'd said for years that he wanted me to be happy, to have a life I enjoy. Used that line to push me to K-State, and only backed off because I'd nearly cried, which was something I didn't do. Except that one time a few weeks back.

"I met several people, Dad." I didn't want to get into it. Jesse was a friend. I was certain that was all this was ever going be. Why would a guy like him—outgoing, charming, and oh yeah, handsome—ever be interested in me? I was sure he had a long list of female admirers, and when he was ready to end his days as the traveling philanthropist roofer, he'd have no trouble securing himself a beautiful woman.

I could picture her. Long blond hair, doe eyes, camera-ready makeup, and probably wearing a dress and those girly flat shoes everywhere she went. The kind of woman who would make the guys on the crew stop their work to gawk and drool. She'd slither her arm around his and lean against his muscled shoulder, a petite princess draped on her knight's proud arm.

My stomach hurt.

"You're keeping something from me, Sarah." Dad kindly punctured the image and brought me back to his dark scowl.

Part of me wanted to thank him for rescuing me from an idea that inexplicably made me nauseous. But I couldn't wrap my mind around what had wound him so tight. "I'm not."

"Why are you going back?"

I sighed. Because Jesse asked me to. Wait, that wasn't the whole of it. Going back and helping Homes For Hope had become part of my quest. I needed to see who I was beyond Dad's supervision. I needed to know what I had inside.

"I liked helping."

Dad frowned. "How is it any different than what you do every day?"

Please, Daddy, please understand. You want me to be happy, right? I stared at him while the words swirled a new storm inside of me. So, this had become a choice. I could continue pursuing a new identity, which apparently was irritating Dad, or I could stay here and never know who I was. How was I supposed to make that kind of decision?

"Dad..."

His shoulders drooped, and he leaned back against the counter. "Forget it, Sarah. You're a grown woman, and you can do what you want."

His concession did nothing to calm my turmoil. I had Jesse's number on my call log. I could have canceled.

I didn't.

Did you meet someone? As the road slipped by beneath my tires that morning, Dad's question continued to knot my gut, pulling the loops tighter with every mile closer to the job site.

What would my dad think of Jesse Chapman?

Lining him up with the important people in my life, I saw him strikingly similar to Rick and Darcy. His cloak of kindness resembled theirs. I could picture Jesse beside them, blending in with natural ease as they went to church.

The image unsettled me. Dad didn't take to that kind. The only reason he tolerated Darcy was because she was his sister.

First time Jesse would ask to pray, Dad would spear him with a *you're pathetic* look, and that would be that. If they ever happened to meet, that was. Which they wouldn't. So, that was irrelevant. Besides, why would I assume that Jesse openly wore his religion everywhere he went?

Because he did. I'd only spent two days with the guy, but I was certain that the God thing wasn't something that Jesse Chapman hid from anyone. Ever.

Coming into Holdrege, I continued on Highway 34 until I passed the heart of old town. After a quick check with Siri, I made a right and then a left. An empty lot surrounded by trucks appeared on the right side of the residential street. *You have arrived at your destination.*

Yep, there it was—but it wasn't empty. A slab foundation had been poured, and in front of it, circled in the dirt, stood a ring of people. Not working. Listening. To Jesse Chapman.

I cut the engine and slid from my truck. With a tentative step, I moved toward the gathering.

"And this same God who takes care of me will supply all your needs from his glorious riches, which have been given to us in Christ Jesus." Jesse read aloud from a small book in his palm. He smiled as he looked back up to the group. "Let's pray."

See? What'd I say? He'd parade his religion in front of everyone, all the time. Dad would have groaned, stomped back to the truck, and pointed it back toward home.

I stood, chewing on my lip and wondering why I was captivated by this odd, good-looking man.

Wait, captivated?

"Sapphira." Jesse left the ring of his followers, striding my direction. Had he prayed already? He held a hand out toward me like I was to shake it.

I did. He pulled me into a *hey, buddy* kind of hug. "Had some foolish fear that you weren't going to come after all. I'm relieved to see you."

"Why?" Oh dear. I said that out loud.

"We need you. See." He gestured to the blank canvas of a foundation. "No walls."

I surveyed the site as if I hadn't noticed the lack of framing and then looked to him. "Why are you here already? No walls, no roof. No need for a roofer yet."

His grin poked a dimple on the right side of his mouth. "I'm part of your crew today. You can be a part of mine in a couple of days."

The man wore audacious like a pro ballplayer would wear a jersey.

"What makes you think I'll stay that long?"

Chuckling, he put a hand to my elbow and started forward. "That's a negotiation we'll work on later. Come on. Meet your workers."

Panic seized my whole body, and I froze. Jesse stopped a step ahead of me, and his smile faltered. "What's wrong?"

"*My* crew?" My heart banged hard against my ribs. I led my dad's framing crew all the time—but I knew them, and they knew me. Remembering what happened with the guy up in Valentine made my chest hurt—not to mention adding pain to my already yucky stomach.

"Yes. You're the master framer. They'll be working under you."

"Where's Mack?"

Jesse shrugged as if it didn't matter. "In town—at the church they've appointed as headquarters. He had some stuff to iron out with the plumber."

He looked at me. I tried to smile. It came across more like paralyzed fear, I was sure.

"Well, don't worry." He chuckled. "I'm compliant. Haven't you ever seen *The Princess Bride*?"

"Uh, yeah?" I cocked an eyebrow, failing to see what the late-eighties flick had to do with framing.

"Consider yourself the newly appointed Dread Pirate Roberts." He nudged me forward. "I'll be your first mate. Everyone else will follow."

Peachy. Now I was a pirate. That helped answer the whole *who the heck am I* question.

Jesse introduced me around. I'd never remember their names. Just impressions.

Middle-aged lady with a pink Under Armour cap. Looked like a runner. Worked like maybe she'd done something like this before. Younger guy, a little on the heavy side, but still capable. Talked like he knew what he was doing. Worked like he didn't. Older man with silver-speckled hair. Quiet, but did exactly what needed to be done. Friendly gentleman, late forties. Reminded me of Jesse, except he told more jokes than he sank nails. That was okay—he was entertaining.

And Laine. I'd remember her name. Distinctly. Younger than me, but not much, I'd guess. Blond hair swept back into a glossy ponytail, bright-blue eyes, and pink lips that smiled the whole day through. Dressed in a tank top and cutoff shorts, she still looked like she belonged on one of those fashion posters I'd seen at the mall.

Her face had been perfectly made up at the beginning of the day, eyes highlighted with a brown pencil, smudged a little— exactly the way Darcy and her beauty-shop buddy had shown me. Contrary to my expectation, by the end of the day she didn't look any worse for the work. No smeared makeup. No sagging disposition. Speckled with a small amount of sweat, her flushed face only added to her youthful appeal.

Pretty sure Jesse noticed.

"Jesse, it's so good to have you back again." Middle-aged Under Armour–cap lady approached him near the end of the workday.

I kept myself busy double-checking the level and plumb lines of all of the walls. Corners needed to be tight, and straight lines were an absolute must. Skip it, and the homeowners would hate us when the drywall started separating at the junctures. It was important. Plus, I didn't have to figure out this unsettled, anxious feeling I had going in my gut if I didn't watch him interact with the other women on the job.

"Good to be back, as always."

Tune him out. It was a private conversation anyway.

"Where are you staying?"

"Over at the Super 8."

Me too. What were the odds? Well, fifty-fifty, since there was only one other hotel in town.

"Oh no." She touched his shoulder.

I only knew because I caught a glimpse of them when I moved on to check a different section of wall. Not because I was watching.

"I can't let you live there for a week. Cameron is gone for the summer. He's working at camp again. You can stay with us."

Jesse chuckled, and his eyes wandered over to Laine, who was sweeping the foundation near the front of the project. I thought he blushed, but I wasn't sure. Because I wasn't watching.

"Thank you, Shari, but I'm already set up there."

"Jesse. I can't have it. You do so much for others—you shouldn't endure a lumpy bed every night."

"Really, the bed's not lumpy. It's cozy. Honest."

He didn't give. This was an interesting development. But why did he keep glancing toward the suntanned beauty, with pink stained across his cheeks? I turned away.

"Okay, but I don't like it." The woman sighed. "In fact, I'm going to have to insist you let me feed you tonight so I feel better about it."

Without looking, I felt his eyes on me.

"I'd planned on eating with some of the crew tonight, Shari. I'm sorry."

Was that a reference to me?

"Bring them all. We'll do a backyard barbecue."

Silence. *Please say no.*

"You got it."

Before I could summon some sense, I glanced backward. He stared right at me. Jesse held me with a look I didn't understand, and I silently begged him not to drag me into this arrangement.

He returned his attention to Shari. "There'll be at least two of us, maybe three."

Mack and me. Which of us was the assumed second, and who was the tentative third?

I should have listened to my dad. I should have stayed home.

Chapter Nine

JESSE

I smelled a setup. They always had the same aroma. Usually the same pattern too. It began with a mom, well meaning and generally pleasant, inviting me over. Without mentioning that her available daughter would be in attendance.

Shari surprised me with this one. Barely a year gone by. I was sure Laine needed more time. Plus, if I'd wanted a date, I'd have asked all on my own. Surely Shari knew I didn't need any arrangements, nor did her daughter.

Perhaps she'd misunderstood the relationship that had developed between Laine and me last year. Laine didn't see me as a potential replacement for her snake of an ex-fiancé. We were friends—good friends—but just friends. I listened while she worked through some of the mess the guy had left her in, knowing without a doubt that she needed an outside ear and an honest guy's encouragement. She'd never hinted romantic interest. I was sure I hadn't either. Not last summer. Not today.

I finished loading my tote of tools in the bed of my truck. Most of the workers had been driven home by rumbling stomachs, Shari and Laine included. Only Alex the resident comedian, Mack, and Sarah remained, all standing in a loose circle near the newly raised stud walls. Fixing a smile, I set my stride in their direction.

Sarah caught my eye and stepped away.

My shoulders drooped. She'd misunderstood. I'd caught her glancing toward me while I talked with Shari. No way she didn't hear our conversation. And she'd also seen me watching Laine. What must she think?

"Sapphira." I caught her attention before she scurried off the job site.

Having no choice, she stopped, but she hesitated before she turned back.

"Hungry?" I grinned, hoping she'd not jumped to some natural conclusions.

She shrugged.

Not an encouraging response. I plunged ahead anyway, addressing the group. "Shari Fulton asked the crew over for a barbecue tonight. Y'all are coming, right?"

"Home-cooked food?" Mack licked his lips. "I'm in."

"Sorry, Jess," Alex said. "My wife probably has dinner on the table. I'd better get to it." He shook Mack's hand, then mine, and started away with a wave. "It's nice to meet you, carpenter-girl. See you tomorrow."

That left only Sarah unaccounted for.

Please come. I didn't want to untangle all the reasons I desperately wanted her there. She needed a friend—that was reason enough. I settled my hands on my hips and managed half a grin. "Well, carpenter-girl?"

That shy, scared look that I'd first seen in her eyes returned. "I promised my dad I'd look over some drawings before I got back," she said. "I think I should work on that tonight."

"The drawings will be there when we get done. Gotta eat, right?"

Mack chuckled, clapping me on the shoulder. He spoke under his breath, moving toward his truck as he did. "You've got a thing for challenges, don't you, Chapman?"

I eyed him, but he already had his back to me. "See ya, old man."

Not stopping, he laughed again. But he'd let it go at that. Mack was an old tease, but he wasn't unkind. He probably didn't get what I was after with Sarah, but he wouldn't interfere.

Sarah didn't move, but her eyes traveled to her truck. Planning an escape.

"Come on, Sapphira." I shoved my hands in my pockets and walked toward her. "Shari's planning on you."

She looked to the frame of the house, to the trees near the property's edge, to the dirt near her feet. Anywhere but at me.

"No more hiding on roofs." I stopped right next to her. "They're just people, is all."

More silence.

"Look, you can walk over with me. You won't be alone."

Thoughts whirled in her head—I could see their movement in her cautious eyes. But I couldn't hear them, which stirred desperation in my gut. *Talk to me.*

With a tiny tilt of her chin, she turned her face to mine. "Why do you want me there?"

A loaded question, one that had too many answers. "Because I don't think you should lock yourself away. Most people are nice, if you'd quit hiding."

"I'm not hiding."

I snorted. "Where'd I meet you again?"

She blushed, but a hint of a smile tipped her mouth.

"Come on." I grabbed her shoulder and gave her a playful shake. "One meal. What do you have to lose?"

Her blue eyes settled on mine, and I heard her silent response through her vulnerable expression. *You have no idea.*

Perhaps she was right. I was always a popular kid, and I liked being around people. But Sarah... I saw a wound in that deep, aching look. Resolution cemented in my heart, and with it, purpose defined what I was pursuing when it came to Sarah Sharpe. I needed to know where that wound came from. More important, I wanted to see it healed.

"They're nice people—I promise." My hand still rested on her shoulder, and I squeezed. "If you hate it, we'll leave."

She pulled in air as if she were drawing in courage. "Okay. But I need a shower first."

Victory. "Done. Which hotel?"

"Super 8."

"Perfect. Me too."

SARAH

Why did I keep allowing him to talk me into things beyond my comfort? Dinner with a bunch of strangers—at their house? And with their attractive daughter, who apparently had something simmering with Jesse?

That shouldn't have surprised me. I knew he wouldn't have an interest in me. Not like that. Laine, beautiful, blond, outgoing Laine fit the Jesse profile.

Why had he invited me? That was weird. And annoying, actually.

I tried to suppress the panic clawing in my chest as we neared the Fultons' home.

They're just people.

Yeah, people who didn't know me, or my dad, or anything about our life. Pretty people whose parents stayed together, whose mother actually wanted to be a mother, and who hadn't managed to reach adulthood without a clue as to who they were.

"Here we are." Jesse slowed his pace and gestured to a property hidden behind two giant cottonwoods. "Ready?"

Um, no.

Apparently that wasn't a real question. He turned up the drive without hesitating. The Fultons' house emerged into view—a vintage Victorian, the type called a "painted lady." The majority of the structure had been painted a mossy green, the trim a burnt orange, and the detail work had been highlighted in a buttery yellow. A wide covered front porch extended the length of one side of the house and wrapped around the back. On the opposite side, a gazebo rounded out the corner, topped with a windowpaned turret.

I stopped to examine the handiwork. The design was complicated and yet functional.

Jesse stopped behind me. "She's a beauty, isn't she?"

I assumed he was studying the house, so I risked a glance at him. He stared at me. Warmth spread over my face, and air stuck in my lungs. *Breathe.*

That was silly. *The house, butch-girl. Not you.*

I cleared my throat. "They don't make 'em like that anymore. Not around here anyway."

Jesse nodded, his gaze still locked on me. "Architecture like that is rare anywhere these days. That's what happens when you place quantity over quality. We lose the charm that comes with artistry."

A well-noted truth. Odd, though, that he thought so. Charm and artistry were unaffordable luxuries for his projects.

"Life sometimes demands simplicity," he continued. "I'm not saying a minimalist approach is wrong. But you know what kills me?"

I expected him to rattle away, answering his question without a breath. He didn't. He waited until I turned my eyes up to his.

"I hate it when they bulldoze the old gems. It's like people can't see the beauty waiting underneath the surface. Some of the best builds from years past end up as rubble because people are only looking at the mess left by neglect."

I froze as his eyes held mine. He spoke in layers. We were talking about houses, but somehow it seemed that he saw me the same way—that he wasn't talking only about houses. That flustered me. Was I a mess resulting from neglect?

I didn't want Jesse to see me as some kind of reconstruction project. While uncertain as to what I wanted from him, whatever it was, I wanted it to be sincere. Was it too much to ask that a person sees me as I was, whatever that may be, and was okay with what he found?

That was a trick question, because I wasn't okay with it. I didn't want to be some guy's project, but I didn't want to stay the same either. Feeling lost was awful. But feeling like a task on Jesse's make-him-a-saint checklist was degrading.

I moved toward the house again. When Jesse set his stride beside mine, I drifted toward the lawn on my right, intentionally widening the space between us.

"You okay, Sapphira?"

"Fine." I looped my thumbs in my jeans pockets. "Why?"

"I think irritation just passed over your face." He closed the gap I'd pried open. "Did I say something?"

"Nope." I drifted farther away.

We encountered the porch, and I set a foot on the first of three steps, when he tugged on my elbow. "You're a tough read, carpenter-girl." The corners of his eyes crinkled, but some kind of concern undergirded his grin. "How about you tell me why you're tucking your head inside your shell again?"

Now I was a turtle? "I'm not."

One disbelieving laugh escaped from his lips, and he stared at me for two more breaths. "Okay, but if I catch you on the roof, we'll take a crowbar to this."

Yep. I was his new project. And here I'd thought I'd actually found a friend.

Mrs. Fulton poked her head out of the glass-paned front door, drawing Jesse's attention.

"Hey, you guys, come on in." She waved us to the house. "Mack beat you here. We're all in the backyard, and the burgers are ready."

With a smile, Jesse nodded and then moved his gaze back to me. "Deep breath, kid. You'll have fun. I promise."

Promise, shmomise. He hardly knew me. Didn't know that I'd really only conversed with a handful of women in my whole life. Didn't know that standing next to the blond beauty waiting in the backyard was going to make me feel like that awkward girl on *Saturday Night Live* who had a thing for smelling her own sweat.

Didn't know that right now I felt like hyperventilating and puking at the same time.

His hand touched my elbow and gave it a little wiggle. My feet moved forward, following him even though instinct said to turn around.

Our walk through the house was brief, but as I glimpsed the hand-hewn trim, the paneled ceilings, and the custom French double doors, I tried to escape into architectural appreciation. Because I was on safe ground there. It didn't work. Our trek through the livable artwork lasted less than a minute, and then we passed through the back door and were dumped into the midst of the waiting group.

"Hey, Chapman." Mack's gravelly voice chuckled. "I see you were successful."

With a sideways glance, I saw Jesse raise a challenging brow.

"It was a good day all around." He shook his head once and held Mack's stare a mite long.

A project, and also a bet. I was worse than an abandoned house.

No more Homes For Hope for me. This whole deal shifted from *good for me* to total humiliation. Worse than dealing with Ed the Ego Man up in Valentine. What was Jesse thinking? My appreciation for this quirky, all-too-good man diminished.

I looked away, thinking back to the two meals I'd eaten with him. He'd seemed so genuine, so happy, and peculiarly kind. Now...now he seemed cruel. The paradox made me dizzy, and suddenly my head hurt.

"Hey, Jess." The blond beauty floated through the back door of the house and straight to his side. She'd showered and fixed her hair so that the glossy, honey-golden strands ran in waves down her back. Her perfect complexion glowed, and I wondered if there wasn't some kind of glitter in whatever she must have smeared over her skin. Black eye makeup drew attention to her pale-blue eyes, which she zeroed in on him. "Glad you came."

He turned his attention to her and smiled. "Wouldn't miss it."

Of course he wouldn't. What guy would want to miss the willing attentions of this young, make-me-feel-like-a-brute beauty? I stepped away, not sure where I was headed, but not willing to stand there feeling like the contrast character in a predictable play.

"Laine, did you meet Sarah?"

Was it rude to keep walking away when you heard your name connected to an introduction? Probably. I stopped, swallowed a sigh, and slowly forced myself to turn back to them.

"No, I didn't get the chance." Laine held her dainty hand out.

I shook it carefully because I didn't want my calloused man-hands to crush her fragile fingers.

"Sarah Sharpe." I pushed my name past my lips, hating that I sounded like a wispy coward with my voice all raspy like that.

"It's nice to meet you." Her thin smile didn't really confirm that. "Do you travel with Homes For Hope too?"

I swallowed. "No."

Her eyes moved from me to Jesse and then back again.

"Sarah lives in Minden." Jesse shifted from one foot to the other and then took a small step away from Laine. "She's a framer. Her dad owns a contracting business, and she's volunteering with us this weekend."

Laine, who had kept her focus glued to him, glanced back to me with subtle relief. "Oh. How nice." A bright smile spread over her face as she returned her attention to Jesse. "So, do you want to meet Sophie?"

And that's my cue. I turned away on my clompy boots and wandered across the grass. How long did I need to stay before my departure wouldn't be deemed rude?

JESSE

Another miscalculation. Two actually. I should have taken Sarah out to that Texas barbecue place downtown.

She'd come to some wrong conclusions. So had Laine. How had I landed in the middle of this pickle jar? See? I got women about as well as I comprehended math.

"This"—Laine reemerged from her parents' home with a bundle wrapped in soft pink—"is Sophie."

Now what? I glanced across the yard and tried not to gulp. No wonder Sarah had skittered away. She probably hated me right about now. Thought I'd drug her here to make her feel awkward and dumb. Maybe even assumed the little bundle of life cooing in Laine's arms was mine.

Nausea turned in my stomach.

Dragging my attention back to Laine, I focused on her four-month-old daughter. "She's beautiful."

It was true. Little Sophie Fulton had her mother's light complexion and blue eyes. A bunny-soft tuft of brown hair covered her tiny head. A genetic trait I would guess originated with her lousy father, though I couldn't say for sure, because I'd never met the guy.

My fists balled at my side as my thoughts passed over the man who'd left this baby girl without a daddy. Miserable excuse for a man.

"Would you like to hold her?" The baby was already against my chest before Laine finished the question.

I liked kids. Shane's girls were some of my favorite people in the world. But this was awkward. My eyes drifted back to the corner of the yard where Sarah had retreated, near the big lilac bushes that marked the property boundary. Mack had found her and stood talking to her. Probably in an attempt to keep her off the roof. *Bless him.*

"She likes you, Jess." Laine's smile softened her voice.

With a small inhale, I refocused on the tiny scrap of a girl in my arms. She studied me, her mouth moving. I grinned as she pushed a fist into her mouth. I did like kids, and this one didn't deserve the life that was thrust upon her.

"Have you figured out what you'll do?" I kept my gaze on Sophie, tracing her face with my index finger.

"No." Laine's voice dipped, and I could feel her sag at my side. "Stay with Mom and Dad for now. That's all I know." She brushed her daughter's downy head and then rested her fingers on my arm. "I'm still praying for a miracle, I guess."

I chanced a connection of our eyes, which I shouldn't have. She wasn't talking about her ex-fiancé's return. At all.

Darting away from her implication, I studied the baby again—because what else was I supposed to do? Involuntarily, I pondered Laine's implication. Two months ago, I honestly might have considered her unvoiced plea. Because I didn't think innocent children should pay for their DNA donors' irresponsibility. And I did like Laine. She was a nice girl who got herself tangled up with the wrong kind of man. But now...

I sought a glimpse of Sarah. Still hiding out by the bushes, she didn't even make eye contact with Mack while they talked. I imagined the conversation was about as fluid as a dry creek bed during a three-month drought. That boat just don't float.

I'd pushed her alone out into the desert. Man, I was such an idiot.

What was my deal with this girl? I'd literally bumped into her, and in the three weeks' time of simply knowing she existed, something in me had changed.

Sophie squirmed, and I looked down in time to see offense contort her little face. Her bottom lip quivered as a squall erupted from her belly.

"I think she wants her mama." I shifted to hand her back, careful to minimize contact with Laine. I'd already managed to plant ideas I didn't intend. Didn't need to water them too.

Laine pressed Sophie against her shoulder and placed a kiss near her miniature ear. "She's a good baby. We had shots yesterday, though."

I smiled but leaned a tad backward. "All babies cry, so I'm told. No worries. I'm not offended."

With her eyes glued to me, I couldn't miss the hope in Laine's stare. Oh heavens. What had I done? And what did I do now? My throat went dry, and I tried to clear it.

I guessed the silence gave Laine the answer she didn't want. Her posture drooped as her look fell to the deck. "I should take Sophie in. She's due a bottle." Her steps were heavy as she covered the distance back to the house.

Wasn't I the biggest jerk? If women had thought bubbles drifting over their heads, I would have been a lot better off. And so would they. I lifted my hat and pushed a hand through my hair. How had I not seen this coming?

Sarah was planted by the shrubs, alone. Mack had gone to fill his plate. Good thing I didn't hope for more than friendship with her. One blind step and I'd shot any chance for more to...Antarctica. Tugging my hat snug down to my burning ears, I stepped down from the deck and headed to her side.

"Whatchya doing here by yourself?" *Brilliant, Jess. Make her feel like the unidentifiable spare part and then ask why she'd run off on her own.*

Sarah shrugged. "I don't know anyone."

"Not gonna either, standing twenty feet from everybody." Did I sound like Dr. Phil? I felt like one of those annoying sports analysts who could only ever say why a particular athlete would *not* be successful. Total jerk.

Her single short glance told me her thoughts ran right alongside the same path.

"I'm not really that hungry." She started moving toward the back gate. "And I'm actually pretty tired. I'm gonna go."

"Wait, Sapphira." I tugged on her arm, and she stopped. I glanced to my hands and drew a lungful of air. "I'm sorry. I know that was really awkward. I didn't expect... Anyway, I'm sorry. Laine and I have known each other for two years. She was supposed to get married last May, but two weeks before the wedding, she caught him cheating. She called it off, and he left. She discovered she was pregnant a couple of months later."

Sarah listened without a show of emotion. "You don't owe me an explanation, Jesse. This isn't my thing, and I still have those plans to look over."

I readied a grin as I searched for something...charming? Hold up. Had I been manipulating her? I shoved my hands into my pockets as my shoulders slumped. "Can I walk you back?"

"The town's not that big. I can find my way." She started off again and then stopped. Her head bent forward, and I saw a sigh roll off her shoulders. "Will they think I'm rude?"

Good work, Jess. "No." I took two steps toward her. "I'll make sure they don't."

She nodded but remained motionless. Like she needed me to let her off the ledge I'd hung her on.

"See you tomorrow, carpenter-girl?"

Her head tipped back, and she studied me, and once again emotion cleared from her expression. "Framing's done. No changes to the floor plan. I'm not needed."

Not a very promising answer. "Roof's still got work."

"I'm pretty sure you can handle it." Without another breath, she left me standing in stupid dismay.

I stared after her for who knows how long. Next thing I knew, Mack was next to me, his rough chuckle rumbling low in his chest.

"Kind of funny to see you squirm, Chapman."

I glared at him out of the corner of my eyes. "Glad you're enjoying yourself."

He let that laugh loose out in the open. "Didn't even see it coming, did you?"

"Did you?"

"You're too nice, boy." He shook his head. "Young ladies and their mamas see you in all your sainthood and start looking for a preacher. You're caught blindsided."

True. Except the sainthood part. I was exasperatingly ignorant with the rest though. "Could have warned me."

"You're too busy trying to calculate the Sarah Sharpe equation."

I blew out a breath. "I'm not calculating anything. Just trying to figure her out."

Mack's laugh bellowed across the yard. A moment later, I heard what I'd said and snickered. It was funny.

Except what I'd done to Sarah today wasn't so amusing.

"Look, Mack. Don't be making a thing out of this, okay? Sarah's..." Sarah was what, exactly? A mystery I needed to solve? A wounded creature I thought I needed to fix? A woman I was compelled toward?

Yes. But no to the last part. Because it couldn't be like that.

"You be careful with that one." Mack crossed his arms and took a step closer. His voice dropped to a whisper. "She's not the kind that'll bounce back, if you know what I mean."

I wanted to pretend that I didn't. "That's not where I'm going with her."

"Right." One eyebrow quirked up, and Mack held a long look on my face. "You're not good at this, Jesse, so trust me on this one. Your head and your heart aren't agreeing with each other, and someone's going to get hurt. I'm pretty sure you'll be okay. But that carpenter girl—"

"No one's getting hurt." I scowled, holding Mack's stare for two more breaths before I strode away.

Something was definitely wrong with me.

Chapter Ten

SARAH

I thought going home would fix everything. Too bad I couldn't develop some kind of selective amnesia. I'd forget the weekend, along with this frustrating quest that nagged me every single waking moment.

Who am I? And is that who I want to be?

Questions I couldn't answer. Answers I needed to find.

I was going crazy. The only way to make this Ferris wheel stop was to nail down that solution.

Jesse Chapman had only complicated everything.

Logic hadn't weighed down that fanciful daydream I didn't want to admit to replaying. A lot. The one where he noticed me as a woman, not just as a carpenter with a fast hammer.

Where logic had failed, Laine had stepped in. Pretty, feminine, and very noticeable. Nothing like me.

Pop. Good-bye, daydream. Hello, reality.

I had packed up as soon as I got to the hotel. Figure that— paid for one night's stay and stayed for less than a day. Waste of time. Waste of money. Waste of foolish emotion. Maybe that'd teach me.

Or not. Because apparently I couldn't voluntarily develop amnesia, and Jesse's green eyes and smile wouldn't budge from my stubborn imagination. Home fixed nothing.

Maybe work would. I buried myself in some files.

Dad was still working in Kearney. I'd been there for three days earlier in the week, installing Sheetrock after we got the building dried in. We hung the drywall abnormally fast, and then I didn't have anything to do because the electrician hadn't finished the second half of the building. I could've gone back and mudded what I'd already installed, but it made more sense to do it all at once.

A whole day to do nothing but think. No thank you.

I shuffled through Dad's upcoming projects, selected a medium bid—a renovation of an old main-street hotel in Aurora—and opened the project file. Clearing the abandoned space would take some time. The three-story brick building had been left to decay for four decades. Some would see the neglect and call it hopeless.

Jesse wouldn't.

Yuck. Go away.

I studied the project proposal. The plans weren't complicated. Most of the interior walls would remain the same. They'd need stripped to the bones to update the electrical and plumbing and then resupported, but the new design maintained most of the original integrity.

It was a job I could take on. With a small crew, I could do it. Without Dad.

My pulse leapt into overdrive, and my fingers tingled. I'd never stepped out on my own. Not for anything bigger than installing a new floor for a local homeowner. Dad had never asked me to, never hinted that he wanted me to. But perhaps that was because I wasn't one to put myself on a ledge, so to speak.

I'd led a crew of amateurs on Saturday. Got the job done. Granted, setting walls for a cracker-box house wasn't the same as taking on a whole renovation, but...

I closed the file. My head had been full of dumb ideas. Time to stay on the firm ground of reality.

Leaning back in my desk chair, I stared out the square window across our shared office. I had a material order to submit. Time cards to calculate. Paychecks to print. Lots of stuff to do.

I shifted my weight forward and propped my arms on my desk. My laptop sat open, waiting for me to become productive. Catching my reflection in the screen, I stared at the girl looking back at me. She had dark-blue eyes shaded by a sweat-stained old hat.

I peeled the hat off, and my hair fell forward. I ran my fingers through the almost black strands, shaking them at their roots. Didn't help much. Maybe a shower would.

With one decisive motion, I pushed from the desk and stood. Payroll could wait—I had nothing else to do with the rest of the afternoon anyway. My long strides took me out the door and to my truck. In less than five minutes I'd driven the ten blocks from our steel building where we worked to our little bungalow where we lived. No. Slept, and sometimes ate. I didn't have a life.

Steam drifted around me as I washed with my drugstore-brand shampoo. After removing the dirt and grease from my hair, I shut the water off and towel dried myself. Clothing next. What should I wear? I hadn't worn more than three articles of my new clothing since I'd gone shopping with Darcy.

I found the overstuffed bag of new duds on my closet floor right where I'd thrown it after that trip. With a quick shove of my hand, I grabbed the first bundle of fabric available and tugged it free. Some kind of pants. I snipped the tag off and stepped into the legs. My nose wrinkled. Were they supposed to reach only three inches below my knees?

Standing half dressed in the middle of my brown-and-blue room, I rewound my mind back to the shopping trip. Had I tried these things on?

Yep. Darcy called them adorable, and not pants. Cappers? Capers? Capris. She'd called them capris. Who knew clothing could be technical?

Okeydokey. Bottom was covered. I giggled. Puns always amused me.

Next contestant. My hand disappeared into the plastic bag and reemerged with something pink. Pink? I actually bought something pink? Holding it by a seam, I let gravity unroll it. A shirt. Blouse. Something.

"You wear it on top," I mumbled to myself, and then I pushed the neckhole over my head. Arms next, and then it draped over my waistband. And now I was dressed. How 'bout that? Same process—almost—I went through every morning. With a pivot on the ball of my foot, I pulled my closet door open to find the full-length mirror that had been in my room when we'd moved in some twenty years ago.

Whoa. Not the same result I got every morning. The startled woman in the mirror snapped her mouth shut and took another pass over my new duds. Huh. I didn't look nearly as manly in *pink.*

I grinned as warmth lined my chest. I ignored the image of Jesse's smile.

My gaze settled on my face. I didn't have Laine's peaches-and-cream complexion. But my eyes were blue. A quick spin away from the mirror, a few small steps to the bathroom, and an easy rummage through the sink drawer produced the small bag of makeup that had sat untouched for three weeks.

I focused on my eyes, because that was all I could remember. After smudging a charcoal pencil over my eyelids, I brushed my lashes with inky black liquid. I couldn't help staring into the mirror.

Sapphira.

What would he think?

I didn't care—much. I was stunned. It took a small hunt to find my blow-dryer, but after five minutes of hot air, a careful combing, and a couple of failed bobby-pin placements, I did another personal inspection.

Couldn't be me.

But it was.

Maybe I could take on that renovation. That woman in the mirror may just have more in her than I'd imagined.

***

"Sarah?" Dad's voice boomed from the back door. "Are you home?"

Oh no. What time was it? I hadn't done my paperwork. Guess it'd be a late night.

Biting my bottom lip, I glanced back to the mirror. What was I doing?

"Sarah?"

I swallowed. "Yeah, I'm here. Hang on a sec."

I searched the bathroom, suddenly frantic. Sweats? Jeans? A baggy shirt? Nope. Towels. Nothing to put over my girly-clad body but towels. That would be ridiculous. I sucked in a lungful of air. It didn't make me brave.

I turned the knob on the door and shuffled a timid exit into the hall.

"Are you sick?" Dad hadn't rounded the corner from the kitchen yet.

"No."

After stepping into the hall, he froze. Except his eyes, which inspected me head to toe. Shock. Then confusion. And finally...anger?

"What are you doing?" he barked.

My throat swelled as heat flooded my face. "I needed a shower."

His eyes narrowed. "What are you wearing?"

My gulp didn't clear that painful lump. "Clothes?"

His jaw worked back and forth, and then his Adam's apple bobbed. His voice dropped to a low snarl. "What's on your face?"

I couldn't look at him anymore. Staring at the floor, I blinked against the hot wetness in my eyes.

"What are you trying to do?"

I swallowed as betrayal saturated me. I was a daddy's girl. Didn't look like one—because I looked butch—but I was. His opinion, or in this case, disapproval, sank into me like a nail into soft wood.

"Nothing, Dad." I squared my shoulders, because good posture projected a good image, a hard worker. Dad said so. But I couldn't look him in the eye.

He began to turn away and then stopped. "Is this what Darcy told you to do?" He scowled as he scratched the rough hairs on his chin. "Did she say you needed to turn into"—he stopped, his eyes grazing my appearance—"into Barbie?"

From butch to Barbie. That was quite a leap. "No."

He'd been the one to call Aunt Darcy, told her what happened at Subway and probably begged her to take me shopping. Where was this hypocrisy coming from?

Boldness streaked through my chest, and I tipped my chin until our eyes met. "No. Darcy didn't tell me to change on the outside. She said what mattered was inside. But I don't feel right inside."

His jaw worked as his dark eyebrows hooded his eyes. "Why? Sarah, we have a good life. What is it you want? A boyfriend? Catcalls at work?" He jammed a hand through his hair and then flung it into the air. "I don't understand what's going on with you."

Me neither. Thanks for the help.

I often wondered if my mother had a soft, submissive kind of personality that finally got worn out. My quiet, take-it-as-it-comes approach to life didn't come from my dad. But at that moment, the brazen tell-it-like-it-is Sharpe trait came rolling to the front and started growing like Jack's beanstalk in the moonlight. "Look, you sent me to Omaha. You sent me to shop. I'm a grown woman, Dad. You can't expect me to cower and comply every time you scowl. At twenty-one, I'm plenty old enough to wear makeup. And if I want to paint my nails, what's it to you? 'Bout time I figure out who I am, and if you don't like it, you can look the other way."

"You think you're going to find who you are in a bottle of face paint?" His voice inched up in volume with every syllable. "Good gravy, Sarah, if you don't know who you are before you paint your face, how do you expect to find yourself in a costume?"

"A costume?" I shouted back. "Maybe flannel and boots have been my costume all these years. You made me into who you wanted. Probably the son you didn't get. But maybe I'm not who you hoped."

"At the moment, I'm pretty sure you're right." An angry stare held mine, and then his features softened. Not with regret, but with something much worse. "The last thing I wanted was for you to turn into *her*."

The blow came hard, splintered with scorn.

***

I didn't know what people did in flights of fury—hadn't had one before. Sure, I'd been mad before, but not like this, and not usually with my dad. So I stormed out of the house, yanked my pickup door open, and climbed in. After jamming my keys in the ignition, the diesel rumbled to life, and I shifted into reverse.

Evidently I was going somewhere.

In a town where there was more livestock than people, options were limited. Bowling. The Pioneer Museum, which was closed. The Circle K corner store. And The Crossing, which was the bar across the tracks. I took the last selection.

I'd been there a few times with my dad and Uncle Dan. They'd knock back a couple of beers, and I'd nurse a "fruity chick drink," as they put it, and we'd share a couple of baskets of hot wings. The life of a carpenter's daughter, I guessed.

I'd never gone solo. Dressed as a woman, complete with makeup and ballet flats. Had not the burn of anger propelled me, I would have stopped short of tugging that wooden door open and turned my pickup back toward home. Thus the term "flight of fury," I figured.

Entering The Crossing, I threw my shoulders back and strode straight to the bar.

"Cosmo." I thought that was what I'd had before.

Joe stood behind the counter and cocked one eyebrow. Probably got the dumb thing wrong. Or maybe I'd been rude?

"Please."

His mouth tipped up in a crooked grin. "Papa-less tonight, huh, Sharpe?"

Cute. Not only was I butch, but I couldn't go anywhere without my daddy. My life kept getting more pathetic. I clamped my mouth shut and let the simmering anger temper my gaze.

"Whoa." Joe held up his hands. "Whoever set you cross must have been some kind of crazy. I've never seen you with emotion."

"Just get me a drink."

"Right." His eyes shifted to the doorway, and his forehead scrunched. "Will I be in trouble?"

I glanced over my shoulder. Dad filled the entry. Peachy. We could continue our disagreement right there at the bar.

After a pointed glare to my dad, I returned my attention to Joe. "Do you need my ID? I'm a grown woman. I don't need my *father's* permission to drink."

"Sure." Joe grabbed a stemmed glass. "Take it outside if it gets rough, okay?"

So flattering. I waited with one foot propped up on the scuffed brass bar running along the base of the cabinetry and both hands jammed onto my hips, any moment expecting my dad to interrupt my effort at not looking at him. One minute ticked by. Then two. No Dad leaning over my shoulder. Joe slid my drink across the counter.

"Thanks."

"Thought only women did the cold-shoulder thing." He shook his head and wandered to the other end of the bar.

I followed his trail with my eyes and found my dad saddled up way the heck down there. Dad glanced at me, his scowl still dark, and then mumbled to Joe. I turned, giving them a view of my back, and pretended to watch the game of pool in progress by the far window.

"Can I buy you another drink?" A deep voice interrupted my concentration on ignoring the two men at the other end of the counter.

Turning only my neck, my eyes landed on Aiden Beck, the most loved guy from my high school days. The boy had played basketball, was voted most likely to succeed in Hollywood, and was probably most well known for his alternating hot and cold relationship with Brenna James, hands down the prettiest girl in our graduating class.

Aiden's dimpled grin faltered a bit as his sky-blue eyes widened. But only for a moment. His lips spread with full-on charm, and he slid onto the stool next to mine. "Sarah Sharpe, you are looking sharp."

Original. Clearly he hadn't been a straight A student.

I'd never actually heard a line directed at me before, so a smile peeked through my prior irritation.

"Aiden Beck, you are looking like…" Oh dear. Had I really attempted to flirt? I didn't know how to do that. Case in point, I had nothing to finish with.

"Looking like it's my lucky day."

Uh, okay, so he was quick on his feet. Cheesy, but not dumb.

He leaned into my space. "So, what are we drinking?"

A throat cleared across the bar. I shifted my attention from Aiden to Joe, who scowled from the other side of the counter.

"What do you want, Beck?"

Aiden glanced to the bartender before he settled that impish grin back on me. "We were just talking about that."

"Sarah's already got her drink." Joe folded his arms over his chest. "Where's your little blonde?"

Good question. I should have asked that. Last I knew, he and Brenna were still *on*. But like I said, that status changed about as often as the Nebraska weather.

"She's doing whatever she wants." Aiden's look flicked to Joe, and he frowned. "And so am I. Right now, I want a beer, and another..." He made a show of looking at my drink. "Cosmo."

Joe looked at me, one eyebrow cocked. "You want another Cosmo?"

I'd barely taken two sips of the one I had. "I'm good. Thank you anyway."

"She's good." Joe nodded, his stare hard on Aiden. "Go fishing for retribution somewhere else."

Retribution? Ah. Now I remembered my place. I slid off the stool and wandered over to the pool table, where the couple who'd been cracking the balls had finished their round. I grabbed a cue stick and racked the balls, ready for my solo night to continue.

"I'll break." Dad spoke behind me.

I swiveled my head to look at him. Our eyes connected, and the tension in my shoulders rolled away. Swallowing, I nodded, and he did too. That was as close to *I'm sorry* as we got.

Chapter Eleven

SARAH

My phone chirped from my back pocket. Pushing my hat back, I reached to answer it, wiping the sweat from my forehead while I looked at the caller ID. Unknown. Weird. Only a handful of people knew this number—most clients called the office, and my dad and uncle Dan were in the shop fifty yards away. That left no one I knew to be calling me at noon on a Friday.

"Hello?"

"Sarah Sharpe." A male's voice seemed to grin in my ear. "Couldn't get you out of my head. Girl, you grew up and were looking good last week."

Who on earth? Where did I go last week?

To the bar. "Aiden?"

"I knew you wouldn't forget me." Somehow the arrogant swagger in his tone made me smile. "I sure couldn't forget you. Got plans tonight?"

Yeah, the usual. Takeout pizza with Dad and Dan, Redbox movie, and a whole lot of nothing else.

"Not really." I sucked in a long pull of air, eyeing my dad across the shop as he squared up a wall. Seemed my way of doing things on the Kearney project finally settled with him, and he took to prebuilt walls like he'd always done it that way.

What would he think of me going out with Aiden Beck? Probably not much of anything good. Wasn't sure that mattered to me. Much.

"Nothing that I can't postpone." I ran my tongue along my teeth, unsure about what I was doing. I'd missed the whole lesson on flirting.

I glanced over to Dad again. He would be furious. Didn't have a good thing to say about Aiden, even back in high school. Not that we talked about him much, but Dad liked to keep track of the basketball team, and Aiden had played. I thought Dad called him a punk. Yep, that was it. An arrogant punk who thought he was a one-man show.

"Good. Postpone it, girl." Aiden had a way of giving a direct order that seemed like a compliment. "You and I are long overdue for a get-to-know-you outing."

Get-to-know-you...how? I wasn't up to speed on those kinds of outings. "Where are we going?"

"Dancing."

Where was that going to happen? Only really drunk people danced at The Crossing. It didn't matter how charming Beck was—I wasn't getting drunk. "Dancing?"

"Yep. Kearney. I'll pick you up at six."

I laughed. "It's four, and I'm at the shop, with sawdust clinging to my skin."

"Oh." His groan prickled gooseflesh on my arms. "I could help with that."

Oh dear. Instinct said to hang up on him. But defiance—or something—kicked in, and I didn't. "No thanks. I can't be ready by six. I work until then. And I don't need picked up. I'll meet you there."

"You don't know where we're going."

True.

Dad stopped firing nails into the studs and turned to look at me. Heat flooded my face, and his eyebrows drew together. I looked away.

"Tell me where and I'll meet you."

"Sarah," Dad barked, "who are you talking to?"

I waved my hand at him while Aiden talked. "Nope. But I'll compromise with you. I'll meet you at The Crossing, and then we can head north. Seven. Not a minute later."

This probably wasn't a good idea. I opened my mouth to turn him down.

Aiden spoke before I got the words out. "Don't stand me up."

Click.

I looked at the screen—*call ended* lit up in red. Great. Now what?

"Sarah, are you going to stand around for the next couple of hours?"

I turned back to Dad. His suspicious glower didn't help the fire brewing in my stomach.

"I pay you to work. Get after it."

JESSE

I pulled up to the local hotel and sighed. Last hotel I'd stayed in had felt...empty. Not that I ever shared a room with anyone, but knowing that Sarah had left early because of my ill-conceived plans carved a pit inside me that seemed to affect my surroundings.

Maybe I had too much on my mind, and that blew everything out of proportion. Avery had dropped a load of bricks on my shoulders this weekend.

I replayed that conversation, which happened on Wednesday evening when I'd been a part of her regular Bible study— something I was usually excited about when I got the chance to go.

"Pastor was telling me about a project his brother-in-law has his hands in out in Omaha." Avery snagged a mitt and opened her oven door. Out came a perfect golden-brown pie, oozing red.

I couldn't resist a long whiff. Oh, so good. My tongue dripped with anticipation. Good thing my mouth was closed. It was hard to think about whatever it was we were talking about, but I forced my mind, and my tongue, to behave. "Yeah? What's that?"

"A project in North Omaha." Ken, Avery's pastor, spoke as if that should mean something.

I wasn't connecting any dots. "I'm not sure what that means."

Ken nodded. "Neighborhood's kind of rough. Not the money hot spot, if you know what I mean. Several churches in Omaha have put a fund together. They bought a block of houses."

"A block? Like a whole city block?"

"Exactly." His wife, Sharon, jumped in, all smiles.

"Okay." I tried to do the math. There seemed to be some variables missing. And I wasn't good with math. "What's a group of churches going to do with a city block of houses?"

"They were crack houses," Ken said.

Wow. Even more intriguing. Still not following.

"Oh, just tell him the whole story, and then say what you're thinking." Avery set plates around the table, each one covered with a monstrous portion of flakey pastry goodness. Did I have to wait to dig in until the conversation worked all the way through?

Sharon spoke before I could push. "They want to convert the houses to something useful, something good. Shelters for single mothers. A recovery house for addicts. Ministry that meets the needs of people who are often overlooked by the church."

"Good plan." I smiled, purposely looking to both Ken and then Sharon, not to the pie that called to my squealing taste buds. "I like it. It involves me how?"

Ken cleared his throat. "The houses are in pretty bad shape. They need renovating."

Aha. I dug my fork into my slice of cherry heaven, which suddenly looked more like bribery baked in pastry. I laughed. "Spit it out, Avery. Whatchya got cooking inside that head of yours?"

"You, Jesse." *She grinned.* "You're perfect for this project."

Not so much. I wasn't my dad.

Exhaustion slid over me. Not normal. I was a hyperactive person. I woke up early, stayed up late, and work somehow acted like a battery for my already high energy level. But that night, I felt tired.

After checking in, I showered and flopped on the sagging bed. We would start another job in the morning. I knew a few of the people around here. Thankfully, none of them were female. No more of that variety for me. I hadn't realized the extent of their...uh, hope concerning me. Not until the fiasco at the Fultons'. They'd pinned me as their knight. Maybe I should've been; heaven knew that baby girl should have a daddy, and I liked Laine, but it didn't seem right. Not with the way my mind always seemed to drift back to Sarah.

Pretty, a worker, smart, and so very vulnerable. That last part had me intrigued. The combination of the first three qualities should have led to confidence, but she wasn't. I got that there were people out there who weren't crowd lovers, but Sarah seemed to shrink inside herself. It was more than shyness, almost like she was lost.

Lost. Yes. She knew exactly what she was doing when it came to building, and she did it well, but even in her element, her eyes held a wandering quality. Like she didn't know who she was.

That was strange, because I felt like I knew her. I stared at the ceiling. How could I really know a woman who didn't know herself?

My phone chirped from the bedside table. My heart did a goofy little hop as I reached for it, unreasonably hoping to see *Sapphira* on the screen. I'd called her last Friday night when I didn't see her truck in the hotel parking lot. She hadn't answered, so I left a message. Short and simple. *I'm sorry.*

She didn't call me back.

Maybe that was why I was so engrossed with her. I hated the idea that anyone wouldn't like me. Too much of a people pleaser, that was what Shane said.

The phone chirped again, and I grabbed it. Mack. My chest caved in, but I made my voice sound like my normal, upbeat self. "Hey."

"Did you make it?"

"Yep." I scanned my room. "Gotta say, Mack, this place is a dive. Even for me."

"I told you to book a room in Kearney."

"Yeah, I know, but I was tired." I pushed a hand through my wet hair. "This'll do."

"Tired?" Mack's gruff chuckle scratched over the phone. "Don't think I've ever heard that one from you. Kearney's only a half hour down the road."

Walked into trouble there. I swallowed, not knowing what to say.

"This has everything to do with the tangled web you managed to get caught up in last week, doesn't it?"

For a guy who generally kept to work and not much else, Mack was getting nosy about this.

"It wasn't that big of a deal."

Mack didn't respond immediately. Awkward.

"You worked by yourself the rest of the weekend and took off for Valentine as soon as the sun went down Sunday. You don't even sound like yourself now. I'd say something was a big deal."

His fatherly tone touched on an ache that had mostly healed. My dad had been quite a guy. Oddly, I found Mack's reminder of him irritating. Not only was I lying in a crappy hotel room brooding about a woman I couldn't pursue, now I missed my parents.

"Look. It's nothing." I came off the bed and stalked to the window. "Maybe I'm coming down with something. Who knows? I'm just tired."

Mack cleared his throat, and my shoulders slumped. Tired. Defensive. Snappy. Yep, there was definitely something wrong with me.

"Did you call her?" His tone sounded soft. Very strange.

I rubbed the back of my neck and allowed my mind to pass over the week again. I loved Avery's house, and her offer for me to land there during a lull had been well timed. It was like visiting a grandparent, and I'd adopt Avery as a grandmother anytime. But always lingering had been the hope that Sarah would call me back.

"Yeah, I called her—apologized." My hand fell to my side.

"Good." Mack's characteristic bark returned. "Is she coming this weekend?"

Ha. That would mean that she'd actually talked to me. "Not that I know of."

You couldn't really pull off casual indifference after a dip into the deep side of a conversation. The air on the line seemed to stretch tenuously.

"Then apologize again." Still the commander in chief. "I need her skills, so fix it."

He hung up. Mack literally hung up on me. No one had ever hung up on me. I wasn't the guy people hung up on. Was he seriously upset that Sarah had ditched us because of me? Maybe that hadn't been fatherly compassion hemming his voice.

Then again, maybe all of it had been exactly that.

SARAH

I brushed the hair out of my eyes and glanced, for like the ten-millionth time, into my rearview mirror. The made-up face of a woman stared back at me. I liked the way she looked. Didn't like the way she felt though.

Lying to my dad—that was new, and it fit like a belt that was two sizes too small. I should've left, gone home. I had no business waiting in The Crossing's parking lot for Aiden like some sneaky, rebellious teenager.

Rebellion?

No. This was a journey. Boys didn't normally look at me like a girl they'd be interested in. They looked at me like a contracting consultant, which was what I was. But there must be more to me than that.

Rocks crackled beneath the weight of a vehicle as a tricked-out Jeep Wrangler pulled up beside my truck. Sitting tall on its lift kit, the bright-orange paint job screamed *I need attention* to anyone near the vicinity.

Was that what my makeup said?

I didn't expect you to turn into her.

I didn't want to be *her*. That was the last thing I wanted. I needed to figure out *me*.

A door smacked closed, reminding me that I wasn't alone, and in the next heartbeat Aiden was leaning on my truck.

"Hello, gorgeous." He spoke through my open window, drawing out the *hello* like he was a game-show host.

The image of a vulture blipped through my mind. I ignored it.

"Hey. I was thinking maybe we could play a round of pool here." I gripped the bottom of my steering wheel, looking at my hands. "I'm not much of a dancer."

"Not a chance." Aiden leaned through the window, seriously invading my personal space. "Always a first time for everything." His whisper tickled my ear. He moved back and opened my door. "I'm a great dancer. You're in good hands."

The hairs on my arms stood straight as warning bells blared in my ears. That was ridiculous. Was I a woman or some thirteen-year-old girl who couldn't even look at a guy without blushing?

A woman. About time I settled that one. Twenty-one was all grown up, and for heaven's sake, I should've been dating long before this. No more of this sheltered, I'm-afraid-of-the-world living.

I slid out of the truck, my black flat shoes crunching on the rocks beneath my feet as I pivoted to shut the door. Aiden opened the passenger side of his glow-in-the-dark ride, and I slid inside.

He stood with the door in his hand while his eyes passed over my form. Twice. I'd worn the dark skinny jeans Aunt Darcy said made my legs look amazing, and a thin fabric tank. My shoulders felt completely naked, and as he perused me with his eyes, I wondered if that much exposure lit a male's imagination.

A low whistle escaped his puckered lips. "Girl, why have you been hiding under flannel all these years?"

Good question. Except I didn't know I'd been hiding. "Maybe you've just started looking."

Huh. This flirting thing wasn't that hard. My face warmed.

A smile crept across his lips, dimpling one cheek. "I see you now." He winked and then shut the door.

My stomach fizzed like it would before one of those thrill rides at Six Flags. I liked those rides. I felt brave when I strapped in and exhilarated when I stepped off.

He pulled onto the highway, heading north, and I sat back against the leather seat, determined to enjoy this ride. We had twenty minutes of pastures and farm ground before we'd reach Kearney. My muscles tensed again. What did I do with twenty minutes in a car alone with a guy? On a date?

"So..." Aiden, who was clearly much more practiced at this than I, flashed a grin. "I see you at the bar for the first time since I've known you, and you're dressed to kill. There's a story there."

Not one I was telling him. "I've been to The Crossing before. Maybe you have bad timing."

He laughed, and then his fingers trailed down my neck. "Or you have perfect timing." His hand covered mine, which rested on my leg. Was I supposed to hold it? I glanced at his profile out of the corner of my eye. His dimples still poked against his cheeks. He squeezed my leg, which jolted my muscles, and then took my hand.

Was this normal? And what did he mean *perfect timing*?

Joe had said something about fishing and retribution last week.

"What's up with you and Brenna?"

He snuck a glance at me that said, W*ell, well, well. We put on bold with our makeup tonight, didn't we?*

Guess I had. I slid my hand from his and waited.

"Nothing. We're done."

I laughed through my nose, which probably wasn't feminine. "Until..."

His smile drifted into a frown. "Until forever. She wanted out, and I'm not sorry."

Clearly.

Okay, so in basketball I think this was what we called hitting the boards. A rebound date...whatever. His compliments weren't a bad exchange in the deal, and maybe I could figure out how this whole scene worked while he figured out whatever he needed to figure out. A win for both of us.

The miles drifted by, and my hand was back in his clasp by the time we parked at Red Lobster.

"Dinner first." Aiden turned the engine off and opened his door. "Things don't get interesting at the club until later."

Maybe I should have asked more questions before I strapped myself into this man's vehicle. Like, *how long are we going to be gone?* My stomach busied itself with knots and bows, making me sure I wasn't going to be able to eat a thing, while Aiden came around to my side of the Jeep. I was already out and had the door shut by the time he made it, so he took my hand again and pulled me snug up to his side.

Was that presumptuous or the expected behavior on a date? I didn't have much time to wonder. His hand dropped to my hip, and then we were moving forward toward the restaurant.

I'd been right about the eating. I could hardly swallow anything. Mostly because Aiden's hands were almost always in contact with some part of my body. He'd toyed with my fingers while we waited for our plates, then somewhere between his first and second drink he scooted his chair closer and found my leg. In between bites, he would lean in close to tell me something he found fascinating about me. Why hadn't he noticed my freckles in high school? And my eyes, so blue. My black hair, so shiny and—he reached up to stroke the ends of my short cut—soft.

His hand cupped my neck, and he leaned so close that I could feel the bristle of his evening shadow against my cheek. "You smell pure." His warm breath tickled my ear. "Do you know what that does to a man?"

Yikes. I pulled away, heat flooding my body.

He got the check and draped his arm over me as we walked to the car. I reached to open my door, but he covered my hand and wrapped me with both of his arms. This absolutely couldn't be normal first-date stuff. The hair on my neck bristled.

"There's something about you, Sarah." Aiden pulled me tight against his chest and whispered just above my ear. "It's driving me crazy. How have I missed it all this time?"

Probably because your tongue's been jammed down Brenna's throat for the last six years.

No, that wasn't it. It was because that night I actually looked like a woman. A surge of confidence raced through my veins. I was a woman this man found attractive, and I did things to him that only beautiful women could do to men.

His lips brushed against my jaw, and I let myself enjoy the tingling sensation. I tilted my head as I leaned into his sturdy body, and he accepted my silent invitation. Light kisses strung down my neck, and when he came to the exposed skin of my shoulder, he groaned. In a breath, I was turned, and his mouth covered mine.

I was pretty sure I was dead-lips for the first few kisses, but as he backed me against the Jeep, his persuasive touch coaxed me into action. His hands moved from my hips to my back and then roamed as they pleased, and without understanding what I was doing, I found myself exploring the hardscape of his chest, his shoulders, his back...

A horn blared. "Get a room!" some man shouted. I froze, and Aiden pulled away with another groan.

"Not a bad idea."

Uh, no. My face burned. I'd left my common sense, and dignity, back in Minden. Making out with a guy in a parking lot—wasn't that...cheap? I couldn't look at him as I pushed against his chest. The pressure of his body eased away, and I felt naked. Humiliated. I spun around and unlatched the door. Aiden waited until I was in before shutting it.

He walked around to his side like nothing unusual had happened and slid into the driver's side. After starting the Jeep, he looked at me, his dimples peeking out again. "Dancing?"

I still couldn't make eye contact. "Sure."

No, I wanted to go home. Aiden's attention wasn't thrilling anymore. I was actually a little scared. I didn't know what to do with men, didn't know what they expected. If that was his idea of a first kiss, I wasn't ready to dive into a second.

We drove north and crossed the tracks. Aiden pulled up to a place I'd never been to before and killed the engine. He took my hand again and pressed the pads of my fingers to his mouth. "If you can kiss like that, you'll have no problem dancing."

They were related? He left the car, and I closed my eyes. Home. Pizza with Dad. A movie. Things that were safe, familiar.

He opened my door and I stepped out. That long arm slithered around me again, his thumb running along the side of my stomach. My abs twitched. He didn't miss my involuntary response, and he moved to kiss me again.

I stiffened, backing away from his descending mouth. "Dancing."

He hovered, his mouth inches from mine, and smiled. "Right." And then he kissed me again, this time gently.

My insides turned to pudding. This was how a girl got into trouble. She went out with Mr. Sweep-'Em-Off-Their-Feet on her first real date, and her brain shut off. I turned away in a slow spin out of his tempting hold and headed for the entrance to the club.

So not my scene. Aiden's club was a Hooters knockoff with a strong dash of gentleman's club mixed in for flavor. Waitresses in uniform, which consisted of bun-huggers and white button-downs kept together by a knot tied at the breasts, sashayed their way in between the bar and scattered pub tables. Neon strobes flashed over the floor, piercing my brain with obnoxious light.

"Don't worry." Aiden leaned over my shoulder to speak near my face. "I only come here for the music."

Yeah. I must've had *stupid* written across my forehead. I eyed him, and my eyebrow quirked.

His sultry grin spread wider. "Or we could find that other place..."

Man, this guy was something. Were all men like this?

Dinner with Jesse crossed my memory. Granted, they weren't dates, but he hadn't acted anything like this. I couldn't imagine he would.

"Two?" A Barbie look-alike sauntered close in her next-to-nothing getup.

Standing behind me, Aiden took my hands and wrapped both his arms and mine around my waist. "Yep."

I sighed, trying to figure out how to pry him off me without looking ridiculous. The waitress didn't seem to care as she tossed her bleach-blond hair—which, by the way, must have been part of the dress code.

"Who's playing tonight?" Aiden wanted to know. Barbie rattled off some band name I didn't care about.

"Aiden?" hissed a female's voice as we passed a pub table.

Aiden stopped, pulling me to a halt. I turned, bypassing his face, and recognized Brenna.

Peachy.

"What are you doing here?" He didn't sound that surprised.

Fishing for retribution. Aha. I was the bait. Would she bite?

Her eyes moved from him and grazed over me. "Who is this?"

"Shows you how self-consumed you are, Brenna." He tugged me close to his side. "We went through four years of high school with Sarah. Think you'd recognize her."

My estimation of his character notched up a tiny bit.

Her brows pinched together. "Sarah Sharpe?"

"In the flesh." His tone was smug.

Was I supposed to speak during this exchange or just dangle there in silence while I waited for the fish to snap?

"It's been a week, Aiden." Tears salted her voice.

He shrugged. "You said we were done. I'm moving on. That's what you told me to do."

"I didn't think you'd move so fast."

Fast—uh, yeah. That was definitely the appropriate adverb.

"Maybe you'll think next time before you deal out an ultimatum." Aiden turned, pushing me in the direction of his retreat, and we moved to the table where our waitress waited.

"Can I get you something to drink?"

Aiden ordered something that sounded dark and dangerous, which matched the way his eyes had shadowed.

"Cosmo, Sarah?"

"No, just a soda." I was not drinking with this man.

Barbie raised an eyebrow. "You over twenty-one?"

Aiden rolled his eyes. "Yes, she's allowed in here."

Why hadn't she carded us before we sat down?

"Sorry, Aiden, I'll still need to see her ID."

Oh, he was a regular, that was why. I flipped open my wallet, which Aunt Darcy had called a *clutch*, and flashed my ID toward Barbie. "Does it matter? I only want a Coke."

"Yeah, that's what they all say." She searched for my DOB and then nodded. With a flip of her hair, she wiggled away.

Aiden took my hand and pulled me off my chair. "Let's dance."

I didn't have a choice as his arm snaked around my body. He dragged me to the scratched wooden floor that separated the bar from the pub tables and spun me against his chest. Feeling like the idiot I was, I moved my feet, trying to match his steps.

Aiden dipped his mouth near my ear. "Just follow me."

No problem. Because I knew how to mirror a guy's moves in close proximity. Something I did all the time.

He tugged me snug against him. Irritated, I glanced up. His head was turned toward the tables, and I followed his eyes. Straight to Brenna.

Worm on a hook. That was me. I stared at his chest and sighed. Aiden didn't notice. Could this night get much worse?

We didn't even get through the song before a manicured finger tapped on my shoulder. "I need to talk to Aiden." Brenna glared at me, and then her look softened when her eyes moved to his.

"We're dancing, Bree." Aiden's arms tensed around me. "You can wait."

Yeah, I believed that was sincere. Apparently Brenna did. Her hazel eyes glazed with tears, and her chin quivered. The fish took the bait. She turned, sniffed, and walked with her shoulders drooping back to her table.

I could have been working on a CAD drawing right then. Or watching the latest Bourne movie with Dad. Or sleeping, for heaven's sake. Any part of my dull life would have been better than being stuck on a hook in the middle of this obnoxious club.

Should have known that the only reason a good-looking guy would notice me was so that he could use me as fishing tackle.

"I should go talk to her." Aiden sighed as if it were actually a burden. "She might make a scene."

Oh, I was sure he hoped she would. I moved out of his arms. "Do whatever you need to do."

Apparently he thought that was genuine. Or he didn't care either way. I walked off the dance floor, slid onto my stool, and sipped my Coke that had been delivered while Aiden had cast his line. Pulling my phone out of my stupid girly clutch, I scanned my contacts. Who to call?

Not many choices there. The only one was Dad. I shut my eyes and slumped against the table. That would be the perfect end to the most perfectly horrible first date ever. I could imagine my dad's scowl as he walked up to this dive, his dark anger stamping a rhythm in his heavy stride. And then there would be the thirty-minute drive home filled with either cold silence or heated words.

Air left my lungs in a long rush, and I leaned against my hand with my elbow propped up on the table. How could I be so stupid? I glanced over to Brenna's table. They weren't there. Knowing I shouldn't look, I did anyway, and I found them huddled in a corner in time to see her pull his head toward hers. He kissed her with a demanding hunger, and she molded herself to his body. The rest...I didn't want to see. I shut my eyes and turned my head.

So, so stupid.

I stared at my phone, still sitting on the table. I didn't have a choice. After sliding my finger over the screen, I punched in my pass code as I prepared myself for the worst. It vibrated against the table before I could scroll to Dad's name. *Incoming call.*

I blinked. Seriously? It vibrated again, and I answered. "Hello?"

"Hey, Sapphira, I was thinking about you."

Chapter Twelve

JESSE

Somehow good sense left me. I imagined her deep-blue eyes, heard that soft, shy voice in my head, and every ounce of logic vacated my brain. Why else would I call her so late?

Mack told me to fix this. That was what I was doing. And that was all I was doing.

"You were..." She sounded a little breathless, which made my heart do some kind of crazy loop-d-loop.

"Thinking about you." On a professional basis. A sudden chuckle threatened to rattle my chest. Lying to myself now. Maybe I should go to a doctor. Something was not right with me.

Music echoed in the background of Sarah's silence. Unexpected. "Whatchya up to?"

I could hear her draw a breath. "Nothing great." She paused, maybe swallowed. "How about you?"

"I'm kind of your way, actually." I leaned back against the headboard of the creaky bed. "We're in Lexington this week."

A snuffly sound fractured the honky-tonk in the background, like maybe she'd sniffed. Something was off. "Where are you?"

An awkward silence pulled on the line. Then, "You're in Lexington?"

"Yeah." I sat up. "Sarah, *where* are you?"

Nothing.

"Sarah, are you okay?"

I could actually hear her gulp. "Can I ask a massive favor?"

Anything. Almost. *No, come to think of it, anything.* "Shoot."

"I'm in Kearney, at a...club." Another long breath. "Can you come get me?"

Alarm prickled over my arms. "Yep. Give me an addy, and I'll be there as soon as I can."

She sighed. "Thank you."

Don't hang up. "Sarah, I need to know if you're okay."

"I'm fine. Just need a ride."

Her voice said she was anything but fine.

I changed from my gym shorts to a clean pair of jeans, thanks to Avery's washing machine, and a fresh T-shirt in less than two minutes. Tugging on my ball cap—which should actually go into the garbage, but it was my favorite, so that wasn't happening—I left the subpar room and jogged to the gravel parking lot.

Why were there speed limits on the interstate in that part of the world? Even in the dark you could see straight on until forever. And seventy-five, during that drive, didn't seem like a reasonable limit.

The Kearney exit finally crawled into view, and I lamented the red glow of the stoplight as I eased off the ramp. It was almost eleven at night. Stoplights were not necessary there at eleven at night.

Green finally illuminated my view, and I took the left turn. Maybe a little fast. Or maybe the asphalt was a tiny bit wet—that could account for the squealing tires. Except it hadn't rained in the last twenty-four hours.

I activated Siri, and she told me where to go, even announcing my arrival when I pulled up in front of the club. A pair of college-aged kids were going at it hot and heavy against the bricks to the left of the entrance, and one glance through the tinted window near the door told me exactly what kind of joint this was.

Nice.

I didn't have to know Sarah long to know this was not her thing. At all.

The door burst open as I hopped out of my truck, and she suddenly stood in front of me. Whoa. Sapphira. My lungs froze, and I couldn't help but stare. Same woman. Same beautiful woman. But...wow.

She looked to the ground as her arms wrapped around her bare shoulders. *Shake it off, Jess.* Except I couldn't make my heart slow to a normal rate. Or my eyes stop gawking at her.

"You look beautiful."

She tried to smile. "That's the story."

Not good. "Are you okay?"

"I already said I was." Her tone cut hard and then cracked. She tipped her face to look at me. "Sorry. I just really want to go home."

How did she get there? I slid my inspection over her one more time. She'd been on a date. My arms tensed. Where was the jerk?

The door squeaked behind her, and her body went rigid. I glanced to see a couple stagger out of the entry—probably looking for a room at the shack next door. Her date? Pawing another woman?

My attention fell back on Sarah. She didn't look behind her. I shouldn't ask. She wanted to go home. I didn't need to know the rest. With a long step, I closed the gap of night between us and pulled her into a hug. "Okay, Sapphira. I'll get you home."

She held herself stiff for a breath and then leaned into my shoulder. Ignoring the warmth that dumped into my limbs, I rubbed her back and then took a step back. Settling an arm over her shoulders—a buddy hold—I squeezed.

"Did you eat?"

She shrugged. "A little."

"I'm starving."

She glanced to the sin trap she'd come out of, and I snorted.

"Not here, Sapphira." I guided her to my truck and opened the passenger door. "You don't belong anywhere near this place."

I thought she'd smile, tell me thanks, but when she glanced my way, anger crossed her expression.

"Do you know where I belong?"

Not really a question, which was good, because I couldn't string together words for an answer.

She shifted so that her face tilted toward her hands. "That's what I thought."

Her lifeless tone sliced at my heart.

Now what? She climbed into the cab, but I couldn't close her door and drive off after a comment like that. I stood there helpless until she turned her eyes back up to mine. Longing, deeper than a yearning to be held, penetrated her stare.

I covered her hands, which rested together on her lap, with one of my own. Even in the summer's warm night air, her skin felt cold against my palm. I still didn't know what to say, but at least she'd know I'd heard her.

God, what do I do?

She slipped her hands away and sniffed. "I'm sorry, Jesse. You don't have to coddle me."

I couldn't tear my eyes off her. They say the need to belong is one of the strongest emotional requirements universal to all of mankind. Didn't know why I remembered that from my psych classes, but the info hit hard as I watched her search her heart. Suddenly, what I hadn't paid much attention to in college looked as clear as a cloudless sky in her striking blue eyes. The hunger to belong growled in her soul.

Strangely, I found that I was familiar with that desire.

The thought set me a little dizzy. It didn't make sense, so I pushed it away. This wasn't about me.

Recapturing one of her hands, I tipped her chin up with the other. "I'm your friend," I whispered.

Her lips trembled as she breathed in. She eased away from my touch. "Thanks."

Window to her soul shut. I dug into my jeans for my keys and set off to take her home, praying, as I pulled into the minimal traffic, that her heart would find the One for whom she longed.

My stomach grumbled as we rolled away from the parking lot. "Drive-through or dine in?"

Sarah pulled her head off her door window. "What?"

"I wasn't kidding. I'm hungry." I was a southern guy. Food always fixed stuff, in our approximation. "There's a Perkins or something up this way, I think. Serves breakfast all night. How 'bout it?"

Her gaze seemed fixed my way, but I got the feeling she wasn't seeing me. Panic stirred in my chest. What had happened before I called? A red light glowed in the distance, and I slowed my truck. If that guy hurt her...

"Pancakes sound good," she mumbled.

I turned to search her profile in the dim light. She stared out the windshield. A queasy feeling rolled through my stomach. "Sarah, you gotta tell me if he..."

"Nothing happened." She didn't shift. "I just needed a ride, okay?"

Green light. Moving on. "Okay." I spotted the restaurant on my left and set my turn signal. Sweat beaded along the back of my neck as the silence persisted, long and hot and awkward. I slid my truck into a parking space and shifted into park.

Sarah still hadn't moved.

I killed the engine. With my fist closed around the metal keys, I reached out and brushed her bare shoulder with my knuckle. She drew a sharp breath.

Yeah, nothing happened. Even if it wasn't physical, the guy had hurt her. I clenched the keys and swallowed. What could I do about it?

Nothing.

I hopped out of my truck and jogged around to her side. Her feet had already hit the ground. After pushing her door shut, I bumped her shoulder with mine. "What's it gonna take to make you laugh?"

Her eyes met mine. "Why?"

"It's good for you."

She looked away. Man, she was tough.

I dipped my head, peeked at her under the brim on my hat, and pushed out my best pouty lips. One side of her mouth quirked up, and she rolled her eyes.

"Halfway there." With my index finger, I pushed up the other corner of her mouth. A tiny mouse laugh escaped from her lips.

Good enough. For now.

SARAH

I couldn't put Jesse Chapman in the same category with Aiden Beck. Didn't think their blood even ran in the same direction.

Then again, Jesse didn't have any interest in me...that way. Even if he had just bought me another meal before we headed back toward Minden. As the blank canvas of open darkness slid past my window, Laine's fair beauty flashed in my mind, and inadequacy sparked irritation afresh. But Jesse had apologized, and I hadn't returned his call. The shame was on me.

"I'm sorry that I didn't call you back earlier this week."

Jesse's hand drifted over the bench seat toward me but then settled on the empty space between us. "I was wondering."

Something he would say—usually with a teasing tone. No teasing tone though. Had it really bothered him?

"It was a busy week," I said.

Liar. More like *I didn't want to talk to you, because you'd tell me I'd got the wrong impression, that you didn't mean to make me like you so much...*

How much did I like him? My glance drifted to his hand still resting on the seat next to me. A sudden strong urge to feel it wrap around mine sprouted, which bloomed into curiosity. How would it feel to be held by Jesse Chapman? Would his kisses leave me feeling naked and frightened? Or would I feel safe against his chest?

Dumb. I wouldn't feel anything against him, because I wouldn't be there. Jesse had much better options, and he didn't need to use me as bait to snag them.

"I really am sorry, Sapphira." His sincere voice ripped me out of my imagination.

My attention moved toward his face and collided with his glance. Longing pulled hard. If only he'd...

He didn't. Settle that now, before you get hurt.

Before? Too late. I had been hurt—humiliated. That was why I hadn't called him back. But it wasn't his fault. I'd been hoping for things I had no business hoping for. Jesse Chapman was way out of my class, and I'd known from the start where I would and wouldn't stand with him.

Time to clear the air. He was a good guy, and a friend. That was what mattered.

"It's all right." I turned to face the dark beyond the windshield. "I'm awkward sometimes, and I don't always see things the way they are."

Honesty gone bold. Somehow though, it felt comfortable.

Jesse chuckled. "You and me both."

Really? I looked back to him, catching his oh-so-friendly smile. If only I could be like him. Comfortable with who he was, he could laugh at himself. Laugh at the rocks in the road rather than stumbling on them. "How come you..." Uh, where was I going with that? *How come life doesn't run over you?* Yeah, that was pretty much it. Did I dare say it?

He sneaked a quick glance at me. "I...what?"

Dare. It was Jesse, right? I pulled in a lungful of air. "Life doesn't beat you up."

He smiled—the *thanks that's sweet but not true* kind of smile. "I've had a few gut shots."

Oh yeah. Parents dying—not a cotton-ball war. I looked at my hands. "I know you have. I didn't mean..."

"I know." His fingers caught mine, squeezed, and then left. Both his hands found the steering wheel and gripped the standard ten-and-two position. "Has anyone ever introduced you to Jesus, Sarah?"

Splat. Like a june bug smacking against a bumper at sixty. Here I'd opened up my insecure little world, and he was going to Band-Aid it with religion.

"No, I've never seen the guy. Hear about Him now and then. But since I've never seen Him show up when it mattered, I've decided He's a bit like Prince Charming. All talk. No show."

Whoa. That was a mouthful for me. A fountain of bitterness had erupted somewhere inside.

"Have you ever actually asked to meet Him?"

"Why would I talk to someone I can't see?"

"Maybe you haven't been looking."

My posture went rigid, and I leaned toward the door. "Where would I look for said hero?"

Jesse leaned forward, his face tilting toward the night sky outside the windshield. "The heavens declare the glory of God..."

Poetry? Definitely an English major. No wonder he couldn't do angles. They were real, not imaginary. Concrete, not abstract.

I stared at him.

"Come on." He grinned, looking back to the road. "You haven't ever looked at a sky like that and thought, *Wow. That's amazing. Where did it come from?*"

"No." Did I have to be so sharp? "I've seen the stars and thought, *It's night. Time to go to bed, because I have work to do in the morning.*"

The joy in his laugh tempted a small smile to my lips.

"Sleep does do wonders."

He paused, and I wondered if he was aligning an argument for Jesus in the silence. That little smile of mine left. Reaching across the cab, his hand warmed my shoulder and then squeezed. "You're awfully uptight about this, Sapphira."

"I don't see the point in pretending a jolly old man in some alternate universe is my best friend. Religion isn't for my kind of people."

"Who are your kind of people?"

How come his side of the discussion sounded so calm, when mine was edgy and defensive?

"The kind that do real work." I huffed. My brain caught up after the words had already left my mouth.

Jesse laughed. "Oh, I see."

The starlit night afforded enough light for me to catch his wink. My face caught on fire.

I. Am. Dumb.

The tires seemed to agree. For the final three miles into Minden, they thumped out a mantra that sounded suspiciously like *you are dumb, you are dumb...*

This was what I got for lying to my dad, sneaking out of town with a guy I knew he wouldn't approve of, and asking another guy—one he might approve of, except for the being a Jesus freak part—for a ride home. No more going out. Ever. I'd stay in my safe world and stick to being the carpenter's daughter. That was what I was. That was all I knew.

Red flashing lights lit up the dark road ahead, and a train horn blared into the quiet countryside. Jesse eased on the brakes as we approached the railroad crossing. The tires quit mocking my idiocy, and the stillness in the cab began needling my eardrums. Stuck at a crossing—could be at least five minutes, swimming in my awkwardness with Jesse sitting nearby to watch.

"Hey, Sapphira?" He shifted the truck into park and moved so that he could face me. "I'm sorry you had a bad night."

I'd smacked him with insults, and he threw me a life vest. My eyes burned as I mashed my lips together.

"Do you want to talk about it?"

"Not really. I've already shown you enough of my stupidity." Again, my mouth went on autopilot. For not knowing how to talk to people, I was overachieving in this conversation.

"Stupid?" His hand grazed my chin and lifted so that I would face him. "So not true. What happened?"

The warmth of his fingers fell away. I wanted to unbuckle, slide over, and curl up against him. "I went out with a guy even though I knew he was on the rebound. His ex-girlfriend was there, and three's a crowd, so…"

Jesse's soft breath came and went in a steady rhythm. I squeezed my eyes shut, cutting off the moisture building in them. I'd wanted a roller-coaster ride, hadn't I?

"Hey." His hand caught mine. "You're not the stupid one."

Another train horn ripped the air, and I actually jumped a little. Red lights faded into quiet blackness, and the crossing guard lifted, leaving a clear road ahead. My truck sat in the parking lot across the tracks. Reality ahead. Proceed with caution.

"That's me." I pointed to The Crossing to the left of the highway. "I'll be good from there, if you'll just drop me off."

His hand still holding mine, he squeezed and then let go.

Come back.

Turning square to the steering wheel, Jesse shifted back into drive, and within a minute we pulled up next to my truck.

"Is this a bar?"

Uh-oh. How did Jesus freaks feel about a bar? I found myself pricked with a desire to bait him. I straightened my shoulders. "Yep. Want to come in?"

"Not tonight. Thanks, though." Nothing changed in his voice.

I thought I'd hear disappointment. Or rebuke. Something that would confirm that he wasn't my kind of people. He parked and cut the engine, and I popped my door open and slid from the cab. Surprise kind of tickled my tummy when he met me beside the door of my truck.

"We could use your skills this weekend." He leaned against the truck bed, kicking his feet out as if we were chatting like old buddies.

"What are you working on?"

"A renovation this time. It'll be a longer job. Haven't even started the demo." His shoe scuffed against the gravel as he poked his hands into his pockets. "Mack told me to make sure you come. We really do need you."

Mack told him? Somehow that was deflating. Crossing my arms, I hugged my middle, wondering when I'd acquired so many mysterious—and annoying—emotions. "I don't know..."

"Please?"

Whoa. Something strong backed that one word, and suddenly I was locked in his gaze. I took a tiny step toward him, and he pushed off the side of my truck, his hands pulling away from his pockets. My heart throbbed as he moved closer.

Light suddenly passed over the both of us as a truck swerved into the lot. Jesse looked away, and his hands slid back into his jeans. What just happened? Did I only imagine the heat in his eyes?

"Sarah." My dad's voice barked from the other side of my truck. A door slammed shut, and the sound of boots slapping against rocks moved closer. "What are you doing?"

Jesse turned, and I looked around him.

Yep. There was my dad. Scowling at Jesse.

"Who is this?"

"Jesse Chapman." He reached across the dim night air to shake my dad's hand.

Dad glared and then stepped around him. "Don't you know how to use a phone, girl?"

"What?" If there was a god, could he just zap me with lightning? Now?

"Past midnight, and I haven't heard from you since you left work." He crossed his arms and stopped right next to me.

I squared to him, crossing my own arms. "Didn't know I still had a curfew."

"Watch it, girl."

Jesse cleared his throat. "I'm sorry, sir." He stepped forward, almost inserting himself between us. "I met Sarah at a Homes For Hope project, and I was in the Kearney area. We were just hanging out. I'm not from around here, and I don't know anyone, so..."

Jesse Chapman, the religious nut, was lying for me?

Dad's glare moved from me to Jesse and then back again. "This is why you keep going to work for Homes For Hope?"

Enough. "I'm all grown up, Dad." I punched a hand into my jeans pocket to grab my keys. Spinning toward my truck's door, I caught Jesse's eye. "Thanks, Jesse. Text me directions, and I'll see you tomorrow." I climbed into the vehicle and reached for the door. Jesse beat me, shutting it calmly. Maybe a good thing—I'd planned on slamming it.

"Real men show up at the door, boy." My dad's voice caught me before I coaxed the engine to life. "They don't slink off into the night with some other man's daughter like they've got something to hide."

I swallowed, glaring at my dad. His dark gaze caught me and held. I shook my head and started the truck.

Jesse Chapman, a guy way out of my class, had just been gnawed on by a guy who was also countless stories beneath him. I doubted he'd text me at all. Which meant I'd never get to see those kind green eyes again.

Chapter Thirteen

JESSE

Ice would have been warm compared to Mr. Sharpe's glare.

"Yes, sir." I was twenty-six, right? Why did I feel like a sixteen-year-old caught making out under a stairwell? Not that I'd ever done that kind of thing. "It wasn't a date kind of thing." My face seared. I wished it had been a date kind of thing.

Mr. Sharpe's scowl deepened. "Don't know where you came from or who you are." He stepped forward, and I could smell chaw on his breath. "Sarah's the innocent type though. And I know the roughneck type. I also have connections that would drop your jaw—so keep yourself to yourself."

Right. How brave did I feel? "I'm not your typical construction worker, sir." Pretty brave, apparently.

"She's not your typical girl."

Right again. Which was probably why this fascination with her wouldn't leave me alone. "No, sir."

What next? My spirit cringed thinking that he believed me to be that kind of guy. Any father would though, right? Daughter out late into the night, no word before she left, then showed up at the bar with some strange man who hadn't bothered to introduce himself? Not a good first impression.

Was it pride or something else that made me really, really wish for a second chance at a better first impression?

Pride. And something else.

"Get out of here." Mr. Sharpe stomped away.

Clearly he'd been boss for a while. A man used to being obeyed.

So I did. Not because I was a coward. Because I wanted to give him some reason to give me another chance.

And because I was a little bit of a coward. I preferred *nonconfrontational.*

I walked to the driver's side of my truck and climbed in. The road stretched an hour in front of me, and my alarm was set for five thirty in the a.m. Could be a long week. Unless Sapphira actually showed up. Then it could be a good week.

The Road Runner's iconic *meep-meep* cut through the silence in my truck. My text sound. After I slid my keys into the ignition, I snagged my cell off the dashboard. One new text. *Please be Sapphira.*

Sapphira. Tapping the text app, I grinned. Some things had to get worse before they get better. That was what my dad always said.

Sapphira: *This whole night was a train wreck. Sorry I dragged you into it.*

Me: *Drag on. I can take it.*

Sapphira: *...nothing.*

She knew I was teasing her, right?

Me: *Are you smiling?*

Sapphira: *Why are you worried about me smiling again?*

Me: *It's good for me.*

Hold up. *It's good for you.* That was what I meant—smiling was good for her. Well, and me.

Sapphira: *...nothing. Again.*

She didn't know what to do with me. By the looks of things, her life was a little confusing. I should have probably saved the teasing for face-to-face conversations.

Me: *Will I see you tomorrow?*

I stared at the screen. "Please..." Talking to your phone when no one else was actually listening was normal. "Answer, Sapphira. Don't crawl back into your cave."

Sapphira: *Send me directions.*

That'd be a yes. I chuckled as I typed the house address.

Sapphira: *What time?*

Me: *I'm starting at six. You up for that?*

Again with the teasing. I couldn't stop myself.

Me: *Teasing. Don't get up that early. Mack wants you to make recommendations for the rebuild. You have a CAD program, right?*

Sapphira: *Yeah.*

Me: *Mobile?*

Sapphira: *Yeah.*

Me: *Good. Mack will do a dance.*

Huge exaggeration. Mack would grunt, point at the project, and tell her to get to work.

Me: *See you in the morning, Sapphira.*

She didn't respond. I kept smiling anyway as I shifted into reverse and left the bar. Ten miles down the road, I realized I was still grinning, and without looking, knew it was the stupid I've-got-a-crush kind.

That was a problem.

SARAH

"Get out here, Sarah," Dad demanded from the front room as soon as the door slammed.

What was the deal with him these days? He'd gone grumpy-control-freak on me. Where'd the guy I'd grown up with go?

I tugged a hoodie over my tank top and adjusted the waist on my gym shorts. Much more comfortable. And me.

"Sarah!"

Snatching the knob on my bedroom door, I growled. "I'm coming."

Dad waited, arms crossed over his chest, in the tiny living room. Grumpy was a nice word. He looked like Bruce Banner as the green guy. Not good.

He set his feet like he was ready to fight. "What do you think you were doing?"

No clue. But he didn't need to know that.

"Dad, I'm twenty-one years old." I mirrored his position. "This is a little past due."

"Don't care how old you are. You can pay me the courtesy of letting me know where you're going and that you're okay."

"That's what this is about?" I snorted. "Not hardly. You're freaking out because I was out with a guy." Didn't need to mention which guy.

"Yeah, some guy no one knows anything about." He shook his head. "Not a good call."

"No." I stepped a little closer. For not having fought with my dad much growing up, I took to it pretty quick. "A guy *you* don't know anything about. I know him fine—and he's nice. But you wouldn't know. Wouldn't even shake his hand."

"At the least, I should know that you're out with him."

Dad's glare made me feel like I was thirteen and had done something really horrible. Like sneaked out at night with a boy. It was different when you were older, wasn't it?

His eyebrow crooked in the most condescending way. "You don't know what you're getting into."

I wasn't thirteen. Even if he was right about my ignorance. "Who's fault is that?"

"I taught you things that matter. How to work. To be honest. Treat people well." The volume in his voice notched up with each item on his list. "Now you're out fishing for the wrong kind of attention from the wrong kind of men. I didn't teach you that."

"Wrong kind of men? Like what? Like you?"

He drew back, but his angry eyes darkened.

I didn't care. "Why'd my mother leave anyway, Dad? You never told me. Was there a reason?" My heart beat hard against my ribs, but I didn't slow down. "Maybe you're afraid because of the kind of guy *you* were. That's not my fault."

Dad's hand cut through the air. "Enough!" He stepped forward and towered over me. "You'll not stand in my house and talk to me like that."

"Fine." I spun on the ball of my foot and stormed away. "'Bout time I went out on my own anyway."

The short hall couldn't pass under my feet fast enough. Once in my room, I ripped a dresser drawer open. Work clothes. Undies. Socks. Hat. All went into my old high school gym bag. I crossed the hallway from my room to the bathroom. Soap. Shampoo. Deodorant. Toothbrush. Makeup? The moment Jesse's eyes caught me coming out of the club flashed through my mind. He said I looked beautiful—and not just with his words. Yes. *Definitely bring the makeup.* And maybe one or two of my new girly outfits.

"What do you think you're doing?" Dad's voice caught me as I left the bathroom. He leaned against the hallway wall with one shoulder, his arms once again crossed.

"Packing."

An eyebrow hiked. "Where are you gonna go at one a.m.?"

"Lexington." I slid back into my room. "I've got a job this weekend. Starts in the morning." I stuck my head out the door and met his eyes. "I'm not completely helpless. And I don't always need my daddy to hold my hand. Maybe it's time we both understood that."

Something passed over his expression—dark and powerful. Anger or hurt? I didn't stand around long enough to figure it out. Shouldering my bag, I stomped into my tennis shoes, snagged my work boots and keys, and headed for the door.

Dad didn't say another word. In cold silence, he stayed propped against the wall, steel in his glare.

Never thought I'd leave him like that.

DALE

She walked out.

Like mother, like daughter.

My jaw quivered. Suddenly I remembered the exact pain that had seized my heart twenty years before. My lungs didn't want to work. Air couldn't reach them, and my chest began to collapse. Pain radiated from my heart to my limbs, and I wished my pulse would stop.

What had I thought would happen tonight? That Sarah would come out of her room, dragging her blankie, and say, "I'm sorry I grew up, Dad"? Not exactly, but I didn't think she'd fight me. She didn't need to get so mad when I was only concerned for her well-being. I wasn't exaggerating—she didn't know what was out there, what she was getting herself into.

Whose fault was that?

How was I supposed to teach her those kinds of things? I was a failure when it came to relationships. Even, apparently, with my daughter. I didn't want her to end up like me and, heaven help me, like her mother.

I stumbled into the front room of our small house and fell into my recliner as our argument continued to replay.

Wrong kind of men—like you?

Exactly.

I'd loved her mother. In the shallow, she-makes-me-feel-good kind of way. I thought I'd be her hero and that would make me something. It was all selfishness. That was a young man for you.

Guilt weighed on me every time I remembered how Cassie died. Alone. Strung out. A used-up piece of garbage, painted to look like a treasure.

I'd failed her. She'd needed a hero, and I failed.

Now it was happening again. To have Sarah go down that same path? I'd die. Felt like I was dying right there in my empty house. I could see it all in my mind—some good-looking kid would pull her close, whisper promises only meant to entice, desire only meant for self-gratification, and she'd latch on to that wisp of belonging. She'd think she'd found herself in his eyes.

It was all very vivid because I'd seen the story play out before in her mother's blue eyes. But I couldn't make Cassie whole or into the person she'd wanted to be. I'd only confused her more and disappointed her dreams. And through it all, what I thought was love had been selfishness. Because young men didn't know what love is.

Chapter Fourteen

JESSE

Coffee. Donut. Now.

I dried my face with the standard-issue white hand towel. Catching the guy in the mirror, I leaned forward and rested my palms against the counter. I actually looked tired. Hadn't looked like that since the year Mom and Dad died.

Thoughts of Sarah had kept me up all night. Her dad was some kind of mad—and strangely that made me feel a little better for her, because that meant he cared. I hoped. It was a little weird though. She was, after all, a twenty-some-year-old woman.

Reading between the lines, I'd guess it'd been her and her dad her whole life, which might explain his angry-bear reaction. Goose bumps rippled across my skin when I thought about what he would have done if he'd seen her come out of that club. Whoever she'd gone there with...she sure didn't want to volunteer that information. Which meant her dad would know who the guy was. Local kid, and not a good one.

Sarah was a nice girl. Why would she go out with a bad boy?

I tossed the towel toward the wall, and it landed on the counter to the left of the sink. This was why I didn't sleep. Couldn't get her out of my head. Not good.

Coffee. Donut. Then work. I needed to find my normal rhythm.

I left my room and wandered to the lobby. The faint light of the sun tickled the black canvas of night as I turned into the tiny breakfast nook. It'd be another twenty to thirty minutes before daybreak spread over the land. Time I'd use in the Psalms.

Leaving my Bible on a table by a window, I straight-lined it to the coffeepot. Once my Styrofoam mug was full, I pivoted to select from the stale day-old donuts laid out next to a bowl of waxy apples and brown-speckled bananas. Man, that place was subpar. I needed to hit a grocery store before nightfall if I was going to survive a full week.

With a glazed cake donut and one of the bananas on my small plastic plate, and the absolutely necessary cup of coffee in hand, I took five steps back to my table. I glanced back to the kitchenette, mentally tracing my path. A perfect triangle. What kind? Maybe a forty-five-degree angle between the coffee to the donut. Was that a ninety-degree angle from my table to the donuts? That would leave another forty-five, right? Sarah would know—wouldn't even need to think about it.

Geometry. Math. Yuck. Why was I thinking about that? Sarah. That was why.

Out.

I ran a hand over my head and anchored it on my neck. I bowed, offering silent thanks for the sort-of palatable food. *Please help me to focus today. Not on Sarah. But, Father, would You touch her heart? She needs You—she doesn't know where she belongs...*

Even my prayers shifted to her. This teetered on obsession.

Coffee in my left hand, I flipped my Bible open.

You have been our dwelling place in all generations.

Dwelling. Home. Pain stirred in my chest as the image of my parents' home collided with the haunting emptiness of Sarah's blue eyes. Weird. The two weren't related, and yet my heart ached because of both. Sarah, I could understand why her searching would pull on me. I wanted her heart to have the home she was longing for. But my childhood home? While there was some sentimental attachment there—my dad built it, and my mother made it amazing—it was ultimately just a house. Not the shelter of my heart.

Jesus was my dwelling place. Why did I picture the house?

Bracing my elbow on the table, I leaned against my hand. I'd sought peace in the Word of God, and I got a puzzle instead. *What are you doing, God?* The moment from a few weeks before swept over me with such force that I almost felt the breeze that had climbed the hill.

Do you trust Me?

I did. Why?

"Jesse?"

My head snapped up when her voice draped around me. Not yet six, and Sarah stood behind me. I looked back, and my eyes collided with those amazing sapphires. Air stuck in my lungs, and I forgot for the moment where we were.

What if every morning began with a cup of coffee, God's Word, and a deep plunge into Sapphira's blue eyes?

I blinked. What if I got my head put back in the right place and stopped imagining the impossible?

"Sapphira." I grinned. It felt like the dumb, teenage-boy-crush kind, which triggered fire on both my ears. "What are you doing here?"

Even with the bill of her hat tugged low over her eyes, I could see a blush spread across her face. She moved toward the coffee. "Came up last night."

Uh-oh.

"You okay?"

She stayed at the coffee dispenser, her back to me, even after her mug was full. Nope. Not okay. I pushed away from the table and moved toward the kitchenette, stopping in front of the donuts.

"Sarah?" My fingers itched to touch her arm. I shoved both hands into my jeans pockets. "You have to tell me if you're hurt."

She glanced to my face and forced a close-lipped smile. "I'm fine." She held up her mug. "Just needed this. See you in a bit." Turning back to the hall, she left me staring at her hunched shoulders retreating from the lobby.

Not fine. That ache tugged in my chest again. A painful puzzle. I glanced back to my Bible.

No wind. No voice. Just a sunrise glowing from beyond the window next to my table. Which meant it was time to get to work.

SARAH

He looked way too good for that early in the morning. And I wasn't right if that was the first thought on my mind.

Maybe I was. He'd rescued me the night before. It was natural to admire your knight. Except, that was how all the girls thought of Jesse—their knight—and he didn't mean for them to. I didn't need to be the next Laine Fulton in Jesse's life. He was a nice guy—a Jesus freak—but a nice guy nonetheless. I could leave it at that.

I sipped my black coffee as I stared at the TV. Some woman with a haircut similar to mine talked seriously about something relevant to society. Katie Couric? Probably. She was pretty. My hand brushed over my hair. Same do. Good thing. Too bad my hat would cover it all day.

Unbidden, Jesse's expression from last night surfaced in my mind again. He'd been dumb-whipped. As if I'd been striking or something. Huh. Quite a few steps up from my normal work look, for sure. Maybe I should lessen the gap between the woman he'd met last night and the carpenter's daughter he worked with during the day.

I didn't pause to think about why I'd want to do such a thing. Instead, I pushed up from the couch and moved to the small bathroom.

Makeup bag in hand, I leaned forward to stare at myself in the mirror. My eyes *were* pretty blue. An asset, I thought. With little effort (because there wasn't much in that little zipper bag), I produced the charcoal pencil Darcy's friend had selected for me. A line over each eyelid, a thinner smudge on the lower lids, and then a quick swipe with my finger over all of them to "blend" the color. Boom. Blue eyes enhanced. I tipped back, inspecting the effect from a distance. Pretty good.

Now, for the mascara. This was a trouble spot for me. I hadn't been practicing this trick for the past ten years like most women my age, so waving a bristled wand near my eyeball in hopes of painting those thin little lashes was a bit like telling myself not to blink in the wind. Some black ended up on the cheekbone under my left eye. Nothing a wet washcloth couldn't fix. Once again stepping back from the mirror, I examined the finished product. With approval.

My heart beat in some kind of mildly painful erratic rhythm for two seconds, which oddly sent pleasure flowing through my veins. Maybe there was something physically wrong with me and I should have gone to a doctor, not a mall, when this whole finding-myself journey started. Drawing a breath, I checked the pulse in my neck. Normal. I was fine. But I needed something more than coffee for breakfast. My fingers combed through my hair while I debated. Hat on or off to go back to the lobby? I'd have to wear it to work—no amount of sunscreen could beat the shade of a bill—but maybe to eat...

No hat.

The narrow hallway wasn't as dark as it had been thirty minutes before. Pale sunlight splashed on the dingy green walls as I passed by the emergency exit. My heart did that funny little kick again as I rounded the corner to the lobby. Pleasure didn't follow this time. Probably because the breakfast room sat vacant.

Should have worn my hat. And not bothered with the dumb makeup. I had work to do, after all. Who wore makeup to a construction site?

153

Laine Fulton. Not me.

Oh well. Food would stabilize my insane web of thoughts. I slapped some kind of donut (didn't care what it was) on my plate and snatched a mushy banana. Breakfast of champions. Making a perfect right triangle, I moved to the seat Jesse had been sitting in and plopped down. What had I been thinking? It wouldn't take him thirty minutes to eat a donut.

But I'd wanted to see that look again. There. I admitted it.

A couple of guys rounded the corner from the hallway and beelined it to the food. Boots, torn jeans, hats. Workers. My kind of people. Didn't make me feel any more comfortable though. There I sat, alone in a shabby hotel, eating stale food as I prepared to work a job for which I wasn't going to get paid. Top it off, I didn't have a plan beyond that. Dad hadn't called me last night, and I sure wasn't calling him anytime soon.

"Crowded in here this morning."

Suddenly I was aware of a large presence standing at my side. I looked around. Five tables, one occupied by only one of the two guys who'd come in.

My brows scrunched together as I looked up. "Come again?"

"Tough to find a good seat." The man standing next to my table winked. "Mind if I sit with you?"

I think my head actually snapped straight. "Uh, no..."

He laughed and slid into the chair across from mine. "I'm Troy."

No. He was nuts. "Nice to know."

"Do blue-eyed angels have names?"

I almost sprayed the coffee I'd sipped all over his Hollister T-shirt. Was this guy for real? "I don't know. Haven't met any."

"Here." He reached across our tiny table and touched my chin, tipping it so that I'd look at the window to my right. "See her? What's her name?"

My reflection stared back at me. Striking blue eyes. No hat. My heart did that thing again, and I couldn't help but grin.

"Cute." I looked back to Troy the Nut. "It's Sarah. But I'm no angel."

"Even better."

Yikes. Maybe Dad was right. I shouldn't be allowed to talk to men. I dropped my attention to my half-eaten donut and concentrated on keeping the heat flaring on my chest from reaching my face.

A chair scraped the tile floor behind me, and another male figure appeared by my side. What kind of a warped scene was this? I wasn't awake. That had to be it. No way in reality I would suddenly be surrounded by men for no apparent reason. Other than makeup. And a missing hat.

"Troy Grey." Jesse's voice, though dark and flat. He straddled the chair he'd dragged to our—my—table. "What are you doing here?"

Troy leaned back and settled a look on Jesse. An image of two dogs circling each other blipped through my mind. Weird. I glanced at Jesse. Not the easygoing face I had memorized.

"Same as you, I guess." Troy crossed his arms. "Didn't bet you'd be back. Again."

"Took the words right out of my mouth." Jesse didn't move. "This isn't your kind of gig, as I recall. Get into trouble again?"

Troy scowled. "Not your business."

"Nope." Jesse stood. "It isn't. Unless you're on my crew." In two seconds he had his chair put back from where he'd taken it, and his hand rested on my shoulder. "Ready to go, Sarah?"

Wait. Was I being dismissed? Summoned? I looked up and found his green eyes steady on me. He squeezed the spot where his hand still rested.

Not the look I'd hoped for, but intense nonetheless. "Sure. Just need to grab my hat." And my food, which I hadn't eaten. Jesse didn't move until I stood, and then his hand slipped to my elbow. He walked with me all the way to my room.

"Do you know that guy?" He stopped me from unlocking my door, his voice low.

"No. You?" Obviously. And he wasn't a fan. Interesting. I thought Jesse the Saint liked everyone.

His hand left my elbow. "Enough."

Enough for what?

"Riding with me?" His eyebrow cocked up as if his question wasn't really a question at all.

Why not? I shrugged. He waited in the hall after I unlocked my door. I snatched my hat and then paused, glancing to the mirror that peeked from the open bathroom door. A woman with blue eyes stared back. A pretty woman who'd been hit on twice in one week. My chin lifted a tiny bit.

Maybe this journey wasn't so awful after all.

Chapter Fifteen

JESSE

The muscles in my shoulders knotted. Workday hadn't even started, and I was wound up like a yo-yo.

Troy Grey had surfaced again. Working with him was one thing, not very pleasant at that, but watching him slither up to Sapphira... The taste of bile tinged my tongue. The guy played women like they were cards in a deck. Seemed to find an identity in his cold game. No way was I going to stand by and watch Sarah slide into that hand.

What was she doing out there again this morning anyway? Half hour before, she'd got her coffee—and had been about as friendly as a badger—before she shuffled on down that hall again. If she wanted to sit and have breakfast, why didn't she sit with me?

I braced my back against the wall, waiting for her to grab her hat. She'd been wearing it earlier. Why'd she show up in that lobby looking all beautiful, setting herself up for a snake like Troy? I wished I could figure women. Sarah was smart and not a game player, so none of this made any sense.

She reappeared in her doorway, hat slapped on her dark hair. Still beautiful. A quick rerun of Troy's fingers on her face made me snarl on the inside. *She's not for you.* Words that had almost broke from my lips as I'd set myself smack in the middle of that unsettling pair. Then again, what claim did I have on her?

None.

Not true. Somehow, that couldn't be true, because thinking it put pressure in my chest until I thought I couldn't breathe anymore.

This wasn't fair. Finally I met a woman who would get me—and I'd understand her, sort of—and she was out of bounds. Why would God do that?

"Ready?" Sarah eyed me as though she'd been standing there waiting for me to check back into reality. Probably because she had.

I pushed off the wall and drank in those eyes set on me. The weight in my chest lifted a little. "Yep. Let's go." Fishing my keys from my pocket with one hand, I tapped the brim of her hat with the other. After that, I shoved the hand closest to her into my jeans. No touching.

A sigh billowed from my chest. Starting the day in a bad mood wasn't par for me, so I wasn't sure what to do with it. Top it off, I was still hungry. After opening the passenger door for Sarah, I walked around to the other side and slid behind the steering wheel. We set off for our latest project. A fast-food sign snagged my attention a few blocks down the road. No sense in going hungry, and maybe some decent food would turn my morning right side up.

"Where are we going?"

"Breakfast." I pulled in between a pair of yellow lines and parked. "That coffee tasted like muddy water, and a day-old donut isn't going to do it for me."

After killing the engine, I sat. Just sat and stared out of the windshield at nothing in particular.

"You're moody this morning."

Oh. So she'd noticed. Did she realize it was her fault?

Not gonna talk about it. "What do you want to eat?"

"What?"

"There's no way that half-eaten donut of yours is going to fuel a work day." I finally turned to look at her.

She wrinkled her forehead. "Wait. How about you tell me what the deal is with you and Troy?"

I looked away. "Eggs? Flapjacks? Some kind of breakfast sandwich? Come on. I'm buying."

"You're flat out grumpy." She unsnapped her seat belt and leaned against the door.

Not getting any better either, thanks. "I'm hungry."

"I've seen you hungry. Doesn't look like a growling bear on you." She crossed her arms over her chest. "You and Troy. What's that about?"

My head hurt. This was a dumb thing to argue about. It wasn't like I had any big secrets. "He showed up on a project two years ago. Had gotten himself into trouble, and the court said jail time or community service. He picked Homes For Hope."

She stared at me, waiting.

"That's it?" She shifted, her eyebrows hiking. "That's all you've got?"

"That's all the story you're getting from me. I don't like him, and I have my reasons, but they don't involve you."

Mostly. And they'd better not involve her with any more depth.

"Seems pretty unsaintly of you." Her tone teetered on the mocking sort. "Can't allow for a guy to mess up without holding it against him?"

Fire flashed through my muscles, and my mouth let loose all on its own. "Not when I watched him mess around with a girl who wasn't even out of high school yet—which, by the way, Sapphira, is *illegal.* And, so we're clear, it wasn't innocent on his part, and he wasn't even a little sorry."

Sarah held me with an angry look for two breaths and then reached for the door. Nice. I didn't normally do this. I wasn't the snarky type. But something with her...she got under my skin and smoldered until I couldn't hold back anymore.

That was my problem, not hers.

"Sarah." I reached across the cab before she could scramble out, and brushed her arm. "I'm sorry. I shouldn't snap at you. And you're right. I should allow for a man to change. It's—"

It was what? That I didn't want him looking at her like that. Touching her. Taking advantage of the fact that, though she'd spent her life around men, she didn't know anything about how they saw a beautiful woman.

She doesn't know she's beautiful.

Whoa. Revelation. My me-centered frustration fizzled. My chest caved as a warm ache replaced hot anger.

I ran my thumb along her arm and over her shoulder. "I want you to be okay."

Her posture sagged as her hand fell away from the door handle, and she looked toward her boots. Not okay. I wanted to slide over, pull her close, and tell her she was amazing. That scenario played out in my head. It didn't end with a hug. *Hands to myself.*

I grabbed the steering wheel. "What happened with your dad last night?"

She tensed up again.

"Seriously, Sarah." My grip reached near superstrength. "You're scaring me."

I watched her profile as her jaw moved. Her face went hard and cold.

My heart stalled. "Did he hurt you?"

"No." Some of the anger drained from her expression. "My dad would never hurt me."

Her eyes slid shut, but only for a moment. I waited, expecting that she'd say more this time.

Nothing.

I wrapped a palm around the back of my neck and blew out a breath. "I need you to explain this to me." I spoke to the dashboard because looking at her kept unraveling my self-control. "You asked me to pick you up from some bottom-feeder club and take you home, which I did. Next thing I know, you're here at five thirty in the morning telling me you came last night. The only thing I've got to go on is the fact that your dad went a little scary when I dropped you off, so you'd better start filling in some blanks, because that's kind of freaking me out."

"We had a fight, and I left. Nothing to freak out about."

All cleared up now, thanks. "He's kind of protective, huh?"

She looked to her hands, which were resting in her lap. "Maybe. Or he sees my mom in me."

Whole new issue, and an ugly one at that. "What happened to her?"

Her hand went to the bill of her hat, and she resettled it over her eyes. "I don't want to talk about this, Jesse. I came up here to get away from it. To work. Can we do that?"

Fair enough—or it should be. Why'd I want to pry this woman open so bad? Like I could fix her, anyway.

I couldn't. Knew the One Who could heal her heart though. There it was—the whole purpose in this relationship. I really needed to keep that in focus.

Sarah popped her door open and slid out.

Time to move on.

SARAH

Jesse in a mood. Wouldn't have guessed I'd see that. Maybe he wasn't such a saint. Which made me feel...something.

This more down-to-earth view made me like him even more. He wasn't so high above me as I'd thought. That something I'd felt was hope. A dangerous thing.

Jesse Chapman saw me as a project. That was all. I hated that I had to keep reminding myself of that. My life was enough of a maze as it was. I didn't need to be adding in emotional confusion concerning this almost perfect guy to the mess.

He bought me breakfast. He was always buying me food. What was that? Pity? A tool? Confusing. We ate in the quick-serve joint with an awkward silence building between us. He'd wanted to know about my mom. I didn't want to talk about her. All I knew about the woman was that she left and my dad hated her.

I left too. Still didn't know if I wanted to go back. Did that mean he'd hate me?

I stared out the window nearest our table and sighed.

"What?" He set aside his breakfast sandwich and leaned both arms against the table.

Too late now. Saying nothing would only provoke his frown. He'd already disapproved of me half the morning. I couldn't take any more.

"She left." My gaze stayed fixed outside.

"Your mom?"

Yep, he'd still been stewing on it. "Yeah. I have her eyes, and she left when I was a baby. That's all I know."

"So, it's been you and your dad all your life?"

I nodded.

"And this fight is a big deal."

Stop. Why was he forever probing? And always right? "You're a lot like my aunt." I looked at his face.

His eyes widened, looking injured. "Is that a bad thing?"

"No, I guess not." I loved Darcy. Except when she was trying to fix me. "You're a lot like her. Especially with the Jesus stuff. Like you think you've got all the answers or something."

The color in his tanned face paled, and his Adam's apple bobbed. I didn't mean it like that—all snotty and insulting. Why did the religion stuff irritate me so much? Wasn't hurting me, and it was actually kind of sweet that Jesse and Darcy wanted me to be okay.

Jesse looked to the table, rubbing the back of his neck. "I'm sorry, Sarah. I don't know everything."

Making him feel bad for caring—that was awesome of me. I groped around my brain for words, hoping to somehow regain our friendship. "I didn't mean it like that. I mean you're her kind of people. The church kind. That's not all bad."

That wasn't anything good. My mouth shut. No more talking. Seven thirty in the morning and I'd already had a terrible day. Please could we go to work?

He chuckled, shaking his head. "That's good to know."

Now what do I do?

Jesse pushed away from the table, wrapping his half-eaten sandwich. "You ready?"

For a fresh start? Yes. Please. Was that possible?

I followed him out the door and to the truck. He opened my side of the cab. He always did that. Southern? Certainly not because I was a lady. Butch. That was me. I tugged on the bill of my hat and moved to hop in. Jesse's eyes stalled me. Pinned right on my face, he stood with a serious, unrecognizable expression and stared. At me. My heart tripped, and I held his gaze.

Breathe.

He looked away, and I inhaled. Blood rushed into my head and over my limbs. I thought I died for a second, and life was resaturating my body.

Staring at Jesse's shoulders as he moved around the nose of the truck, I wanted to die again. He kept his eyes away from mine. Had he died too?

No way. Maybe he'd seen me go, though, and was appalled. Much more likely.

He started the truck and shifted into reverse. I shifted back to normal. Butch girls didn't swoon. I hoped the job ahead was demanding. Hard, sweaty, exhausting physical labor. No more thinking, and especially no more feeling.

JESSE

A buzz of silence filled the cab as we rolled down the road to the job. That moment our stares collided in the parking lot flashed. An urge to touch her—her fingers, the warm skin on her work-muscled arm, or her face—had crashed over me. That'd be throwing water on a grease fire, wouldn't it? I swallowed. Logic didn't smother the desire.

An eternal five minutes of silence stretched out before we pulled up to a place that looked like the creepy farmhouse everyone would want to throw rocks at. Judging by the shattered glass in the window frames, they had.

The house had been green tagged. Condemned. Homes For Hope took on fixer-uppers? This was a new one on me.

We'd beat everyone to the site, including the coordinator. Time to use wisely. I'd messed up the whole morning—the best part being that now Sarah thought me a religious know-it-all. Was that really how I came across?

I parked along the street and shut off the engine. "Can I ask you something?"

Sarah unbuckled her seat belt. Clearly she didn't want to be in the truck with me. "What?"

I was batting a big fat zero that day. Maybe I should've let it go. But I couldn't. "When you said religion back there, you kind of...snarled."

She stared at me, her expression cool. "That's not a question."

"Why?"

After a breath, her focus turned to the disaster house outside her window. "I just don't like it."

"Religion?"

"Yeah."

Did I do the dance of semantics here? An overdone approach, but true nonetheless, and I didn't see many other options. "Most people don't like religion. My relationship with Jesus isn't about religion."

"It's not?" She snorted. "Seems there are way too many churches filled with religious people for that to be true." Her eyes flashed back to me, bright with silent accusation. "Saints. Pretty people dressed up, with all their ugliness tucked safely away, who scorn the ugly ones who haven't cleaned up their messes."

"Saints?" My eyebrow hiked toward my hat. "Like me? Like your aunt?"

Her mouth snapped shut, and she looked away again. I searched for words. Nothing brilliant flashed through my brain. *God, you're going to have to help me out here.*

"I didn't mean you—I can't imagine you have anything ugly to hide." Her voice took on a flat quality. "Some people are just good. Maybe that's the real issue. Religion is full of people who don't get my kind."

I was nice, and that was the issue? Maybe she needed to know how much I resented the way I felt manipulated by people. How I really wasn't at peace all the time with my dad and mom's death. How hard it was to forgive the man who'd taken their lives. If she knew the mess inside me, would that change things for her?

I shifted, leaning toward her. "What does that mean, your kind?"

Her head rolled back against the seat, and she glared at me. "The blue-collar, trying-to-make-ends-meet kind. Dirt under the fingernails. Sunburned-and-not-always-put-together kind. The working kind."

"Oh." Huh. Not what I was expecting at all. That was a strange resentment. "So church is for rich, cushy people?"

She didn't look at me as she shrugged. "Yeah. I guess."

I laughed, and she turned a glare to me. Inspecting my hands, I shook my head. "Guess I better scrub my hands a little better on Sundays, then."

Pink crawled over her face, and she dropped her sheepish look to her hands. "Sorry. I didn't mean..."

"It's all right. I live on an inheritance, right? That puts me in the cushy class." Getting defensive while sharing Jesus. Always a good strategy.

"Jesse, that's not—"

"I know." I sighed. "I'm sorry. That was cheap, and I know you weren't thinking about that. But I think that you have some prejudice—maybe because of a bad experience or something—

but you shouldn't let that paint a picture of what God is like. It isn't true."

"He isn't the perfect God in a pristine heaven ruling over all things?"

My shoulders drooped. "Well, yeah. He is. But—"

"How am I supposed to relate to that?"

"By knowing that's not the entirety of who God is. You can't boil down His character to a flippant statement like that."

"This is a weird conversation." Sarah frowned at me and then opened her door. "We're here to work. Let's do that."

I looked up and down the street. No one there yet. But she'd already made her escape. A storm of confusing emotions brewed inside me as I stepped out of the truck. Frustrated that she wouldn't listen—and that she wasn't making sense. Confused as to why she was so irritated with me this morning—not only about this conversation but all morning. And disappointed. So very disappointed. For her and for myself.

The last part I needed to cut off. This wasn't supposed to be about me. I'd let this emotion—the powerful one that would grip my whole body and squeeze—take over. Wanting her to know Christ should be about her and about Jesus. I wasn't supposed to figure into that.

I moved to catch up with Sarah, who had gone to examine the mess we were going to work on. "Sapphira." I should probably quit calling her that if I was going to remove my emotions from this pursuit. Probably.

She glanced at me, a storm in her eyes. She was confused too.

"Have you considered that Jesus wasn't one of the cushy people?"

Her eyebrows scrunched together. "What do you mean? He was a religious guy."

I shook my head. "He was born to a carpenter. Like you."

The play of emotions crossing her face strangled my heart. Open for a moment, and then she shut it off and turned hard. "What do you know about my life?"

Her cold voice nipped my determination. Another truck turned off the main street and headed our way. Mack's. Time to shelve all of this and move on.

With my hands shoved into my pockets, I tried stifling a sigh. "Mack wants you to work with him this morning." I couldn't summon any positive energy.

We both needed some space, I guessed. I'd spend my morning scraping the roof, and she'd spend hers on the ground.

Her back faced me, but I watched as her shoulders sagged. "He does? How do you know that?"

"He told me to get you here." When had things between us gotten so...complicated? What happened to easy dinners at the burger joint? Maybe we'd find our normal selves somewhere in the work. We'd grab a burger tonight and everything would be fine. "He's got some ideas for the redesign, but he wants your input."

"Mine?" She turned, her face pinched as if any of her input would be inconsequential.

How did she not know what a valuable asset she was to Homes For Hope—to anyone in construction? "You do drafting, right? Know the codes. Know what walls can go, what needs to stay, and how to make the place livable again. Right?" I glanced at her but wouldn't connect with her eyes. That lost-woman look would be too much, and I'd forget why I was supposed to be her friend. "Mack wanted you here. Said he needs you."

I might need you too.

Whoa. Need? My chest locked down hard. I couldn't go there with her. Needing Sarah in a way that physically hurt was a blueprint for a long spell of recovery. I'd been through one of those in the not-so-long-ago past. Didn't feel up to another one.

With her mouth drawn down, Sarah stepped away. Almost as if she knew what I had been thinking and was making her opinion known. She didn't want me to need her either. I wasn't her kind.

Chapter Sixteen

SARAH

Mack wanted me here. That was the reality I needed to grasp. I left home because Dad and I had a fight. I came here because Mack wanted me on this job. Jesse had nothing to do with it.

Jesse had everything to do with it. I looked back at him, hungry for those green eyes. He met my glance, but his expression was closed. In less than twenty-four hours everything had changed between us, and I guessed he wished we'd never met.

Another truck pulled up, and the two guys from the hotel stepped out. Troy and whoever Troy's buddy was. Without actually looking directly at Jesse, I checked his reaction. He didn't acknowledge either one of them, but strode up the chunked-up sidewalk and pushed through the grimy wooden door. I followed him because I didn't know what else to do. Troy and his sidekick cut a trail right behind me.

"So you're a Homes For Hope donor too, huh?"

I glanced back at Troy. Conceit slathered his grin.

"Do you travel with Chapman?"

"No." Wait. How much should I let him know about me? Jesse didn't like him, and no matter what I'd said earlier, that was a big fat black mark against him. I reached for the door and pushed. The hinges had long since rusted, and the top had pulled away from the frame.

With a big hand anchored on the trim, Troy stopped right behind me. "Huh."

I looked up. He smelled like he'd bathed in some kind of junior-high kid fragrance, and that confident smirk met my inspection.

"Good to know, Sarah." He sealed his implication with a wink.

"You here to work?" Mack's normal bark came from the epicenter of disaster within the house. Broken furniture, boxes, outdated clothes, and heaven knew what else littered the room off the entry. It looked like a crime scene. Maybe it was. Jesse stood beside Mack. Jesse crossed his arms—the muscles tight against his short sleeves. He nailed an ice glare on Troy.

"We'll start on the roof." He spoke without moving his stare. "It's a no-brainer. Needs to be stripped and redone. Once the layers are off, we'll be able to tell how much repair the skeleton needs." After a slight pause—I was pretty sure meant as a silent challenge to Troy—Jesse turned back to Mack. "Let me know what you and Sarah decide after lunch, and we can plan demo from there."

Stepping around the obstacles, he moved toward the door. His shoulder brushed mine as he passed, and I fought a crazy impulse to lean into that little bit of contact. What would he do if I lifted my hand, trailed my fingers over his arm?

Put up more distance. Exactly the way I'd seen him inch away from Laine last week. Was this a game to him? That didn't add up. Jesse the Saint who traveled around building other people's houses for free? Not probable.

With a long breath as an attempt to clear my unreasonable thoughts, I picked my way around the battlefield toward Mack. He smiled, but not with an actual smile. Hard old men did that. They had a way of looking at you with approval that wasn't really a facial expression.

"Glad you came."

A generous amount of words, and complimentary at that. If he was anything like my dad, which I was pretty sure he was, in construction-man world that was equivalent to an elaborate thank-you speech.

"Jesse said you wanted me to." I pushed my hands into my pockets and let my inspection wander the condemned dwelling. "This doesn't look like a Homes For Hope job."

One nod. "It's what we got."

Yep. *So let's get to it.* "Jesse said you wanted me to help with the reconstruction design?"

"You do that?"

"Not what I normally do. But I can work up the drawings if that's what you need."

"Good." He turned to the wall opposite the entry. "Take that wall out." He swiveled and then pointed. "And figure out how to make this more open."

I didn't have a chance to ask what was behind those walls. Mack tromped over the mess, set on a mission, and I followed, mentally tallying everything he wanted done. Two more rooms—could we make them bigger? Check the header, make sure the load-bearing joists would hold. Make the front window wider. Stairs needed redone—wider and more open.

We stopped at the front door, near the area where we'd started. I surveyed the mess again. "Wouldn't it be cheaper to build new?"

"Don't know the story." He spit into a box near our feet. "The town wants this place cleaned up and made useful. The local Homes For Hope committee took on the financial planning for it, and they have buyers. We're here to make it happen. So make it happen."

Got it. This kind of communication I knew—I understood. Direct. Simple. Clear. No guessing, no wondering what the guy was thinking and if I measured up to whatever standard he had. Why'd Jesse have to go and get all complicated on me?

Mack moved out of the house, and I trailed him again, glad to breathe in clean air rather than the stench of must, decay, and urine. He stopped on the sidewalk and looked back at me. "Make sure it passes inspection." His gaze traveled up and settled on the guys scraping layers of beat-up shingles, and then swooped back on me. "And whatever you did to Chapman, fix it. Three years, I've never seen him go dark. Boy doesn't deserve it, and you ought to have enough sense to know that."

Hold up there. Why would he assume Jesse's sour condition was my fault? I settled back on my heels and crossed my arms. "Jesse's not my problem."

"Yep." He spit into the mostly bald lawn and then walked away.

I rolled my head back and huffed toward the sky. Just like my dad. Could say a whole mouthful of insults with one little syllable.

Whatever. I had work to do. A few more pickups and a handful of cars had smattered the street in front of the project house. Mack made his way to the far corner of the yard and called for attention. My cue to get busy.

Smacking the cracked concrete with the soles of my work boots, I set off for Jesse's truck to retrieve the tool belt I'd tossed in this morning. I snapped the hook around my waist, ripped out the small notepad I kept behind my tape measure, and moved back to the house. After I had a rough footprint sketched and all the things Mack wanted done listed, I got down to the dirty work.

Sweat rolled down my spine by noon. With the help of a few volunteers, the front room was cleared by chucking junk out of the broken window. Mack instructed the crew to continue the cleanup. Maybe he meant me too, but my frustration needed some quiet space and demanding work. I took a crowbar and a sledge to the plaster wall, slamming pockmarks and tossing debris as I went. The morning rolled over in my mind as my muscles slid into autopilot.

Jesse *had* been in a mood. And I'd pushed him there. But it wasn't my fault. Didn't he understand how humiliating it was to be someone's project? Not a lot of difference between me and this ugly old house, apparently. Both in desperate need of a redo. Or a teardown. With that thought, my nose stung. I threw my energy into the demo because crying over my injured pride in front of a bunch of strangers wasn't an option.

I had a six-by-six opening well underway when Jesse came in and picked over the mess.

"Lunchtime."

Great, now he was down to minimal communication too. Before long, we'd be at the grunt-and-point level. Men.

"Is there a gathering out there?" I kept pace with my destruction, unwilling to look at him. "I don't do those, remember?"

Jesse bent to grab the crowbar I'd thrown on the floor and went to work on a stud that I hadn't cleared yet. "I remember."

He worked silently after that, which was worse than his prying at breakfast.

Why did his lack of attention matter so much? Every sensible wrinkle in my brain told me his interest in me wasn't really in me at all. But somehow I'd snagged onto some dumb hope that he saw me—not only all of the things that were wrong with me—but me. Stupid butch girl. Why would he do that?

Moving away from him, I reached up to the highest part of the wall, whacking the jagged plaster that still clung to the joint at the ceiling. The chunk shook on impact, and the plaster crumbled into a fall of white ash. I moved back, but even before the flakes landed, I knew it'd been a dumb move.

Safety glasses. Should have had them on the whole time. Dust covered my face, and as I squeezed my eyes shut, tiny granules scraped against my eyeballs like sandpaper rubbing against soft paint.

One hand flew over my eyes as the other flung the hammer against the partially demoed wall. "Damn it," I hissed, still unable to blink the invasion clear.

"Whoa." The crowbar clattered to the floor, and in the next instant, Jesse's hands gripped my shoulders. "Stand still. Let me see."

He turned me, and I tried to pry open my eyes. The intrusion felt like blades, and I squeezed them shut again.

"Forget it." I pushed his fingers away from my face. "I'm fine."

With one eye squinted open, I followed the wall I hadn't yet destroyed to the nasty bathroom I'd seen on my earlier tour. Not that it'd help much, but maybe I could extract the foreign offense on my own. Stumbling over the warped floorboards, I made it to the germ-laden sink and leaned toward the wall. No mirror. Only a sliver of reflective glass still clung to the stained wall.

By then tears had dropped from the eye I was squinting, and most of the dust had washed from that socket, so I could see a blur of reality. But something large and abrasive was stuck in my right eye. After brushing away the tears seeping from my left, I pressed my fingers against the other.

"Don't rub it." Jesse slid into the tiny bathroom space behind me. "You could damage your eyeball." With one hand, he turned me away from the sink to face him. In the other, he had a water bottle. "Silly girl. Plumbing's been shut off for years." He twisted the cap, and holding the bottle over the sink, he dumped some water over his fingers.

Thanks. I feel less dumb now. "I know that," I snapped. "I was after a mirror."

His fingers cupped my chin and held fast. "Don't move. Let me get it."

Water droplets transferred from his thumb to the corner of my still-closed eye and seeped between the lids. I blinked, but the sharp burn of the chunk of plaster still scratched my eye.

"I see it." His hand left my chin, and the next thing I knew, he'd taken my hat and turned the bill backward. "I can get it." With two fingers he pried my lids open, and then the pad of his finger came straight at my eye. "Do you wear contacts?"

"No." It took a concentration of discipline not to pull away.

"So your eyes are really that blue all on their own?" A smile carried in his voice.

I didn't know why that annoyed me. Probably because it was drawing that soft spot inside of me to the surface again.

"I told you they're from my mother. The only thing she left me."

His first attempt at removing the offending body proved unsuccessful, but he'd moved the speck over my retina, and I blinked.

"I'm sorry," he whispered.

For not getting the flake out of my eye or for the fact that my mother ditched us?

He reset my eyelid and brushed his thumb over my vision again. Felt like he'd pulled a branch out of there. His hands left my face, and my fingers covered both eyes, rubbing as moisture smeared over my cheeks.

"Better?"

I expected he'd have backed off. He didn't.

"I'm fine."

Again, my chin became captive to his hand, and he lifted my face to inspect it. "You've got black all over your cheeks." Shaking his head, he grinned. "Why'd you wear makeup to a job site anyway? You know better than that."

Heat crawled up my neck and oozed into my cheeks. I pulled away from his fingers and looked to the puke-yellow sink still clinging to the wall. My eyes burned again, but the tears weren't helpful this time. The air between us became heavy, almost painful. That had happened a lot that day.

"Sapphira..."

His nickname for me—spoken with a warmth I'd never heard or felt—sent a rush of tingles over my arms. When his fingertips slid over my cheek, I couldn't resist his silent plea to look back at him. Intensity burned in the green eyes focused on me. My breath hitched somewhere between my lungs and my throat as he grazed my cheekbone with his thumb. I swore his head tilted toward mine first. I was sure of it, because warm moisture fanned my lips when he whispered "You're beautiful" right before his mouth brushed mine.

Kissing Jesse was nothing like kissing Aiden. Aiden had been forceful. Demanding. Jesse was warm and gentle. Safe. In a pulse-throbbing, make-my-knees-weak sort of way.

My hand covered his and then followed the bend of his arm to his shoulder. His other palm slid over my hip to my lower back, and I was pulled against him. Heat traveled over me, and my heart hammered as he slid his fingers into my hair, sending my hat tumbling to the ground.

The stiff bill clattered against the hardwood, and suddenly our kiss was over. Jesse stood straight, breaking all contact. His nose flared, and his eyes, wide and bright, had a wild and alarmed look.

"Sarah." His voice cracked, and his hand cupped his neck. He studied his feet and rolled his lips together. "I shouldn't have done that. I'm sorry."

Regret, heavy and serious and awful, weighed his husky voice, and he refused to look at me.

Why would he want a butch carpenter's daughter?

He didn't.

The house could have crumbled over top of me. It would have been less painful.

JESSE

I kissed her.

Biting my lip and staring at the floor, I fought against the dizzying heat that billowed over me. Unable to calm my pounding heart, I focused on finding a normal breath.

Why had I kissed her? I knew better.

A quick glance at Sarah, and desire flared hot again. Every cell in my body screamed to draw her back, to curl her body tight against mine. I shut my eyes, willing away the phantom sensation of her lips responding to my kiss.

She sniffed, and I forced myself to look at her again. Her arms wrapped around her middle, and she huddled near that awful sink, like a girl who'd been kicked in the stomach. I had wanted her to know—to feel how amazing she was. Now she sank under the humiliation of rejection.

Nice work, Chapman.

"Sarah..." My voice hitched. "Please don't think—"

The tips of her fingers swiped at the black under her eyes, and then she bent to retrieve her hat. "Don't think what?" She replaced the hat, pulling the bill low over her eyes.

Think that I don't want you...

I couldn't tell her that, because then I'd have to explain why I *couldn't* have her. The wrong move for so many reasons. Swallowing, I straightened my concave posture and stepped toward her again.

Touching her was dangerous, but not optional. My fingers brushed her shoulder and traveled down her arm until they settled on her elbow. "Don't feel like..." I cleared my throat. "We're—I'm just not ready for this."

Liar. If I tossed logic and boundaries aside, there'd be no air between us, that kiss wouldn't have ended, and she wouldn't think that I didn't ache to hold her.

She jerked away from my touch. "Right."

My hand fell to my side, and an empty, helpless feeling cooled the place in my chest that had been on fire moments ago. I'd blown everything—my testimony for Christ, our friendship, any hope that someday she'd be saved and...

That was the problem. I'd had an agenda attached to what should have been my purpose. If I'd cut off that selfish desire and stayed focused on the mission God had given me, we wouldn't be drowning in awkward pain at that moment.

"I can run you back to the hotel." My fingers curled into my palm. Even after knowing what I'd done, and how wrong it was, the desire to touch her almost overruled my self-discipline. "You can wash your face, and I have saline. Rinsing both eyes would be a good idea."

"I don't need you to fix me, Chapman." Her chin lifted, and a sharp stab sank into my gut when her blue eyes settled on me. "I don't want your pity."

She brushed past me, the contact between her shoulder and my chest harsh. With a pace more suited to a gym than a construction site, she left the bathroom and cleared out of the house.

I shut my eyes as my head fell forward. You'd think by twenty-six I'd have outgrown stupid.

Chapter Seventeen

SARAH

Walking with my face covered in smeared charcoal makeup wasn't conspicuous at all. What choice did I have? Wasn't letting Jesse take me.

How come I confused his pity for actual care? The day had been awful from the get-go. I must have had bad karma coming at me—probably from fighting with my dad and then leaving.

I should call him.

The sound of dusty brakes squeaked behind me, and I felt the presence of a running engine crawl nearer. I kept up my pace as I stalked down the sidewalk. Jesse was something else. Couldn't he leave me alone?

"Hey, Sarah." Not Jesse's voice. "Where you headed?"

I stopped, keeping my back to Troy. Not someone I wanted to talk to, but not someone I was refusing to talk to at the moment either. His truck eased parallel to me, and the brakes gave one last squeal as he stopped.

"Going for lunch?"

Could I talk to him without actually looking at him? "Yes, but I need to go wash up first."

He chuckled. "A prissy carpenter. That's new."

Turning my head, I scowled at him. "I got junk in my eyes, and I need to rinse my face off. Nothing prissy."

"Oh." Somehow his grin came off as a smirk. Maybe that was his normal. "Hop in. I'll drop you off."

I glanced back down the block I'd covered. Jesse came out of the house, and his gaze tracked my path and landed on me. Heat simmered in my stomach. "All right." I turned back to Troy. "Thanks."

Once I slammed the door shut, he pulled away from the curb.

"Chapman couldn't run you back?"

"I don't know. I didn't ask." This lying thing came pretty easy. And this time, I didn't feel the tiniest brush of guilt.

"So..." Troy hooked his arm over the steering wheel and glanced at me. "You two are..."

"Nothing." I cocked a *that's a dumb question* look on him. "We've worked a couple of jobs together. That's all."

He snorted. "I think you may have a stalker, then." His eyebrows hiked. "I'd watch out for that guy. He's wound up tight."

Yeah, Jesse Chapman was wound up. Today. Every other day, he was the most easygoing person I'd ever met.

"Matter of perspective, maybe?" I pushed my back against the seat, not sure why I was defending the guy who'd just pushed me into a well of humiliation. "Said you were trouble."

One side of Troy's mouth tipped up. "Maybe." We came to the only stoplight between the house and the hotel, which was red at the moment, and Troy anchored a look on me. "How about you decide that for yourself."

Huh. If attracting male attention was the female goal in life, I was having a good week. Except for the fact that I'd managed to snag the attention of the guy I actually liked, lip-locked with him, and lost him all in less than a minute. Heaviness sank through me. Jesse didn't want me as anything more than a fixer-upper. I couldn't get that nail out of my chest.

So I ignored it.

"Does that work on all the girls?" Flirting as a default in uncomfortable situations. This was an interesting development in my personality. Who'd have guessed?

The light turned green as Troy managed the most innocent face a player could mask. "What girls?"

A tiny grin spread over my lips. Not because I thought he was cute, but because he thought he was clever. Games. That was all this stuff was. Men and their games.

Even Jesse? Laine's face flashed through my memory—she'd set her hope on him, and when he silently pushed her away, her downcast eyes said more than any words. He'd messed with her heart.

Yes, Jesse played, no different from the rest. An invisible grip wrapped around my heart and squeezed. He'd been messing with me, and he was better at it than either Aiden or this transparent Troy guy. I swallowed, willing away the burn in my stomach. They all did it, some with more layers than others.

Troy's right hand left the steering wheel, and he draped his arm over the back of my seat. "So..." His jaw moved as if this conversation had already played out in his head and he knew exactly where it was going and how it was going to end. "You and Chapman are nothing. Which means you're free tonight, right?"

Tipping one eyebrow up, I gave him a sideways glance—the same kind he'd given me when I'd first climbed in his truck.

His grin spread full. "I'm thinking you, me, a couple of beers, and a round of pool."

"That's what you're thinking, huh?"

He answered with a wink.

"I happen to have work to do tonight."

His confident grin faltered. "Work? That house doesn't have electricity. What kind of work are you going to do after sundown?"

"Drafting."

"Are you getting paid for it?"

I didn't have anything clever to say.

"Thought not." His fingers brushed my neck. "Girl's gotta have a life, right?"

Sure. Why not? "You're buying?"

"Of course."

I smirked. "One round. Then we'll see."

Troy chuckled under his breath. I had some kind of smug satisfaction smooth the ache from earlier.

Let the games begin.

DALE

My phone finally rang at seven. Not that I'd been waiting.

Like hell I hadn't. Sarah hadn't ever taken off like that, and she hadn't called since she left.

I punched the Accept button. "Where are you?"

She drew a breath and held silent.

I white-knuckled the phone. "Sarah, damn it, I asked you a question."

"Lexington." She cleared her throat, and then her voice, which had been soft, flipped to the foreman kind she'd learned from me. "I'm on a job with Homes For Hope."

I'd kill Dan for getting her into this. "You're with that guy, aren't you?"

"No."

Fire seared my gut. Where had my girl gone? My daughter didn't do things like this—fight with me, take off with some guy, and then not come clean about it. "Don't you lie to me, girl."

"I'm not *lying* to you." Her voice cut hard on that word. "Jesse's here, but I'm not *with* him."

I heard her shudder, and the fire spread to my arms. He'd hurt her. I knew it. That jerk had led her on, got what he wanted, and left her more messed up than she'd been before she met him. The muscles in my arms rippled, and my free hand fisted. "Come home."

Her sigh sounded agitated. "I told you, Dad. I'm working here. I can't come home."

The protective anger flipped, turning icy and hard. "Fine. Stay. Leave me out of this circus though. Let me know when you've figured out whatever you think it is you need to figure out."

"Dad..."

"Don't 'Dad' me." I'd been through this before. All my efforts to raise her to be different, and none of it mattered. She was becoming *her*. "I'm not doing this. So stay or go or whatever. I don't care."

"What does that mean?" Panic underscored her words.

I should back off. She wasn't Cassie. This wasn't the same thing, was it?

Hurt the same.

"It means I don't want to go through this. You do what you need to do. Leave me out of it."

She didn't answer. I wondered if she'd hung up. Seemed like something she'd do at that moment—although it wasn't something my old daughter would have done.

"Okay, Dad."

Her breathy response melted my frozen resolve. And then the line went dead. Frost resettled over me, which suited better. I didn't want to feel that kind of pain again.

JESSE

Sarah didn't come back after lunch. Panic had my heart throbbing, and when Troy showed up alone, I stopped him near the west wall of the house.

"Where's Sarah?"

A grin—the kind that curdled my lunch in my stomach—slithered over his face. "What's it to you?"

I'd never been in a fight. Didn't know how to go about it—but at that moment you couldn't tell. I had his T-shirt wrapped up in both my fists and his back slammed against the wall faster than he could wipe that horrible smile off his face. "If you hurt her..."

"You'll what, Preacher?" He struggled against me, but I held him pinned with my forearms. Guess roofing every day had some payoff.

"She doesn't want you," he hissed.

My grip uncurled. He didn't know anything, and this whole afternoon had been my fault. "Did you take her to lunch?"

He rolled his eyes like a stupid teenage punk. "What, are you like her dad or something?"

I stared at him. "I'm like your supervisor, smart guy, and the judge will ask me to sign off on your time." Not completely true. Mack would have to verify. But I had a pretty solid connection there.

He straightened himself to his full height, which was a good two inches taller than mine, and hovered. "I dropped her off at the hotel. She said she had to do some kind of drawings or something."

Like two inches were supposed to intimidate me. "Get on the roof."

I pivoted on my boot and strode away from him, heading for my truck. I should have taken Sarah back to the hotel, but causing a scene out in the open seemed like a bad idea. I'd already made her feel awful. Didn't think adding an audience to it would be a good call.

After opening the driver's side door, I reached under the seat for my phone. A swipe, a tap, and then another tap brought up *Sapphira* on the screen. Her name summoned those blue eyes, and my heart pooled in a way that hurt.

She didn't answer. Been through this drill before.

"Sarah, I'm really sorry. We need to talk." I rubbed the back of my neck, imagining her averted face and replaying how she'd pushed me away earlier. "Please. Call me."

She wouldn't though. I knew it before I'd called. Sarah was the hiding kind. From people. From pain. And now, from me.

The afternoon dragged by. I threw myself into the work. No conversations. No breaks. Not Jesse Chapman–style at all. By the end of the workday, my clothes were soaked with sweat, the roof was bare, and Mack had me cornered.

"Wanna talk?"

With him? That was laughable. Conversations with Mack were quippy and mostly work related. Mostly.

"Nope."

"Where'd she go?"

Asking *who* would be a childish game. "To work on the drawings." Glad I knew where she was. Made it all sound so much more amiable.

"You two gonna figure this out?"

I snorted. "You're paddling in an ocean with a twig, old man. Better stick to what you know."

"I know." His eyebrows flickered, and he crossed his arms.

How was it he could say things louder by not saying them at all? "Don't know what to tell you, Mack."

"The truth." There it was again. Two words. Two solid pounds that sank the nail in deeper than a dozen little raps ever could.

Glancing up to the burly old guy, I suddenly saw my father standing there, and my defenses dropped. "I messed up, and I don't know if I can fix it."

He nodded. "She hurt?"

My chest locked down so tight I couldn't draw in air. Hanging my head, I nodded.

"Yep." He uncrossed his arms and looped his thumbs over his pockets. "Better find a way. Life's short."

And thus ended the motivational wisdom of a seasoned contractor. Sometimes good advice poked up from the most interesting sources.

I followed Mack's trail to the street, hopped into my truck, and started the engine. Being by myself in the cab of my vehicle had never felt so lonely. Mack was right. Life was too short to let this slide, but I still hadn't a vague inclination as to how to fix it.

Shower first. Then a face to face. *God, write something wise on my heart, and let it cross my lips.* Certainly on my own I'd make the mess worse.

My stomach rumbled by the time I toweled my hair—which still needed cut. Would Sarah let me buy her dinner?

Not a good plan.

Oh. So, being kind was confusing things?

Maybe it was being manipulative. Hold up—was I manipulative?

Somehow I hadn't expected that this relationship with Sarah—this *friendship*—would hold a mirror up to my unrealized flaws. That was not cool. So, being kind but having a hidden agenda driving the act of kindness was manipulative. Right. Everyone knew that. Didn't know I was doing that though.

How did you separate kindness for kindness' sake from agenda-driven kindness?

No concrete answers. But tonight, no dinner. Because it was manipulative.

I called in an order for pizza with a local place, tossed a clean T-shirt over my head, and wandered down the hall toward Sarah's room. My pulse accelerated as I drew closer to the door, and my tongue seemed to swell. What was I going to say? Nothing brilliant had struck me yet.

Rapping with my knuckles on the door, I leaned a shoulder against the frame opposite the knob. Seven heartbeats—in only about two seconds—pulsed in my chest until Sarah opened the door.

"Hey." I didn't try to force a smile. That would be manipulative.

She drew back, placing a hand on the door like she was thinking about closing it. "You."

"Yeah, me." I swallowed. "Can we talk?"

Her eyes burned into me. Angry still, but the intensity seemed to be more than that. I drew away from the wall and slid a palm on the door. "Please, Sarah. I can't tell you how sorry I am. I wasn't thinking."

"You mentioned that already." She stepped away from the door but didn't push it closed. Was it okay for me to go in?

Wisdom, God. Please?

I pushed the door back and filled the entry frame, which gave me a full view of Sarah. Whoa. Dark slim jeans that hugged her long, feminine legs, flat shoes, and a gauzy white flowing top. So beautiful. Energy surged through my veins, and a replay of our kiss passed through my mind. My lips tingled, and hot desire flooded over me.

"You look..." Amazing. Tempting. Why did she look like that? Oh. Heat froze. "You're going out."

Her mouth twisted to the side. "Seems I clean up well. Been a good week for me." The flat tone of her voice said exactly the opposite of *good.* She tucked one side of her hair behind an ear and drew in a long breath. "Look, Jesse. Forget it, okay? It was just a kiss."

My chest collapsed. I couldn't forget it. And people said *it was just a kiss* all the time. It was never true. You didn't get to go around messing with other people's emotions and have it not mean anything. That was not the way life worked.

"Sarah..."

"No." She held a hand up. "I don't want to dive into it, okay? You didn't mean to. Fine. I don't want to be your next Laine Fulton."

"What does that mean?"

"Forget it."

"No. What do you mean by that? I told you what happened there—which was nothing. She needed a friend, and I was it. That's all."

"That was not all." Fire sparked from her eyes. "I'm ignorant about a lot of things, but I saw how she looked at you—both before you brushed her off and after. That wasn't all."

Every heartbeat hurt. She thought I was... "I don't play games, Sarah."

She blew a contemptuous laugh through her nose. "Right. Everyone plays games. Some don't know the rules, but everyone plays."

I took a step toward her. "Do you?"

Crimson poured into her cheeks, and she looked to the floor. "I'm still new on the field."

Now breathing hurt. Cynicism hadn't been a part of her character before today. I'd done this.

"You're not that kind of woman." She moved back as I came closer. "And I'm not that kind of guy. Which is why I'm trying to make things right between us."

A silent shudder moved over her shoulders, and she sniffed. Suddenly I understood that an explanation, no matter how well put, wouldn't help. Only a sincere acknowledgment of what I'd done would maybe bridge the gap I'd carved.

"I'm so sorry I hurt you, Sarah." I reached to touch her arm and then thought better of it. "I do want to be your friend. Please forgive me."

Her lips worked under her teeth. I forced myself to endure the silence as she worked through her emotions.

A knock at the door—which I'd left open on purpose—stole the awkward moment. Sarah looked up, and I turned my head.

Troy.

"Hello, hottie."

No. After a hard, long look at the womanizer, I turned my gaze back to her.

"Hey," she said, avoiding me. "I'm about ready."

No she was not.

Troy slithered into her room, smelling like a boy's locker room, and slid a hand around her narrow waist.

I wanted to vomit. Right after I broke every one of his trespassing fingers.

"What are you doing here, Chapman?" He tugged her against himself. "Evangelizing?"

My eyes found Sarah's and held. A tiny peek of remorse darkened her stare before she looked away. "He was going to check over the drawings for me. We'll only need a minute."

She was forgiving me. I took what seemed like my first breath of oxygen since Troy had tainted the room.

"Can't he do it later?" He turned Sarah flush against his chest but pinned a glare on me. "Like during work hours?"

Sarah pushed away from him and removed his arm from her body. Amen. "No, we work on the house during work hours." She scurried toward the laptop sitting closed on the desk.

"Come on, gorgeous." Troy stepped behind her. "Fun times await. Don't let the Bible drill sergeant rule your every waking hour."

Sarah leaned to open her computer, and Troy's tentacles vined around her waist again.

Enough. "Knock it off, you oozing bundle of hormones. The grown-ups are having a big-people conversation."

"You're tighter than a spring, Chapman. Chillax, dude." With a mocking grin, he nuzzled her neck and kissed the exposed skin under her ear. "I think your stalker is jealous."

My fists clenched tight as fury exploded in my chest. I'd never wanted to hit something so badly in my life. However, before I could blink, Sarah stood straight and pushed him away again.

"Troy, just give us a few minutes." She caught his advancing hands and pushed them back. "I'll meet you in the lobby."

Ha. Dismissed. His haughty expression fell, and I couldn't help but smirk.

He kept a grip on her hands. "How about you show me the drawings?"

Great idea. Have the *can't keep out of a bar fight, didn't graduate from high school, forever seventeen-year-old* guy look over house plans. "Are you a master?"

He scowled. "Are you a loser?"

Oh, that was so low. I might never recover. "And that's why you don't need to be in on this conversation. Good-bye, Troy."

The air in the room froze, and both of us looked at Sarah. Her eyes collided with mine and then darted away. "Two minutes, Troy. I promise."

He snagged her chin with one hand and brushed her lips with his thumb. "I'll be counting." That horrible, satisfied grin of his settled on his mouth, and then he brushed hers with it.

My gut burned, and every muscle coiled tight as he passed by me. *Breathe. Deep. And don't explode.* I waited until the door clicked and then faced Sarah. She stared at the computer screen as if that was actually what I was there for. Careful to control my movements, I stepped next to her until our shoulders touched, and mirrored her leaning posture as we both braced against the desk.

"What are you doing, Sarah?" A hoarse whisper was all I could manage.

"Going out." She continued to stare at the screen. "You knew that."

"With *him*?"

Her bottom lip went under her teeth.

"Why?"

Stoic. Nothing. Except her jaw moved—hard.

I swallowed, the desire to wrap her in my arms making my biceps quiver. "Don't do this."

She inhaled and then stood straight. "Do what?"

"You know what he wants." I kept both my palms glued to the desk.

"So?"

Agony ripped through my chest. Had I done this? Pushed her into his razor-sharp talons set on soul destruction? Slowly, I pushed off the desktop and turned to hold her gaze. "You won't find what you're looking for in his bed."

Though her brows shot up in a challenge, a sheen of tears glazed her eyes. "And what am I looking for, Jesse?" She stepped nearer, the heat of her body tempting mine. "Will I find it in your bed?"

"No." *God, help.* I curled my fingers into my palms.

Silence wrapped around us, somehow invisibly cording us closer. Looking into her eyes, nothing else mattered. Her beautiful, aching, searching soul reflected there, and helpless longing pulsed warm through my heart. I wanted so much more than to hold her. What could I do to make her whole, happy?

Nothing. Wholeness was not mine to give.

Chapter Eighteen

SARAH

It happened again. I died. Staring at Jesse, standing near enough to inhale his just-showered scent and to feel his body heat, I left the reality of my life and discovered a place that felt warm and mysterious and safe all at once.

But then he blinked, broke our connection, and cast his gaze to the side. *No.* He was saying, *You can't stay there with me.*

My heart dropped, splattering all over the reality of who I really was. A butch carpenter girl. Not a woman Jesse wanted. Why did he keep doing this to me?

Fine, Jesse Chapman. Someone wanted me though. Even if it was only for tonight, I'd take it. Didn't care about Jesse's moral compass. Didn't do me any good. No, worse than that, whatever it was inside of him that was dictating his actions was killing me—and not in the good way anymore.

I straightened my shoulders, swaying away from the alluring aura of his warmth, and grabbed my little clutch thingy off the hotel bed. "Shut the computer down when you're done, and make sure my door's closed." Wishing the space between him and the exit was more than a narrow hall, I moved to pass him.

His hand caught my wrist, and he tugged me to his side. "He'll leave you in little coiled-up ribbons scattered on the ground." His breath fanned over my neck as he leaned in to whisper. "Don't give yourself to him."

I stared at the door. Not because I didn't want to see the intensity that was pouring from his voice and rippling off his solid body. But because if I saw it, I'd crumble. I'd throw myself against him and beg him to want me.

He didn't. Whatever this emotion was that was winding him tight and turning him into something I wouldn't have expected, it wasn't jealousy. Holy fire, maybe? Self-righteousness? Probably. Not desire—not for me.

I twisted free from his grip. "Have a nice night, Jesse."

Three more steps took me to the door, and I didn't look back. Brushing back the hair that fell over my eyes, I strode through the hall to the lobby. He was messing with me in a game I didn't understand. What was he gaining by drawing me in and then pushing me away? At least with Troy, I knew the rules—mostly. I knew what he wanted, and I could play him back. Mutually beneficial, that was what this interlude would be. Two adults satisfying their desires and moving on with life.

Don't do it.

I shut the echo of Jesse's voice out. What did he know? He didn't know what it was like to be the only woman in a group of men and yet never be noticed. Didn't know what it was like to hear other women questioning what you were. For one night, I wouldn't be the carpenter's daughter. Not the butch reject. I would be beautiful, desired. And it would be amazing. Like dying in Jesse's heated stare.

My breath hitched as that feeling washed over me again. Why did he look at me like that?

My pace slowed as I neared the lobby, and I glanced over my shoulder. The hall was empty. Had I hoped he'd come after me? Stupid girl.

Rounding the corner, Troy came into view. Leaning up against the wall, arms crossed over his chest, he smiled. Jesse's smiles washed me in warmth. Troy's smile sent a chill through my arms.

No, it didn't. The air-conditioning vent was right above me. Probably. I didn't check.

"Hey, sexy." Troy pushed off the wall and sauntered to me, his eyes unashamedly wandering over every inch of my body. One arm slid around my waist, and his thumb anchored in my jeans pocket. "Let's go."

I ignored the way his touch made me stiff. Wasn't used to it, that was all.

He tugged me to his truck, opened the passenger door, and then dropped both hands around my waist. His thumbs moved in circles over my abs, which made them jump without my permission. I sucked in a breath, and he chuckled from deep in his chest. He closed the space between us and then backed me up until I bumped into the side of his truck.

Games. I could play. My hands slid over his arms and under the sleeves of his T-shirt as I tossed my look up to him. His grin...so self-satisfied. As if he thought *he* was playing *me*. I smirked, which he must have thought was an *I want you* look. His mouth pushed hard against mine, and he dove in full force.

Games. I could play. I kissed him back, noting that his heart rate shot up. Mine didn't. At all. When his hands began to explore my body in more detail, I nudged him away. "Were we going somewhere?"

A cockeyed smile fixed on his smug face. "It's going to be a good night."

Yep. I leaned in so that my mouth was close to his ear. "I'll hold you to that."

The vein in his neck jumped. So easy, this little game we were playing. I spun away from him and climbed into his truck. Lust smeared over his face. He shut my door and held eye contact as he rounded the front of the vehicle. With one motion he climbed in, leaned over the center console, and gripped the back of my head. Another heavy kiss. He moved like he thought he'd set my world on fire.

I let him think that he did before I pushed him away again. "I'm hungry."

That dark, throaty chuckle escaped from his chest again. "I can tell." He winked and then started his truck.

We finally pulled away, leaving that scared, innocent carpenter girl behind.

JESSE

What had I done? I stared at Sarah's computer, trembling. *Please protect her.*

Nausea swirled hot in my stomach as I unplugged her laptop and shut the screen. I'd take it with me. She'd have to come find me to get it. Wouldn't be tonight though.

The image of her body coiled against Troy's forced the bile into my throat. I moved for the bathroom and coughed over the toilet.

What would I do when I saw her in the morning?

Wiping my mouth with a handful of toilet paper, I leaned against the counter. Troy would use her and be done with her. On to the next conquest. Did that really not bother her?

No. She could put up a wall of indifference, but deep in her human soul, she'd writhe under the rejection. She wasn't calloused. She was lost, and this would cut deep.

Pain seared in my chest, as if the wound she was about to submit to had sliced across my heart too.

What would I do? My head fell forward, and my eyes slid shut. *Help me show her Your love.* Harder than it would seem. Because while I was standing there feeling sick, knowing exactly what she was getting herself into, I also felt a burn of anger. I'd warned her—and she knew even before that. She flushed it. Didn't care. Was willing to give herself to some guy in exchange for a couple of drinks and a night of being held. Why would she do that?

How did I get into this? Pushing my hand into my hair, I stared up at the ceiling. Pain continued to throb over me, and it hit me. Like a bundle of shingles tossed off a roof, the truth pounded hard and sank deep into my heart.

I looked up to the ceiling of Sarah's empty bathroom. "I love her."

I. Loved. Her.

That kind of realization was supposed to be sweet. Mine was riddled with agony.

"God, I love her." My voice shook, and I dug my fingers into the counter. What was He doing to me?

Me too.

Hold up, what? Oh. Yeah. He loved her too—loved her first. Loved her best.

"Does it have to hurt like this?"

That night on Avery's deck stirred in my soul again.

Do you trust Me?

The answer didn't come as readily as it had that evening. Yes, but...but why? What are You doing? If I'd written this story, Sarah would have been interested in the Jesus that had been born to a carpenter when I told her about Him earlier that day. She would have asked about Him, gotten to know Him, ultimately accepted Him as her savior, and she wouldn't be chasing wholeness from some abusive, self-seeking vulture. And I wouldn't be left alone writhing through all of it. Why couldn't this be that kind of a happily ever after?

Sometimes life just didn't make sense.

SARAH

"Have you played before?" With a bottle in his fist, Troy snugged an arm around my waist.

I'd been scoping the cue sticks, looking for a shorter one. Guess he took that as ignorance. At least, I assumed he was talking about pool. "Not much." Enough to know how to choose my weapons, but I was trying a whole new game plan here.

Troy reached with his other hand to the rack and chose a stick that was too long for me. "Here."

I looked up and he winked. "Don't worry. I'll show you."

I bet he would. After a swig of my hard cider, I twirled out of his hold and took the stick. "Hope you're a good teacher."

That snake of a grin slithered over his face. "Oh, don't you worry, honey. The things I'm good at, I'm really good at."

My stomach shivered. I thought about the phone in my little purse thingy, and pictured Jesse's name in the contacts. He was just a few minutes away...

Not an option. I could play *this* game with Troy. Jesse's game—too dangerous. He'd already made me feel too much of nothing good.

Troy racked the balls, and the game commenced. I painted stupidity on my face, and he draped himself all over me to *show* me how to shoot. I'd never been touched so much by another human being in my life. Didn't particularly enjoy any of it. But his interest assured me that I was at least somewhat attractive.

"That's the game." He'd sunk the eight ball in the side pocket. I still had four stripes scattered on the tabletop.

I blinked and then gazed up at him, fixing what I hoped looked like some version of adoration. "I'm not good at this."

Sauntering toward me with his cue stick posted over his shoulders, Troy zeroed a heated look on me. His body pushed against mine, sandwiching me between him and the table. With slow, deliberate movements, the cue stick came over his head and lowered behind me until he had it flat on the table.

Pinned. His head lowered. "I can show you a few things." His fermented whisper brushed hot across my mouth.

"I'll bet." My stomach rolled. What was I doing?

His mouth crashed on mine, and the weight of his body pressed against me. He demanded. I gave, even while the sickish feeling inside me swirled fiercely. His hands roamed, landing on my waist. For a tiny moment, his body shifted away, and I was lifted to sit on the pool table. The muscles in my thighs jumped when his fingers made a trail from my knees upward. He wrapped my legs around him and quickly closed the small space separating us.

Heat poured over me. The bar was crowded, and the sounds of people and music and glasses clanging together seemed to increase as I became more acutely aware of how obnoxious this scene was. Yet I kept kissing him, letting him believe his desire was mutual. His fingers found the hem of my shirt and slid beneath the fabric. I squeaked in my throat. What was I getting into?

That dark laugh of his rumbled through his chest. "Hungry little thing." His mouth moved against mine as he spoke. He leaned against me, and I was forced to cling to his neck as he dipped my back closer to the table.

"Hey," someone barked from the bar. "No sex on the pool table."

I jerked away.

Troy laughed, pulling me upright.

Humiliation dumped over me, and I started to tremble. I wiggled off the table, but he stayed in front of me, his hands back on my hips. He leaned in again. Really? But instead of kissing my mouth, he trailed his lips over my jawline until his mouth was near my ear. "Let's get out of here."

Yes. Let's. Quickly, before I had to look at anyone in the room. I nodded, sliding through the very narrow space between him and the pool table to grab my clutch. Troy stepped right behind me. Right. Behind. His hand landed on my hip to guide me out.

We got to the truck. More kissing. Eventually I pushed him away.

He nuzzled my neck. "Back to the hotel?"

Don't do this. Jesse's whisper buzzed in my mind. What did he know?

"Yes." My voice quivered.

What was I doing?

We got to the hotel. The side parking lot was not well lit. In the semidarkness, Troy pinned me against the wall beside the entry door. His hands explored without reservation, as if my body belonged to him. Because I was giving it to him. My heart slammed against my ribs.

What was I doing?

I ducked from his insistent kisses, bowing under his arm and sliding away from his rigid body.

His hand caught me and slid over my stomach. With my back to him, he pulled me hard against him. "Upstairs?"

My room was downstairs. But I nodded.

Don't do this. Had there been pain in Jesse's plea? Why did he care?

Troy barely had me in his room before he tugged my shirt off. I trembled violently. *Don't give yourself to him.*

Nausea rolled in my stomach.

"Stop." I pushed Troy's shoulders.

His hands fell away, but only to pull his own shirt over his head. His hot skin stuck against mine as he pulled me against him again.

This time I centered a hand on his chest and pushed harder. "Stop, Troy."

"Come on, baby." His hands dropped to my jeans, searching for the button. "You can't do this to a man."

Guilt soured inside me. I'd done this. Made him think this was what I'd wanted. But it wasn't. "I'm sorry. I can't do this."

He pulled away, his heated eyes roaming over my half-naked body. I wanted to huddle under a blanket far away from his lecherous gaze.

A slow, ugly smile carved his mouth. "I see." One finger grazed over my shoulder and down my chest. "It's okay, little girl. I don't mind your inexperience." He slithered closer, tugging my hips against his. "I'll be gentle."

Was that why I was afraid? He tipped my head to the side, kissing my neck, my shoulder, and then my chest. I shut my eyes, sinking my fingers into his arms. Every girl was afraid her first time, right? Maybe it'd be best to get it over with. It would be okay. Plus, he wanted me. Bad, apparently.

Don't give yourself to him.

Jesse didn't want me. Why should he care?

Don't do this.

Tears lined the seams of my eyelids. Why was I so messed up?

"Troy." With both hands I pushed him away again. "Stop."

He stared at me, his face reddening, his jaw moving hard. Both of his palms braced against the wall beside me as his eyes fired with anger. "Didn't pin you for jailbait."

I blinked, pushing into the wall as much as possible.

"Fine, you ugly little tease." He pushed away and turned his back to me. "Get out of here before I lose my self-control."

I bent to grab my shirt, quickly placing it over my trembling body. "Troy, I'm—"

"I said get out!" His bare muscles rippled as he turned.

Fear tied a frozen knot in my chest. My bottom lip went between my teeth, and I darted for the door.

Nearly running down the stairs, I felt like trash. I should have just slept with him. Seemed my insides were going to rot either way.

Chapter Nineteen

JESSE

For hours I'd played at distraction. Spent a good sixty minutes or more staring at Sarah's drawings. Her vision would transform that trash pit of a house, and when we were finished, it would make someone an amazing home. So talented, that little carpenter's daughter. Really, she ought to be doing this kind of job more.

After shutting her laptop down, I took myself to the mom-and-pop grocery in town. Sarah's sad, desperate blue eyes came with me, and I begged God to intervene tonight as I replayed our standoff in her room. My gut knotted again as I imagined Troy pressed against her.

"Have a thing for yogurt?" Some stranger—an older woman—stopped next to me in the dairy aisle.

"Huh?" I glanced to her and then to the basket I was gripping in my left hand. At least twenty little containers had been piled in there. I must have checked out of reality. "Oh. No. Well, yeah, I guess. A couple for breakfast. You know."

She cackled and patted my arm. "No wonder you're such a looker. Healthy boy."

Yeah, I was a looker. That was why, up until that day, I hadn't kissed a woman since college. Well, actually that was mostly a choice. I hadn't found anyone who made my heart simmer the way Sarah did. I shouldn't have kissed her though.

I pressed a half smile to my mouth and looked at the woman. She grinned back and shuffled on her way. What was it about me that the older women were drawn to? I was such an oddball.

After I replaced half of the yogurts I'd stacked in my basket, I found the bread, some lunch meat and cheese, and a bag of chips. I swung back around to the dairy section for a gallon of chocolate milk and headed for the front to check out. The liquor aisle distracted me. I was not opposed to a drink here and there. Preferred something mild though. Shane always laughed at my choices. He'd rather taste his liquor than disguise it, which was fine. He hadn't been drunk since he was a teenager. Dad had fired him once back then—showed up to a job late and hungover, and Dad cut him loose on the spot. We lost him for a year or so, although Dad kept track of his doings during those months. One day Shane showed up on a build. Said he was ready to work, was done being stupid, and please, would Dad give him another shot? The rest...well, Shane ran the company, and I was glad of it.

Not a common story though. The path of rebellion seemed to be the long, twisted, sharp-drop kind. I paused in the middle of the store, shut my eyes, and pictured Sarah. Bile churned around inside, and my chest ached. If I hadn't been so selfish, maybe she wouldn't be going this direction. She wouldn't have gone out with Troy.

God, please...

I went through the checkout and then back to the hotel. After several hours of *House* reruns, I flicked the TV off and pretended I could go to sleep. Sarah's face waited for me, surfacing vivid and piercing every time I shut my eyes. Alternately, she looked heartbroken and then angry. Because of me? Or because of the scene that I was sure was playing out between her and Troy?

Quit. Nothing I could do about it. I flipped from my back to my stomach, punched the pillow down, and folded my arms under my head. Sleep.

Every muscle in my body was tense, and I couldn't make any of them relax. I tried all the techniques I remembered from my required stress-management class from college. Nothing worked. Every time the sound of a vehicle pulling into the parking lot rustled outside my room, I had to beat down the urge to sneak to my window and peek through the blinds. Why would I want to see them together anyway?

I rolled to my back again. Maybe if I stared at the ceiling, eventually sleep would force my eyelids closed. So I stared. About as relaxed as one giant muscle cramp, and calm as a cornered tomcat, I stared. Nothing.

Flip over and repeat. The cycle lasted for who knew how long. Finally I sat up, tossed the worn-out blankets aside, and planted my bare feet on the floor. The red numbers on the clock said 12:35.

I growled in the dark room. Why couldn't I forget all of it? Sarah was a grown woman and could make her own choices. Not my problem. I flicked on the bedside lamp and stomped to the bathroom. After splashing my face, I ripped open the pack of water I'd bought earlier and grabbed a bottle. The cap twisted off and fell out of my grip. Might have been a little aggressive with the twisting part. It landed on the table and bounced around about fifty times before it dropped to the floor.

Insomnia and messy. Who was this guy? Definitely not me.

With the bottle at my mouth, I threw back my head to chug. Warm. Yuck. Tasted like plastic. After throwing on my green zip-up hoodie, I grabbed the ice bucket and my key card.

I had to pass Sarah's room on the way to the ice machine. I looked the other way and forced myself not to tune in. I didn't want to know. Halfway down the stretch of hall, a passage opened to my left—the side stairwell and vending area. Looking at my feet more than anything else, I turned. A small figure huddled against the wall on the bottom step—dark-blue jeans, white top, short dark hair.

Sapphira.

My chest caved even while I sucked in air. "Sarah?"

Though her head barely moved, those blue eyes looked up and locked on me. Sad, lost sapphires that squeezed my insides until tears burned against my eyelids. The wolf had done what a wolf would do, and now she sat with her insides shredded.

How do I respond? Surprisingly, I felt only pain—for her.

She sat in silence, dropping her gaze to stare at nothing in front of her. I stepped to the stairs and eased onto the riser beside her, setting my bucket to the side. She didn't move, didn't speak. Just sat with her eyes glazed, peering into space as if she'd find the answers she ached for in the silent emptiness of the night. I studied her as quiet cocooned us with a surreal sense of intimacy and understanding. The skin on her cheeks, neck, and chest were splotched red—the burn marks left by the sandpapery texture of a man's evening shadow. A darker mark on the exposed part of her shoulder demanded my attention— red and purplish. A hickey. A sick feeling swirled inside my gut, and I moved my eyes away from the bruise. The tag of her white top stuck out, and I moved to poke it back into place, but stopped before my fingers touched it. The seams were out too.

I swallowed. Hard. My insides continued to wring tight. Unzipping my hoodie, I tugged my arms from the sleeves and draped the sweatshirt over her small frame.

"Did he hurt you?" I could hardly force my whisper past the knot in my throat.

"No." Her lips quivered, but that vacant stare persisted.

Yeah. Clearly not.

There were moments in life in which nothing said could ever make the pain less. Like in a hospital after your parents were pronounced dead. Or in a stairwell after you'd sold your body for a moment of human warmth. Words couldn't penetrate the solid mass of complete and suffocating heartache.

Sarah was in that place. Hurting, but not understanding the pain. Hungry, but not knowing why. Nothing said—that was my best move. So I put an arm around her and carefully drew her close. She turned her face into my shoulder, pressing her forehead in deep. My other hand came up, and with fingers combed into her soft hair, I held her.

She didn't cry—no sniffing, no warm pool of tears soaking into my white T-shirt. She just stayed—worn out, used, and lost—tucked in tight against me.

Somewhere in the hurt I felt for her, a strange calm washed warm and clean in my heart. I thought of Peter, the traitor who'd denied Christ. Redeemed. Paul, the church slayer. Redeemed. The thief on the cross who, at the moment of death, recognized Christ for Who He was. Redeemed.

Nothing was unredeemable in the hands of the redeeming God. I'd blown it earlier. He could still work in Sarah's life, even if it wasn't through me. Sarah had made a heart-shattering decision. God could still seek her lost soul and heal it. His call was still on her life, and neither she nor I could render it void.

I blinked back tears at the same moment she pulled away. After a long intake of air, she sighed, put her hands on her knees, and pushed up to her feet.

"Still have a full day of work in the morning, right?" she said, still not looking at me.

I stood, reclaiming my ice bucket as I moved. "Yeah."

Her nod preceded a moment of silence, and then she moved for the hall. "Good night."

"Night, Sapphira." I turned to the ice machine to fill the pail. Small chunks clinked together as I held the dispense button, willing myself not to watch her go.

"Jesse." Sarah's hush voice cracked.

I looked up, releasing the button so she wouldn't have to talk over the falling ice.

Tears glazed her stare. "I didn't sleep with Troy."

Relief surged over me so strong I was almost ashamed at how selfish it seemed. After setting the bucket on the floor, I closed the gap between us and wrapped her in my arms.

Her shoulders trembled, and then her arms twisted around me. Her fingers dug into my back as she gripped my shirt. She was crying, and I got how desperate she was to feel special. Loved. How horrible she felt to be treated as a cheap diversion, as someone unworthy of sincere affection. I'd been a part of that, but maybe, in this silent, emotional moment, she would understand that I hadn't rejected her like she'd thought.

She wasn't ready yet. Maybe neither was I.

SARAH

I'd never cried in a man's arms before. Tough girls didn't— butch girls, that is. But I'd never done a lot of what I'd done that night, and all of it balled into one giant storm of hurt.

I'd behaved like a cheap thrill. Like my mother, probably. And I'd done it partly to hurt the man who held me. Why did I do these things? Any of them, recently? Storming out of the house, leaving Dad without telling him where I was going, flirting with a man I knew was as shallow as a Nebraska puddle—and then nearly sleeping with him? This wasn't me. It couldn't be me—I wouldn't feel so miserable if this were who I really was.

Jesse rubbed my shoulder with his thumb. "It's going to be okay, Sapphira."

I loved that he was calling me that again. There, in his arms, I could believe that. I was okay with him. Was it desperate to beg him to make it okay—for always? My heart twisted. He wasn't in this for that. I really needed to plant that truth and let it grow, because even if he wouldn't ever want me, love me, I needed him as my friend. For some reason he understood me and wanted the best for me.

What if I told him I thought he was what was best for me?

Warmth washed over my face, and then I connected the dots. He was this magnetic, medicinal sort of man. He had a way about him that made a girl feel special and okay with life, and I wasn't the only one to experience that. Laine had too, which was why she was hoping for forever. Jesse hadn't played her. She'd hoped for his heart in ways he hadn't intended. I needed to learn from her—because if I let myself hope that way again, well, tonight would be a calm prologue to what would play out in my life.

I moved away from his shoulder and rubbed my fingers over my eyes. "I'm sorry, Jesse." Sorry for things I didn't want to put into words.

For the tiniest moment he cupped my face in one hand, and then moved away as if he knew that would tie up my heart. He dropped his touch to my elbow and squeezed. "Sapphira, you were created beautiful." He paused, his green eyes plunging me into his stare. "God loves you."

Not what a girl wanted to hear after a heart-dropping look like that. *Can't you?* I wasn't able to squelch the poisonous thought before it formed. This was what he could offer, and only this.

Breaking our connection, I looked at my shoes.

Jesse released my elbow. Felt like when the sun set on a chilly day, leaving my skin begging for its warmth.

"Walk you to your room?"

"You don't have to." I peeked at him with a meek smile. "I know the way."

His eyes glazed, which triggered questions in my unsettled heart. Why did he care so much, yet not enough? How could he seem to feel so deep and not drown in it?

He retrieved his ice, which suddenly struck me as strange. An ice run after midnight?

"Why aren't you sleeping?"

With a hand on my back—again with the touching. Didn't he understand how that would make me long for more?—he nudged me back into the hall. "Couldn't sleep. I was worried about you."

We stepped off several paces in the dim-lit corridor. Shouldn't surprise me—he didn't want me to go in the first place—but confusion sneaked back into the spot I'd been trying to resolve.

"Why?" I stopped, and he did too, and we faced each other. "Why would you lose sleep over someone like me?"

That look. Again. Made my insides puddle and my confused brain swim.

"You're worth so much more than a one-night stand," he said.

My eyes leaked again, and he pulled me against his chest.

Please, can't you love me? I let him hold me—no, I buried myself against him. I'd probably regret this taste of what I'd longed for but couldn't have, but at the same time, at least I'd know the flavor.

He stroked the back of my head. "Sarah, that carpenter's kid I was telling you about earlier today?" Pausing, he nudged me away and then tipped my chin to look at him. "He thought you were worth dying for."

Jesus? We were talking about Jesus in a moment enveloped with intense emotion? Maybe the intensity level on his part didn't match mine. Certainly not. I pulled in a shaky breath as I studied his expression. Seemed every bit as severe as the storm in my heart. Why would he bring up God in such a moment?

"You confuse me."

His look softened but didn't shy away. "I know." He reached for my hand and then squeezed. "But I'm praying that you'll understand. Soon."

Suddenly I wanted to understand. Desperately. "I think you'd better pray harder."

Chapter Twenty

JESSE

You know the rain that continues after the fiercest part of a storm passed? It was like a soft soaking that let you know life would continue, no matter how much damage the winds had done earlier.

My life had changed that night. Forever. I loved Sarah, and realizing it had resculpted the landscape of my heart. But I wasn't sure what to do with it. She was a fragile rock. Tough, solid, and yet prone to shattering. If I loved her selfishly, I'd likely break her. Or maybe worse, I'd smother the drive she had right now to find what would truly make her whole.

I tossed aside the covers that had twisted around me in the few hours of sleep I'd found. My feet on the ground, I leaned onto my knees. This thing with Sapphira was a tricky business.

"God, help."

Sometimes the most powerful prayers were short. Because you had nothing in you to dress up the need. I needed help. Sarah needed help. It was really that simple.

Inhaling a long breath, I pushed off the bed and found my work clothes. The sky outside my window had become layers of promising colors—orange, which bled into a light blue, which built in intensity to a darker hue as the dome of sky reached upward.

Breaking day. A new day. I found myself praying that it wouldn't be as emotionally charged as the one before. I couldn't do roller coasters like that all the time.

Snagging my ice bucket, which still had a few cubes swimming in the cold water, I drained the liquid and filled it with four yogurts. The hall was dim and empty when I stepped toward Sapphira's door. She'd been up at this hour yesterday, but I hesitated with my knuckles poised to knock. It'd been a long night. Maybe she'd finally drifted off to sleep, and if that was so, and she was still out, I didn't want to wake her.

Without permission, I wondered what it would be like to hold her while she dreamed. The muscles in my shoulders jumped, and warmth spread through my chest.

Couldn't go there—not right then.

Your love, God. Please, help me show her Yours.

I looked down as I prayed. Light touched the outdated carpet that ran under her door. She was up.

Pushing away the image I hadn't invited and now didn't want to let go, I rapped on her door. After a moment of rustling, the light poking through the peephole darkened, and then she opened the door.

"Hey." Her soft voice drifted over me like a warm spring breeze.

Every molecule in me begged to reach for her, to pull her close and hold her. *Self-control.* I curled my fingers tight and leaned against the doorframe.

"Morning." I swallowed, tipping the bucket toward her. "Breakfast?"

"Sure." She wouldn't make eye contact. "I need to brush my teeth. Want to wait, or should I meet you down there?"

I crossed my feet in front of me. "I'll wait."

She left the door open, and I stayed propped up against the frame, examining her profile while she applied toothpaste to the brush. Her face seemed to sag—tired, but more than physically. Soul worn.

That overwhelming urge to wrap her close rushed over me again. I shut my eyes and pressed my back harder against the wall. Her image remained behind my closed eyelids—tanned complexion, cute straight nose, high cheekbones, soft dark hair.

Not helping the self-control front.

"Tired?" She shut the water off.

I opened my eyes again. She tapped her toothbrush against the sink and placed it back in her plastic bag. She'd been looking at me, but her eyes darted away as soon as my vision landed on her.

"Just a bit." I pushed away from my leaning post.

With sagging shoulders, she came back to the spot where I waited. "I'm sorry you stayed up because of me."

Her sad whisper, drawn expression...an irresistible need to touch her saturated me. With one knuckle, I traced the outline of her face and tipped her chin up. She hesitated, refusing for a moment to meet my gaze.

Can I please take her in my arms? Please, can I fix this breaking heart?

Wholeness. That was what she needed more than my feeble comfort. Wholeness wasn't mine to give.

Those deep and glassy sapphires finally settled on me. A breathless moment passed, and I hoped that she would sense my heart even if I couldn't share it with her right then. Wouldn't it help to know that she was wanted? Loved?

My chest squeezed at the thought of the *L* word. What would happen if I blurted it out?

Love her enough to let her love Me first.

The air caught in my lungs. The demands of unselfish love...harder than I'd imagined.

She blinked and started to pull away from my touch.

"Sapphira..." I caught her before she could retreat entirely. "We're friends, right?"

The sheen in her eyes spilled onto the corners near her nose. She bit her lip, and I felt her disappointment like a sharp slash across my heart.

I'm not rejecting you.

My gaze moved from her eyes to her lips. *If I kiss her...* Blood pulsed hot through my veins, and that warm, tingling desire washed over me.

Why was self-control so hard? I looked to my feet, moving my hand away from her soft skin.

She touched my arm. "Yes." Her weak smile did very little to disguise the ache. "We're friends."

SARAH

Jesse vulnerable. I hadn't seen that coming. When I didn't answer him right away, he retreated, as if I'd rejected him.

If he only knew how humiliated I was for the way I'd behaved. Maybe then he would have understood why I'd hesitated.

He tipped the ice bucket he carried toward me. "Ready?"

I nodded. Guessed we were moving on.

We walked toward the lobby, the halls of the hotel quiet and mostly dark. I prayed—I think—that Troy wouldn't show up this morning like he had yesterday. If I never saw him again, that would be okay. I glanced to Jesse as we passed the stairway. He was looking at the stairs. Did he see me sitting there where I'd been the night before, or was he looking for Troy?

Somehow I knew right then. Jesse would shield me, and this time I'd let him. He knew things I didn't understand, and while I would have liked it better if I wasn't clueless, I'd hide under his wisdom when I didn't get it.

Jesse's hand brushed my arm, and reassurance settled my rolling stomach. It occurred to me that I'd never known someone like him. Mysterious and yet safe. Guarded and yet open. I realized again how badly I'd made him out to be yesterday. I still didn't understand our kiss and then his regret, other than he didn't mean to give me the impression that he wanted me when he didn't, but my trust in him as a good person had rebounded and solidified. Jesse Chapman was the best person I knew.

What would Aunt Darcy think of him?

We sat at the same table he'd taken yesterday. He placed his bucket in the middle and settled a look on me. "Would you mind if I pray for you this morning?"

We'd been praying over meals since I'd met him, but this was a first. "For me?"

"Yeah."

I shrugged, wanting to ask why but figuring I'd find out if I just let him roll with it. Which he did.

"Jesus, You're good. Thank You that You love us. Please, let Sarah see You. Let her know You know her and love her. Amen."

Huh. That was it? Jesus knew and loved me. I didn't even know me, so that seemed strange.

Wait. Could Jesse actually see this Jesus guy?

"Isn't He dead?"

Jesse paused, his hand in the ice bucket. "Who?"

"Jesus."

A grin tugged on one corner of his mouth. "Nope. Alive and reigning over creation."

I felt my forehead scrunch, and then cynic me took over. "I thought you said He loved me enough to die for me. Or was that just one of those exaggerated claims people make about emotions?"

He sat back, a yogurt container in hand, unrumpled. "He did. On a cross, for you and me and every sinner, which would be all of us. But lots of men died on a cross throughout history. Doesn't make them all saviors. Jesus proved He is God, and the Savior, by rising from the grave."

I pictured zombies wandering the dirt roads of ancient Rome. Very weird. "You really believe that?"

"Yep." His stare stayed on me for several breaths. Sincere, no gimmicks, his silence felt convincing. What if this rock-solid peace and balance he lived with had something to do with this conviction I felt taking me captive?

What if my aunt Darcy had been right?

What if God had allowed this gaping wound in my heart so that I would start paying attention—looking for Him?

My pulse skipped. Did wounds bring healing? Did God work in contradictions?

Seemed like a wild stretch. But...if giving this carpenter-Jesus-God a chance meant finding out who I really was and being okay with it, then maybe it was worth a chance.

JESSE

She didn't turn cold and shut down. Hope began to rise in my heart, but I had to put a tether on it. That hope was more me-focused than her-focused. This couldn't be about my emotions, what I wanted for me. This was my point of failure over the last few days.

I breathed deep and plunged into my breakfast, shifting into work mentality. We had the roof stripped and needed to replace a few of the truss beams before we could resheet it and get the shingles on. It'd take a couple of hours to get that first part done. From my back pocket, I retrieved my phone to check the forecast. *New message* flashed. It was pretty early in Tennessee. Maybe one of Shane's girls had gotten ahold of his phone. I'd check it later.

AccuWeather said rain was in our future. Like tomorrow night. That put a pinch on things, and I could really use Sarah's hammer. Except, I didn't want her up on the roof if Troy's community service wasn't done.

Dilemma.

I set my phone down and leaned my arms against the table. "Do you know what Mack has you doing today?"

"No." She scraped the bottom of the yogurt container. "Did you need me?"

"Just trying to formulate a plan."

Her head bobbed slowly, and she didn't look up. I watched while she twisted her mouth, and her skin shaded a warm pink. Finally she drew a long breath and spoke. "Do you know how long Troy will be around?"

And there was my answer.

"No." I almost spit the word out. Anger solidified in my chest so suddenly that it took me back. Man, I had to get this situation with my emotions under control.

She nodded again, and her jaw moved.

I reached across the table and brushed her arm. "I'll take care of it, okay?"

She didn't answer. Just looked out the window—or maybe in the window. I wondered if she could see the beautiful woman I saw.

I doubted it.

We finished breakfast in silence. I gathered my gear and met her at her door, and we left for the rehab house. She worked on her laptop, which I'd brought because I hadn't returned it yet, as we made the short drive, and then stayed in my truck to "fix a few flaws" after I parked.

Seeing Mack's truck parked a bit down the street, I figured he was already orchestrating a strategy for the day. I found him inside, near the demoed kitchen, writing a list on a bare stud.

"Morning."

He looked from the frame to me and back again. "Is it?"

Man, he was really set on this deal. "Sure. Same as always." Only not really.

"Bring that carpenter girl back?"

"Yeah."

He stopped writing and nailed a look on me that said *Did you finally fix whatever you did?*

No, I hadn't. It wasn't fixable. We'd moved on, that was all I could do. That'd be an interesting conversation with a monosyllabic kind of guy.

Evasion was a solid tactic. "What's your plan for the day?"

"You'll be on the roof."

Yeah, no kidding.

Mack started scribbling again. Some things had to be taken on directly.

"I want Troy up there with me."

His fingers stopped, and his eyebrow cocked. "You're friends now?"

A loaded question, and he knew the answer. I didn't respond. Mack lowered his hand again and turned back to face me. "And the carpenter girl?"

"Figured you'd have her working in here."

His eyebrows hiked even higher.

"I don't want him near her," I blurted. That hard anger inflated in my chest again.

Mack studied me. "What's gotten into you?"

I was a hot ball of emotions, that was for sure. Talking about them with Mack seemed like a humorous left turn. I didn't feel like laughing, so I walked.

"Jesse." Mack didn't leave his place, and he still faced me when I looked back. "I'll keep an eye on her."

Chapter Twenty-One

SARAH

Mack was pleased with the drawings. He'd come to the truck while Jesse was unloading his equipment, but he was looking for me, not Jesse. Something warm and exciting bloomed in my middle as I went over my ideas with him. I hadn't done this before—a total home reno. But as I walked him through the drawings, I could see the finished product, the open spaces where walls had been, a brand-new home where a total disaster had once stood. Except that total disaster hadn't been replaced. It had been made new.

He grunted after I finished the virtual tour. The air felt thick—like those moments at school when you had to give an oral presentation, and at the end everyone in the class sat in frozen silence waiting for the teacher's reaction.

"You did this?"

"Yeah." Who else would have done it?

"Done it before?"

"No." I swallowed. "I mean, I do CAD drawings all the time, but for new construction. I've never done a reno before."

He studied the screen again. "Will it meet code?"

"Should." I nodded. "Just gotta make sure we get the load-bearing walls supported correctly. Might have to reroute some plumbing. We'll have to see what's inside that kitchen wall for sure. But the structure in the drawing is sound."

Another grunt. "I'll need printed copies by tomorrow."

"Yes, sir."

He fist-bumped the side of Jesse's truck and then started away. Two steps, and then he paused. "This is good, carpenter-girl. Thanks."

He hadn't turned toward me, so he couldn't see my grin, which was fine. That way I didn't have to feel embarrassed. I looked through my drawings again and then back to the disaster house. My mind's eye stripped away the ugly and saw it for what it would be. Taking in a long breath, I felt light and...happy.

This. I could do this job every day and love it. What would Dad think? We had a similar project lined up in Hastings. If I asked, would he let me take it?

As I shut my laptop and stepped out of the truck, a conversation between Jesse and me flashed through my memory. The one where he'd been talking about houses like the one we were working on—old homes that needed someone to look past the mess to see their value and potential. I'd been so offended to think that he saw me like that. But now...

Now I hoped he saw potential in me. Surely he did—he said nearly as much last night. That I was worth more than a one-night stand.

What if this total disaster of a heart that had defined me for twenty-one years could be made new? What if I could be defined by something beyond my history, my work, and my appearance?

Wasn't that what I really wanted?

JESSE

Troy sauntered onto the job site round about 11:00 a.m. Add lazy and incompetent to the long list of reasons I really didn't like the guy.

Did I have to forgive him? Standing on an anchored piece of new sheeting, I sighed. People were messed up—I was messed up.

Watching him as he cut a path toward the front door, my muscles coiled.

Nowhere near her, jerk.

Mack intercepted him on the front walk three feet before he reached the entry. I knew I could count on him. Their exchange was brief, involving Mack pointing up, Troy crossing his arms and shaking his head, Mack throwing a *whatever, but I'm not signing off on your time if you don't cooperate* shrug. Troy tossed his hands down and stomped toward the east side where the ladder was.

His buddy, who'd actually shown up when he was supposed to, punched Troy on the shoulder as soon as he'd steadied himself on the roof.

"Hot date musta gone well, eh, killer?"

Troy looked from him to me and then sneered. "You know it."

What a dog. I stepped to a roll of roofing felt, kicked it, and then looked back to them. "This needs to cover the sheeting." I grabbed a staple gun and moved toward Troy. After shoving the tool into his chest, I nailed a hard stare onto his face. "Make sure it's flat, the seams match, and you're paying attention. The ground hurts when you hit it after a twenty-foot drop."

"Yes, Dad," Troy said.

Such a grown up. Bet the girls loved his toddler act.

Skip it. I had work to do, and so did he. I turned my back and snagged another piece of sheeting to drag into place near the peak. This part wasn't complicated, just awkward, but I didn't want any help. I had to scurry over the rafters to shimmy the square into place, making sure the seams met snug, but by the time I had my first anchor nail sunk into place, the two junior high kids in man skin barely had the plastic off the roofing felt.

"Do you boys need help?" Sarcasm edged my voice.

"Yeah." Troy looked up from his kneeling position and cocked an eyebrow. "Send that blue-eyed carpenter girl over."

Heat crawled over my skin as I glared at him.

"Come on, Preacher." Troy crossed his arms over his chest. "I know it's killing you. She's got a tight little body under those baggy work clothes, and you know it's the shy ones who are the hungriest."

I couldn't remember the sequence that followed. All I knew was within five breaths, I had Troy pinned against the roofing velvet, one knee buried in his chest and the other pinning an arm down. The staple gun he'd been using lay beside him. I grabbed it, and without pausing to think, I stapled the shoulder seam of his T-shirt to the sheeting.

"That's enough, you disgusting excuse for a man." I leaned in closer, pressing the metal of the gun against his face. "I mean it, punk. One more word about it, and this gun will find something far more valuable to you than your preppy shirt. Got it?"

His eyes blazed, and he struggled against my weight. It suddenly dawned on me how out of character this whole scene was. For a guy who hated confrontation, I sure dove in head first.

Still glaring at him, I stood and moved away. Emotion made my body tremble, and I needed to breathe by myself for a few minutes. With a couple of solid swings that sank the nails in deep, I finished placing the piece of sheeting and then scrambled down the ladder. Most of the activity on the ground was happening inside the house, so I was able to slip away unnoticed.

The neighborhood moved with a life of its own. Kids running, playing ball, or digging in sandboxes. Dogs barking every now and then. A woman here and there hanging towels on a clothesline, or weeding gardens. Occasionally a mower cutting paths through thick grass. Typical small-town life. The part of life I'd been avoiding for the past few years. I remembered digging flowerbeds with my mom, working by her side while she taught me that smelling the dirt, weeding a flowerbed, or pruning roses could all be acts of worship.

I feel Jesus here with me most, like He's right beside me, listening to me as we work together, she would say. *I tell Him how amazing His creation is, and thank Him for putting beauty into everything.*

That single memory opened the door for a whole lifetime of moments with my parents. Dad worked with precision, because he said God wanted his best every day. He loved to quote Martin Luther: *The Christian shoemaker does his duty not by putting little crosses on the shoes, but by making good shoes,* and then he'd twist it to fit our life. *Our duty then, son, is to build well, for the glory of God. He'll take our work and make it useful. We simply must be faithful to work.*

Though I knew he never intended it, I felt failure in his shadow. Today, for example. Or this whole week, actually. I'd kissed Sarah when I knew I shouldn't—had made her feel worse than she had when she'd left home. I hadn't offered an ounce of grace to Troy, and maybe if I had, he'd have left Sarah alone. And that scene on the roof? Deplorable.

God, I'm sorry. I keep failing.

Again, the steamroller of emotion passed over me. I couldn't do this. I couldn't love Sarah the way God called me to love her. Not when my selfish desires kept getting in the way. Honest confession: *I* wanted to be her everything. But what if she took that and settled? That would be tragic. Like soda on a hot day, it would quench the immediate thirst but wouldn't meet the real need. I'd be sugar when she needed life-giving water. Long-term, I really did want her to find that spring of life.

I wanted both. More than I knew how to put into words. God and me. Couldn't we both claim her heart?

I reached a park and found an isolated bench under a locust tree. The sweat that had gathered at my hairline chilled as I stepped under the shade, and I sagged onto the seat, propping my elbows on my knees. Three months ago my life made sense. Granted, I didn't have a clear vision for the future, but my everyday living made sense. Now I had a picture of what I wanted for my future, which included a blue-eyed carpenter's daughter close by my side, but my every day didn't make any sense. Because that future didn't seem possible, and life seemed to go sepia toned in that light.

What now, God?

He'd asked me to trust Him, and I thought I did. Now I stood on what felt like a precipice, and I wanted to turn and walk back to the safety I'd known before.

My phone vibrated against my jeans in my back pocket. Probably Mack wondering what the heck happened with Troy and why I wasn't working. That should be a fun chat.

I sighed as I shaded the screen. It wasn't a phone call, but a text alert. Actually multiple texts—eight to be exact. Then I remembered. Shane had sent me a message this morning, and I hadn't even checked it, let alone responded. Yikes.

They were all from him. Couldn't be good.

6:20 a.m. *Jess, big storm came through. Call me.*

6:50 a.m. *You need to call me.*

7:15 a.m. Pic text. My parents' house. Shutters askew, major roof damage. Tree limbs everywhere. My mother's gardens... A lump swelled in my throat.

7:20 a.m. *Turn your phone on and call me.*

8:30 a.m. *Are you sick?*

9:30 a.m. *Dead?*

10:30 a.m. *Seriously, Jess. It's important.*

11:55 a.m. *At least text so that I know you're still alive.*

My shoulders folded, and I tugged my hat off and pushed my fingers through my soppy hair. I needed to go home. Not exactly the answer I'd been hoping for.

SARAH

My wet hair dripped onto my neck as I stared at my phone.

Showered after the full day of work, I sat on my bed and debated. I should call my dad. The thought kept surfacing in my mind. Especially after talking to Mack this morning about my drawings. The idea of doing this kind of work full time had taken firm root as we continued demo today. Tomorrow we'd start rebuilding, and I'd see my vision come to life. Butterflies did swirlies in my stomach. I couldn't wait to have the vision in my head become reality. Disaster redos. Maybe this was me, my sweet spot in life.

I was desperate to share my newfound burst of joy with my dad. But we weren't on good terms at the moment, and if he had any idea what I'd done the night before, how I'd behaved, he'd be livid. Maybe disown me. Because I'd behaved like my mother, I was sure.

Where was my mother? Would he tell me if I asked? Would he hate me if I contacted her?

Three days had passed since I'd left, and I had kind of expected that he'd call me, even though our last phone conversation hadn't ended well. The fact that he didn't... Fear squeezed hard in my chest and made my heart rate jump. What would I do without my dad? He was the only sure thing I had in my life.

Except Aunt Darcy. And maybe Jesse.

Was Jesse a sure thing? I snorted in my empty room. Not even close. He kept me confused at almost every turn. Heated stares, a passionate kiss, and then rejection. Followed by more looks that made me melt and words of value whispered against my hair while held securely in his embrace. What was I supposed to do with all of that?

I wanted him to be my friend. He made it clear that was all it was ever going to be between us. Except for when he felt it was okay to bend that friendship line. Was this normal?

Pushing against the mattress, I got up from the bed and stalked across my room, replaying every touch that had danced across my skin, every wisp of breath that had warmed my face and neck. And that kiss...

One sweet, emotion-filled kiss with Jesse superseded all of the sultry lip action I'd experienced with Aiden or Troy. Theirs meant nothing except that I was an object of their lust, which I had settled for in those empty moments.

But Jesse's kiss... My insides melted, and my heart kicked hard at the memory.

Why was I torturing myself?

Pacing from the bed to the door and back again, I fisted my hair and moaned. *Stop.*

A hollow knock interrupted my monologue. Jesse? Of course that would be my first hope. I was in too deep, and I didn't know how to swim. Maybe it was time to go home. Patch up with Dad and forget the whole summer. Besides, I hadn't seen Jesse most of the day except for when he drove me back to the hotel, and he'd been silent. Completely silent until we parked, and even then all he said was, *I'll see you, Sapphira.*

Cryptic for Jesse. Which meant, *I really shouldn't have held you the way I held you last night, and once again I want you to know that I'm really not interested in you.* A good reason for me not to have been replaying that kiss. I wasn't going to get over it by reliving it. And I wasn't going to slip into that mess again.

Whoever stood in the hall knocked again.

Grow up, Sarah. I gripped the handle and tugged. And then forgot everything I'd just reminded myself of when I found his green eyes waiting for me on the other side of that door.

Down I went. Again.

Chapter Twenty-Two

JESSE

Wet hair on an attractive woman...someone ought to explain to the female population what that does to a guy.

Not her fault. I'd come without warning, so how was she supposed to know?

"Hey..." She leaned against the door, which she'd only opened partway.

"Hi." Staring again. I was always staring at her. I could have the most convincing pep talk before I saw her—which I did before I left my room—and feel confident that I wouldn't act like an idiot when we were face to face, and then I actually connected with those blue eyes. I was lost.

Her mouth twitched, and then she looked down as if she needed to escape. "I didn't see you much today." She cleared her throat. "You okay?"

No. Nowhere in the neighborhood of okay. "Do you want to do something tonight?"

Her head whipped up. Reminded me of when I first asked her to have a burger with me. What had it been, four, five weeks since then? Hadn't known how complicated this would get.

She searched me, and I couldn't understand the questions passing through her mind. I probably should leave her alone, but I couldn't. I was heading south in the morning. Then what? I didn't know how to define this relationship. We had one more evening, and I wasn't going to spend it staring at the ceiling of a crappy hotel.

"Come on." With a hand on the doorframe, I leaned toward her. "Please?"

"Where are we going?"

"I don't know." I stood straight. "We'll find something fun. Let's get out of here. Okay?"

She studied me a little longer, and this time I understood the question. *Are we friends, or is this going somewhere else?*

Friends. Who couldn't find their way back from somewhere else. How did I love her up close from a distance? Was that even possible?

I nudged the door, and it gave. With a jerk of my head, I beckoned, and she gave.

"'Kay, but I can't do another late night."

No late nights. No hugging. No kissing. Got it—anything else?

With her hand on the door, she began shutting it. In my face. "I have to change. I'll meet you at your truck."

"Why?" My eyes took a once-over. Gym shorts, T-shirt, bare feet. "Put on some shoes, and we're good to go."

She scowled. What was wrong with that?

"Give me one minute."

Door shut. I was left standing, still staring.

Did she really think she had to dress up? I remembered the first day I'd run into her—literally. Not high maintenance. That was what drew me.

The door popped open again, with me still standing there scratching my head. There she stood, jeans that hinted at her body shape and a plain white T-shirt cut a little closer to her small frame than the baggy work shirt she'd been wearing.

Still not fussy. But I had to admit, wow. A grin poked at my mouth.

"What?"

Staring. Man, I needed to quit that. "Nothing. That was quick."

"Huh." Her mouth twisted in an ornery sort of way. "Didn't know you'd be hovering. Glad I didn't decide to do something better with my hair."

I glanced to those black tresses. Still damp, she'd pinned the front out of her face. Simple. Beautiful.

"Me too." That didn't require an explanation, did it? "Let's go. We'll find a drive-through and then head to Kearney. I've heard they've got laser tag."

Her mouth lifted into an all-out grin. "Laser tag? You don't know what you're getting into."

"Aha." I chuckled. "See, I told you we'd have fun."

We did. I loved that I could eat any kind of garbage my taste buds requested, and not only did Sarah not mind, but she dove in too. By the time we pulled up to The Big Apple—the local fun center—we'd both wolfed down two not-gourmet tacos and had emptied a pound of tots. She didn't groan about how she'd have to run so many miles to work off those calories or insert that she'd make an exception in her strict diet for me. Hallelujah! A girl who lived.

"So, based on your comment earlier, I assume you've played before." I lifted the harness over my head and clipped the buckles at my waist.

Sarah smirked. "Guess you'll find out."

"What if we're on the same team?"

"Oh, I'm sure you're hoping so."

Fascinating. Which way should I hope? Same team meant we'd get to work together, concocting strategies together. Opposition...could also be interesting.

The lights on our shoulder straps blipped. Sarah's were red. I was green.

Interesting could be fun.

Thirty minutes later I followed her back into the equipment area with sweat rolling down my back. Rivulets ran down the sides of her cheeks, and the ends of her short hair were wet.

"Sapphira, you smoked everyone in there."

She had. I barely racked up half the points she'd accumulated. And her team won all three rounds. Losing to her...still fun. And I loved seeing her come to life. Full of confidence, from the bright glow in her face to the bounce in her step.

She lifted her harness over her head and smiled up at me. Somehow, I forgot how to breathe. *Not a date.* Right. My lungs decided to work again.

I settled my equipment on the proper post and waited for her at the door. She passed through while I held it open. The cool air and bright lights took my senses by storm, and I paused near a table.

"Now what?" Sarah stopped a few steps away, her smile still lifting her lips.

"Bowling?"

"I stink at that."

"Good." I brushed her elbow, moving forward. "I don't."

She did stink at it. Which was also totally fun. Best not-a-date ever.

By the eighth frame she'd managed to rack up a grand score of sixty-five. She rolled yet another gutter ball, and I grinned as she slunk off the wood floor and dropped onto the chair beside mine.

"I told you. Stink." She tipped her head back and growled.

"Not competitive or anything, are you?"

"Shut up." Her tongue poked out of her mouth.

I laughed. "You know, for a girl who can whack a nail straight through a stud in three swings, you sure have a noodle wrist." I grabbed her forearm and wiggled it. "Keep it straight, and the ball will go straight."

Time—life—froze when you least expected it to. Sarah reached to push me away, but then everything seemed to stop the moment her palm touched my chest. Our eyes met. And held. Tunnel vision faded everything from my periphery. In that silly-turned-serious moment, I only saw her. I was lost in those beautiful eyes that pleaded for significance. Identity. Love.

227

I love you.

The words almost fell out of my mouth.

With a jolt, my heart began to throb, and reality blasted my brain. I couldn't tell her that right now. What if she was satisfied with it—settled for the love my imperfect heart could offer? She'd miss agape—God's love.

Slowly I uncurled my fingers from her arm and pulled away from her touch. She looked at the floor by her feet.

No. If I could only make her understand...but I couldn't. There weren't words to make this make sense.

I pushed up from my chair, and we finished the game. Best not-a-date ever took a nosedive.

See, God? I told you I can't do this.

SARAH

He was killing me. How could he look at me like that and then push me away in the next breath? Didn't he understand what it did to me?

No more looking into his eyes. No more being silly with him. And definitely no more touching.

Jesse clobbered me in bowling. I didn't even look at his final score—which was well into triple digits by the sixth or seventh frame. By the time we were done, the fun of the night had been snuffed out, and I felt stupid yet again.

Which was worse? Giving your body to a man you knew didn't care one ounce about you, or wanting a man who seemed to care about you in every way except that?

If only I were prettier, more feminine. Would he feel different then?

We climbed into his truck, and the thirty-minute drive back to Lexington was quiet until he took the exit.

"Are you okay, Sapphira?"

Now we could talk. Because it was safe. We were almost back to the hotel, and he could retreat to his room without getting mixed up about me again. Frustration gripped my chest.

"Fine."

He turned onto the main road leading to town and then into the parking lot of our hotel. "I don't think you're fine." The truck stopped, he shifted into park, and then shut off the engine. Turning toward me, he hooked his elbow on the seat in between us. "It's been a bumpy week. What about things with your dad?"

I swallowed. Why did he dig around in the tender spots of my heart? "I'm fine."

He shook his head, and then it happened again. Jesse's look took on that warm, intimate quality that made my insides melt.

I looked away. "We'll be fine."

"Have you talked to him?"

"No." I stared out the passenger window at the nearly empty parking lot. Moths flitted around the lamppost standing near the corner of the building. "I don't think you need to worry about it."

The upholstery on his seat rustled as he shifted. "I am worried. First time we talked, sounded like you and your dad were pretty close, and I know this fight is a big deal. What happened between then and now?"

I pulled in a long breath. "I'm going through some stuff he doesn't get. It makes him mad."

"Because he's afraid he'll lose you." Jesse's matter-of-fact tone drew my attention. "I would be."

Our eyes collided again, and like the force of gravity on a massive boulder, I couldn't pull away. My heart fluttered, and shallow breaths were all I could manage.

I was dying again, and it wasn't fair. "Jesse, you can't keep doing this to me," I whispered. Breaking our gaze, I looked at my fists, clenched in my lap. "You're killing me. Don't look at me like that when you don't care."

His hand came to my head, and he stroked my hair. "Sarah," he whispered, tucking a lock behind my ear.

My lips trembled, and I shook my head.

"I'm sorry." His fingers brushed my chin for the smallest moment, then moved away. "I do care. So much."

My eyes felt wet, but I glanced at him anyway. "Then why…"

I'd never seen that look on a man's face before. Some kind of mixture of pain and desire and…love? No. I wouldn't know what that looked like, so I must have been mistaken.

"I can't explain it right now, Sarah." His hand covered mine. "I don't know how to make it make sense to you. I care. Deeply. But we can't go there right now."

A tear slipped over my eyelid. "Are you married?"

"No." He blew out a small laugh. "No, Sapphira. There's no one else. I promise."

I pulled my hand away from his, missing the warmth of his touch the second it left. What did you say in a moment like that? I had nothing. I looked at my knees, then squeezed my eyes shut. Hot tears slid down my cheeks. The silence seemed to pull us in opposite directions, and my ever-present loneliness grew larger, deeper.

Why did I have to fall for a man who refused to fall for me?

"Sarah." Jesse's hand rested on my back. "Please…please trust me. I desperately want the best for you."

"That doesn't make any sense." I lifted my chin and turned to look at him. "You don't want me to be with anyone else, but *you* don't want me either. What is best for me in your opinion, Jesse Chapman? To be alone? To be the butch carpenter girl no man would ever want?"

I was crying. Full-on sobs of resentment and confusion and pain. Why all the crying this year?

He winced as if I'd punched him in the stomach. "You are *not* butch. I told you—you're beautiful."

I remembered that—couldn't forget it. Or the kiss that came after that conversation. I couldn't take anymore. I clawed at the handle to the door, and as soon as my feet hit the ground, I slammed it shut. Three steps were all I managed before his hands gripped my shoulders.

"Stop."

Folding in on myself, I couldn't help but comply. His arms circled me from behind, and he pulled me against his chest. I continued to cry, leaning my head against his arm. He stayed quiet as he held me, and as confusing as it was, his solid embrace also softened the ache in my heart. I couldn't understand why he held his heart away, but his compassion—this different kind of love—somehow lent me peace.

When my tears stopped falling and I didn't feel so smashed, I pulled away.

He let me go and rubbed my back. "Jesus loves you, Sarah."

I glanced back at him.

The dim light of the lamppost above us bounced off of the sheen in his eyes. He swallowed as his hand gripped mine. "He loves you more than anyone on this planet ever could."

How did all our conversations work back to that? I looked up, and the moths around the lamp caught my attention again. They swirled around the light. Suddenly I saw myself flitting around every meager source of light and warmth—hoping for something better than a 60-watt glow.

When would the sun break over my horizon?

Jesse couldn't be my sun. That was what he was trying to tell me.

For the first time ever, I really wondered about this Jesus. Was He just another light bulb flickering in the night—or could He burn through the darkness?

JESSE

Sarah studied the lamp above us. I wasn't sure what she saw or what she was thinking, but she seemed intent on it.

I squeezed her hand. "He does love you, Sarah. Don't ever forget that, okay?"

Jesus loves you. That was all I had to give her. Maybe not much—except it was the most simple, profound truth she could know. If only she'd believe it.

She sniffed and squeezed my hand back. That was something—she didn't argue, or come back at me with some sarcastic comment about religion or white-collar people or church. *God, please...* My prayers for her built up with urgency. *...set her free.*

Her attention came back to me for a moment, and then without a word she moved toward the hotel. I forced my fingers to unwrap her hand, and walked beside her. Silence accompanied us as we passed inside and down the hall to her door.

She slid her key card into the door, but I stopped her from opening it, with a hand over hers. I had more to say. Needed to say. "Sarah, I have to go tomorrow."

Her face darted up to mine. "What?"

"I have to go back to Tennessee. There was a storm, and my parents' house was damaged." I sighed, moved my hand away from hers, and rubbed my neck. "I'm not sure how long it will take, so I don't know when I'll be back up this way."

Her eyes drifted away from mine, and her body sagged. Officially, this had gone from best to worst not-a-date ever.

I rubbed her arm. "Will you answer if I call you?"

She pressed her lips together and blinked, then nodded.

Tugging on the arm I still touched, I pulled her into a hug. Words wouldn't form in my head, so I simply held her.

What if I never saw her again?

I closed my eyes as ache throbbed deep in my heart. I wished I knew the future—or that I could write it the way I wanted it to work out. Then I would know that she'd be in my life forever; she'd be saved and whole and happy. And mine.

I couldn't know any of those things.

In reality, I only knew one thing for sure.

Jesus loved her.
And me.

Chapter Twenty-Three

SARAH

We finished demo by lunch the next morning. Mack found me before break, which was a first.

"Carpenter-girl, you coming out back to eat?"

In the middle of unbuckling my tool belt, I didn't bother to look at him. Found it a relief that I was occupied, because that was a weird request—he hadn't cared much about what I did, unless it concerned putting Jesse in a bad mood.

Had Jesse put him up to it?

Could be. Troy was still around, pounding nails into the roof above me—without Jesse's supervision.

Strange. The past couple of days I hadn't worked right beside Jesse, but that day I really felt the void of his absence. Couldn't hear his laughter while he joked with a volunteer. Couldn't sense his eyes on me when I wandered to the truck to grab a water bottle. The lack of his presence felt like a chilly breeze against my heart.

What was I supposed to make of our friendship? He cared—deeply—but we couldn't go there right now. What did that mean?

"Sharpe," Mack snapped, "you gonna answer me?"

Oh yeah. That was why I was thinking about Jesse—he must have told Mack to watch over me.

I shook my head. "Thought I'd run into town."

"Not today. The new owners are here, and they want to meet you."

What? No. I didn't do introductions. Recent weeks had proven that to be a disaster.

"Let's go, carpenter-girl." He nodded to the back door. "Your fans await."

My fans?

Twenty or more sweaty people milled around the dirt-patched backyard, the hum of their conversations saturating the air. Anxiety wound a cord around my chest and cinched it down tight. Stupid as it was, I glanced around, looking for Jesse.

"Relax, kid." Mack leaned so he could speak near my ear. "You're fine on your own."

Wait. Mack? The gruff supervisor-contractor guy giving me a pep talk? What had Jesse told him?

"Mr. and Mrs. Brown." Mack reached a hand to a man who was probably in his late twenties. "You were asking about the designer. Here she is. This is Sarah Sharpe."

Designer—ha! I was no designer. I was a carpenter. A drafter and framer. Not a designer.

"Sarah..." The woman next to the man gushed my name. "Mr. MacKenzie showed us your plans for the renovation. They're amazing! I can't believe you can do all that to this rickety house. It's going to be beautiful."

I stared at her. It wasn't an amazing plan. I blew out a few walls, made the kitchen and bathrooms bigger, and added a nicer window to the front of the house—which wasn't even my idea. There was nothing special about what I'd done. Except that I'd enjoyed doing it.

"This is Sarah's first renovation project with us." Mack filled my rude silence. "You can bet it won't be her last, if I have anything to say about it."

Mr. Brown laughed. "I would think so." He set his look squarely on me. "Clearly we're happy with your drawings.

Thank you. We didn't know you could do so much with a condemned house."

I managed a smile. I hoped it looked like a smile, anyway. Mostly, I was dumbfounded. My mind drifted to the project my dad had waiting on the bottom of his to-bid list. What if...

Mack nudged my shoulder with his large hand.

Oh yeah. I was supposed to be having a conversation.

"I'm happy you like it." I reached for Mrs. Brown's hand. "I hope it turns out exactly like you hope."

She hugged me. In my filth, grunge, sweat, and stink, that woman gripped me in an all-out hug.

"We can't wait."

I tried to smother the sudden intake of breath and pushed out another grin.

Mack directed me to the food table with a tip of his head. "Eat up. More work ahead."

Crazy how one tiny, inconsequential conversation could change the color of the sky. Well, not really, but as I left the work site later that evening, after an energized afternoon filled with much accomplished, I honestly thought my world seemed clearer, less gray.

I hoped that Jesse would call that evening so I could tell him about it.

JESSE

The house was a mess—and it was more than storm damage. Guilt soured in my gut as I walked through the home my parents had built. A hint of mold sat on the damp air, and a thick film of dust covered every surface. Evidence of mice scattered over the floor in the kitchen, and green slime had grown around the sink and on the bathroom fixtures.

Negligent. I'd been one of *those* people. For five years I'd spent my time fixing livable places for people across the Midwest, and all the while had allowed my parents' home to slip out of repair. It didn't have to be that way. I just hadn't wanted to deal with it.

"Pretty bad." Shane startled me from the front door. The plan was that he'd meet me here first thing in the morning. I'd made it into town somewhere around 1:00 a.m., maybe after, and had thought to stay at the house. Right up until I pulled next to the curb and found a massive hole punched into the front wall and a foot-diameter tree limb lying on the front porch. While I lived most of my life in hotel rooms these days, not being able to stay in my childhood home stapled a cold reality onto my heart.

It wasn't my home anymore. They weren't there, and my life... Well, I didn't know how to define my life, exactly. But it wasn't in this house. It had moved on.

I hooked my thumbs over my jeans pockets. "Yeah. You didn't send pictures of the front." I frowned. "Thanks for that, by the way."

Shane shrugged and stepped over the refuse scattered across the wood floor. "I told you to get here—figured you'd see it for yourself soon enough."

"Storm damage says roof damage to me, not holes the size of a giant's fist in the side of the house."

He crossed his arms. "Does it matter?"

I rubbed the back of my neck. No, it didn't make a difference, really. But everything had gone heavy the past week, and this felt like one more brick to add to the pile.

Shane finished his trek across the front room, sidestepping furniture that had been knocked out of place, and crunching shattered glass under his boots. Water damage colored the wood floor and crept up the drywall under the peeling paint and warped base trim. The room would need to be gutted. Completely redone. Strange, gutting a house in Nowhere, Nebraska, hadn't bothered me—seemed fun, actually. Thinking about gutting this house, though, even part of it, sank like a hot rock into my stomach.

I growled under my breath. "Where to start?"

Shane's hand clapped on my shoulder. "With coffee. You're a grump, which is not normal, so let's get some grub and a hot mug of joe, and we'll figure it out over breakfast."

Mack's scowl passed through my memory. He'd called me a grump—or something like it—a couple of days ago. Man, I was a hot mess these days. I thought that was left to the realm of women.

Speaking of which, Sarah's blue eyes replaced Mack's image in my head, and my heart squeezed. She was one giant question mark in my life, which felt more like that hole in the front wall of my parents' home than a harmless punctuation mark at the end of a sentence.

As if I needed any more frustration first thing this dreary morning.

Maybe I'd call her. With that thought, some kind of overwhelming demand steeped me—like I *needed* to call her. That instant. Except Shane was standing next to me, waiting for my answer.

"Breakfast would be good," I said.

He nodded. "Mia will have it ready. The girls are anxious to see you."

I pushed out a tight smile. "I'll be right behind you."

Shane turned and started weaving through the damage again. I pulled my phone from my back pocket and scanned for *Sapphira* in my contacts.

Shane paused at the door. "Thought we were leaving?"

"One second."

He hovered at the entry. Dang. No phone call. A text would have to do.

Hey. Miss you. Call me.

I took in a breath of musty air and exhaled. Didn't settle the rumpled stirrings in my heart. Maybe Shane was right—I needed some coffee and food.

SARAH

Hey. Miss you. Call me.

I stared at my phone, which had buzzed in my back pocket while I was unloading my tools.

How did all this work anyway? And what exactly was *this?*

We just can't go there right now.

So, that left us where, exactly? Somewhere in a friendship zone...

For being levelheaded, nice, and everything good, Jesse was sure tying me into knots.

I hit the little green phone icon on the screen. Call sent. Why hadn't *he* called *me?*

He didn't pick up. So, I was supposed to call, he wasn't going to answer, and I was stuck leaving a message I hadn't prepared for. I huffed.

"Hey. Hope you made it okay. I'm about to dive into work, so I guess we'll talk later. Or something."

I stabbed End and glared at my phone.

I was making this too complicated. Air slowly released from my lungs, and my shoulders relaxed. He was a friend. That should be good enough, because I needed a friend. And I had wanted to talk to him—especially after meeting the Browns yesterday, which was part of the reason I was irritated. He said he'd call, and he hadn't. But having worked around men all my life, I knew that was standard. When they said they'd call, they meant eventually. There was a long expiration date on that promise.

My phone chimed. New text.

Jesse: *Sorry. In the middle of a thing. I do want to talk to you though. Call me when you have a break?*

I smiled, and heat tickled my face—not from the morning sun.

Me: *Okay. A couple hours?*

Jesse: *Sooner?*

That warmth turned hot. See, this was why things were confusing.

Me: *We'll see. Gotta get to work.*

Which meant that Jesse couldn't occupy my mind. A good thing. Probably.

"Sharpe."

Mack's bark ripped my attention from the phone. I slid it into my pocket.

"Yes, sir?"

"I picked up those Lam beams last night. I need you to get them installed."

"Yes, sir." Except I couldn't set massive headers on my own. The group of workers we had over the weekend wouldn't be showing up today. I walked to his truck, assuming we'd need to unload the two-by-twelve laminated wood beams. "Will you be around to help?"

"Can't make any promises." He slid the first of six wood planks out of the truck bed. "Grab any of the guys. All you need is muscle, right?"

Yeah. Except the thing of it was, simply grabbing one of the guys on this kind of job didn't always work out well for me. Jesse, in fact, had proven to be about the only man who took me seriously from the first hello. Probably because I'd pirated his nail gun.

It was a man's world, and—even if I'd lived in it every day of my life—it remained a man's world.

Huh. For some reason, resentment didn't pool thick and icky in my stomach with that thought. Determination, yes, but not resentment. I knew what I was doing, had shown myself capable beyond my dad's supervision, and had gained Mack's approval. All good things. Plus, and this still ballooned inside me, I'd found something I was particularly good at. I could do that reno job in Hastings. I knew I could, and I'd be good at it.

Except one little hang-up. I hadn't discussed my plans with Dad. *Pop* went that balloon.

"Hey." Mack snapped his fingers at me. Twice. "Work, girl. Loads of work."

Right. I put two hands to a beam and tugged, sliding it over the metal runners of the truck bed. Mack caught the back part, and we marched it toward the house. After leaning it against the house, we spun in unison to get the next.

"Jesse make it to Tennessee?"

Whoa. Number one, small talk? From Mack? And two— why'd he assume I'd know?

"Guess so. Haven't heard otherwise." I exhaled slowly, quietly—and dang that dumb heat on my skin!

Mack glanced at me and then bowed his head as a grin chiseled onto his scruffy face. "You two..."

Wasn't going to touch that. He didn't have a clue about it— because I didn't, and I was pretty sure Jesse didn't either.

He tugged another beam loose, and this time I followed him with the tail. We continued to unload the lumber without another word. When the beams were all accounted for and placed next to the house, I moved to retrieve my tools, which were still sitting in the grass by my truck.

Mack squeezed my shoulder—also strange—and gave it a little shake. "Tell him hey." He patted the spot he'd squeezed, then walked toward the front door. Chuckling.

I assume he meant Jesse—and for some undefined reason, I smiled. Reaching for my back pocket, I found my phone again.

Me: *Mack says hey, and did you make it okay?*

I waited...he said he was in the middle of a thing, but maybe...

Jesse: *Hey back. Yeah, shipshape. The house isn't though.*

Me: *Uh-oh. That doesn't sound good.*

Jesse: *No. Could use your skills down here.*

Um...was that a hint? An invitation?

Jesse: *You there?*

Me: *Yeah...*

Jesse: *Your face is red, isn't it?*

What?

Me: *Why would you say that?*

Jesse: *You always blush when I say something you don't know what to do with.*

I touched my cheeks—which were hot.

Me: *I don't know what to do with you.*

Maybe too honest.

Jesse: *I know. Sorry.*

If he were standing in front of me, his fingers would brush my arm. Or my face. And I'd look into those green eyes and...

Me: *Maybe someday I'll understand?*

Jesse: *I hope so.*

I drew in a long breath as the warmth drained from my face. My heart, which had felt light and fluttery two seconds before, squeezed hard and dropped.

Jesse: *Sapphira...*

I shut my eyes, hearing his husky voice as if he were standing with me. When I opened them, I found my hand shook.

...you are loved.

Loved...by him? No, Jesus. That was what he'd said the other night. My bottom lip went under my teeth. Jesus loved me...did I care?

My heart twisted.

Do you love me?

My silent question wasn't for Jesse, which sort of shook me off kilter. This Jesus, the carpenter's kid Jesse talked about, He must be real. Jesse wasn't stupid—and his compassion surpassed most. Because of this Jesus?

I remembered what Darcy had said all those weeks ago about pouring yourself out for others. Counterintuitive to the human drive, I thought. Why would she tell me to do that? Because of this Jesus she followed. The same Whom Jesse followed.

The same Who loved me? My thumbs wobbled as I punched in a simple text.

Me: *By Jesus?*

Jesse: *So much.*

Me: *How do you know?*

Jesse: *He died for you. He's calling you. He's what you're aching for, Sapphira.*

Not for Jesse? Also counterintuitive...if a man saw how a woman hungered for him, wouldn't he take advantage of it? Jesse wasn't that kind of guy.

I want what is best for you...

Not normal. My phone chimed again.

Jesse: *Keep listening, Sarah. You'll hear.*

Hear what?

A hammer pounded from inside the house. Work. I was supposed to be working. Still off balance in my heart, I shoved my phone out of sight, wishing Jesse wasn't so odd.

No. That wasn't what I wanted. I wished I could understand him. Maybe that I was more like him.

Chapter Twenty-Four

JESSE

"What's her name?"

My head snapped up. "Who?"

Shane chuckled and Mia smirked.

"You're cute, Jess," she said.

Cute? I wasn't a puppy. I scowled. "I don't know what you're talking about."

Shane shook his head. "You've never been one to text during a conversation. Because it's rude."

Oh. That. I shifted my attention from him to the plate I'd scraped clean.

"Please tell me it's not another sixty-year-old woman inviting you for a meal next time you're in town."

I sent him a *shut up* look. "No."

He grinned like he'd just pried open my secret. "But there *is* a woman on the other end of those texts."

Dang. The sneak.

"It's nothing."

"Yes." Mia snagged my plate. "We can see that it's nothing. You typically drift into another world, ignore the girls, and have that concentrated look for no reason. Totally normal."

With a long breath, I rubbed the back of my neck.

Mia laughed. "Do you have a picture?"

I held my tongue.

"Come on," she said. "We've been trying to set you up for ages. You have to let us get a glimpse at the woman who finally snagged your attention."

This wasn't going to end. I looked first to her and then to Shane. "No. Let it go, please?" I set my phone facedown on the table. "It's not anything right now, because it can't be. Okay?"

They exchanged raised eyebrows.

"That doesn't sound good, bro. You're not..."

I sighed. "She's not married. Not weird. Not a convict. She's actually quite amazing—but not a Christian."

Silence hung over the table until Shane leaned against it with his elbows. "Ouch."

Mia slid onto the chair next to me. She looked first to Shane and then back at me. "You never know, Jess. Maybe you could—"

"Save her?" I shook my head. "Not my place. Not in my power." And things were too complicated.

"Mia." Shane's soft tone rebuked her.

"It works out sometimes," she said. "You never know what God can use."

I cleared my throat. "And if it doesn't?"

She stilled, looking at her hands. "I don't know."

Exactly. She didn't know. But I did. It'd break my heart. I couldn't imagine spending my life with someone—loving her like this—and knowing she'd never see heaven. Worse, wondering if I'd superficially filled her search for Christ by getting in the way. I wasn't going to live like that, and I didn't want Sarah to either.

"What's her name, Jess?"

I pulled my gaze off the table to meet Shane's. "Sarah."

He nodded, and that was all.

Good. Subject dropped.

Shane reached for the notepad he kept on the sideboard behind his chair. "Let's get to work. Repairs..."

Finally. If only my heart could shift so easily.

Mia pushed away from the table, finished the dishes, and left the area. I could hear the girls squealing in the basement, and wondered for a moment what this kind of life would feel like. Home every night, a wife to hold as I drifted to sleep, kids to make every day interesting. Not something I really imagined much. Because it looked too much like the life my parents shared.

Why did that bother me?

"...the front room will take most of the time and money." The foreman in Shane easily stepped forward. "I know you're a roofer, but I think hiring that job out would be best. You can't do both at once, and as this is Tennessee, leaving either job to wait is a bad call."

Right. I tried to stick my mind to the list Shane was writing out.

"You could also hire a cleaning company." He leveled me with a disapproving look. "Rephrase. You *need* to hire a cleaning company. You let it go too long."

Ouch. I clenched my jaw and stared at him.

Shane set his pen on the pad and spread his palms on the table. "Rough morning or not, Jess, we have some things we need to discuss."

My shoulders knotted. Shane wasn't that much older than me, but every now and then he took on this big-brother, dad-ish persona that I probably needed but didn't want at the moment.

"Not now."

"No. Now." He paused, the shift of his brow daring me to argue. "You're not home more than two weeks at a time, usually in the winter, and often in my basement. Which is great. We love having you, and don't want that to change. But it's time to deal with some things."

Some things being the rest of my parents' estate. I cleared my throat.

"It's past due," Shane said, "and you can't keep ignoring it."

I kept myself still, because fidgeting was a sign of discomfort, and I didn't need to show how uncomfortable this was.

"Level with me, Jess." Shane leaned forward again. "Why do you keep avoiding this?"

Good question. I didn't know. All my memories of my parents were good. Happy childhood. Solid home. Successful parents. A great life.

Not the life I saw for myself. At least, I hadn't been able to picture it before. But as I sat there, the sounds of that same sort of life filled Shane's house, and a new picture bloomed in my mind. My house, my wife—whose blue eyes had mesmerized me from the first day I'd bumped into her—and some kids who looked something like both of us.

Not fair. I'd never had that vision with anyone before. I pushed it away. Love hurt too much. Couldn't hold it. Couldn't keep it. At some point, you had to let it go.

Let it go, and see what happens.

Where did that come from?

"Listen, bro." Shane shifted in his chair. "I knew your dad. Loved him. And I know this: He didn't leave you everything they'd worked for so that you would feel obligated. He and your mom chased their dreams. They wanted you to have the freedom to chase yours. If this—the house, his business, all of it—if it's not part of *your* dream, then let it go. It's okay."

Was that it? Warm moisture stung my eyes. Wouldn't that make me ungrateful?

I wasn't the owner-manager type; I wasn't my dad. I liked the work I did, the way I did it. I didn't want to be in charge. Mack did it just fine. Shane did it well. Me? Not so much.

"It's okay, Jess. You don't have to be him. He's proud of you as you."

I swallowed, drew a long breath, and then released it. "Seems disrespectful to sell it."

He shook his head. "It's disrespectful to let everything go to waste. Bless someone else with it. That was what your mom and dad were all about anyway. Being a blessing to others. Which is why you love to do what you do. You learned from them. Just do it as you."

I lifted my eyes to him. "What about you? What happens to you if I sell?"

"Mia and I..." He shrugged. "We'll be fine. Your dad built a life, and there's something good about that, don't you think?"

I did, and he had. That was one of the things I admired most about my parents. They had a plan, a goal, and they worked for it. It didn't come easy, but it was theirs. And then it was mine, to do with as I chose. I looked up to Shane, an idea solidifying as soon as it struck.

"Do you want it?"

Shane's expression pinched in question.

"Dad's company. Do you want it?"

He chuckled. "You know I can't."

"That wasn't the question."

His silence revealed the answer. "You run it anyway. There's no reason not to sell to you. You've worked for the company since you were sixteen."

He rubbed a hand over his head. "There's no way I can pay you what it's worth."

"We'll figure it out. If it would be a blessing to you and Mia." I paused to pull in some more air. "It'd be a blessing to me if you took it."

Another stretch of silence pulled between us, but somehow a weight I didn't realize I carried slipped from my shoulders. All this time, I felt in the far reaches of my heart that I would need to come back, to carry on Dad's work the way he'd done it. It had pressed on me, and I hadn't understood until this moment why.

I wasn't him. But he didn't expect me to be. My lips quivered as I looked to my legs. Why had I carried that lie all these years?

Dad hadn't fed it to me, but I always measured myself by him, and I was sure I'd never reach his stature.

Dad hadn't. He measured me by love, and it was always enough.

Love didn't leave. It grew.

I'd clung to expectations that were never meant for me, belittling the real love that had been there. Now it unfolded, covering me until the fears of inadequacy drowned under love's sufficiency.

Sarah... If you could only know this love.

Clarity sank deep as I shifted my thoughts to her. This was why God had crossed our paths. I understood her better than I'd realized. We shared the same fear—that we would never know who we were, or if we did, it wouldn't be enough. My heart seemed to explode with the full impact of truth.

Jesus loves me—this I know.

As I was. As she was. He loved completely.

I am listening. Please, let her hear too.

SARAH

I rolled my tongue around inside my dry mouth. I hated dehydration. It made my head pound. Time for a break.

After looping my hammer, I inspected the beam we'd installed. It went in without a problem. The guy Mack had left to work with me was reasonable and willing, which had painted the sun brighter in my world. That, and the fact that Troy wasn't present. Guess his community service had been met. As I exhaled, satisfaction tugged on my lips. Finally. A good day.

"Take five, Sam." I turned, looking at the thirtysomething guy I'd been working with. "I need some water, and I'll bet you do too."

"Yes, ma'am."

Military, probably. Gotta like that. My grin grew as I strode out the front door and to my truck.

I had a water bottle half chugged when my phone chimed. Thought he'd call already—it'd been a couple hours. If he had, I missed it.

Nope, no missed calls. But he did text.

Jesse: *When you get a break, go here.*

Below was a YouTube link. Huh. Must be on vacation if he had time to surf the Tube virals.

Me: *Kicking back today?*

He didn't answer. Maybe he was busy watching ESPN or something. The life.

"Did you talk to Chapman yet?" Mack spoke as he walked from his truck toward me.

The fire-flood started in my face again. How did you train a blush? Was it possible to disconnect it? Mack kept me blazing like a prairie fire with his constant poking.

"No." I met his eyes, just so he wouldn't think he had me flustered. "You?"

His gravely laugh prompted a grin on my mouth. Mack was unexpected. What was his story? He was a lot like my dad, and yet nothing at all like him. Dad was a good man usually, but he wasn't too concerned with others. If they did their jobs, he let them be. Everyone needed to keep their lives to themselves— that was his philosophy.

Mack seemed to be of the same sort, except with this. Curiosity unhinged my tongue.

"What's with you and the meddling?"

The old man shrugged one shoulder. "He's a good kid. Deserves to be happy."

And I figured in...how?

He cleared his throat and spat in the dirt. "You're a unique one. Don't come across a gal like you all the time. Pretty sure he knows it too."

Huh. Almost sure that was a compliment.

"How long have you been doing this, Mack?" By this, I meant Homes For Hope. I assumed he knew what I was talking about.

"Ten years, more or less."

"Why?"

"Healing."

Back to one-word answers. Would he get mad if I pushed? I chewed on my bottom lip and let a space of quiet extend between us.

"My wife, she was a good woman. Lot like you, actually. Special." He spat again. "When she died, I didn't know what to do with myself. She'd been on the local Homes For Hope committee, and one day they asked for my help with a build. Thought I'd do it, to honor her. Strange as it may be, working that build..." His voice trailed onto the summer breeze, and he looked at the house in front of us. "It was the first time breathing didn't hurt."

Mack married—and loved that strong?

"She was a Christian woman. Always tried to get me to love God like I should. Seemed unnecessary to me. She loved me. That was enough. But when I didn't have her anymore..." He swallowed and then cleared his throat. "I still don't understand God. I keep listening to Chapman—from a distance, and he probably doesn't know it—but I can see that he's the real thing. Maybe I'll figure it out. I do know this though: Alice lived to serve. God and other people. And serving does heal. I don't know how or why, but I do know that it's true."

I stared at him, which probably made him uncomfortable, but I couldn't help it. Shock had me dumb-whipped. This man who grunted more than he used the English language had just spit out the most touching story I'd ever heard. And it echoed what Darcy and Jesse had been telling me. To live beyond myself.

Why would that heal or bring wholeness? Everything you heard on TV told you to make "me time" and to prioritize yourself. Why would acting the servant rather than the master give restoration?

My gaze slid to the house we were working on. Our restoration project. But the restoration wasn't so that the house would continue to stand empty and useless. If it did, the work would not only be a waste of time and money, but the house would crumble.

Restoration has a purpose. To serve.

Whoa. Did I just think that? I wasn't that smart or deep. Where did it come from?

The phone in my hand chimed again.

Mack took a step away as if he was going back to the house, and then he paused. "Chapman is something, Sarah. You both are. Seems only right..." His shoulders turned, and he continued up the walk.

Seems right and *is* right weren't always the same. Clearly there were things about Jesse that neither Mack nor I understood. A weight of sadness settled in my chest. I longed to understand.

I brushed the heaviness away and checked the phone.

Jesse: *Kicking back? Only if you count gutting my parents' house as kicking back.*

Me: *Yikes. That bad?*

Jesse: *You'd be appalled. I've been negligent. There's a story there...one I'll tell you. Later.*

When? Did that mean he couldn't talk right now, and I was supposed to call him later? *Please quit shoving me into awkwardness!*

One more chime.

Jesse: *Call you tonight.*

I blew out a breath. Thanks for that.

Water break done, I met Sam back in the house, and we worked for another two hours, getting another span of opened wall structurally secured with a beam. The headers we'd placed allowed for six- to eight-foot openings, and the transformation to the house was impressive. From the front door one could see not only into the front room but into the kitchen beyond if they looked left.

On the right, another large room had been opened with a six-foot case to expose a fireplace on the far wall. The staircase in the middle had been stripped of its enclosure, and Mack had been working on a code-approved banister that would complement the open feeling of the new floor plan. The third header, which we hadn't secured, would go on the backside of the staircase where we'd opened the wall that had separated the kitchen from the formal dining area.

An open concept in a traditional, loaded-with-character home. *Perfect. Ask the Browns.* Pride puffed in my chest as I walked through the progress.

We quit for lunch, and I actually stayed on site to eat along with Mack and Sam and three other men. Mack had ordered pizza, and some woman dropped off a bag of oranges and a pack of flavored drinks. It struck me as I was eating how a community could make a difference if its members chose to. Simple acts, like providing fruit and drinks, could make life mean more. Was this how it was supposed to work? Me serving with what I knew, the resources I had, and others doing the same?

That was how Jesse's life worked. I loved that about him.

Uh-oh. There was a word in that thought that shouldn't be there. I *admired* that about him. Better.

Mack's voice drew me out of my mental slipup. "Will we have the structure sound by the end of the day, carpenter-girl?"

"Should. Sheetrock should start tomorrow." A couple of days' work, if we had a decent crew—but then the mudding might take more time. Depended on the humidity. Then the floors. Old oak. After a good sanding and a few applications of stain and poly, they'd be beautiful.

While I was making a mental checklist, Mack nodded, bit off another massive chunk of pizza, and turned away. I looked down to my food and grinned. A man of few words, unless it was really, really important. I could work with that.

If it weren't for finances, which I did have some saved, I could see myself doing what Jesse and Mack did.

As quickly as the thought rose, it fell. Dad wouldn't understand or approve. And as much as I was still mad at and hurt by him, I couldn't handle the thought of his complete disapproval.

Call him.

Not now. I pushed off the tree I'd been leaning against and moved back toward the house, shifting my mind back to the list I'd made. Thinking about this project, seeing my vision come to life, was way more thrilling than contemplating the next conversation with my dad.

Why hadn't he called me?

Forget it. Work at hand, that was what I needed to focus on.

And so I did. By the end of the day, every header had been set. The stairway had been redone and was ready for stain. We'd even managed to get the cabinetry in the kitchen unhinged so that volunteers could paint cabinets while the drywall was being hung.

Mack caught me as I reached for the door to my truck at the close of our workday. "We'll need a layout for the kitchen in the next couple of days."

"I don't know anything about that." I didn't cook. Me and a microwave were pretty good pals. Which meant kitchen geography was about as familiar to me as the Himalayan mountains.

"Learn." One solid pat on my shoulder punctuated his demand. "You're my girl."

Well, glad I was somebody's.

Guess I knew my plans for the night. I'd go back into my original structure plan and get the dimensions for the kitchen and somehow figure it out. How hard could it be? Kitchens needed what—a sink, a stove, and a fridge?

Something heavy lodged in my stomach. The Browns had been so pleased with what I'd done so far. What if I messed it all up with a half-baked kitchen? Pun intended.

I had to get it right. This was where more architect and design classes would have come in handy.

As I eased up to the red light ahead, my phone rang. An actual call.

What if it was Dad? My muscles bunched tight. I checked the ID. *Jesse.* Even while I smiled, because I was glad he called, disappointment sagged through me.

Did Dad really hate me now?

I brushed away the question and answered my phone. "Hey."

"Finally."

"Finally?" Had he been trying to call me?

"Yeah, finally," he said. "Couldn't wait to talk to you."

Hmm. Could have called last night. This morning. At lunch...

"Did you go to that link I sent you?"

Oh, so that was what this was about. "No. I was working. Just got done and am heading to the hotel. What is it?"

"Oh yeah. I forgot about the time difference." He paused. "Be sure to go to it tonight, okay?"

Weird. "Why? What is it?" I repeated.

"A song. I needed to hear it today, and I wanted you to hear it too."

Very weird. "Are you okay?"

He laughed. "I'm good. Have a ton of work down here—the place is a huge mess. But I'm good." Again, he stopped talking, and the air between us hung. "I decided some things this morning. Some stuff that has been dragging on me. I'm selling my parents' house and my dad's business."

The light, which took forever, finally turned green. "You're not leaving the country or anything, are you?"

"No."

His chuckle made me smile.

"Why sell?"

"Because neither the house nor the business are a part of who I am anymore, and I've neglected them both. If I don't need them, someone else should enjoy them."

He sounded almost giddy. "You're not sad?"

"I'm relieved." I could hear him take a long breath. "I don't know if this will make sense, but I've been afraid to let go because they were a part of my mom and dad, and I thought they'd be disappointed in me. I wish you could have known them—they were amazing. But all this time, part of me has been afraid that I'd live in their shadow forever. But I don't have to."

Wait. Jesse Chapman was afraid he wouldn't measure up? He had to be kidding.

"Jesse, you're the best person I've ever met." Oh boy. I said that. Out loud. My ears began to burn. Did I need to qualify it? "I mean, why would you think you stood in someone else's shadow?"

Again, he chuckled, only this time much softer. "Everyone struggles with inadequacy, Sapphira."

They did? How about those women at Subway who sat like perfect little peacocks, scorning the undignified slobs? Did they struggle with inadequacy?

"Are you there?" Jesse said.

"Oh." I sniffed—which I found annoying that I would need to. "Yeah, sorry."

"Do you believe me?"

No. "Yes."

"About to the hotel?"

Nice shift? "Pulling in right now."

"Call me after you shower. We'll have supper."

"We will, huh? How's that going to work?"

For some reason I felt his smile over the digital air. "Talk to you soon."

Chapter Twenty-Five

JESSE

It probably wasn't right how much I enjoyed making Sarah wonder what I was thinking.

With a grin, I sprawled across the bed in Shane's basement guest room. Interesting. It'd been a long time since I called Tennessee home. For the first time in a while, that didn't bother me. I was free to seek a life of my own.

Phone still in hand, I scrolled through Chrome looking for a Jimmy John's. Of course there wouldn't be one in Lexington, Nebraska. Closest was Kearney. At least twenty miles. Not gonna happen. I glanced to the wrapped sandwich still waiting for me on the side table.

Still, worth a shot. I tapped the phone link and waited.

No. They couldn't deliver to Lexington. Yes, there was a manager on duty. Groan...I suppose you could talk to her.

I sorted through my brain for a reasonable explanation for my ridiculous request. They all sounded dumb. Or cheesy. Or desperate. By the time the woman's voice touched my ear, however, I decided I had nothing to lose.

"I'm in Tennessee, but..." And I plunged in.

She listened politely until I finished with a definitively desperate, "Please? Help a guy out here?"

The line paused in awkward silence.

"You want me to send a delivery a half hour away because you can't be there to take this woman out to dinner?"

"Right." *I. Am. Pathetic.*

A soft laugh rustled over the phone. "Wow. That's really sweet."

I grinned. "So..."

"Don't advertise it—I can't be doing this all the time."

"You'll do it?"

"Tonight. Because it's sweet." She paused, and I could hear rustling in the background. "Wish I'd meet such a nice guy. Okay, give me your order."

I took a stab at what Sarah would like. Should be fairly easy—she wasn't picky. "Charge me whatever you need to, and put a sandwich on there for the delivery person too."

"Got it." She rattled the bill, which wasn't that bad, considering. "Should get there in about thirty minutes."

Thirty minutes... Tick. Tick. Tick. Twenty-six minutes. Tick. Tick. Tick.

Time was torture.

At twelve minutes till touchdown, my phone rang. Smiling like a schoolboy, I rolled to my stomach and answered.

"Hey."

"Hi. So, how's this going to work?"

Delay tactics. I didn't have any of those. Surely I could make some up. "How was your day?"

"Huh?"

"Your day. What'd you do?"

She didn't answer right away. I imagined her eyebrows drawing inward, which made me laugh silently. I was ridiculous.

"We put in Lam beams for all the expanded openings. Mack worked on the stairway." Her voice sounded hesitant, like she thought I was a nut.

Not far off the truth.

"Who'd you work with?" I felt comfortable with that question because Mack assured me that Troy would be gone.

"Sam."

I'd met him. He'd helped strip the roof Saturday.

"Nice guy, in the reserves—Air Force, I think." I reached for the soda that was sweating down the sides of the cup, leaving a ring of moisture on the napkin beneath it.

"How do you know these things?"

I almost snorted out my soda. "I talk to people, Sarah. They're actually interesting—and not that scary."

"Except Troy."

Why'd she go there? "There are some exceptions, I guess."

"Yes. Always, it seems."

What did I say to that? This girl, she had a fun side. I'd seen it. How did I pull out the warrior woman who'd taken the laser arena by storm the other day?

"I wish you were here..." she said.

I nearly dropped the phone.

"Why?" Did I dare ask that? Guess I did. "Something up?" There, that should lighten it. Maybe.

"I'm supposed to get a layout for the kitchen done tonight. I don't have a clue about kitchens."

I snorted. "Like I could help there. I live in hotels, remember?"

Her long draw of air wisped softly over the phone, as did her exaggerated exhale. "I might be in over my head."

"Nah." I sipped my Coke and then set it aside. "You did a great job with the overall plan. You've got skills, carpenter-girl."

"Not in this."

Why did this little bump throw her like this? One little challenge shouldn't bum her out quite this much. "What's really eating you?"

She left me with silence for a few breaths.

"Sapphira?"

"I had an idea—a plan." The words tumbled from her in a rush. "Now I'm not so sure."

A hint of direction for her life? That was a good thing. "What's the plan?"

"Well..." Her voice trailed off. "Never mind. Forget it."

"Nope. Talk."

She growled. Which I thought was adorable.

"I'm waiting."

Two more beats of nothing, then she let her guard down. "There's a place not too far from home that is looking for bids. An old mansion that the new owners want to turn into a bed-and-breakfast. I was going to..."

"Do it." I pushed off my stomach and came to my feet. Her own reno project—she'd be perfect. "Pitch a bid. Why not?"

"It's on my dad's bid list."

Oh. That was why not. "Have you talked to him?"

Nothing.

"Sarah..."

Something in the background rustled.

"Hang on," she said.

I grinned and kept listening, though the sounds had been muffled. Probably by her hand over the speaker.

More movement. The door, I think. Then, "I didn't order..."

A man's voice drifted to my hearing, but I couldn't decode the mumbling.

"But..."

More male speak.

"Jesse?" Her voice carried loud and clear.

I choked back a laugh. "What?"

"Did you order me Jimmy John's?"

Okay, how to play this... Own it with a confident *Yep?* Roll out evasion and make her drag it out of me? Or let silence answer.

"I can't believe you did that. There's not a Jimmy John's for...wait." Her voice was muffled again. "Where did you come from?"

The man answered. My smile stretched—silence was a good choice.

SARAH

I stared at the guy standing outside my door. "Come again?"

"Kearney." He tugged his hat. "And I've got to go back. Have a nice night."

If stupid had a face, it was mine in that moment. I stood with my mouth hanging open, my phone hovering somewhere near my ear, staring at the delivery guy's back as he retreated down the ugly green hall.

"Hello?" Jesse's voice beckoned me back from shock.

"You bought me dinner? From Tennessee?"

The smile I couldn't see penetrated the silence over the phone. My insides warmed, then turned to mush. Who knew there were men in this world like Jesse Chapman? Some girl would be a lucky woman someday...

But she wouldn't be me. I reshaped my puddled insides, wrapped them with dignity and resolve, and shut the door to my room. "That was really..."

Nice? Way more than nice. Thoughtful? How impersonal did that sound? Amazing? Yeah, but if I said that, the heart I'd just stood upright would melt into goo all over again.

"I told you we'd have supper tonight."

Yes, he'd said that. Another extraordinary Jesse move that made him unbelievably attractive, even if he didn't mean for it to.

"Will you pray with me?" he asked.

I bowed my head and squeezed my eyes shut, even though it occurred to me that doing so was stupid, because who was there to see it?

Jesse said amen, and I heard the wrapper, on what I assumed was his own sandwich, crinkle in the background.

"Why do people bow their heads when they pray?"

"Huh?" His *huh* sounded like it came out around a mouthful of bread and meat.

Okay, so it was left field. But with Jesse, nothing was dumb, usually. "Bowing and shutting your eyes. Why is that a rule?"

He swallowed—I knew because I could hear it. "It's not a rule. I don't always bow. Or shut my eyes. I'll talk to God right out loud on top of the roof while I'm nailing down shingles, if there's something on my mind."

He did? Did that qualify him as crazy? "But I've seen you—when you pray over the food. Does it guarantee good digestion or something?"

He snorted. "No. You're hilarious." A pause hung between us—I think so he could take a drink.

I took the moment to rip into my own dinner. Turkey, beef, and ham. No way he'd known that I didn't like ham. I opened my sandwich, peeled off the yucky stuff, and put the bread back together. Perfect.

"I think we bow because it's a way to show God honor. He is the King, you know."

No, I didn't know. "King of what?"

"Everything. All of life, everything we know and don't know. All of it is His."

Someone that big and important wouldn't be interested in one confused, minuscule woman.

Jesus loves you.

Strange how echoes whispered at such moments. Jesus, this carpenter's kid Who was apparently God—which I didn't get—was also the King of everything...and yet He loved me? Not likely.

Jesse's voice, clear of food garble, drew me out of myself. "What are you thinking?"

He didn't want to know. Pretty sure. Maybe he did. Would he be offended?

Huh. That thought demanded a pause. The only time I'd seen him offended was by Troy, which still kind of baffled me. But even when he thought I'd slept with the creep—and I was sure that was exactly what he'd thought—he wasn't offended by me. Was that hypocrisy or something else?

"Sarah, in this kind of situation, you have to use your words, because I can't see you, so I have no way of guessing your thoughts."

Cute. I wasn't sure he'd be able to guess my thoughts if he was sitting across from me.

Actually, probably he could. He was keen like that. So why not? "Why would a king care about my little life?"

I spit the question out like I'd just tasted vinegar. But not because the idea of that sort of love was sour. The opposite—the idea was too sweet, and it made the reality of it being impossible bitter.

"Because He made you."

Jesse's words cut through me like fire and landed in my chest. Was it possible that he was right?

"Think about this," he continued. "That house you're working on—are you happy with it?"

A smile poked my mouth up. "Yes." This project was turning out to be one of the most thrilling jobs I'd ever done.

"And even though someone else will live there, own it, will it matter to you what happens to it?"

Yeah, it would matter. A whole lot, it would matter. They'd better take care of it. Love it. It'd break my heart to see it neglected and run down again.

Guess my silence gave him his answer.

"Do you think it'll be any different with that mansion you're going to bid on? Or any other project you put your hands to?"

Probably not. My work—I put myself into it. This house would have part of me in every corner. Indifference didn't come with an investment like that.

"Why would you think the God Who created you—designed you according to His delight and plan—would feel anything less?"

That burning sensation stirred in my chest again. But he was operating on assumptions here—the first of which was, did I believe there was a God?

Yes.

Two months ago, I wasn't so sure, but meeting Jesse... I was changing. Everything about me was changing.

Who am I, and is that who I want to be? That had been the question that had launched this whole journey. For the first time since that day, I felt like maybe the answer to the second part of that question could tilt closer to yes than no.

Maybe because I believed there was a God. And was he King? Did He have a name?

Did He love me?

"Sapphira, did you go to that link I sent you?"

He probably had his whole sandwich gone in the space of my reflection. Didn't seem to mind though.

"No, I didn't have a chance."

"Promise me you'll pull it up tonight and listen, okay?"

Now we were making promises...this was the strangest relationship ever. Not that I'd had many to base that claim on.

"Okay."

"Promise."

I laughed. "Okay, okay, I promise."

I felt his grin in his pause. "Good. One more thing."

I looked to the food he'd bought for me, shut my eyes, and pictured him sitting there beside me, his fingers brushing my arm. Tingles rushed over my skin, and my head felt light. I'd promise anything to this quirky, amazingly good man.

"Name it."

"Call your dad."

Not what I was expecting. The light-headedness dropped, as did my heart. That was the last thing I wanted to do.

Chapter Twenty-Six

SARAH

Two promises. One I didn't want to keep. But that one kept swirling in my head, spinning a demanding mantra. *Call your dad. Call your dad. Call your dad.*

I groaned. Or snarled. "Fine," I barked at my phone, which was still in my hand. But in my head I kept arguing. Why should I call him? He was the one who exploded the night Jesse came. He was the one who was pushing me away right when I needed him most. He should be calling me.

I promised Jesse.

My shoulders drooped. Okay, calling Dad. Should be fun. I slid my thumb across the phone screen. Less than two seconds later, the call was going through.

What was I supposed to say to him?

"Yeah?" snapped his choppy voice.

I swallowed, forcing away the urge to hang up. "Hi, Dad."

"'Bout time."

Now wait one minute... "You have a phone too, you know."

"Haven't talked to you in almost a week, and you only called to argue?"

"No. But you could have called me."

"I told you to let me know when you've figured this out." He stopped long enough for me to open my mouth, but not long enough for the reply to make it out. "Are you done chasing illusions yet?"

"What illusions?" My empty fist curled at my side. "What exactly is it you think I'm after, Dad?"

"I don't know!" His shout made me tremble. "Twenty-one years you and I have lived in peace. I don't know what the hell is going on with you now."

My lip quivered, but I wasn't ready to back down. "I go out on a date, and you freak out. I wear clothes cut for a woman, and you go nuts. I'm not sure the problem is with me."

Silence gripped the digital air between us. Where was Jesse when I needed him? Oh, he was gonna hear about that—some brilliant plan this was.

He's afraid he's losing you...

Huh. That was a peachy sentiment, except Dad was shoving me over a cliff. More like he was trying to get rid of me.

Dad's calm, low voice destroyed that theory. "Come home, Sarah."

I bit my lip and dropped onto the bed.

"We don't fight like this, girl."

"I know." I had to push the words out. "I hate it. But I can't come home right now. I need to finish this job."

I waited. He gave me nothing.

"I *am* working, Dad. I promise I am."

"Doing what?" Though his voice remained low, a snappy current ran through it.

My defenses regathered. "Building. Remodeling, actually. What did you think?"

Silence yet again. What did he think? That suddenly I turned hooker on him?

I sighed. "You know what, Dad? Think what you want. I may not know exactly who I am, but I have a pretty good idea of what I'm not. Apparently you don't. I'll be back when I can, and then I guess we'll figure out what's next."

"What does that mean?"

"It means that my life and yours have apparently developed an incompatibility. Maybe it's time for me to move on."

He mumbled—pretty sure something unsavory. "If that's what you want."

The connection fell, and that was the end of that.

DALE

At least she was alive. God knew doing what.

When Sarah was twelve, we would watch movies together on Friday nights. *Star Wars. Indiana Jones. Pirates of the Caribbean.* Good movies. Action, adventure. She loved them. One night she plopped down next to me on the couch, a full bowl of popcorn in her hands, and with uncharacteristic directness, she blurted out, "Most girls need a mother, Dad."

I sat shocked—didn't know what to say. Fears stacked in my mind like lumber coming off a delivery truck. Twelve years old, wasn't that when girls started...changing? How was I going to handle that? No answers. None. I didn't know what to do or say.

She rescued me. "I'm not most girls though, am I?" She shook her head, answering her own question. "I only need you."

Right then I knew we'd do okay. Still didn't have a clue how to navigate through teenage girl stuff, but I knew she'd give me a whole lot of room to figure it out and together we'd get through it. And we did.

How could we make it through all of that, and yet this... We couldn't do this?

She's turning into her mother.

Fear had an inaudible voice that made your hair stand on end and your skin feel like you'd hit a hot wire. I could handle Sarah moving out, standing on her own. Truly I could.

But becoming her mother? I couldn't handle that.

JESSE

There was a place between asleep and awake where reality became uncertain. Sometimes I felt like I was floating, though I could feel the mattress at my back. Sometimes what I hoped for and what was true blurred into a surreal oneness, and I felt the satisfaction of grasping a dream.

That night, in that haze, I felt Sarah at my side, her head resting on my shoulder. With my eyes shut, I imagined fingering her glossy dark hair, smelling the hint of vanilla I remembered filling my truck the night we went to Kearney.

Probably a good thing there were a thousand-plus miles between us. But still. Was it that wrong to hope that someday...

The text *meep-meep* from my phone pulled me out of my dreamworld and back into the land of reality. I reached for the cell, which was resting on the nightstand.

Sapphira.

The corners of my mouth lifted into a smile, and I opened the message.

Sarah: *Called my dad. Not good. Thanks for that.*

Oh boy. Should I call her?

Me: *I'm sorry. Are you okay?*

Sarah: *Peachy.*

Me: *Want to talk?*

Sarah: *No. Need sleep.*

Yeah, that was why she texted me. I drew a long breath.

Me: *I'm really sorry it didn't go well.*

I stared at the phone, waiting for her reply. Just kept staring. And staring.

Nothing.

Me: *Did you listen to that song I sent you?*

A whole lot of more blank screen. Maybe she shut her phone off.

Me: *Here's another. Found it today. Listen to both. You promised.*

After sending the new link, I turned the phone over and replaced it on the table. She wouldn't text me back tonight. Which gave me time to pray.

A much better use of my presleep time.

SARAH

Texting my anger out to Jesse didn't fix it. I was so mad at my dad.

Jesse's solution? YouTube. Terrific.

I wasn't sure why I didn't want to tap the links Jesse sent me. Knowing Jesse, the link would have something to do with love or Jesus or something. What if I tapped those links, they promised the longings that tugged on my heart, and I found them to be wrong?

I couldn't handle any more emotional disappointments.

But I did promise.

My thumb scrolled up to the conversation we'd had earlier and hit the link. There, I opened it. Was that good enough?

I knew it wasn't.

The advertisement played itself out, and then a male voice sang as words scrolled over the screen. I didn't latch on to any of it until he got to the chorus part of the song.

Jesus, He loves me...

See? Jesus and love. Jesse was predictable.

Was he right?

Jesus, He loves me...

Suddenly Jesse's question from an earlier conversation resurfaced.

Would it still matter to you what happened to that house?

Yes. It was only just a house, but it was my workmanship, and I loved it. Wanted it to be loved.

269

My breath caught hard in my chest.

Do You love me?

That Chris guy on the video kept saying so. But I wasn't him. I wasn't Jesse. I wasn't Darcy or Adam or Jeff.

Do you love me?

The corners of my eyes itched. I rubbed at them and found wetness. The most important question of my life transformed from *Who am I?* to *Do you love me?*

I needed an answer. Now.

Because the answer to the second question would determine the answer for the first. I didn't know how or why, but I was certain of the connection.

I scrolled on my phone to the second link Jesse had sent minutes before. This time there was no hesitation. Open. Skip the ads. A beautiful woman named Kari started into the song. *I am not alone.* I hung on every lyric and wept.

If Jesus loved me, then I was not alone, and I was His. Or at least I wanted to be His.

How?

I squeezed my eyes shut. *Please show me how.*

Was that what Jesse meant when he said he prayed whenever he felt the need? Could it really be that simple?

I leaned back against the pillow, tapped repeat on the YouTube link, and shut my eyes. When the song ended, I closed the link and settled back again.

Please, Jesus, if You love me, please show me how to be Yours.

Chapter Twenty-Seven

JESSE

A distinctive *meep-meep* woke me before my alarm chime went off. Who texted before coffee?

Sarah: *Is it true?*

I rubbed at the sleep weighing my eyelids down. Only six in the morning, which meant it was earlier in Nebraska. Had she stayed up all night?

I assumed she was talking about the songs I'd sent her.

Me: *He loves you.*

Pushing off the bed, my bare feet scuffled on the carpeted floor to the bathroom across the hall. A small ball of frustration bounced inside of my chest. Why did she have to form this serious interest in the things that were so important right when I had to be here and not there? I reviewed everything that had happened over the past couple of days while I'd been gone. She'd found her passion—rehabbing houses. Wanted to pursue it, but was afraid. She fought with her dad, again. What was his deal anyway? Now this.

Sarah was on some kind of emotional roller coaster. Maybe my being there would only add more twists.

I brushed my teeth and stared into the mirror for a few moments. My own life had turned into a bit of a ride too, and

Sarah had been the major catalyst. Once again, I found myself questioning my motives, because, let's be honest, we all had a selfish bend.

Please, let this be about You and her, not her and me.

More awake, I walked back to my room, looking for my phone. She'd responded.

Sarah: *I want to believe you.*

Not about me.

Me: *Believe Him.*

Waiting for her to text back, I tugged on my work jeans and shoes. The *meep-meep* sounded as I tied the second set of laces.

Sarah: *I have to go see my dad this weekend.*

Hold up, that was an interesting switch. Had we been talking about the same thing? Another message flashed.

Sarah: *He hates religion. I don't know what I'm doing.*

Okay, so we were sort of on the same page. Close, anyway.

Sarah: *He's really mad at me, and I don't understand why. I don't know what to do.*

Was that her asking for advice? I didn't have any good advice—I didn't understand what was going on either. Who got mad because his grown daughter went on a date or wanted to stand on her own two feet? There had to be more mixing into that mess, but if Sarah didn't know what, there was no way I was going to figure it out.

Sarah: *Are you there?*

Me: *I'm here. Thinking. I don't understand the situation.*

Sarah: *Me neither. He's never been mad at me like this.*

I sighed. What if I could be there, go with her? Not an option, and apparently not the will of God. Maybe I'd make it worse or get in the way.

Me: *All I know is that we're supposed to love God and honor our parents. I don't know how that will play out for you, but I think you're doing the right thing by going to see him.*

Even as the message was flying over the digital waves, hesitation—no, actual fear—gripped my insides. Was her dad a violent man? What would happen if they fought again? Did she have anyone else to run to? And what about the *love God* part? Was she there, or were we still tiptoeing around the whole idea?

I would have given anything to be there with her. Sometimes God and I didn't share the same blueprint.

SARAH

Friday came before I wanted it to. I'd told Mack I wouldn't be around for the weekend, sort of hoping that he would pressure me to stay.

"Most of my workers have other responsibilities, carpenter-girl. I appreciate all you've done."

That was that.

I really wanted to see the house finished, but my presence wasn't really necessary anymore. The design and the framing were done. Other experts and volunteers would have the project wrapped up soon, and the Browns would be able to move in the following month.

The project house was void of noise and workers by the time I packed up my toolbox. Alone, I toured through the redesigned space, touching the smooth wood of the cased openings, running my hand over the new island we'd anchored in the open kitchen, admiring the airy bathroom we'd connected to one of the bedrooms to create a master suite.

Shutting my eyes, I pictured it complete. Wasn't hard. The drywall crew had hung Sheetrock throughout half the house. The shell was taking on skin, and my drafted design was coming to life.

My work.

I loved it. Loved this house. Loved knowing what it had been and seeing it become so much more.

A house renovated.

A heart renovated.

Could Jesus do this to my heart? Would I find the satisfaction in His work like I found satisfaction in this?

And, most important, would *He* find satisfaction in it? Could He love me?

I turned and meandered to the front of the house again. Eyeing the entry, which had been fitted with a new steel door inset with a window that gave it a semi-craftsman feel, I sat down on the third riser of the open staircase. I pulled my phone from my back pocket and slid through my texts until I found the links Jesse had sent.

Chris Tomlin and Kari Jobe sang to me in the stillness of that house. It was their voices, anyway. But—and I couldn't really fathom this, but felt it as sure as I felt the wood beneath me—Jesus was singing to me. Those words were His.

I love you, Sarah.

You are not alone.

I love you.

With my eyes closed and my lips trembling, I leaned back and listened. Though the music ended, I remained still, soaking in a voice I couldn't really hear, and wondering at this presence I couldn't see.

"I'm scared," I whispered in the silence. Of these things I didn't understand. Of how powerfully tied my heart felt to Jesse. And of going home to face my dad.

Did this Jesus understand what I meant?

That presence remained, but I couldn't hear the voice.

Maybe I'd imagined it. Quite possibly I'd gone nuts. Crazy people heard voices that weren't there.

I pushed forward and pulled myself to my feet. Time to go. For better, or, more probable, worse, it was time to go home.

An hour later, I couldn't decide if I wished the drive had been longer or shorter. A longer drive would have kept me away until dark, and then my dad would be in bed, and I wouldn't have to deal with him until the morning. But then I'd have to lie in my childhood bed, imagining all sorts of scenes that would play out when I saw him again.

A shorter drive meant that I'd have made it for supper, and that would have been awkward. Somehow sharing a meal with someone you were not on the best of terms with was...well, horrible. I'd enjoyed my supper in the peace and safety of my truck, thank you very much.

Now it was time to face it—all the bad stuff between Dad and me that had somehow developed over the summer. I pushed through the screen door, my bag slung over my shoulder.

Dad was where I'd suspected. Sprawled out in his oversized recliner, remote in his right hand and a Big Gulp in his left, with the paper remains of a takeout burrito from the Circle K crumpled up on the table beside him.

I stopped two steps inside the door, and we stared in a silent deadlock while blood pounded through my veins.

Why was I here again? *God wants us to love Him and honor our parents.* Right. Because...why, exactly? My mother left, so she was not even around to play that one out. And my dad—what the heck was going on with him? All of this anger and silence. Was that honorable? I needed him, and he was rejecting me. Was that worthy of my respect?

Jesse hadn't qualified his advice, which probably meant honor whether you wanted to or not. Whether he deserved it or not.

My thoughts caught me off guard. Where were these insights coming from?

Didn't matter. I was standing there like a statue while the strain between us continued to build in the silence. I'd come home. Might as well make an effort.

"Hi, Dad."

He frowned. "Didn't expect to see you."

Tonight? Here? Ever?

"Thought we needed to sort this out."

He grunted.

I dipped my shoulder, letting the duffel strap slide down my arm. The bag dropped to the floor.

"Words, Dad." I stepped forward. "I need you to use some words. Why are you so angry with me?"

His look was like a laser into my eyes. "You left. Didn't call for days. Think that's acceptable?"

My head lowered, and I focused on the spot nearest my shoes. "No. I'm sorry."

Another grunt.

Holy smokes, did the man know how irritating that was? I looked back at him with a glare. His focus was back on the television. My temper spewed like a volcano. "You flipped out on me for no reason. What did you expect from me?"

He glanced at me and then returned to his stupid show. *NCIS.* Yes. Way more important than talking to your daughter whom you haven't seen in over a week.

I marched over to the flat-screen, punched the Power button, and then turned to stab him with a look.

He scowled for two breaths, then flipped the foot of the recliner down. Without a word, he stood and left the room.

Three seconds later, his bedroom door smacked hard against the frame.

Welcome home to me. This was a terrific idea.

Maybe he needed to sleep on it. I didn't. Sleep, that is. In the hollow silence of the house that used to feel like home, I fumed. About my dad. About Jesse and all of his brilliant, saintly ideas. And about how now I felt trapped. I didn't have anywhere to be, anywhere else to go.

My life in this small town had been completely entwined with my dad's. Six months before, I didn't think about it, let alone mind. Now I hated it. I couldn't stay there, live like that.

The sunlight finally reached a level of brightness that would make it acceptable for me to be up. Dad was already about, slumped over a newspaper at the table, with a half-empty mug of coffee near his large hand.

"Coffee hot?" I asked, skirting him just enough that it wasn't obvious I was keeping my distance. I hoped.

"S'pose so."

Yay. We could use words.

I slopped enough black bitterness to fill three-quarters of my mug and then went to the refrigerator.

"No creamer." Dad's gravelly voice stopped me from opening the door.

"What?"

"Ran out last week."

"How?" I was the only one of the two of us who used it.

He gave me nothing. Not even a grunt. I glared at him, willing him to look at me or to move at all. Nope. He stayed like a cement blob staring at a paper I knew for certain he wasn't actually reading.

"You dumped it, didn't you?"

His jaw jumped, but he still wouldn't look at me.

"Why would you do that?"

His fist curled on the table. "You left."

"So you dumped my creamer?" I slapped my coffee mug onto the counter. "Did you empty my closet too? How about my tools? Are they gone? Maybe you should change the lock, make it official."

The paper crumpled in his hand. "Maybe you should think twice before you take off. I swear, Sarah, the more you chase after this *finding yourself* crap, the more you become like your mother."

I had to force air into my collapsing lungs. He *hated* my mother. Every single memory I had of her coming up between us, all of which I could count on one hand, screamed his absolute contempt for the woman. And I had hated her too. For him. Because my daddy didn't deserve what she did.

But then again I didn't know the whole story.

"How the heck would I know anything about that?" I pressed my palms against the counter and leaned forward, toward him. "I know nothing about the woman. Everything I know comes from a man who apparently has a dark side I'd never seen until now. Maybe I hated a faceless person who didn't deserve it."

He finally looked up, fire smoldering in his eyes. "That what you think?"

"I don't know what to think!" Anger trembled through me. "How is anyone supposed to handle you when you're like this, Dad? I came home because you asked me to, and I got all of a two-sentence greeting followed by a door in my face. You bit my head off for wearing clothes made for a woman, and you came unglued because I'd gone on a date. That's not reasonable, so it makes me wonder what really happened between you and my mom."

One tightly bound fist slammed against the table. "It's not your business."

"She's my mom!"

He stood, sending the chair beneath him flying against the wall. "We're not talking about this."

We were never talking about it. How many things in my life did we never talk about? Had I missed the signs of a split personality all of these years?

"Why are you being psycho all of the sudden?" I bolted around the counter, catching my dad by his elbow before he stomped out of the room. "Where is she? At least tell me that."

He stared hard at the wall opposite me, his features cold, his lips set like iron.

"Come on, Dad," I thundered. "I deserve to know where my mother is. You owe me that much."

His eyes shifted, pouncing on me. The fire in them burned my heart, nearly melting my courage.

"She's dead." His voice, flat and cold and heartless, made me wilt. He ripped his arm from my grasp and moved toward the hall. After stopping just outside his bedroom, he returned that awful death stare to me. "Your mother is dead, Sarah."

The trembling started in my chest and radiated outward. Was he lying? Did my dad just look me in the eye and lie? My hands shook violently as I brought them over my ears. Truth. I desperately need the truth. And it wasn't here.

But I was pretty sure I knew where I could find it.

JESSE

I stood at the front door of my parents' house and surveyed the progress. We had the damaged room stripped to the studs, and the roofers were finishing up the last of the shingles. It'd all be okay.

Everything in my life was going to be okay.

Per usual, my mind shifted to Sarah. I hadn't heard from her that day. She'd gone home the night before, which apparently hadn't gone well. Surprise. What kind of grown man gave the silent treatment?

It hurt her, more than she knew how to put into words. Her whole world for her entire life had been that man.

An angry knot hardened in my chest.

But other than that, everything was going to be okay. Sarah was believing—starting to believe—that she was loved by God. That was huge. And it changed things for us. Me.

Impulse pushed fiercely through my veins. What I would give to skip this project and head north. Drawing a long breath, I smothered the longing with logic. A few more days, a week at the most, and I could do just that.

I pulled the front door shut and set the lock with my key. Shane had recommended a Realtor, and I was supposed to meet with her in the morning. So many balls to juggle in this letting-go business, but it would all be worth it in the end. I finally saw a future that was worth releasing the past. And more and more, it included a blue-eyed carpenter girl whose tough exterior belied a fragile heart.

Could I take care of that heart the way she needed?

After hopping behind the wheel of my truck and shutting the door, I let my eyes slide closed. I was way ahead of myself. And no, there would be times that I would fail. That was why she needed Jesus first.

Help me to be patient...

Even while the prayer lifted from my mind, I reached for my phone. Sarah's number sat first on my list, and I hit Call instead of Message.

"Hey." Ache saturated her voice.

I sat up straighter, gripping my steering wheel with my free hand. "What happened?"

She delayed, and I could hear her breath waver. "Another blowout. I'm in Omaha now."

Omaha? Wasn't that like a two-, three-hour drive from Minden? This running away thing of hers—where'd she get that? "Sarah..." How did I go about this? "Did you talk to him at all?"

"I tried," she clipped, irritated.

"Tell me about it."

"I asked him about my mother—what happened. He locked down until I demanded to know where she was." She paused, clearing her throat. "He said she's dead and then stormed away."

Oh boy. So many wounds festering in this. I was in way over my head. "So...you left?" I kept my voice soft, hoping she wouldn't read accusation in my question.

"I need the truth, and he's not going to tell me."

Ah...her aunt lived in Omaha. The one who was like me. "What did Darcy say?"

She seemed to calm, her voice settling back to normal. "I haven't talked to her about it yet."

I studied the dashboard of my truck, not really seeing it, trying to sort through what I should say. "Are you okay?"

Of course she wasn't, but I couldn't think of anything else.

Her voice came soft and uncertain again. "I don't know what to think. Or what to do."

That impulse to leave that instant, point my truck northwest and make my way to her side, surged over me again. I ached to hold her, to whisper against her ear that it'd be okay, that we'd figure it out together.

But we weren't there yet, and God had me here on purpose.

Why was that again?

Focus on the reality of the moment. "What do you mean when you say you don't know what to do?"

"I can't live there anymore. I've got to figure out a future for myself that isn't dependent on him."

True. Except for the running away part, because severing her relationship with her dad wouldn't bring the peace she was looking for.

"I'm not disagreeing with you, Sarah, but don't shut him out. He is your dad, and that's important."

Bitterness gripped her words. "Apparently not to him."

Chapter Twenty-Eight

SARAH

Dad was lying. I was sure of it. He didn't want me to look for my mother—to find her.

Frustration boiled inside me. Talking to Jesse hadn't helped, because he was disappointed in me. Well, he wasn't there, so he didn't know, couldn't understand. I couldn't stay in the same house with my dad when every second had become a thunderbolt of anger. I wasn't going to live like that. And I wouldn't live with a liar.

Inhaling a long, steady breath, I worked to calm my irritation. Time to think about something else.

My phone still in hand, I scanned through the pictures I'd snapped earlier that day. The brick two-story house looked creepy in its deplorable condition, and the property was overgrown. Some kind of vine almost completely covered the north side of the structure—hosting who knew what kind of vermin. Native grass and weeds stood tall and thick across the three acres of property.

Not a lot of hope in that scene—if I wasn't willing to look for it. But I was looking. The house had been a solid build, once upon a time. Brick exterior, covered front porch, which would need to be replaced but was architecturally appealing. The foundation didn't seem to sag too much, and the windows were all still in place, offering hope for the interior.

The little red rectangle sign posted in the front yard had snagged my attention as I'd left town earlier that day. For Sale by Owner. I'd snapped a picture of that too, because it had the owner's phone number.

It'd be daring. Where would I stay while I made the place livable? Located just outside of Minden, if Dad and I were on friendlier terms, it'd be easy to work on it in the evenings and weekends while I continued living with him. But that didn't sit well in my stomach at the moment. I wanted out. Immediately.

Uncle Dan lived across the road from the shop. Maybe...

That would probably cause a big rip between him and Dad. I wasn't looking to damage my father's life, only to get out from under it.

My mind shifted back to the conversation I'd had with Jesse. He disapproved. He was being cautious about it, trying not to offend me, but he disapproved. Because I wasn't honoring my dad, probably. That made me want to scream. Dad was being mulish, Jesse was being subtly pushy, and I was lost as to what to do next.

Emotion whirled through my head, making me feel dizzy and frightened. I couldn't handle this anymore—feeling alone.

You are not alone.

Whoa. That voice...not really a voice, yet words pressing into my heart, clear and strong. My eyes slid shut as I yearned to hear—or feel it again. It didn't come, but the impression remained deep. It had been there, spoken. I wasn't crazy.

My attention moved back to the phone in my hand, and I switched the app to my texts. It took three breaths before I found what I was looking for, and a few more before the link loaded onto my screen.

I am not alone.

Those words sank into my soul. I eased back against the pillow on Darcy's guest bed, shut my eyes, and held the phone against my chest.

Please, let it be true.

A tear seeped out of the corner of my eye, trickled over my cheekbone, and soaked into my hair. I lost myself in the music. The depth of those words and the singer's rich voice carried me to a different reality.

Or maybe it was to the true reality.

My world shifted, as if the life I had been living had been a gray shadow of the life I'd been intended to live. Living, but not alive. Taking in oxygen, but not really breathing. Like watching an old *Andy Griffith* that had later been imposed with color—I thought my life before had the various shades of reds and blues that were natural and normal. Now I could see—I'd been shown what real color was. Bright. Vivid. Saturated color that came from the inside out.

Not alone. Alive from the inside out. How did I hold on to this reality?

The song ended, and the other one picked up a few seconds later.

I stayed where I was, afraid to move, because if I did, this beautiful place would dissolve, and I'd be back in the superficial zone of black and white smeared with false colors.

Jesus, He loves me...

I looped the words in my heart, wanting them to plant there. Take root and grow.

"Good song." Darcy's voice, soft and a little amazed, drifted from the doorway.

I blinked, and more tears dropped from my eyelashes.

Darcy passed through into the room and sat on the edge of the bed. I watched her, somehow feeling exposed by my display of raw emotion, and yet safe. That was new—and amazing.

Her hand fell to my socked foot, and she squeezed. "How did you come across that?"

I glanced down to my phone and tapped the Pause button. "A friend sent it to me."

"Good friend." She smiled.

"Yeah. He is. I met him while working with Homes For Hope. He's a roofer."

I stared at my hands as discomfort intruded into the sliver of peace I'd enjoyed moments before. The words continued playing in my mind...*He loves me*... I was desperate to know if it was so. The question grew, my longing inflating it like a balloon until I could no longer keep it inside.

"Is it true?"

"That He loves you?"

My lips quivered, and I was afraid to speak again. I nodded.

"The truest thing you'll ever know." Darcy scooted closer and reached for my face. Her thumb brushed away the fresh tear that had escaped my lid. "He. Loves. You."

I squeezed my eyes shut, pushing away every doubt that threatened to smother the words. *If You love me, I want to be like Darcy, like Jesse. I don't know how, but I want what they have...*

"Just believe, Sarah." Darcy spoke as if she knew my thoughts. "Believe that He is God, that He died to save you, and that He'll keep you. Believe that He loves you."

"I believe." I did. I believed.

Arms surrounded me. Darcy's. And somehow I knew Jesus held me too. Because He loved me. That changed everything.

DALE

Dad, I'm in Omaha. Please stop being mad. We need to talk.

It had been three hours since Sarah had texted me—and I ignored it. How did a guy—a dad—stop being mad when his daughter kept running off like some...

Never mind.

I squeezed my eyes shut. They burned with exhaustion. I hadn't slept since she left yesterday morning. Glossy images printed on tabloid pages kept surfacing from my memory and antagonizing me every time I'd closed my eyes.

They'd released Cassie's final photo shoot two weeks after she'd been found dead. Grotesque. That beautiful girl I had married straight out of high school had been chewed up by a monstrous world and spit out for the paparazzi to mock. Her shallow face, sunk in with the hollow trademarks of a meth addict. Her blue eyes—the very eyes that had made her famous—sucked into the sockets, still open, glazed over, and lifeless. Scars littered her body. Cutting, most likely, although definitely some from needles as well. And abuse. Certainly many marks left from a man's brutal hand.

Her final cover story—sad, hopeless. *And, dear God, if You're actually real at all and You aren't the awful monster Cassie's dad believed in, please don't let it be the prelude to Sarah's life.*

That was what killed me. Those images from the magazines burned into my mind, except they morphed until it was no longer Cassie lying dead in that junk house. In my mind, it was Sarah.

My beautiful, talented, hardworking daughter. Used. Abused. Trashed.

Dead.

How could I get past that image? From all I could see, she was slipping down that path, and she wouldn't listen to me.

We need to talk...

That line froze my heart. It almost never came before anything good.

But maybe this time she'd listen.

Dropping into my recliner, I thumbed the remote waiting for me on the side table. I tugged my phone from my belt. One more chance. She'd have to listen. If I had to shout it into her head, I'd get through to her.

Select. Call.

She had to hear me...

Two rings.

"Hello?"

"Sarah." I cleared my throat.

She hesitated. "Hi, Dad."

My tongue seemed to swell. Where did I begin? "What are you doing in Omaha?"

Her sigh rustled the air. "I'm staying with Darcy."

"That guy there?"

"What guy?"

Playing stupid? Anger began to swell. "Don't act dumb. You know what guy."

"Jesse?"

"I don't know his name."

"Dad." Sarah stabbed my name. "Why is that your first question? Am I okay? Yes, just in case you were actually wondering, I'm fine. Will I come home? Eventually, but we need to discuss that. But no. Your first question is, am I with a guy? No, Dad. Jesse's not here. He had to go back to Tennessee. And even if he was here, he's not the kind of man you've pinned him as, and I'm not the kind of girl you've decided I've become."

Her snappy tone hammered against my ear, busting that balloon of anger. "I have no idea what kind of girl you've become. You keep running off, so what am I supposed to think?"

"You're supposed to trust the daughter you raised, and ask real questions, not ones laced with accusations."

"This is why you texted me?" I slammed my fist against the table, sending the remote flying across the room. "So you could sass your old man over the phone? What are trying to prove?"

"I'm not trying to prove anything." Though heat tinged her voice, it cracked. "I'm trying to make things okay. Why can't you see that? Why won't you try, Dad?"

The emotion in her voice tugged hard at my chest. I shut my eyes, and those magazine images surfaced. *God, please, no...*

"Dad..." Her voice, now soft, cut through those silent omens. "Please, please, hear me. Or talk to me—for real. What are you afraid of?"

My core trembled. If I spoke, she'd hear me break. Men didn't break. Dads didn't break.

She sighed again. "It's about my mother, isn't it?"

Not her. We couldn't talk about her.

"Who is she—what did she do?"

Sarah didn't ever need to know who gave her those blue gems. Didn't need to know the fate that had been laid out for her.

"Dad..."

I drew a deep breath. "I told you not to bring her up." My fingers squeezed hard against the phone. "Don't ask, Sarah. Not ever again."

Silence vibrated between us, though I could hear the muffled sound of her breath. Not good enough.

"Do you hear me, Sarah Jane? Not. Ever. Got it?"

"Sure." She paused, and then her voice became cold and distant. "Nice talk, Dad. Have a good night."

Once again, she wasn't listening.

Those magazine pictures continued to taunt me long after she'd hung up.

SARAH

I glared at the wall beyond my bed. Knowing Jesse would call tonight, that he would ask if I'd talked to my dad, and that if I hadn't, Jesse'd be disappointed in me—knowing all of that, I'd talked to my dad.

Jesse couldn't understand. His parents weren't around to make him feel like a failure or a reject.

Not so. He'd just told me the other day he'd been afraid he'd never live up to his dad's reputation, and that hadn't been his father's fault. Were all parent-child relationships doomed to friction?

A question I couldn't answer—and was fairly irrelevant anyway. Nothing had doomed my relationship with Dad outside of Dad himself. He'd gone control-freak psycho with this stuff about my mom. I wanted to know where she was, who she was, so I would know where I came from. What did I have from her besides blue eyes? Was my physical build Sharpe, or was it from her? Did I do anything that she did? What if she was a house designer? She could teach me how to plan a kitchen, what trends leave a lasting impression. Or she could be a businesswoman. She could show me how to structure a plan to set out on my own and succeed.

So many possibilities. Dad must have known. There had to be a reason he wouldn't tell me—and it didn't seem probable that whatever that reason was, it was a good one.

Maybe my mother had wanted me, and Dad kept us apart. Would he do that?

Secrets. They were never good.

Fueled by a new conviction that my dad had betrayed me, I whipped off the bed and snagged my laptop. My anger built as I waited for the screen to light up. Google knew everything. Dad couldn't keep his secrets forever.

My home screen lit up, and with a quick move of the mouse, I became Sarah Sharpe, private investigator.

Dale Sharpe. I stabbed the letters of his name on my keyboard, taking my anger out on the little buttons. A long list floated to the first page. Common name, which meant this could get tricky.

Dale Sharpe, Minden, Nebraska. The new search narrowed the field. Dad's construction company came up, along with his cell phone number.

A paid site drew my attention. *Find People.* Lucky for me, I knew tons of personal info about my dad, including his DOB and his social security number. Taxes. I was that girl, and it was going to pay off.

I entered the information and slid my debit card from my clutch thingy that I was still carrying around for no apparent reason.

Who needed a real detective?

Dale James Sharpe. Graduated from Minden High School in 1993. Basketball scholarship to Kansas University, revoked. (That was news—I'd have to find out why later. I doubted it was relevant to my cause). Marriage...now we came to it. *Married: 1993 to Cassandra Holtz. Children: Sarah Jane Sharpe, born 1993. Divorced 1994.*

Cassandra Holtz. Cassie—that was what Darcy called her.

I cleared the Google field. *Cassandra Holtz, Minden, Nebraska.*

The search brought a barrage of photos. Like a gazillion of them. All of the same woman with dark hair and vivid blue eyes.

The woman in all of those professional, model-type photos looked a little like me. Only way prettier. And her name...Cassandra von Holtzhausen. I clicked on the first link. It took me to a magazine article.

Cassandra von Holtzhausen, A-list bombshell model famous for her ever-revolving relationships, edgy lifestyle, and most notably, her striking blue eyes, was found dead in a rat-infested house...

Dead.

I stared at the computer, not seeing anything but the letters D-E-A-D.

Dad hadn't been lying. My mother was dead.

Chapter Twenty-Nine

SARAH

One should cry when she finds out a relative was gone, shouldn't she? My eyes remained so dry that they itched. Anger had scorched away all possibility of tears. I glanced back to the top of the article, searching for a date.

June 2003.

My mother had died when I was a child, and my dad didn't think I should know that? Why would he hide that from me? What did he have to lose if I knew my mother—apparently a runway model—had died of a drug overdose in some scumbag, roach-infested, bottom-feeder house?

I picked up my phone, stabbed at it until Dad's number floated to the screen, and hit Call.

He barely had a hello out before I laid into it. "How could you not tell me?"

"Tell you what?"

I whipped the computer screen so that I could see it from my standing position and began to read. "Cassandra von Holtzhausen, A-list bombshell model famous for her ever-revolving relationships, edgy lifestyle, and most notably, striking blue eyes, was found dead—"

"Where did you find that?" His voice sank low and hot, and he barely paused before he continued. "Did your aunt show you that?"

"No, Dad." I slapped the laptop closed. "I Googled it. Wasn't that hard. How could you hide that from me?"

"It's not your business. I told you to leave it alone."

"She was my *mother!*"

"Was, Sarah." His voice moved from hot and livid to dark and cold in one breath. "Was. And she wasn't a good one. We were better off without her—you were better off. There's no reason you needed to know then, and no reason to talk about it now."

I couldn't think of an argument. But I wanted to know. "What happened? Please, Dad, just talk to—"

"No!"

The stillness after his shout made me dizzy. I shut my eyes against the spinning reality of my life.

"Never again, Sarah." Dad's tone sent an icy chill over my arms. "Don't bring her up ever again."

Silence returned, followed by the empty click of a dropped call. He'd given me an ultimatum. If I wanted a Dad, I'd have to forget I'd ever had a mother.

JESSE

Shane supplied a crew, and we made a lot of progress in little time. The listing would go up on Monday, but I didn't need to be there for it. That meant I could wrap things up in a few days and head north. Now...to concoct a reason to do that.

I had a reason, right there in Omaha. The evening spent with Avery, Ken, and Sharon flitted through my mind. Ken's brother-in-law had a job for me. A big one, and it was the kind that Sarah would be amazing at. Perfect. We'd go tackle the job together and work on the other stuff between us too. One phone call, and the wheel would be rolling.

Finding my phone in the kitchen where I'd left it this morning, I saw I had two new texts.

I grinned. Both from Sarah.

9:54 a.m. *Jesus loves me...I believe.*

Air rushed from my lungs with such force that it hurt. I leaned back against the counter, my eyes closed. She believed. *Thank you, Jesus...*

My hand clutched the phone—of all days for me to not have it on me, it was this one. I couldn't wait to talk to her, to find out what happened, and to be sure she meant what I thought she'd said. My fingers actually trembled as I moved to call her.

But there was another text. Right. *Read that first.*

4:26 p.m. *My mother is dead.*

Oh no. How did she go from *Jesus loves me* to *my mother is dead* in less than twelve hours? My heart squeezed hard. What was God doing?

I tapped her number and hit Call, wondering how to start this conversation. Did I want the good news first, or the bad? Did the bad news negate the good news?

"Hey."

Her defeated tone sealed a decision. I didn't need an excuse to go north. I'd leave first thing in the morning. Or right after I got out of the shower that night.

Chapter Thirty

SARAH

Jesse: *Where are you now?*

I was pretty sure it was rude to text in church. But Jesse's message distracted me, and I couldn't help myself.

Me: *At church. With my aunt. Shouldn't you be in church somewhere?*

Jesse: *Yes. If I wasn't driving. Which church?*

Driving? Air caught in my lungs. Where was he driving to? Determined to look casual, I turned over the folded paper thingy I'd been given when I passed through the entry doors. Bethany Bible Church of Omaha. Shifting my attention back to the pastor, the argument ensued in my head. Texting right now was like carrying on a conversation during class. So rude. How long did church last? Jesse could probably wait.

My phone vibrated again.

Jesse: *Sarah, I need an addy.*

Oh, an addy too? He was coming... It was wrong how adrenaline raced through my whole body at the thought of seeing him. Today. Soon. Friends didn't physically respond that strongly, did they? Yeah, that whole *friends* deal was becoming foggier with every text.

Me: *Where are you?*

Jesse: *South side of Omaha. Need to know which direction to go. Addy please?*

Me: *You're texting while driving? Bad call.*

Jesse: *Voice command.*

Me: *Still a bad call. Pull over.*

Jesse: *Give me an address and I'll stop bothering you.*

Me: *Pull over and I'll give you an address.*

My phone stayed still for a few moments, during which I glanced to my cousin. Adam's eyebrows lifted, and his mouth moved in a knowing smirk. Eavesdropper.

Peachy. Not only was I completely distracted, muddled by the fact that Jesse, my *friend*, had apparently spent the night driving to Omaha, but judging by the wave of heat that just washed over my skin, I was beet red as well.

Adam shifted, taking the bulletin I'd balanced in between the folds of my dress, which I'd worn for the first time ever today of all days. With one hand he held it tilted so I could see, and with the opposite index finger he traced the address to the church.

My eyes darted from the words to his face. He grinned and then leaned to whisper. "It'll probably take him twenty minutes to get here. We'll be about done by then."

Focused on his eyes, I let the silence ask the questions rolling in my head. What did I do? Would Aunt Darcy be okay if I invited him over? Would Adam and Jeff take him in?

Adam's smile softened, as if he understood all of those fears. "YouTube guy, right?" he whispered again.

I nodded.

He slid my phone from my hand and tapped against the screen, sending Jesse the address. When he was done, he set it on the space in between our seats and then squeezed my shoulder. "Mom wanted to meet him."

As I was drawing a long breath, my phone vibrated again. I didn't pick it up, but I could read Jesse's message anyway.

Be there in twenty.

JESSE

Sunday mornings in Omaha left the interstate system fairly quiet. Good thing, because I really couldn't focus on the road.

With one fist wrapped around my lukewarm coffee and the other gripping the steering wheel, I let my mind traipse over the past week. Or rather, over the summer that had nearly passed behind me.

There were some seasons in life that redefined you.

The summer my parents died, for example. I'd suddenly realized how amazing I'd had it after that truck took them away. And in that, I found a paradox of comfort and agony. Their legacy was a gift, and somehow, without realizing it, I'd twisted it into a burden.

Funny, five years later and nearly to the day of that transformational moment, I bumped into a woman who would once again shift my life's paradigm. God had interesting methods, I guess.

Like that change half a decade before, I couldn't make out the next steps ahead of me. I knew what I wanted the future to look like, which was like a lifting of the fog I'd drifted through over the past few years, but this moment—these upcoming days? Not a clue.

Maybe once I saw her, everything would become clear.

Take ramp to 680 north on right.

Good thing Garmin kept track of where I was. I'd have ended up in Lincoln before I realized I'd missed my exit.

I glanced to the hand that was white-knuckling the steering wheel. When was the last time I'd been this tied up? *Be anxious for nothing...* Did that include Sarah? Tough call, because not only was I in love with her, but I had no idea what to expect from her. Talk about a roller coaster. Was she still on the ride, with those steep highs and deep drops, or had this last chunk of news she'd uncovered kicked her to the ground? The answer would be nice to know, because her ride had become mine, and I didn't know if I was supposed to buckle up or prepare to carry her through.

Maybe both.

Garmin chirped another direction in her computerized, know-it-all voice, and as I took the designated exit, a large church building appeared in the horizon. Destination ahead.

Deep breath.

Sarah ahead.

Stop shaking.

Future on the horizon.

Please, God, let that be the truth.

Guess I was about to find out.

As I pulled into the large parking lot, a steady trickle of Sunday best-dressed people seeped from the front doors, which meant service had just let out. Placing the cup I'd been clenching into my cup holder, I parked in a far corner and took up my phone again.

Me: *Garmin says I'm here. Are you?*

I scanned the scene beyond my windshield, searching for a raven-haired beauty in jeans. Plenty of young women milled around the front sidewalk, but none had the definitive solid-yet-feminine build of my Sapphira.

My Sapphira.

I tried to chide my own thinking—we still had some things to work through. My thoughts wouldn't listen. She was mine. My heart declared it. My thoughts seconded it. Now, to carry the motion...

The phone buzzed in my palm.

Sarah: *Yes. Getting ready to go. Where are you?*

A grin moved against my cheeks.

Me: *I'll find you.*

Grabbing my keys and leaving my coffee, which hadn't been any good anyway, I stepped from the truck and across the blacktop, still searching for a woman with short black hair, straight posture, work-molded shoulders, and dark-blue jeans.

A small group emerged from the door, an ebony head between two solid young men. Teenagers, more accurately. Maybe. The taller of the two looked to be twentyish. The cluster stopped to talk to a man in a tie—the pastor, most likely—and the woman stepped back enough so that I could get a clear view.

Dark hair, cut like I remembered. Square shoulders, solid arms.

And a teal dress.

I squinted. Definitely Sarah.

In a dress. Huh. No. Wow.

Without consciously deciding to, my pace doubled. All I could think about was my hunger for those blue eyes. My focus stayed solely on her, as if blinders to everything else had draped over my vision, until a masculine hand fell to her lower back.

Tall guy tugged her forward, his hand still resting where it had landed.

No.

He turned to the pastor-looking man, clearly making an introduction. He looked at her with a proud smile when the pastor moved to shake her hand.

No! No, no, no.

I jerked to a stop fifteen feet from the scene of a nightmare I didn't know I'd had before. I could actually hear my pulse, which was painful as it surged blood unnecessarily fast through my hot veins.

The man dropped his hand—finally—and Sarah drifted away from the loose circle again. Her attention lifted, and she began scanning the people beyond.

This was my deer-in-the-headlights moment. I was too close to hide, running would only draw more attention, and I most definitely did not want to meet whomever she was with.

Why hadn't she said something about another guy?

Why would God tease me like this?

Why...

I ran out of time for empty questions. The sapphires I'd been starving for landed on me, piercing my heart with a new and horrible kind of ache I'd never experienced before.

My Sapphira.

Didn't she know?

She had to know. I wasn't that discreet.

Was this another Troy she'd picked out to torture me? I hadn't done anything this time.

Not. Fair.

Our silent stare must have caused a scene. Suddenly I was aware of Tall Guy's attention on me. He took me in, eyebrow hiked, before shifting to look at Sarah. A smirkish grin spread over his face as he turned back to me.

Punk.

Panic gave way to pure irritation. I wasn't some passerby with a sudden infatuation. I knew this woman—her heart, her pain, her wanderings...

Her future.

Who was this guy to interfere? To smirk at something of which he knew nothing? Sarah was mine—should be mine. He was nothing.

He leaned down to speak to her, which flushed a fresh wave of heat over me. Sarah glanced up to him, her shy, sweet smile tightening the knot around my heart. She was supposed to look at me that way.

And then she did.

Hold up, what happened? Tall Guy, with his dang hand on her back again, guided her my way, and Sarah's smile landed on me.

"So you're the roofer." Tall Guy's hand left her body and stretched toward me.

The roofer? She didn't even give me a real name?

His grin widened. "Jesse, right?"

Oh. My lungs expanded. Air. Breathe. "Yeah, I'm Jesse Chapman."

Again, he looked from me to Sarah and back again. "We were hoping we'd get to meet you. I'm Adam—Sarah's cousin."

Cousin. One word, and my world shifted right side up. I mentally stepped outside of myself, witnessing my reaction. Crazy jealous. Psycho guy. Hopefully, I hadn't blown this first impression, because I was already on the blacklist with her dad.

And the reality was that Sarah wasn't really even mine.

Yet.

SARAH

My stomach wouldn't stop fluttering as I climbed into Jesse's truck. Climbed...not the right word. What a day to wear a dress for the first time in my whole life.

Had he noticed?

I shifted on the bench seat, much like I had when I sat down at the beginning of church, wondering if everything that should be covered was, and if I looked like madame troll, ruining a perfectly good dress.

I should have worn jeans. Much more comfortable, much more me. Except, maybe Jesse noticed.

With a sharp intake of air, I glanced to him as he settled behind the wheel. He met my gaze, and a half smile tugged on his mouth.

"That was quite a scene."

My heart squeezed and then dropped. I looked ridiculous, then.

He chuckled. "Your cousin must think I'm psycho."

Wait, what? "Adam?"

Jesse shook his head and inserted his key into the ignition. "Yeah, sorry about that."

Uh, what were we talking about?

"I should have called you first." He started the truck and shifted into drive. "I decided last night that I'd come." We eased to a stop at the intersection where the lot would dump onto the main road, and he looked at me again. "I was worried about you."

Melt into those green eyes and hope he would forgive me, or look away. Those were the options. I took the second, because I remembered how awkward things had gotten after our bowling incident.

"Thanks." I brushed my cheek with one hand, feeling the feverish heat and agonizing that he could see it coloring my skin. "I'm okay though."

A horn blipped from the car behind us, a little nudge forward because, hey, it was lunchtime, and the rest of the world was hungry.

My stomach had wound itself too tight to even think of food.

Jesse guided the truck forward and held quiet for two blocks before he spoke again. "I hope I'm going the right way. I lost track of your cousin's car."

Directions. Right. A perfectly sane and legitimate distraction. I squared my shoulders, kept my eyes trained on the road ahead, and hoped that he was too busy driving to notice that I was avoiding visual contact while I issued driving orders.

As we neared the final turn to my aunt's house, Jesse veered off course, cutting into a large parking lot at a busy grocery store.

"What are you doing?"

"I'm southern."

"What does that mean? Southern guys don't know how to follow directions?"

He parked and then reached across the cab, tweaking my nose. "You're so cute."

I mentally beat down both the heat and the desire to make that little gesture actually mean something.

"Yeah, that's what all the guys say." Yikes, not the best way to make nothing out of it. I rushed to fill the air before he could respond. "What does being southern have to do with going the wrong way?"

"Well"—he tipped his imaginary hat—"my mama taught me never to show up at someone else's house for a meal empty handed, especially someone you don't know."

My eyebrows pushed against the skin above my nose. "She did, huh?"

"Yep."

And with that syllable, he was out of the truck.

I thought about the scene that was about to ensue at Darcy's house. Adam had been nice, though his emphasis on the word *friend* when he first spoke with Jesse unraveled all sorts of frayed edges in my stomach. Jesse was a friend, and Adam didn't need to make it sound like I'd made him out to be more. What must Jesse think of me?

"Hey." He stood a few steps outside my door, which he'd opened for me. "You coming?"

"Yeah." I scooted out, acutely self-conscious about the stupid dress. How did you get out of a pickup in one of these things without flashing the world behind you? How did you keep everything pinned down discreetly while the wind stirred the skirt wherever it willed?

No more dresses. Ever.

Jesse's hand cupped my arm as I touched the ground, as if he was escorting an actual lady.

"You look nice today." The warmth of his hand remained even after he shut the door and we started across the parking lot. "Did I tell you that?"

No. He hadn't. But saying so would tell him that I'd noticed that he hadn't and that I hoped he would.

"I don't know." I pushed a smile onto my lips. "Thanks."

That was smooth, right? Nothing desperate or presumptuous or idiotic. I could handle this.

The AC slammed against my skin as we passed through the sliding doors, almost giving me a headache from extreme temperature shock. I pulled in a lungful of air, noting that Jesse had yet to remove his hand, and schooled every facial expression to look passive. Relaxed. Normal.

Yeah, this was normal stuff for me...I always wore girly clothes, and having a man escort me was par in my life.

Jesse stopped by the produce area. "Okay, so what do I get?"

I looked up to him. Oh goodness, those eyes. On me. Smiling.

Nope. We were friends, this was normal, and I didn't have any reason to feel...dizzy? That was dumb.

I shrugged. "Oranges?"

He snorted. "Cute. I'm not showing up to your aunt's house with a bag of oranges. Try again."

"I don't have any idea. I don't know this practice."

"What do they like?"

I stood mute, feeling my eyes round. "Food?"

With a headshake, he rolled his eyes, which for some stupid reason, I thought was adorable.

"How about dessert? Did your aunt already make something?"

After a mental rerun of the stuff I saw Darcy gathering this morning, I shook my head. "No, I don't think so. We were going to grill kabobs. Don't think I saw anything sweet."

His satisfied smile, pinned right on me, made my stomach swirl, which only intensified when his hand moved from my arm to my back as he guided me deeper into the produce department.

"Have you ever grilled peaches?" he asked.

"No."

"Good. You'll love it." He bagged eight of the fuzzy things and then guided me toward the frozen section. "We need whipped topping. Gotta have whip."

"Okay..."

And then he stopped, well before we reached the freezer.

"What's your favorite color?"

He was always taking U-turns on me, and I never knew what he was thinking. With a glance at him, I found him looking across the aisle at the—

Flowers?

My favorite color? Must have been a slip. "Darcy likes yellow."

He looked at me. "That's not what I asked."

The throbbing pulse thing started again. What was he asking? "Color, Sapphira."

I couldn't beat down the heat sprawling over my face. "Depends on what we're talking about. I like white on a house. Deep browns for floors. Light blue on walls..."

His laughter halted my list. "Such the carpenter's daughter." Then he stepped across the aisle, away from me, and snatched a handful of mixed blossoms.

"Here." He held them out to me.

I did nothing but stare.

He took my hand and pushed the bunch into my palm. "Study them, and you can tell me later which one you like best."

Why would I do that? I swallowed, wishing my head wasn't spinning with confusion. A man didn't just get a girl flowers. Not in my world. But it couldn't mean anything. Jesse had been clear about our boundaries, and I was going to respect them.

Wished he would too.

Silly girl, those blossoms weren't for me. He'd meant them for Darcy. He'd only wanted to know my favorite color because he was quirky. That had to be it.

He finished his shopping, paid—and made sure the flowers landed back in my hands after the clerk was done with them—and then we headed back in the right direction.

Darcy and Rick welcomed Jesse like it was nothing unusual for me to bring a guy to their house. Thank the great big heavens. Seriously. I couldn't handle any more awkwardness wrapping around me. They chatted about his traveling, how he got into it, and why he continued, while the kabobs sizzled on the grill.

"I know a guy that would want to meet you," Rick said as he transferred the sticks of veggies and meat from the grill to a platter. "He's got a project north of here—a big one. Actually, it's a joint project. Several churches in the area have come together to purchase a block of houses in a rough area of town..."

Jesse grinned, nodding. "I know this one. I work with a guy back in Valentine who was telling me I needed to contact his brother-in-law about that project. That's why I'm here."

Oh. That was why. As reality dimmed my daydreams, I glanced back to the colorful blossoms Darcy had inserted into a vase of water.

"How 'bout that." Rick laughed. "Sounds like your friend's brother-in-law is our associate pastor. Can I introduce you to him?"

So, did God plan these things, or did they just happen? I sat back in my wicker chair on the deck, listening to the men as they grew more enthusiastic about this coincidence, wondering how the theater of life scrolled out. Did God plan for me to meet Jesse? If He did, what was His purpose, exactly? I was glad I met him, and as the song that had become my anthem the past few days played through my head—*Jesus, He loves me*—I was so enormously glad I'd met the Carpenter's Son as a result.

But this life right now...

What did I do with Jesse? I couldn't make my heart stop lifting with a hope that things could change between us—had changed. That terrified me. With things between me and my dad being so rough, and finding out that my mother—the rock-star model, apparently—had died when I was still a kid, I couldn't handle any more emotional trauma.

Rejection from Jesse would require emotional life support. Best not go there.

We gathered around the outdoor table on Rick and Darcy's deck and prayed for our meal, and I tried to feel normal while I pulled my food off the skewer. Jesse blended as Jesse always blended. Easygoing. Lively. Comfortable.

I fell into my usual silence, trying not to sink under the ache of disappointment. Surely I'd get over it.

Adam and Jeff both had plans. Something about sand volleyball somewhere not there. Rick promised to call Grant North—the associate pastor whom Jesse apparently needed to meet, and then he and Darcy left for their Sunday walk.

Did they always take a Sunday walk?

That left me on the deck alone with the guy who had become my best friend—something I'd never had—and my deepest disappointment.

I stared at my hands. Silence swirled in the warm summer breeze. *God help, because I feel too much to be indifferent.*

Jesse leaned against the table, his forearms pressing onto the glass. "Talk to me, Sapphira."

I glanced to him, the pain building inside me. "You still call me that."

He sat a little straighter. He looked down to the table, and I thought there was a hint of fire on his face. "Does it bother you?"

Yes. But not because I didn't like it. "No. I—you hadn't for a while."

Silence again. I hated it.

"You drove a long way." There. No more silence.

His head came up, and when those green eyes landed on me, there was no way that I could convince myself that I could just be his friend.

He shifted, brushing his fingers against mine. "I was worried about you."

Emotion built so thick in my throat that I wondered if I'd suffocate. "Why?"

"I told you. I care about you."

Yeah, he did. Right before he said we couldn't be more than friends. Clearly he did care. I shut my eyes, not wanting him to see how much I wanted him to be more.

His voice dropped, soft and deep and threaded with concern. "Tell me about your mom." His hand warmed my shoulder. "What happened?"

Steady, there, my fragile heart. "I Googled her because my dad wouldn't tell me anything." I stopped, pulling in a cleansing breath.

"You wanted to meet her."

"Yeah. I don't know why." Pushing my shoulders back, I lifted my gaze from the table. I wasn't defeated. This life, this week, wasn't fair. But I wasn't beat. Not by my dad, or my dead mother, or by Jesse Chapman. "Now I know though. She's dead. Has been for years."

"Sarah..." Jesse studied me, the concern on his face deepening as a shadow of confusion passed through his eyes. He stared at me, as if trying to read my thoughts.

Read them, Chapman. I'm not beat. Whatever this was between us, it wasn't going to take me down.

He pushed away from the table and stood. Leaving again.

Immediately I regretted the way I'd mentally slapped him, because he seemed to feel it, as if I'd struck him with my palm.

His retreat paused after two steps, and then those tanned arms circled around my shoulders. "I'm so sorry."

After a sharp intake of air, I worked to unscramble my thoughts. He wasn't leaving. He was holding me, and that pulled all of the emotion to the top again. Not just about him, but about my mom, about my dad. I didn't know what to do with it all, and I didn't want it to crash over me anymore.

"I didn't even know her, so..." It shouldn't matter to me if she died.

"You wanted to."

I did. I had no explanation for why. Why would I have searched out a woman who had abandoned me?

"It's okay that it hurts, Sarah."

Was it? "I wish my dad had told me—" The words caught. I was going to cry? Because of a dead woman I didn't even know? Yes. And because my dad had lied to me, and because of it... "Maybe it wouldn't have stung quite as much when she never reached out to me on my birthdays. No Christmas cards. No graduation call. If I'd known, then—"

With his arms still around me, Jesse kneeled beside my chair. "I know. It's okay."

"No it's not," I spat. "Why wouldn't he tell me? What good was it to keep it secret, to make me find out from the stupid Internet?"

Darcy's voice, soft and tentative, came from behind us. "Guilt and pain and fear do strange things to people."

We turned in unison to find her at the deck door.

"I'm sorry. I didn't mean to spy." She stepped toward the grill. "Just forgot my sunglasses." After grabbing what she'd come for, she turned, settling her eyes on me.

Jesse's hold loosened, and he dropped the arm closest to Darcy. But the opposite hand found my shoulder, and his thumb ran small, soft circles into the muscle. For a moment, Darcy looked at him, and she seemed to smile without really smiling before she slid her attention back to me.

"Your dad..." She sighed. "He's had a hard life, and he doesn't know what to do with all of the baggage. And the stuff with your mom—there's still a lot of guilt and pain there. He does love you though, Sarah." She moved close enough to reach a hand across the table to cover one of mine. "Truly he does. And he's scared to death of losing you."

After squeezing my fingers, she settled her sunglasses on her face and headed for the door, touching Jesse's shoulder as she moved by.

The air felt heavy as I processed my life all over again. I couldn't talk about my mom with my dad. He'd never tell me about her, what it was he liked about her, why they fell in love in the first place. Pushing him was severing our relationship. I didn't want that.

I didn't want to keep living as I was either. My life needed to be mine, to mean something, and to move forward.

Again my eyes slid shut, and a new wave of emotion crashed over me.

"It's okay to cry."

I shook my head.

He turned me to face him, cupping my cheek in his palm. "I know grief, Sarah. I know it's not the same—our stories are very different—but I also know this: When everything goes dark and lonely and sad, one thing is still true. Jesus loves me. He loves you."

My lips trembled, and when he pulled me to his shoulder, I leaned against him.

"I promise you," he whispered into my hair, "it's enough."

Chapter Thirty-One

JESSE

Heartsick, but not alone. Still a hard spot, but not the awful bleakness that Sarah had been living in. Praise God for that.

I leaned back against the padded seat of Rick's Pathfinder and shut my eyes. The long night of driving had caught up with me, and it was tempting to doze off. I'd need to find a hotel after this meeting. Tomorrow, I'd figure out a plan, which would most likely include renovation houses in North Omaha. Avery would squeal in her Dolly-pitched voice and say something like, *The Lord is moving, isn't He?*

Yes, He was.

About this Sarah deal, Lord...I don't know what I'm doing. Could you move there too?

Rick interrupted my prayer, drawing me back from the hovering place between reality and sleep. "Darcy has been praying for you the past few days."

"Few days?"

"Yeah, I know we just met you, but she heard Sarah listening to that YouTube video you sent her the other day, and she asked about you."

Aha. That explained "the roofer" comment from Adam. "Thanks. Tell her to keep praying."

Rick cleared his throat. "Are you in a sticky situation?"

"Not sticky. Delicate. And foreign."

"Wanna tell a near stranger about it?"

I chuckled. "Sarah's talked about you and Darcy, so I'm not sure you're really a stranger. I'm just not sure what to do with her."

His shoulders jerked straight. "Careful there. Dars and I love her like a daughter, so if you're—"

"I'm not." I met his look with a quick glance between us, hoping he could see my sincerity. "I wouldn't drive all night without a place to stay if I was just testing the waters. But I'm not sure where she's at."

With his focus back on the road, Rick nodded. "With you, or other things?"

"All of the above."

Rick paused, tapping his steering wheel. "With you...I don't think you need to wonder. Those other things, I think she's getting it."

I wondered if we were talking about the same stuff—and given the fact that I already messed up with her in Lexington, I did have to wonder about things between her and me. There were always consequences, even when you were not sure what they'd look like.

"She's still a little unsteady—and her life is such a maze." I glanced to him to make sure he wasn't misunderstanding me. His expression stayed open. "I'm not scared of that. I just don't want to go stepping into places I won't be able to fill."

He nodded. "Understood. And I respect that. You've already made such a difference in her life. She actually asked us if she could come to church today. That's never happened."

Dangerous, that kind of attribution. "That wasn't me."

He smiled. "No. Guess not. But God's been using you, and Darcy and I are grateful." He glanced at me again. "And you do have a place to stay. Whether Sarah's around or not."

"Thanks. I might need it, and you might regret it if this job is as big as I'm guessing."

"Oh, it's big. And if you can't take it on, you just say so. I don't mean to volunteer you for a ball and chain."

Pretty sure we were talking about the North O project, not Sarah. "I volunteered myself." For both.

I thought he understood that, because he chuckled again as he pulled into a drive belonging to another split-level home. Man, these Omaha driveways...steep and short. I'd hate to be around in the winter.

"Okay, here we are." Rick cut the engine and unsnapped his seat belt. "Grant's high energy, and he's got big visions that don't always touch any sort of reality, so if you need to ground him, just go ahead and do it. You're the expert, not him."

"Actually, we should have brought Sarah."

With a cocked eyebrow, Rick paused to look at me.

"She's really good at renos. She has vision, not to mention the skills to make it happen."

Approval swept over his expression, which kind of bothered me. I wasn't handing Sarah unwarranted compliments. After shutting the door, I met Rick on the other side of the truck, and we started up the set of long stairs to the front door.

"You'll do her good," he said.

"She can do good all on her own." I bumped his arm so he'd look at me. "Serious."

"I know she's got the skills. But the confidence... You're exactly the guy for that job."

My heart skipped uncomfortably. I'd love to be that guy... But it was time to change the subject.

Rick reached for the doorbell, and I stood back. Grant North was exactly the kind of guy Rick had described. Energetic, a bit of a dreamer, and determined. Had me figured for the coordinator before I'd laid eyes on any sort of building or plan, and wanted to give me a full tour of the project that very moment.

"Hold up, Grant." Rick snagged the man before he could grab his car keys. "Jesse's had a long drive. Plus, it's Sunday evening. I just wanted to introduce you, maybe give you a chance to set up a time to meet this week."

"Right." Grant grinned, his enthusiasm undeterred. "How about tomorrow? We can do lunch, and then I'll take you to the site."

Tomorrow. I had to mentally tell myself not to let my shoulders droop. Actually had visions of hanging out with Sarah for one whole, uninterrupted day. Guess not. Maybe she'd come with me.

Either way, I couldn't really say no, because I knew in my gut that I'd do this job. This was where I was needed next, and that was the commitment I'd made when I took on my parents' dream.

I nodded, holding out my hand. "I'll meet you at the church."

Grant returned my handshake, and that was that.

Cicadas buzzed their vibrating symphony as Rick and I pulled up to his house.

"I assume you have some stuff?" he asked after we both shut the doors to his vehicle.

I nodded. "I didn't assume you'd take me in though. It's not a problem for me to find a hotel."

"Nope." He shoved his hands into his jeans pockets. "That won't do. We have room, and you can stay as long as this project takes. If you're taking it on."

Strangers took me in quite often. It didn't usually feel awkward. This did. I wasn't sure if it was because I didn't really know what I was getting into here—I'd never coordinated a whole project on my own, let alone one this size—or if it was because of the hazy stuff between Sarah and me.

"Thanks." I glanced to my feet, wondering if I sounded as strained as I felt. "Mind if I talk to Sarah before I decide?"

"No problem." He tipped his head toward the house, a *let's go* kind of gesture, and my heart picked up its pace. I wasn't sure why.

Darcy was in the kitchen, emptying the dishwasher when we came in. She offered me tea, asked how it went with Grant, and then finished with the last clean plate.

"Sarah's downstairs." She smiled and then turned toward the back door.

Permission to depart. I took it.

I found Sarah on the couch in the family room, dress replaced by gym shorts and a T-shirt. Her feet were tucked around her, and her laptop was perched on her legs. She stared at the screen, her eyes sheened.

Easing next to her, I brushed a bare foot. It flexed but didn't jerk away.

"Not ticklish?"

A tiny smile poked onto her mouth. "Not there."

I lifted my eyebrows and waited for her to look at me. When she did, she wore a locked-down, *there's no way you're going to find out* kind of smirk.

Mack had said I liked a challenge. Apparently Mack was correct. I lifted my hand, intent on testing her neck, but she intercepted my fingers.

"Don't." The small smile faded completely, and her eyes shifted from playful and daring to closed and almost hurt.

Confusion draped heavily over me. I wanted so much to be close to this woman, to see her smile, hear her laugh. To show her how much I cared. Loved.

Studying her profile while that thought passed through my mind made my chest squeeze, and our kiss rushed through my memory. I had acted purely on desire that day. It had been reckless, and now she didn't trust me.

Or maybe she didn't want me anymore.

No. I couldn't accept that.

I shifted, respecting her space but not willing to abandon my hopes. "What are you doing?"

She sighed. "Reading."

Not for pleasure, apparently. I tipped the screen of her computer so that I could see. An article from a popular gossip publication filled the space, the date long since passed.

Cassandra von Holtzhausen...

The story didn't matter much to me until I scrolled down. On the bottom right of the page, a photograph changed everything. The eyes of the dead woman were strikingly similar to the eyes I'd seen in my dreams.

I could have sworn I was looking at Sarah.

SARAH

Jesse pulled in a sharp breath when my mother's picture settled on the screen. He stared like he was looking at a ghost.

"You look just like her."

I actually snorted. Me? Cassandra von whoever was a national spectacle in the world of modeling. I was a butch-looking carpenter girl in the world of nowheresville.

Beyond our blue eyes, I looked nothing like the woman. Jesse was insane.

His fingers left the screen of my computer and came to my chin. He turned me to face him—so that he could do a closer inspection.

"Just like her."

The intensity in his gaze set fire to my skin. I pulled away from his hold and turned back to the screen. "Doesn't matter. She's dead."

His hand covered my foot again, though he didn't try to tickle it this time. "Why are you reading this again?"

A question I'd been wondering myself. I'd been staring at the horrible image for close to an hour, rereading the story, wondering why Cassandra von whatever chose to die in a rathole rather than be my mother. Childish thoughts for a full-grown woman.

"I don't know."

He reached for the laptop again. "How about we check out something else?"

Before I answered, his fingers pecked at the keyboard, and the autofill on Google found what he was looking for before he finished typing.

Jesus, He loves me.

The loading wheel spun, and I closed my eyes in the pause. The dead woman who had given me blue eyes still stared vacantly back in my mind. Jesse shifted, and suddenly I was gathered against him. The music began, and he stroked my hair against the backdrop of lyrics I had memorized over the past few days.

"Do you believe that He loves you?"

"Yes." Didn't I? I swallowed. "I want to." My mouth quivered. "I just wish I knew who I am."

"You won't find who you are in a story about your mom." Jesse spoke softly, still holding me against his shoulder. "You won't find who you are with a man, or in a job, or in your dad's past, or your aunt's church. These things may shape you, but they aren't the core of who you are."

Jesse moved, his hands gripping my shoulders and pushing me so that he could look into my face. "The truest thing about who you are is that you are loved." Rough and warm, his palms slid against my jawline to frame my face. "Do you believe that?"

Biting my lip, my eyes slid shut. I nodded. I did believe—and a ray of warmth slid over the barren chill of my heart. Loved. By God. This was truth. No matter what my dad did. No matter who my mother was. Whether or not my life would intertwine with Jesse's. Whatever path my future would take.

I was loved.

"Yes." I whispered. "I believe."

His thumb brushed over my cheekbone, and then his hands fell away. "Let that define you."

I sniffed, opening my eyes to search his. Whatever feelings we had or didn't have between us, this was more important. He was desperate for me to hear him, and I ached to understand.

"Everything else may shatter. Life is unpredictable like that. But if you define yourself with the truth of God's love, you will always have an anchor. Because His love will never change."

His words settled around me, in me. I ran them over and over in my mind, memorizing them. Letting them sink deeper until they planted in my heart. I was loved by God, and His love would never change.

There were moments in life that redefined everything. That was mine. Nothing really changed on the outside—my mother was still dead, my dad was still not talking to me, I still didn't know what kind of future I had, and my heart still ached for the man sitting next to me.

Yet, everything changed on the inside.

Love did that, I guessed. It gave hope where there was only hurt. It redefined life. Or maybe it rebirthed what was dead.

Because of love, I had life. That was what changed.

Chapter Thirty-Two

JESSE

"What do you think?"

I'd managed to snag Sarah by the elbow and discreetly held her back in the doorway of the crumbling, horrible-smelling house we'd just toured. One of four. Wow. They were more than a project. To Grant, they were almost an obsession. For me? They were the next twelve months of my life, at least. Overwhelming would be putting it mildly.

Sarah looked over her shoulder back into the house that screamed abuse from every corner. "It's a big undertaking."

"Yeah." I snorted. "Maybe they need a stick of dynamite."

One eyebrow hiked on her beautiful face.

"Seriously," I said. I meant it. It'd be easier to build from the ground up on all of these houses. "The electrical, the plumbing... Let's not even think about what's living in the attics and inside the walls. These are the worst houses I've ever seen."

Staring at me, she swallowed, a hint of rebuke in her eyes. "Can't see past the neglect?"

Ouch. I'd been so poetic about old houses and reno projects back when I was working on new builds and wasn't in charge. I rubbed the back of my neck. "Yeah, only this isn't neglect. It's abuse."

She turned away and stepped toward the staircase that divided the interior into two equal parts. As she drew closer to the first riser, her hand settled on the fluted newel post that should have been holding the railing solid. It quivered beneath her palm.

"Grant has vision."

I knocked against the doorframe with my foot. "Borderline crazy."

She chuckled and turned back to me. "Imagine coming through that door when it's done. Seeing it restored. That would be something."

"It would. Except it sounds exhausting. And did I mention crazy?"

Her head moved from side to side as she stepped toward me. My fingers suddenly itched to remove her hat, to trace the determined lines on her face and to draw confidence from them. Rick's words seeped through my mind—that I'd be good for her, give her confidence. Wasn't true. Here we were, in a house that was literally crumbling around us, and she knew without a doubt what it could be—what it should be—and that I could do it.

"Imagine, Jess, that you were here not as a contractor but as someone else." She scanned the space, a ramshackle of broken furniture, old drapery, and garbage. It smelled like sweat and urine and decay...and maybe even death. A sheen glazed her eyes as her look transformed into a distant stare. "It looks like the place in the picture."

Picture? Picture...picture. The one on the Internet. The one where her mother's lifeless eyes stared into the camera lens.

This was more than a renovation. This was a way to transform the legacy that she'd been handed. Her mother's life ended in a house just like this.

She wanted to take the ugly and transform it, to make it not just useful but beautiful. Because she was the Carpenter's daughter, and she had her Father's heart. Emotion swarmed me as I watched her. Everything she'd wrestled with that summer, and the work God was doing in her, now swirled in my heart. I pressed my trembling lips together and reached for her shoulders.

I couldn't find the words to tell her I knew what she was thinking, or that in that moment she was the most beautiful woman I'd ever seen. Or how much I loved her. So I tugged her toward me, wrapped my arms around her, and held her against my chest, hoping she'd hear it all in the rhythm of my heartbeat.

I thought maybe she understood, because she leaned against me and after a moment, circled her arms around my waist.

This. I wanted a lifetime of this. We could conquer this house, and the other houses, and any other disaster we stepped into. Together we were a complete team.

Sarah lifted her head and started to pull away. "So you'll do it?"

I wasn't ready to let her go. "Are you going to help me?"

She leaned back to study my face, which was bold for her. I couldn't read the questions there, but I knew she was asking them.

"I need your help." No. *I need you.* That was what I should have said.

A small smile settled on her mouth. "You know I can't say no to you." She turned away and skittered out of the house.

Not fair. That kind of conversation was not supposed to end with her back to me.

I had no choice but to let it go and to follow her toward Grant's waiting car. Putting away the desire to taste her lips, however, was a much more demanding task. Why'd she run away like that?

I'd ask her. As soon as we got back to Rick and Darcy's.

Didn't work out that way. Sarah's aunt and uncle had all sorts of questions about the project, and somewhere in the mix, Sarah announced that she was going back home.

She sat across from me on a wicker chair in the shade of a locust tree as the four of us talked. "I haven't talked to my dad in a few days," she said, refusing to look at me. "I need to go back."

True. I wished she'd told me earlier. How was all of this supposed to work?

SARAH

I folded the last of my clothes and slid them into my bag. Hadn't brought much, so it didn't take long to pack, but I'd been hiding in my borrowed bedroom in Darcy's basement for nearly an hour.

I just couldn't face him anymore.

Knowing he'd come for the project houses set my daydreams straight, but Jesse drew out the vulnerable parts of me that were raw and tender. It'd be easy to slip into the temptation to stay here under the guise of helping him like he wanted, while hoping the whole time his hugs would become more frequent and tip his heart toward me.

But that would be foolish hope, and I couldn't tell him that. Leaving was the only option. And I really did need to see my dad.

"Knock, knock." A set of knuckles tapped on the doorframe to my room, and Jesse stood in the opening, his hands shoved into his pockets.

I glanced away before we made eye contact, and focused unusually hard on zipping my bag. "Hey."

"You're not leaving tonight, are you?"

Shrugging, I tossed the bag onto the floor. "Yeah. I want to catch my dad when he's not working, and I don't know what project he's on right now, so I don't know what time he'll leave in the morning."

Jesse wandered in, looking uncomfortable, and slowly sat on the end of my bed. "When did you decide you were going?"

"I don't know." I crossed my arms and leaned back against the wall. Something felt strained between us. Why was this friendship so emotionally demanding?

He looked at me, and it seemed that his face hardened. "Wish you'd said something earlier."

"What?"

"I just got here, and..."

And what?

One hand pushed through his hair—which had been cut—making it stand up. "It's just that...well, I mean...I need your help. I thought we'd do this together."

Together. A word with barbs hidden within its syllables. But he couldn't have known how that one statement would needle me.

"I've got the pictures. We got the footprints down on paper. I'll work on it."

"But—" He pushed up off the bed and took a step toward me. "It'd be better, easier if you were here." Another step closed the gap between us. "I need you...on this project."

The fact that he had to qualify his need was exactly why I couldn't stay. "I need to get things straightened out with my dad."

"I know."

"Do you?"

"Yeah, I do. It's just..."

"Look, I'll help you, okay? I promise I will, but I can't be here now."

"You seem to run away a lot, Sarah."

I pushed off the wall and stood straight. "Run away?"

"Yes."

"What am I running from?"

He stared at me, blinked, and then turned away. The way his shoulders caved made my heart sink. Why was he doing this? Because he wanted me on a job? That wasn't fair.

"I feel like you're manipulating me."

His shoulders rolled back, and he turned his look back to me. "What?"

"You can't make me feel bad about this, Jesse. It's not fair. My dad...he's all I have. I can't lose him. You're making me feel bad about a job when I am on a slippery slope with my father. I have to go back, and I thought you'd understand that."

Jesse stared at his feet as he rubbed his neck. The moments pounded by with heavy silence, and then he sighed. "I know. I'm sorry. I didn't mean to be manipulative."

The look he pinned on me was both disappointed and sincere. What was I supposed to do with this man? He managed to touch on every emotion possible in my heart.

He pushed his hands back into his pockets and swung around to leave my room, shoulders drooping again.

Guilt pushed forward. "Jesse, wait." He paused but didn't look at me. I darted a look around my room, searching for something to make our unease die. My vision settled on my laptop. "We could work on those drawings for a bit, if you want."

He turned, an attempt at a smile on his mouth. "You should hit the road."

"No. I can give it another hour." I reached for my computer. "Okay?"

His eyes slid shut, and he didn't respond for the longest moment. How was I supposed to read him?

JESSE

Drawings? Couldn't have cared less about them. All I wanted was to fill my arms with her.

But she'd called me manipulative. I was having a serious problem with that personal flaw that only recently had come to my attention.

Why was she leaving all of the sudden? To fix things with her dad—which if I thought was the truth of the whole deal, would be a good thing. But I felt like she was running. From me.

I'd come back. Made the trip in a straight-through-the night drive. That should have counted for something.

My heart felt whiplashed. But if drawings would buy me another hour...

"Sure." I tipped my head toward the couch in the room beyond hers.

After grabbing her laptop, she followed me to the family room, and we settled on the cushions. She on one side, me on the other. Not going to work. So while she flipped open the screen, I slid over. Confidence had siphoned from me over the past hour, but I worked up enough boldness to lay my arm on the space behind her. She didn't seem to notice.

With the pads of her fingers, she tapped the file marked *Reno*, and a picture bloomed on the screen. Only it wasn't of any of the houses we'd looked at earlier that day.

I leaned forward. "What's this?"

"Wrong file. Sorry." She moved to close it.

I snagged her hand and held it. "No, wait. What is it?"

"A house."

Yes, Sherlock. Next clue please. "Do you have another project in the works?"

"No." Her answer came fast, and then she hesitated.

I also noted that she hadn't tugged her hand from mine. "No?"

"Yes."

"Yes?"

"What?"

I chuckled. She wiggled away from my grasp, but her hand fell limp rather than closing the file. With a reverse pinching motion, I expanded the picture.

"For sale." I glanced to her. "Looks like a project."

"Yeah."

"Where is it?"

"Outside of Minden, toward the interstate."

I grinned. "Are you bidding on someone else's project or buying your own?"

"I'm not doing anything at the moment."

"Why not?"

She shrugged. "I saw it on my way here. I was curious."

Moving the picture so I could see the details more clearly, I examined the house. Not nearly the disaster I was taking on. Actually, it looked like a nice place. Well, like it had a whole lot of potential to be a nice place.

I shifted to grab my phone from my pocket, and the movement pushed me toward her. A hint of warm vanilla filled my nostrils. I breathed deeper.

"You smell good."

One dark eyebrow hiked over her blue eyes. "I do, huh?"

"Yep." I leaned closer again and sniffed. "What do you wear?"

Now both eyebrows raised. "Clothes?"

I laughed. "Yes. What is that smell, ornery?"

"Soap, I guess. I don't know what you're talking about."

See? This was why I loved this girl. So not fussy. Simple.

She pushed my shoulder back as if I were invading her space. "You ask weird questions."

Yes, I did. But maybe she'd feel special knowing I noticed her—everything about her. And heaven knew I wanted her to feel special.

I returned my attention to the phone in my hand and leaned toward the computer on her lap so that I could make out the numbers on that sign.

"What are you doing now?" She snatched the cell and looked at the five numbers I'd managed to punch in. "You can't call."

I covered both her hand and the phone. "Why not?"

"Because you don't know anything about it."

"I would if you told me."

She tugged the phone free again, hit the Home button, and then closed the file on her computer. "This isn't what we were working on."

"Tell me."

With a determined set of her jaw, she ignored me, focusing instead on the screen, and opened the file with the Omaha project in it.

Nope. That wasn't going to slide. With my thumb and index finger, I turned her chin so that she'd look at me. "Tell. Me."

Her expression widened and then fell into a soft gaze. Kissable. So, so kissable. But then she lifted her chin and moved away.

"I thought maybe I could buy it." She sighed. "It was just an idea, that's all."

"To live in?"

A growl curled from her chest, and she set the computer onto the table. "Yes. To live in. You're just like my dad."

I was pretty sure I was nothing like her dad. "What does that mean?"

She pushed off the couch and moved two steps out of my reach. "You don't think I can do it."

"That is *not* true." I stood too but didn't move toward her. "Why do you think I was calling?"

Her bottom lip went under her teeth.

"Know what I think?"

She wouldn't look at me.

"This doubt or fear or whatever it is, it isn't coming from me or from your dad."

Quiet settled between us as she still refused to meet my gaze. I stepped forward, letting my hands drift over her arms. "I learned something last week, Sapphira."

She finally lifted her eyes to mine. "What?"

"Gifts aren't meant to be ignored."

A tiny smile lifted the corners of her mouth, but then she looked down again. "What if I fail?"

"You'll learn something along the way, and then you'll try again."

"But my dad—everyone in Minden—will think I'm nuts."

I shrugged. "God won't."

"How do you know?"

"Because even if *you* don't know you completely, *I* know you. And I know that God has given you a gift of vision, and He's equipped you with skills. He didn't do that so that you would never use them. This desire to try, that's not a mistake, Sarah. He gives us wings so that we can fly."

She searched me as if looking for validation, or maybe strength.

I was that guy—the one Rick said she needed. The one to build her confidence. I didn't know the words to describe that kind of honor.

"You can do this, Sarah Sharpe." My fingers slid over her arms again, this time anchoring on her hands. "You're not going to fail—not in the long run."

Her eyes closed and she whispered, "I'm scared."

"That's okay. I'll help you. I'll be right there with you."

Those blue eyes flew open again. "What about the Omaha project?"

Yeah, that.

I leaned until my nose brushed hers. She inhaled sharply and then froze.

"We'll figure it out," I whispered.

Her eyes slid shut, and I brushed her mouth with mine. The hands that I'd enclosed gripped mine, but she didn't kiss me back.

She didn't pull away either.

We had a lot to figure out. But we would. Together.

SARAH

I wondered if he knew what he was doing this time. I forced my eyes open, determined to ask. I didn't need to. His gaze, soft and deep and completely open, stayed fastened on me.

One hand left mine and gently cradled my face. "I'm not trying to manipulate you."

Closing my eyes again, I leaned forward, and his lips grazed my forehead.

"You have to be straight with me, Jesse. I feel too much to play games with you."

His other hand came up to frame my jaw, and he tipped my head back just enough so that I would look at him. "No games."

But two weeks ago he said this couldn't happen.

He pulled me forward again, and before I could put voice to my questions, I was lost in his kisses. Thoughts melted away, and I responded to the slow, gentle pressure pulsing warm pleasure over me. I gripped the tails of his button-down shirt, which he'd left untucked, and moved closer, molding myself against him.

"Sarah..." His mouth left mine, and he moved to grip my shoulders.

No. Déjà vu. I drew in a quivering breath and moved to step away.

With his hands still holding my arms, Jesse caught my retreat and found my lips again. For a moment, and then he pulled away again. "No games, Sarah."

I sought his face, trying to understand. What would this relationship look like? I had very limited—and bad— experience. I didn't know what he expected. Why would he kiss me like that and then push me away?

He raised a hand and traced my mouth with his thumb. "I promise."

My fears must have been palpable. Jesse tucked my head against his shoulder and wrapped his arms around me. After a moment's hesitation, I moved to hold him, and he kissed the top of my head.

"I want to get this right, Sapphira."

I loved when he called me Sapphira.

"Okay." What did right look like, exactly?

"I need to meet your dad." He leaned back, capturing my chin. "Proper this time. Can I come with you?"

My smile was genuine, even if hesitation swirled underneath it. Jesse meeting my dad "proper" sounded pretty serious.

It also sounded like a disaster looming in the distance.

Chapter Thirty-Three

DALE

The *boy* stepped through my front door, and I actually heard the fight bell sound in my head. *Round two.*

That was all she needed right now—some Romeo following her around like a puppy. And I *thought* he was in Tennessee. That was what Sarah told me.

Lies. More lies.

I bypassed Sarah, who'd barely stepped in the front room, to confront the punk. "What are you doing here?"

"Dad," Sarah hissed. "Stop it. See if you can act like a grown-up this time."

I turned to glare at her, noticing uncertainty cross the boy's face as he glanced her way.

He cleared his throat. "You said real men come to the front door." His hand stuck out in the space between us. "I was hoping you'd give me a do-over."

I looked hard at that hand, which showed signs of work. Construction. Sarah said he was a roofer. I didn't care, and I didn't want him in my house. I shifted my glare to him.

"You're not staying here, boy, so you can drop your hand and head back out the door."

Sarah gripped my sleeve and tugged me her direction. "Dad. Stop."

"You said he was in Tennessee."

"I was, sir. I came back up—"

I stepped toward him. "I wasn't talking to you, boy."

Sarah inserted herself between us. "He has a name, Dad. This is Jesse Chapman."

Didn't care. I grunted, then moved away.

Silence frosted the room, and I felt both their eyes follow me as I moved back to my chair. When I turned to drop onto my seat, I caught the boy's hand run down my daughter's back before he squeezed her hand.

Not in my house. The pit bull in me snarled.

Apparently he couldn't read my total contempt—which made him an idiot—because he moved forward, farther into *my* house, and opened his mouth again.

"I think maybe we have a misunderstanding, sir." He made it two steps in front of me and shoved his hands into his pockets like a guilty little punk. "I never treated your daughter with anything but respect."

He paused, rolling his lips together. A sure sign of dishonesty.

"I think it's important that I introduce myself—"

"Are you stupid, boy?"

His eyes widened.

"Dad!"

I ignored Sarah, even as she once again put herself in the small space between me and the roofer.

"I said get out."

"No." Sarah gripped his hand, staying his leave.

"It's okay, Sarah." He turned and rubbed her shoulder, clearly going to fly the scene. The coward. "I'll find a hotel and come back tomorrow."

Good luck with that.

"No, I told you—you can stay with my uncle Dan." Her mouth twisted, and she set her look on me. "He's not nearly as psycho as my dad."

She tugged on his hand, moving toward the door. He shot me a look of confusion. How hard could it be to understand that I didn't want him here and definitely didn't want him touching my daughter?

I scowled at him and then called to Sarah. "Be home by ten, or don't bother coming at all."

She stopped and pivoted to face me. "Ten? It's nine thirty, Dad, and I'm not fifteen."

My jaw set hard as I planted an *I mean it* look on her before I shifted my attention back to the TV, bypassing the boy.

"She'll be back, sir."

Patronizing. The spineless puppy wouldn't last. Sarah would be better off without him.

JESSE

Holy control freak, what was that?

"Jess, I'm so sorry." Sarah's hand trembled inside of mine.

I pulled in a long breath. Losing it because Sarah's dad was a spoiled five-year-old in a big man's body wasn't going to help her. Tracing her knuckles with my thumb, I pulled her hand up to my lips.

"It'll work out."

She gnawed on her bottom lip, refusing to look at me. With my other hand, I tipped her chin so she'd make eye contact—so she would know I wasn't going to run off because her dad was crazy.

What was with him though? Couldn't be a good idea for Sarah to stay with Angry Arnold in there.

"I'll take you to Uncle Dan's." She still wouldn't meet my gaze.

"I can stay in a hotel."

"Not unless you go to Kearney. There's only one in town, and it's usually full."

Going to Uncle Dan's held about as much appeal as sleeping in a rat-infested shed—especially if he was anything like his brother. I could stay in my truck. That'd be cozy. Way more safe than going back into the grizzly's den.

Seriously, was Sarah going to be okay?

"Guess we should have called and given him a head's-up, huh?"

Sarah shrugged and looked away. "Wouldn't have mattered. He'd be a bull either way."

"Sarah, I don't know if you should—"

"I'll be fine." She shifted and looked me in the eye. "I told you, my dad would never hurt me."

Yeah, well, maybe not physically. Every muscle in my body coiled tight as I looked at this wounded woman. For a moment, taking her away, telling her to never look back, seemed like the right idea.

Except it would chisel hurt deeper into her heart. Running wouldn't fix that. She'd been trying it for months, and it had only made things worse.

Which left me standing there in the semidarkness wondering what I was supposed to do.

"Bet you wish you hadn't come." Emotion wobbled in her voice.

I folded her close and held her. "Not at all. We'll figure it out, okay? One day at a time."

She nodded against my shoulder, and I wondered what it would be like just to hold her. Tonight. For the rest of my life.

One day at a time.

"Come on. Let's see if I do any better with Uncle Dan."

She breathed a soft chuckle. "Can't do much worse."

Right. So we went.

Dan was actually sane. That meant of the three siblings—Darcy, Dan, and Dale—Dale got all the crazy. Lucky me.

Poor Sarah.

"Bed's old and lumpy, but it's yours." Dan nodded toward a half-closed door just off the small front room. "How long you here?"

I looked at Sarah. She was already watching me, clearly wondering the same thing.

"Can you put me to work?"

He grinned. "Always need a grunt."

I smiled, mostly at Sarah. "I told Grant I'd be back on Monday. Guess that gives us a week to get some work done."

Maybe after a few days of driving nails with the Sharpes, I'd have a chance to build a better trust with Dale.

If he'd leave the crazy out of it.

Big if.

***

By Friday that *if* had dwindled to *not likely*. Dale avoided me nearly every minute of every day, refused to let me cross the threshold of his house, and had demanded that Sarah be home by ten every night.

I was at the end of my patience. And Sarah had all but quit on him. She brought dinner over to Dan's every night and stayed until 9:53—giving herself just enough time to get home at exactly ten.

This family dystopia was completely foreign to me. I remembered Friday-night pizza and movies. Games of Scrabble and Pitch and Ticket to Ride. I had no idea what I was supposed to do with the iron curtain Sarah called *Dad*.

The thought of leaving Sarah there on her own the following week left my stomach more uneasy as the days ticked by. Maybe there had never been any stability between them. What if Sarah had only thought that they'd been okay all those years? Did she realize that his rock-hard grip on her wasn't normal?

What if I was leaving her in a disaster all by herself?

I couldn't unravel it all, and my time was cutting short. I'd agreed to the Omaha project and had made a commitment to Grant. Starting Monday.

Sarah sat at her uncle's table, clicking away at her computer. Working. The woman was always working. My chest sort of caved at that thought, because she was more than likely working on drawings for my project, which made me feel guilty.

Instead of setting her free to pursue her passion, I'd heaped a load of responsibility on her. That was swell of me.

Moving from the counter, where I'd landed my paper plate loaded with slices of supreme pizza, I wiped my hands on a napkin and moved to stand behind her. With both hands, I gripped her shoulders and leaned to kiss her head. Soft dark hair tickled against my nose, and I inhaled deeply.

Vanilla.

I drifted lower until my mouth neared her ear. "It has to be your shampoo."

"What?"

I nipped at the spot just below her ear, and she twitched, shrugging and turning into me. A low laugh rolled from my chest as warmth spilled through me, and I wrapped my arms around her. "You smell good."

She leaned into me. "Hmm...you weren't saying such nice things about me two hours ago."

I moved to kiss the soft part of her neck, which was exposed just above her T-shirt collar. "Come on now. All I said was that you had sawdust in your hair."

"Because someone stole my hat."

"It's filthy."

She snorted. "Like yours is any less gross."

Chuckling, I rocked her side to side. A powerful feeling surged over me. Anxiety that I didn't know I carried drained from my muscles, and a sense of rightness—of security—covered the places that had been tense.

Home. Here, with her, I was home.

"I love you, Sarah." The words fell off my lips, as natural as breathing.

She turned to look at me, but when our eyes met, there were no questions, only trust. Her head rested against mine, our noses brushing, and she smiled. "I love you too."

SARAH

I hadn't seen a lot of chick flicks in my life. Didn't fit in with the *Bourne* series and *Die Hard* movies that typified our viewing selection growing up. But I do remember a few romances I'd caught here and there, mostly with Darcy.

When the guy told the girl he loved her, there was always this explosive kissing scene. Tense, energetic, and, to be honest, a little awkward for a girl like me.

This moment with Jesse—the heartbeats after he said he loved me? Not that. Yes, my heart hammered, and the surreal feeling of amazement washed over me. But it felt safe and good and wholesome.

It was exactly what I didn't know I'd hoped for in such a moment, and I knew I'd forever remember the warmth and safety of his arms wrapped around me, the honesty of his simple sentence, and the sense of belonging that all swirled together as our hearts intertwined.

He loved me.

The music I'd come to cherish in the past few weeks hummed softly in the background of my mind. *Jesus, He loves me.*

Kind of a strange reaction to romance. But I melted into it. Explosions were bound to die. Energy fizzled. And then what was left?

This beauty. This knowing.

Security.

I am loved.

We stayed there for I didn't know how long. I knew Jesse felt it too—this steady anchor in what had been a tumultuous sea. I wondered, as the joy of security gripped my heart, if my dad ever knew this kind of love.

Probably not.

I suddenly understood why he was acting the way he was. As that knowledge lifted a little bit of the fog around him, the longing for him to grip this anchor of hope took firm root. My dad needed to meet the Carpenter I'd met.

"Jess, my dad needs to know Jesus."

He pulled away just enough to look at me, but my seemingly left turn didn't throw him. He knew exactly where my thoughts had gone, and he smiled.

"It makes all the difference, doesn't it?"

I nodded. "He won't listen though. I know he won't. He hates religion."

Jesse studied me, and I wondered if he were replaying the conversations he and I had about that topic just a few weeks before.

I wasn't exactly an open receptor either. Maybe there was more hope than I'd thought.

He shifted and then pushed his fingers into my hair and tucked my head into his chest.

"One day at a time, Sapphira."

His new mantra, apparently. I made it my own.

DALE

I'd been replaced. Nothing could prepare a dad for that kind of blow. She used to say I was all she needed. Now she was always with him.

She loved him.

Dan said I should be relieved, that she could do a whole lot worse. Those were his words, not mine.

Jesse seemed okay to the unwise. He'd spent the week working with us, and he definitely knew how to swing a hammer. He also spent the week saying things like "praise God" and "I've been blessed."

Religious verbiage oozed from his lips and dripped on me like the poisoned nectar it was.

Memories of Cassie assaulted me all week. *Father says we must stay on the path of righteousness, or condemnation will consume us. The penitent person is only blessed when they walk in purity.*

Honestly, I had no idea what half of those words meant. But I remembered Cassie saying them as she tried to explain—to *defend* her father's abuse. All the while I could only focus on the purple bruises coloring her knees, and the scars that lined her arms.

Words like *blessed* and *righteous* and *god* were as ugly to me as anything I'd ever heard in the crass world of construction.

But the untried didn't know that.

Sarah didn't know it. She didn't know what she was stepping into. And so help me, I wasn't going to nod and smile at a man who could put her in the same bondage that had stolen Cassie's mind.

No father would.

Sarah came out of her room at seven thirty Sunday morning, dressed like the attractive—no, the knockout—woman she was.

I glared at her above the rim of my coffee mug. "What are you doing?"

She slipped a slice of bread from the Wonder bag and dropped it into the toaster. "Jesse and I thought we'd go check out that little church downtown."

"What?"

She raised her eyebrows and turned to the coffeepot.

I slapped my mug onto the table. "I knew it."

Looking over her shoulder at me, she frowned. "You knew what?"

"I knew he wasn't right."

She drew a breath and rolled her eyes.

The chair beneath me screeched against the floor as I jumped to my feet. "I mean it, Sarah. Don't blow me off. A guy like that, he can't be trusted."

She turned and leaned back against the counter, her look saying she thought I was behaving like a junior high girl. "Jesse is the most trustworthy man I've ever met."

Including you.

"You don't know what you're getting into."

"I know exactly what I'm getting into. You don't know him at all, because you'd rather act like a spoiled bully than give him an honest chance. He's a good man—"

I leapt forward, slicing the air with my hand. "He's a religious freak!"

"Whoa." A man barked behind me. "What's going on in here?"

Every muscle coiled as I curled my fists and turned. "Get. Out."

The boy shook his head and looked at Sarah.

"It's fine, Jess." Her voice held more irritation than fear.

"I could hear him from the front door."

I stepped toward him. "I want you out of my house."

He didn't move.

"Boy—" I lifted a hand to jab my finger into his chest.

With one hand, he intercepted mine. "That's enough."

"Dad, just stop." Sarah pulled on my elbow, forcing me to look at her. "Why are you acting like this? He hasn't done anything wrong."

I glared at him and then turned to her. "You don't know what they'll do. They'll mess with your mind, tie you into so many knots you won't know the difference between sky and dirt. He's leading you into hell."

I could see her pulse throb against her neck as she studied me like I belonged in the old institution over in Hastings.

I wasn't crazy. I'd seen crazy. Crazy was offering your own blood as atonement and spending hours on a concrete floor waiting for some angry god to let you up again. Crazy was sitting in a dark inner room in some church, quaking while some mouthpiece of god roared over your impurities, real or imagined. Crazy was ending your life in a crack house because

339

nothing else could erase the sound of your father's voice condemning you to eternal fire.

"Dad, you don't know—"

"I *know*, damn it, Sarah!" I moved to hover over her.

The boy took her elbow and moved her behind him so that he stood in between us.

"You'll kill her." My jaw went hard, and I began to shake. "You'll take her mind piece by piece, and she'll end up just like her mother."

His eyes, which had smoldered up until that moment, widened as if confused.

As if he didn't know.

"Sir."

"Shut up." I stepped to the side so I could look at my daughter.

Her eyes glazed, and she mashed her lips together. "Daddy, please..."

I shook my head. "I'm not watching this." I had to swallow, because I couldn't let her hear my voice crack. "If you choose him, don't come back. I can't do it again."

Her jaw quivered, and a tear slipped onto her cheek. "Fine," she whispered. "If that's how it has to be."

She drew another long breath and turned her back to me. I'd never forget the sight of her walking out the door.

Chapter Thirty-Four

JESSE

What happened to that man?

I sat in church wondering what to do. I didn't pay attention to the sermon or to anything else, for that matter. All I saw was Dale's beet-red face, rage carved deep into his expression. I didn't know what to do with that.

One moment I was sure I needed to get Sarah out of Minden. Omaha seemed the perfect solution. With that North O project, we had plenty of work to do, and she could stay with her aunt and uncle.

She couldn't stay here. It wasn't safe. Dale wasn't reasonable, and none of it made sense.

But there was part of me that had been woven with a thread of undefined compassion. There had to be something behind Dale's rage. Anger that fierce didn't just erupt without having been fueled by something.

What would I do?

Somewhere in the midst of all the wondering, it became clear. She needed to stay, and I needed to step out of the way for a little while. If Sarah lost her dad, she'd lose part of herself, and she'd

341

be devastated. I'd seen how much this war with her dad had been messing with her all summer. If she chose to come with me to Omaha, and I was pretty sure she would, she would definitely lose her dad.

I couldn't possibly force Sarah to choose between me and the man who'd raised her. I'd never be able to live with it.

Whatever it was driving Dale into this madness was deep and painful, and though the realization was a little on the terrifying side, I was pretty sure Sarah was the only person who would be able to reach into the ache and bring him back.

With the love of Jesus.

Even as this decision (which I didn't really think I actually made on my own) settled over me, my anxiety climbed. *What if* arguments swirled in my head, and I was pretty sure they were directed at God, because this against-my-instinct plan had to have originated with Him. *What if something really bad happened? What if her dad turned violent, and despite what she said, he actually did hurt her?*

I couldn't live with myself, and frankly, I'd be pretty mad at God.

That small voice, the quiet, peaceful, and yet commanding voice came to me again.

Do you trust me?

For some reason, the more something mattered, the harder it was to trust. I wondered if this was universal. But at that point I was dealing with me, and I had to answer the question. Did I trust him? Yes, I did, but I was going to need some help with that kind of demand-my-whole-heart faith.

Please?

Me trusting God wasn't the only issue at hand. I had to figure out a way to bring it up with Sarah. As sure as I felt the seat underneath me, I knew that conversation was going to be a fight.

SARAH

Church, lunch, and then home. A someday home, for a someday life.

The run-down farmhouse before me tugged hard on my heart. Nothing had changed in the week since I'd first seen it. Weeds still swallowed the three-acre lot, the roofline of the front porch sagged dangerously, and the windows all screamed *abandoned.*

But not for much longer.

A small smile slowly pulled on my mouth. This could be home, and I could make it amazing. Jesse and I could...

He leaned into me from the side, and the hand that held mine squeezed. "Do it," he whispered.

My little grin broke into an all-out smile.

His chest moved against me as he laughed. We were crazy. Between his massive project in Omaha and this top-to-bottom renovation we were looking at, we'd be busy for the next two years, at least.

The smile that had just broken free faltered. "Maybe now's not the right time."

He pulled away. "What?"

After a long breath and an attempt to put on a positive face, I turned to him. "I want to, but you've already told Grant that you'll be there on Monday to start the North O renos. If I buy this now, it'll drive me crazy to have it just sitting here—"

Jesse's mouth twisted, and he shook his head. "Hold on, Sarah. I've been thinking about Omaha, and I think you need to stay here right now."

"What?" My heart dropped.

His hands cupped my shoulders. "You need to be here. I'm going back to Omaha. Alone."

"No." I blinked. "No. We were going to do that job together. You said—"

"I know. But that was before I knew your dad, before I saw…" He looked over my shoulder, pulled in a long breath, and looked back at me. "Remember what you said? That your dad needs Jesus? He does, and he also needs you. Right now, I'm in the way, and it's tearing you two apart. The last thing I want is for you to have to choose between him and me."

What was happening? My eyes stung. "He'll get over it, Jess…"

"No. This thing with him is serious. You told me that before this year you two were fine. Close. This morning was not fine, and if you walk away now, you'll never be able to go back. You'll regret it."

"He's making his choices, and I can't change that."

"We make our choices too, Sarah." His hands left my shoulders and came up to frame my face.

A tear leaked over my cheek.

Jesse rubbed it away with his thumb. "He's scared of losing you."

My voice came out ragged. "He's the one pushing me away."

"Don't let him."

What if in the process of trying to keep my father, I lost Jesse? This wasn't supposed to be like this. Why were the men in my life tearing my heart in two?

"You have to try, Sarah, and I have to go to Omaha. That's just the way it is."

Really? Like I couldn't make up my own mind. With my spine rigid, I stepped away, and Jesse's hands fell limp at his sides. I looked away, focusing on the house that had become my new dream. The fantasy faded. It would be work. Hard, dirty, make-me-ache-and-frustrated work.

I wasn't sure I was up for it.

JESSE

She wouldn't even look at me. We climbed into the truck,

with an icy silence expanding between us.

I should have handled that differently. Except, I didn't know how. Her dad's ultimatum had swirled in my mind all morning and into the afternoon. The lunch we bought after church tasted sour in my mouth and sat like a slow burn in my stomach.

My core trembled as we wordlessly drove back into town. *God, please don't let me make the biggest mistake of my life.*

I made the three turns necessary to reach her house and then pulled up to the curb. After setting the truck into park, I looked over to her. She stared straight ahead.

"Sarah..." I reached to touch her face.

She jerked away. "You leave tomorrow, right?"

Air emptied from my lungs, and it seemed that they wouldn't fill again. "Please, Sarah—"

"Just go." She stabbed me with a glare before she hopped out of the truck and marched to her front door.

Like father, like daughter? I had no idea what to do with that.

DALE

Jesse's truck pulled up to the curb somewhere past 4:00 p.m.

Round three. Or was it ten? The boy was as hardheaded as I was. At that moment, that was all irritating without a trace of admirable. He'd won. Sarah went with him, chose him. Hard anger locked in my shoulders. He had no business coming back here.

A car door slammed, jolting my attention back out the window. Sarah stomped up the walk alone.

That was a twist. One that, for some reason, turned the notch higher on my temper. First sign of trouble, and the boy was going to run.

She'd be better off without him.

I caught a glance of her face. Pain twisted her expression, and when she walked through the door, she went straight to her room.

After two steps toward her room, I switched directions. The punk. I'd kill him.

Just like the coward I'd known he was, he'd already pulled away.

Chapter Thirty-Five

JESSE

My head ached. Not as much as my heart. All this time—ever
since we'd met up in Omaha—I thought I understood. God
graciously allowed me to be a part of Sarah's life, used me in His
plan for her salvation, and opened the door to my heart's
greatest desire.

Except, not that last part.

Yesterday afternoon flashed through my mind again. The way
she looked at me, so hurt and so angry. The hardest thing I'd
ever done was drive away, praying that she'd understand and
that somehow we'd figure this out. And that Dale would
miraculously gain some sense.

After snagging the coffeepot from the twenty-year-old maker
Dan kept in his kitchen, I dumped enough black mud to fill my
mug and slid the carafe back into place, not caring that it
clanked under my none-too-gentle hand. I dropped into the
chair I'd tugged away from the table and stared at my unopened
Bible.

"Rough night?" Dan's deep morning rumble came from the
archway separating the main part of his house from the two
bedrooms.

I cleared my throat. "Guess so."

I had work waiting for me, and I couldn't keep putting it off. Omaha, here I come. Without Sarah.

I slouched against the table, my insides sagging as if coated with lead. *Why, God?*

No answers. Not that I was owed any. But this uncertainty hurt. A lot.

Dan stepped toward the kitchen, grabbed his own mug, and came to the table. "Bed okay?"

"Yep. Everything has been good." I sipped the strong brew. "Thanks for keeping me. I've gotta get going though."

Dan's gaze focused on me. "Going..."

"Got a job in Omaha waiting on me."

A long, thick pause hung over the table. "Is this about Dale?"

I couldn't look at him. Or at anything, really. Just the Bible, still unopened in front of me. "I don't know how to answer that. I don't know what to do."

DALE

The steel door to the office squeaked open and then slammed shut. I glanced at the clock on my computer. Seven a.m. was pretty early for Dan. Didn't usually see him till round about eight. No doubt he had more opinions to fill my ears with about that boy.

He did seem to have a point. Not that I'd tell him that. This Jesse guy...had I met him on a job, I'd have probably liked him. Hard worker, knew his stuff, dependable, respectful, and easy to be around.

Without the religious crap, he'd be okay.

Except whatever had happened between him and Sarah had taken her from me. Unforgivable. Not to mention, she'd cried last night. I was sure she didn't know I knew—thought I was sleeping—but I heard her sniffing. Most definitely unforgivable.

"He's leaving today."

Dan sure knew how to make an entry.

"That boy?"

"That *boy* is a full-grown man, and a good one at that. He happens to be the best thing that could happen to your daughter."

Nope. Jesus freak, that was why. And he made her cry. "Then why is he leaving?"

"You want his answer or mine?"

Where did Dan get his temperament for meddling? Stay out of other people's business, that was my creed. Dan was always into other people's stuff.

"Are you giving me a real choice, or are you just leading up to a lecture?"

His glare narrowed on me. "Fine, you get both. He says he's got to get to that job in Omaha. Without Sarah. Today. He's needed there now, and she's not going."

"That's life. Work. Not my problem."

"No, that's not your problem." Dan marched closer to my desk. "Here's your problem. You're so sure that Sarah's life will be a rerun of Cassie's that you're bullying the man she's in love with out of her world."

I dropped my pen and pushed away from my desk. "What's that supposed to mean? If he were that great, he wouldn't be running."

"That right?"

"Yes, that's right."

"Even if he doesn't want to be the reason she loses her father?"

"You're giving him too much credit. You don't know anything about it."

Dan's face turned an angry shade of red. "Then why is he leaving a girl he clearly loves more than the sunshine on his back?"

Dan and poetry.

Did Jesse love her?

Dan's glare softened. "Look. Jesse wouldn't say what happened last night, but he's not skipping around with joy this morning,

349

and last I knew, they were taking on this project in Omaha together. You're her dad, and you've done everything short of jabbing a shotgun into his chest to get rid of him—which neither Darcy nor I can figure. If you could handpick a man for Sarah, you know it'd be him. Maybe it's time you stop living in the past and take a risk for the happiness of your daughter."

After a long glare, certainly meant as a stamp on his rant, Dan turned and marched his way out the door. Which left me staring at the gray steel he'd slammed behind him.

I did care about Sarah's happiness. That was how this whole thing started. I'd wanted her to be happy. Thought that a weekend shopping with Darcy would set her world okay and we could move on. I'd never imagined the way the past four months had played out. Homes For Hope, then fights, and running off, then Jesus, and now Jesse. What kind of a crazy trail was that?

But I still wanted her to be happy. And Jesse seemed to light her up.

The night Sarah asked me to tell her about Cassie stormed through my mind. Man, I'd come unglued. Didn't have a good reason for it either. It was long overdue, actually. It was natural for anyone to wonder about who gave them life. I hadn't wanted to talk about it, to remember her. Hurt too much.

With my elbow on the desk, I rested my head in my hand. I *was* locked in the past and afraid Sarah would relive it. Which meant that I wasn't allowing her to live at all. That wasn't right.

I pushed away from the desk and walked to the window. Scanning the lot out front, I tracked the sidewalk across the road to Dan's house. Jesse stood on the curb, checking the toolbox in his pickup.

Getting ready to leave.

Maybe this was my one more chance. Careful not to appear hurried, I walked out the door and across the gravel lot. *Sarah's happiness, Sarah's happiness, Sarah's happiness...*

Jesse heard my footsteps when I was about ten feet from his truck. He looked up from his packing and then back to his hands.

"Hear you're taking off." I stopped at the tailgate.

"Yes, sir." He still didn't look at me.

"Sarah know?"

"Yes, sir."

My mouth felt dry, and words wouldn't form in my head. Jesse made no effort to rescue the silence. He finished organizing whatever he'd been arranging and shut the toolbox. With one step, he retrieved the duffel waiting for him on the sidewalk and then tossed it into the passenger side of the cab.

Must have been a doozy, whatever had happened.

I crossed my arms and cocked my head. "So leaving is how you're gonna handle this?"

He turned toward the bed of the truck and pushed both palms against it. After one long breath, he slammed a palm against the metal. "What it is you think I should do, Dale?" After straightening, he anchored both hands on his hips. "Tell me what to do here. You gave her an ultimatum. Did you want me to take her to Omaha? You want her out of your life? I can't be that guy."

Heat sparked in his eyes, and I began to wonder if I'd been wrong.

With a step forward he continued. "This cold war you have going on with Sarah is crushing her. I've watched it all summer. Every slam of anger you hammer against her drives the pain deeper. You're her dad. She *loves* you. As much as I want to take her away, because you're being a little scary right now, I can't. I don't want to be the final blade that severs the little bit of relationship she has left with you. She'll regret it, and I won't be able to live with myself."

They fought about me—and Jesse was on my side? That didn't add up. Guilt began to weigh heavy in my chest, and I couldn't push aside the image of my daughter, shoulders slumped, shuffling to her room yesterday. I thought her heartbreak was Jesse's fault.

Turns out it was mine.

Jesse sighed. "Look, I don't know what it is you think you have figured about me, but I'm pretty sure it has something to do with Sarah's mom. While I'm not sure what happened there, I can promise you I'm not what you think I am. I want Sarah to be whole and free. I want her to be happy."

Whole and free. The exact opposite of what Cassie's father had demanded from his daughter. I stole a glance at Jesse's face. He looked about as honest as they came, and like he was in as much turmoil over this whole thing as I was.

What if he was telling the truth? If Darcy and Dan were right, and Jesse was really what he appeared to be, then I was an idiot.

Sarah loved him, and he wasn't taking her from me. Would he change, show a different side of himself if I trusted him?

Jesse exhaled, and his shoulders drooped. "I have a job to get to," he mumbled as he stepped away.

My fists balled at my side, and I found that my muscles twitched. I didn't trust much. But...

"Did you say good-bye?" Heat crawled up my neck as I pictured myself as some little old meddling woman.

He stopped, his back to me, and his hand anchored on his neck. "No."

I drew a breath, long and deep, digging for courage and honesty. "I did that once."

Jesse turned, looking back at me.

"Left after a fight. Didn't say good-bye." I swallowed, the memories pounding me with ruthless cruelty.

Crazy, I hadn't remembered that part all these years. That Cassie and I had fought the night before she left. Even in that moment, I didn't remember about what, likely about her father, but I knew we fought, and I went out. Didn't come back until late, slept on the couch, and then left early the next morning before she and the baby were up.

I glanced back up, finding Jesse still looking at me. Waiting.

"Never saw her again." Emotion surged over me, and I had to grind my jaw to cap it. When that didn't work, I turned away.

All these years, I'd blamed everything on Cassie and her father. Now I knew. I had been wrong too.

JESSE

Dale turned away, his shoulders hunched tight. I thought his jaw quivered before he turned his back to me and walked across the street. His confession had been costly.

I scanned the neighborhood, quiet in the warmth of the late summer morning. "Sir." My voice broke the stillness.

He turned but didn't really look at me. I moved forward, not realizing until I reached him that I'd jogged across the way.

"Where is she?"

He lifted his eyes, which were sheened. "Left this morning. I'm not sure where she went."

I had a guess.

After a moment of careful study, Dale nodded. I waited, feeling like he wanted to say more. When he didn't, I moved back toward my truck.

"Jesse."

My real, actual name. That was a big deal. I stopped to look at him.

"Be a better man than me." He didn't wait for me to respond. Just continued to the office door, his shoulders tucked in as if to protect his heart.

Because it was broken.

A fresh compassion washed over me, one which I should have maintained in the first place. Strange how love could draw out the best and the worst in a person.

I chewed on that as I hopped into my truck and pulled away from the curb. More proof. Without God, we were lost. Even in the most amazing gift—love—we were destined to make a mess of things.

But, and this was amazing, but God...He was able to heal what had been damaged.

Please make this right.

SARAH

The sun kissed the eastern sky, making the semidark horizon blush a beautiful pink hue. I hadn't slept at all, and I wasn't ready to face my dad again. Desperate to see Jesse, I pushed down the impulse to drive to Uncle Dan's, and drove in the opposite direction.

The house stood quiet and sad in the early morning dimness. It needed new life.

Do it.

I didn't know how he talked me into things, but I was certain he had. I planned to bid on the house that afternoon.

Despite my tears that had everything to do with Jesse and my dad, my heart jolted with erratic kicks. I pulled onto the weed-filled driveway of my dream house. Not much of a dream house, if you were judging by HGTV standards. But as I wandered into the front yard filled with overgrown neglect, I could see the dream unfold. Jesse was right. I did have vision. He said it was a gift. I still thought maybe I needed medication.

I loved that project in Lexington though. And those houses in Omaha...seriously, I couldn't wait to witness their transformation.

This house in front of me was so much more than a project. It would be my first home, the one that was mine to go with the life I was beginning to see.

A fresh vision for a fresh me.

Strange. I'd been me all along. Over the summer, I really hadn't changed that much. All of the searching, and I'd been there the whole time. That day, however, I *felt* different.

The sound of a vehicle slowing down on the highway snagged my attention, and I watched Jesse's truck pull in behind mine. He knew. Warmth stirred in my chest as I caught his profile before he parked. He was some kind of looker, that roofer. And he could puddle my heart with one heated glance.

But I was complete. Even in my anguish through the night, not knowing how this complicated thing with Jesse and my dad and me would work out, I'd felt it. I'd be okay. I'd live. Not just survive, but *live.*

Jesus loved me. I was not alone. God gave me wings so I could fly.

"Hey, Sapphira." Jesse's soft call drew a smile to my lips. "You okay?"

I turned slowly, letting my vision cast over the rest of the acreage. The dream continued to unfold in my mind.

I laughed, free and truly happy.

"Yes." I met his gaze. "I'm good."

Everything was still messed up, but we'd work on it. Life with Jesse wasn't clear, but we'd take it one day at a time. And in it all, I'd be good.

I knew who I was, and the Carpenter's daughter was exactly who I wanted to be.

Epilogue

SARAH

Morning light eased over the horizon, soft and warm with the orange and pinks of a Nebraska sunrise. The cup of coffee I'd set to brew gurgled finally, and I wrapped my hand around the mug, letting the warmth seep into my palm. Moving to the granite bar-height countertop we'd installed a month before, I wrapped my free arm around my shoulder and buried my nose into the T-shirt I'd slept in.

His. Smelled like Jesse. I smiled and inhaled again.

My laptop sat closed on the counter. With my smile still pulling on my mouth, I opened the screen. After a quick slide of my finger, I had my latest file open. Cottonwood Farm. The house was a two story—a four square. Simple in design, but had been neglected. Not anymore. I had plans. I'd show our newest clients later that morning.

I'd never dreamed of loving life like this. Hadn't known it was possible.

It wasn't just the job. Not Jesse either. Both were good, but they weren't the heart of it.

Who am I? The driving question that had haunted me just over two years before. Now it had been answered. All of those things I had used to fill in the blanks faded away. The carpenter's daughter, a girl abandoned, the daughter of a woman who had died in shame... All of these things had been a part of my life, but they were not the complete picture. Even being Jesse's wife wasn't the whole of me. Strip all of that away, and I was simply Sarah.

That made me smile all the way down to my soul, because as simply Sarah, I was the daughter of the King. That was amazing.

Footsteps scuffed softly against the floor behind me, and then strong arms encircled my waist.

"What are you doing in the dark?" Jesse nuzzled my neck and then tucked me close against his bare chest.

I wasn't sure it was called snuggling when you pushed your back up close to your husband's chest, but that was what I thought of it as. He kissed a spot beside my ear.

"The sun's not up yet, silly girl." One hand moved from my waist and tipped the computer screen so that he could see it. "Dreaming, are we?"

I tilted my head so that I could see his silhouette. "Thinking."

"They're not the same?"

"Not today."

He moved to capture my chin. Soft light seeped through the east window as the sun broke free from the night.

Jesse studied me, then tipped his face until his nose brushed against mine. "Keep thinking whatever it is you're thinking. It makes you glow."

I felt his cheeks rise as he smiled before he brushed my mouth with his lips.

"I was thinking that I am loved."

He turned me flush to him and pulled me close again. "You are. So much."

Rest there, my soul. That is enough.

THE END

***

Did you enjoy The Carpenter's Daughter*? I'd be so grateful if you'd take a moment and write a review. Thank you!*

Dear Reader,

We meet here at the end, and I am fiddling with words to express my gratitude. I am still floored that anyone would want to read what I write, and am amazed that God allows me to learn through the vehicle of story. He knows me so well.

This was my third published novel, and to be honest, the one that I struggled the most to write. I quit on it twice. I rewrote the end several times. I stalled. I debated...maybe this one wasn't one for the books. Why? Because it really hit me deep. Who doesn't wonder, at some point or another—and usually more than once—who the heck am I?

So, thank you for taking this journey with me, because for me, it was deeply personal. As I struggle in a season of redefinition—one that has happened before, and I'm sure will happen again—I have come to this:

Jesus loves me. That is enough.

My earnest prayer is that you will come to that same place as well. Maybe now, as you've walked with Sarah, or later, when you reach your own crisis of faith.

In the end nothing could be more precious.

Praise God.

With my heart and love,

Jen

PS—for those in construction, if I miffed the real deal, as I probably did, I ask for your grace. You're amazing. I wish I could do what you do.

About the author...

Jennifer Rodewald is passionate about the Word of God and the powerful vehicle of story. The draw to fiction has tugged hard on her heart since childhood, and when she began pursuing writing, she set on stories that pointed to the grace of God.

Jen lives and writes in a lovely speck of a town where she watches with amazement while her children grow up way too fast, gardens, and marvels at God's mighty hand in everyday life. Four kids and her own personal superman make her home in southwestern Nebraska delightfully chaotic.

She would love to hear from you! Please visit her at www.authorjenrodewald.com or connect on Facebook at www.facebook.com/authorjenrodewald.

More from Jen...

BEST FRIENDS—MAYBE MORE—UNTIL ADDICTION SHATTERS EVERYTHING.

Andrew and Jamie have always been best friends—maybe more than friends—until addiction shatters everything. Caught between loyalty and fear, Jamie realizes she cannot be Andrew's miracle and makes a decision that rips them apart. Can the hand of grace reach into their broken lives to bring redemption to all that has been lost?

LAND OF HER OWN AND THE LOVE OF A GOOD MAN.

SHOULDN'T THAT BE ENOUGH?

Left wounded by a marriage cut short, Suzanna Wilton leaves her city life to start over in a tiny Nebraska town. Her introduction to her neighbor Paul Rustin is a disaster. Assuming he's as underhanded as the other local cowboys she's already met, Suzanna greets him with sharp hostility. Though Paul is offended by Suzanna's unfriendliness, he can't stop thinking about her, which unsettles his peaceful life. A hard-fought friendship slowly kindles something more, but just as Paul's kindness begins to melt Suzanna's frozen heart, a conflict regarding her land escalates in town. Even in the warmth of Paul's love, resentment keeps a cold grip on her fragile heart.

Will Suzanna ever find peace?

Made in the USA
Middletown, DE
19 June 2025